Praise for
LINDA CARDILLO's
Dancing on Sunday Afternoons

"A superbly nuanced, emotionally rich tale of one woman's journey from turn-of-the-century Italy to America in which Linda Cardillo beautifully blends women's fiction, romance and historical fiction into one unforgettable story."
—*Chicago Tribune*

"A fresh and original storyline...a 'must-read' for anyone who enjoys family drama. In the style of LaVyrle Spencer, Jude Devereaux or Danielle Steel, author Linda Cardillo has penned a wonderful debut novel."
—*Contemporary Romance Writers*

"Deeply touching and rich with period detail."
—*RT Book Reviews*

"This is a stupendous book! Don't miss this story. It will move you to tears with the pain and joy you find within each page."
—*The Romance Readers Connection*

"Linda Cardillo makes a fine debut with this unexpectedly tender and engaging love story."
—Barnes & Noble *Heart-to-Heart Newsletter*

"Based on her own family history, Cardillo's beautiful love story will be cherished by readers."
—*Booklist*

"...a beautifully told story...Warning:
You may shed a few tears before you read the last page..."
—*Romance Reviews Today*

Dear Reader,

I'm often asked where the inspiration for my stories comes from. I tell people I'm a collector—of images observed and fragments of conversations overheard, of dreams and memories (my own and others). I also collect rocks—the stones that wash up on beaches, tossed by the ocean until their jagged edges are rounded and elegant and satisfying to hold in the hand. I sort my ideas in much the same way that I sort my rocks, looking for patterns that repeat themselves and themes that converge.

It was the convergence of two recurring themes in my writing that inspired and informed the story you are about to read—Italian family life and food. For the resilient Rose Dante, her talented but risk-averse daughter, Toni, and her emotionally reckless granddaughter, Vanessa, food is love, change, forgiveness and salvation. Their restaurant, Paradiso, is the soul of the family and the scene of those moments that define a lifetime—homecoming, marriage, celebrations of birth and death, betrayal, reawakening and redemption.

Across the Table is a celebration of family and a recognition of what is most valuable in our search for connection and happiness. It has its origins in the spirit and stories of my mother and her sisters and sisters-in-law—the aunts who helped to raise me and my cousins as we all sat around the tables of my childhood. They were the first generation of the family to be born in America—young women who saw their husbands and boyfriends and brothers go off to war; young mothers who faced the challenges of raising children in a culture and a time that was changing rapidly; wives who loved passionately; and finally matriarchs who anchored their families with a mixture of humor, wisdom and love expressed through the bounty on their table.

As Rose would invite you, come sit at my table. *Mangia!*

With warm wishes,

Linda Cardillo

P.S. If reading about the meals prepared by Rose in *Across the Table* and by Giulia in *Dancing on Sunday Afternoons* makes you hungry, you'll find the recipes on my Web site, www.lindacardillo.com and in my blog, http://linda-cardillo.blogspot.com/. I'd love to hear from you about your own family recipes.

LINDA CARDILLO

Across the Table

HARLEQUIN®

TORONTO • NEW YORK • LONDON
AMSTERDAM • PARIS • SYDNEY • HAMBURG
STOCKHOLM • ATHENS • TOKYO • MILAN • MADRID
PRAGUE • WARSAW • BUDAPEST • AUCKLAND

Recycling programs
for this product may
not exist in your area.

ISBN-13: 978-0-373-23078-5

ACROSS THE TABLE

Contents

ACROSS THE TABLE   9

DANCING ON SUNDAY AFTERNOONS   303

LINDA CARDILLO

Across the Table

To my aunts—Angie, Beulah, Carmella, Cathy, Clara, Corinda, JoAnn, Kay, Lydia, Mary, Rita, Rose, Ruth and Susie

ROSE

1939–46

A Lifetime Ahead of Us

I HEARD THE SCREEN DOOR slam shut against the wooden doorjamb and the crunch of Al's work boots on the conch-shell fragments that surrounded our cottage a quarter mile from the Chaguaramas airfield on Trinidad. It was 5:00 a.m. The tanagers that nested in trees beyond the field where we enlisted men's wives hung our laundry had just begun their morning song.

I rolled away from the empty hollow on the bed where Al had been sleeping only fifteen minutes before. The sheets were damp with his sweat. Nothing stayed dry in that climate.

I figured I might as well get up, too, put on a pot of coffee, start cooking before the temperature climbed. Thanksgiving Day and it was already seventy-five degrees outside. It would rise to one hundred and twenty degrees in the shade before the day was over. Al had hung a thermometer for me outside the bedroom window so I'd know as soon as I opened my eyes how hot it was. I'm not sure why it mattered so much, but it helped. Gave me a little piece of knowledge that let me feel some control over my life. Hah!

I wrapped myself in the navy blue embroidered kimono Al brought me last year when he was on furlough at Christmas and managed to get back to Boston for ten days. It seemed like a ridiculously impractical gift at the time, the middle of winter in the Northeast. I was wearing flannel nightgowns and wool socks to bed, for God's sake.

But then he'd asked me to marry him. Al Dante and I had been keeping company since we were in high school. He was a year ahead of me, one of my brother Carmine's friends.

The ring was in the pocket of the gown.

"What's this?" I asked when I felt something hard and lumpy against my heart. I'd just put the kimono on over my powder-blue sweater set in my parents' living room.

I slipped my hand into the pocket and retrieved a velvet box.

"Open it, Rose." He was sitting on the edge of his chair. He had his uniform on, the petty-officer stripe he'd earned a couple of months before neatly displayed on his arm below the Seabees construction insignia. He looked sharp, my Al did.

I held my breath as I lifted the hinged top of the small box. Inside was a diamond sitting high on four silver prongs. I let out a quiet gasp and my eyes filled up—for all the nights I'd lain awake, wondering how he was doing so far away, building an air base as the world descended into war. Trinidad. Al told me the U.S. Navy had leased territory there from the British because of its strategic location in the Caribbean, a base for planes that escorted convoys and patrolled the sea lanes. I had to go to the library to look up where it was.

My nose started to run. I was a mess. Tears streaming down my cheeks, me sniffling. Who knew this was what love does to you.

"Will you marry me, Rose?"

We didn't have much time. But I wasn't going to let him go back to Trinidad for God knew how long before we could walk down the aisle at St. Leonard's. Neither of us wanted to wait. We talked to my folks that very night. They were wary about the rush.

Mama got me alone in the kitchen for a few minutes.

"Rosa, be honest with me. Are you gonna have a baby? Is that why you gotta go to the priest so fast?"

"No, Mama, no! I swear on Nonna's grave that I'm as pure as the snow that's falling outside. It's just—I can't bear for him to go away again. The navy will let me go with him if we're married."

"He's gonna take you away to that island! Your papa will not agree to that, Rosa. You belong here, with the family. It's too far. Too strange. Another country."

"Mama, you left your parents to go with Papa to another country when *you* got married. America was a lot farther from Italia than Trinidad is from Boston. Please, Mama. Understand. I love him. I've waited already, worrying about whether he'd come back alive. I don't want to wait any longer. Talk to Papa. Give us your blessing!"

Mama put her hands on her hips and looked at me, measured me. She was from the old country, but she'd been in Boston a long time—thirty years.

"I didn't want to leave back then. It broke my heart to say goodbye to my family. I was pregnant, don't forget, with your brother Sal. But the last thing I wanted was to be separated from your papa. I'd seen too many men leave the village on their own and get lost in America, find another woman, forget the family they left behind. I was scared, but I knew I had Papa to depend on, protect me and the baby. With his skill as a stonemason, he knew he could find work in America. But when we left, my mother cried and cried as if it was my funeral. I won't do that to you, *figlia mia*. I'll talk to Papa."

She made the sign of the cross on my forehead and went to talk to my father.

We got married on New Year's Day. I wore my mother's veil and my sister-in-law Cookie's dress. My best friend, Patsy, stood up for me. It snowed the morning of the wedding. Huge flakes came in off the harbor and by the time we went to church there were three or four inches on the ground. I had to put on galoshes and hold my skirts up as we walked the two blocks to St. Leonard's. Fortunately, Father Giovanni had gotten somebody to shovel the front steps. My cousin Bennie, with the voice of an angel, sang the *Ave Maria*. Instead of his overalls covered in granite dust, Papa had on his good black suit and waited in the back of the church while I changed my shoes and Patsy fixed my veil. She licked her thumb and wiped away a fleck of soot that had settled on my cheek. I peeked into the sanctuary through the little glass panes in the doors and could see Al up at the altar in his uniform.

I bit my lip, squeezed Patsy's hand, then took Papa's arm. I stepped across the threshold and headed into my new life.

After the Mass, we went to a restaurant on Salem Street that had closed for our private party. The meal wasn't elaborate; after all, this was still the Depression, and the rest of the world was at war. But they did a nice job for us—escarole soup, manicotti, a cacciatore made with rabbit, fagiolini and broccoli rabe on the side. The wedding cake came from Caffe Vittoria, but the cookies Mama baked herself. It took her three days. Mostaciolli, anise cookies, pignoli cookies, honey fingers. She even managed to find sugar-coated almonds, and I sat up with Patsy two nights before the wedding and wrapped the pastel-colored nuts—blue, green, pink, lilac—in circles of white netting that we tied with thin strips of white satin ribbon as wedding favors.

Al and I spent our wedding night at the Parker House. They brought us a bottle of champagne and a fruit basket on the house because Al was a serviceman. I'd never had champagne before. It was New York State, not French, of course, because of the war. It wasn't what I expected. But then, most of what's happened in my life wasn't what I expected.

The hotel wasn't far from the North End, but it might as well have been a foreign country. Very old Boston, with a snooty bell captain and a dowdy lounge. Not that we wanted to spend any time there. It was all we could do to get up to our room and get the key in the door, we were so excited. I was nervous, with a lot of butterflies in my stomach. I'd hardly eaten anything at the reception. I'd been busy moving from table to table, kissing and being kissed, thanking everyone as they slipped their envelopes into my hand and I put them carefully into the satin-and-lace *borsa* Mama had carried on her own wedding day. We didn't count the money until the next morning. We had other things on our minds that night.

Although she'd given birth to seven children and therefore must have known *something* about the sexual side of marriage, Mama had offered me nothing in the way of preparation. Her only advice to me was, "Don't ever go to bed angry. When you fight, make up before you fall asleep."

But right then, I couldn't imagine fighting with Al. I'd known him since we were kids and never in all those years had we ever said a sharp word to each other.

My sister-in-law Cookie, in addition to handing down her dress, had given me a smattering of advice, although I tried to avoid the image of my brother Carmine doing to her what she was trying to describe.

"That was the first time I'd ever even seen one," she said of her wedding night. "You'd think, growing up with five brothers, that sooner or later I'd have caught a glimpse. So it was kind of a shock. Try not to react too strongly when you see it, 'cause men are very sensitive about that. And try not to worry or build the whole experience up into something that's got to be perfect the first time. More than likely it won't be. But it does get better." And she smiled this knowing, secret smile and patted her belly. She was just starting to show.

So we made it into the hotel room with these goofy smiles on our faces. We looked at each other and then Al swooped in, picked me up and carried me to the wing chair by the window and sat down with me on his lap. We looked out at the city, coated now in a thick blanket of snow that softened the edges of everything and hid the shabbiness.

It was magical, that whiteness. The world seemed fresh, unmarred by weary footprints. A good omen for us, I thought.

Al nuzzled my neck in the spot he'd discovered when we were sixteen and he first kissed me. He'd begun with my lips, but then moved to cover my face with his kisses—my eyelids, my cheeks, my earlobes and, finally, right below my ear. It had sent shivers through me then, and he'd known ever since that was how to make me melt.

He lingered there for a few minutes and I leaned back against his chest. All the nervous energy that had gotten me through this frantic week dissolved into his tenderness and strength.

"Oh, Rose," he whispered.

And then he began to unbutton the twenty satin-covered buttons that ran up the back of the dress from below my waist to my shoulder blades. I knew he wanted that dress just to slide off me like the waterfall in the middle of the island he'd described for me—heart-stopping ice-cold water plunging from cliffs so green you thought they'd been colored by a child-giant with a box of crayons.

But there were so many buttons! Not only up my back, but on the sleeves, as well, marching up to my elbows. Painstakingly, one by one, he slipped the loop fastener over each button to release it. While he unbuttoned, he continued to nuzzle my neck, his breath hot and urgent against my skin. Finally the buttons were all undone and he drew the bodice off my shoulders. I stood and let the whole thing drop to the floor and turned to face him in my bra and slip and panties.

I had a negligee in my suitcase that I'd bought at Filene's the day after Al proposed, all filmy white nylon with pale blue flowers embroidered around the neckline. But I could see from Al's eyes that I wasn't going to put it on that night.

Those eyes swept over me from head to toe and back again, coming to rest on my breasts. He broke into a broad grin.

"You're beautiful, Rose!"

It brought tears to my eyes, how adored I felt at that moment.

He picked me up again and carried me to the bed. Nothing Cookie had told me prepared me for the rest of that night— for how I felt lying against the pillows, watching him undress; for all the revelations about my body and his that followed; for the absolute peace of sleeping in his arms.

As he stood by the bed, undressing, the stiffness and formality of his uniform gave way to the soft curl of black hair against the smooth browned muscle of his arms and chest. The work he'd been doing on that tropical island had given him a sleekness and a strength I'd never seen in him before, not even when we'd gone to Revere Beach during the summers we were in high school. He wasn't a boy anymore, not in his body, not in the way he wasn't embarrassed to have me watch him, not in the way he touched me when he got into bed next to me. I wondered—fleetingly—if he'd gained that confidence from being with another woman. But he dispelled any doubts I had about being the only one in his life from that moment on by his tenderness and his passion. His patience with the buttons had only been the beginning of his willingness to take it slow for me.

We didn't sleep much that night. It was as if we had to fill ourselves up with each other, fill that emptiness that had gnawed at us all the time he'd been away. We didn't fall asleep until early morning, the sheets twisted around us. I woke up first, disoriented by the strange bedroom. I eased myself out of the bed to wash. There was a bit of blood, but not as much as I'd thought there would be. I looked at myself in the mirror over the sink. The bride who'd anxiously bitten her lip and walked with nervous hope down the aisle was still there. We still had a lifetime of unknowns ahead of us. But one question had been answered for me during the night. I had the certainty—don't ask me where it came from—that if things were okay in bed, a couple could weather whatever else life threw at them. We were going to do all right, Al and I.

We couldn't afford more than one night at the Parker House, so we spent our last night in Boston and the second night of our married life at Al's parents' apartment. My mother-in-law, Antonella, invited my parents over for dinner. We'd spent the day walking around the city, arm in arm, Al helping me over the snowbanks, as we talked about the life we hoped to have. God willing, the war would end before the United States got pulled into it, and we *could* have a life.

When we got to my in-laws', my cheeks were red from the cold and I heard a lot of ribbing from both the Vitales and the Dantes about being the blushing bride. Al just took me in his arms with a grin and planted a big one on my lips in front of everybody. Then everyone had to kiss me.

Eventually we sat down to eat. Al's mother is Calabrese, so her cooking is slightly different from Mama's. She made tripe in a pizzaiola sauce and her own fettucine. Papa had brought a jug of Chianti filled from the cask in our basement, the wine made from my uncle Annio's grapes that he grew in his garden in Everett. The toasts were endless, each family raising their glasses to our safe journey, long life and many babies. The meal was raucous, a celebration but with an undercurrent of melancholy as the evening wore on and our mothers, especially, worried about our departure the next day. Nobody wanted to say good-night. But at last, Antonella, Mama and I cleared the table and began washing up and putting the kitchen back in order. Around eleven, with another round of kisses—and, by now, tearful embraces—my family headed down the stairs. I went to the front windows, Al's arm around my waist, and watched them walk down the block. Before they rounded the corner, Mama turned and looked back. I blew her a kiss, but I don't think she saw me.

We sailed early the next day, first to Miami and then on to Trinidad. Off in the distance we could see the escort ships protecting us. We weren't allowed to photograph them, a reminder that even on this side of the Atlantic, the world was a dangerous place. I was seasick the whole twelve days of the trip, throwing up in the cramped stainless-steel toilet in our cabin. When we had a practice emergency evacuation drill, I crawled up to the deck with my life jacket on, but at that moment, I didn't care whether I lived or died, I was so sick. The tugboat horns indicating that we were in the harbor were the most beautiful music I'd ever heard.

Little by little, I made a home for us on Trinidad. The first thing to adjust to was the heat, since we were practically sitting on the equator. I pinned my long hair up on top of my head and made a few sundresses out of some cotton I found in a shop in Port of Spain. But before I sewed the dresses, I cleaned.

The cottages assigned to the married couples were newly built, like the airfield Al and his platoon were carving out of the peninsula. But left empty for even a few months they became overrun with wildlife, large and small. Our cottage had two rooms, plus a small kitchen and a lavatory. The shower was outside. When I first saw our home, I hadn't held down any food to speak of in more than a week and I was covered in a layer of dust from the open jeep ride to the base. The sweat was pouring down my neck, leaving a trail of narrow brown rivulets.

Inside the cottage, cobwebs hung from every corner, the husks of giant beetles and unidentifiable insects trapped in the sticky silk. Something had made a nest under the kitchen sink. Geckos slithered along the edges of the floor. If there'd been a clean place to lie down, curl up and cry, I would've done so. But there wasn't. So I put my bags down on the porch and immediately dug out a housedress and a bandanna to tie up my hair.

"You got a broom, some rags and a bucket?" I said to Al.

God bless him, he scrounged around while I changed and came back with the basic necessities. He told me he had to report to his commander and then left me for the afternoon.

I put all my years of Mama's training as a housekeeper to use that afternoon and for days afterward, sweeping and scrubbing that place until it was something I could be proud of. It was my first home, after all—but let me tell you, it wasn't like anything I'd ever imagined.

The blue of the sea, the purple of the bougainvillea, the red of the Chaconia trees—I'd never seen anything like them. The colors of the land, the smells of the sea and the flowers—everything was heightened by the heat and the moisture. The same was true of the food. The tastes were both strange to me and exaggerated.

The base had a commissary where we could get tins of evaporated milk, peas, potted beef and Spam. But I longed for fresh, so soon after I arrived I walked down to the little village that was halfway up the hill between the base and the harbor. I'd seen chickens pecking around a yard the first day, and vegetables I didn't recognize growing in a field. I knocked on some doors, talked to the old mama who had the chickens and walked away with a basket of greens, some eggs and a packet of spices—cardamom, cilantro, some dried chili peppers.

They eat spicy in Trinidad. Al was used to Calabrian cooking and that was spicy, so I gave the local things a try. If I had to open another can of Spam and make it into something recognizable, I thought I'd shoot myself. Or we'd both starve.

But fresh eggs I knew what to do with. I had some potatoes and onions and made a pan of frittata, with the greens on the side. Al came into the house and smelled the familiar aromas. He ate that night with gratitude and pleasure.

By Thanksgiving, I'd had almost a year to poke around the markets of Port of Spain and find things that were close enough to what we'd known in Boston or learn how to cook what was totally unfamiliar. We weren't going to have turkey, for instance, but I'd gotten a nice capon the day before, all plump and with lots of flesh on its breast even after I'd plucked the feathers. I used breadfruit instead of sweet potatoes. I found a sausage maker, and although the taste wasn't like my uncle Sal's fennel sausage back home, it was still pork and hot. I couldn't make lasagne, like Mama always did for Thanksgiving, because I couldn't find any cheese similar to ricotta. But I bought some cornmeal and made *pastelles* instead, an island dish we had one night in a local tavern and Al liked so much I got the owner's wife to show me how she made it. I used the sausage and a bit of beef I was able to get my hands on, chopped up and browned with onions and garlic and carrots and then simmered in broth and the local spices Imelda, the old lady in the village, supplied me with. At the end of the simmering you toss in olives and raisins. With the cornmeal you make dough with water and shape it into balls that you flatten with your hand. You put a spoonful of the meat mixture in the middle and mold the cornmeal dough around it, then wrap each little pie in banana leaves coated with oil and annatto powder. You tie up the leaves like a package and then steam the packets. Oh, when you unwrap those leaves, those *pastelles* are just bubbling with red juices and that spicy flavor that wafts through every kitchen in Trinidad.

There was a lot of homesickness on the base, and the only way I knew how to dispel those feelings was with food. I invited all the married couples in the compound and the single guys in Al's platoon to Thanksgiving dinner. Each of the girls offered to bring something; several of them had gotten packages from home, so we had a real feast that afternoon. We set up two long tables out in the courtyard between the cottages and covered them with bedsheets. Everyone brought their own chairs and dishes, since nobody had enough to set a table for eighteen.

I think it was the first holiday any of us had spent away from our families. But you know, that day, sitting across the table from one another, we *were* a family.

Despite the heat and the strangeness, I got used to tropical life. I found an office job working for the navy and rode my bike to the base every day, along roads lined with pale blue and yellow shacks with rusty corrugated tin roofs and curious children watching me as their mamas spread laundry out to dry in the sun.

Children. Al and I both wanted a family. Who didn't? But two years went by in Trinidad, two years of lovemaking in the humid night, breezes drifting over us carrying the fragrance of frangipani or the roar of the night rains. Two years of waking up every month to renewed disappointment. I'm not one to dwell on missed opportunity. When the milk spills, I mop it up and refill the pitcher. But as time wore on, as I washed blood out of the sheets for yet another month, I couldn't help myself. I cried. I wondered what was wrong with me.

I didn't think it was the tropics. If anything, the heat seemed to make everything and everyone around me *more* fertile. Two of the girls who lived in our compound had already given birth and three more were pregnant.

One day when I was in the village picking up my eggs and greens from Imelda, I had to wait for her because she had another customer. But instead of filling the young woman's basket with provisions, she pressed a packet wrapped in brown paper into her hands.

"Remember, make a tea, let it steep for five minutes and then drink the whole cup. Every morning."

I watched the young woman take the packet nervously with a shy smile. Imelda patted her belly.

"You'll be carrying something in there in no time."

I felt a sharp longing and a desperation to try anything— even Imelda's potion. I didn't tell Al. I didn't think he'd understand. Besides, I didn't want him to feel inadequate—that somehow, because we hadn't been able to make a baby, I wasn't satisfied with our life.

So I bought the packet of herbs from Imelda in secret that day, along with okra and onions, and made myself a tea of hope.

The next morning the Japanese bombed Pearl Harbor. We'd known we were preparing for war, but the horror of the attack and the chilling reminder of our own vulnerability—on yet another navy base on a tropical island—brought urgency and renewed purpose to the work at Chaguaramas.

For the next three months the construction crew made an intense push to finish. Al worked long hours, coming home at night and collapsing into exhausted slumber after supper. He had no energy for lovemaking, and I was so afraid I was barren it was all I could think of on those few nights when we managed to reach for each other in the bed. I can't say our lovemaking wasn't passionate. But it wasn't the same as the early days when we couldn't get enough of each other. Besides my own worries, which I kept to myself, we had others, as well. My brothers Carmine and Jimmy had both been drafted. And with the completion of the base we realized new orders for Al were coming soon. God only knew where he'd go.

When the orders came, I should've been glad that I'd at least be going home. I hadn't seen my family in two years and the timing meant I'd get to see my brothers before they shipped out. But leaving Chaguaramas also meant leaving Al. I wasn't going with him on his next assignment, because he'd be on a ship heading across the Pacific and into war.

I was so busy packing up I didn't notice that I hadn't gotten my period. I wasn't very regular, anyway, so I didn't give it a thought. The navy flew us out of Trinidad to Florida instead of transporting us by ship. It was my first time in a plane. Al made me sit by the window and—oh my God—what a sight as we lifted off and circled the island. There was Al's work below us, the long, straight landing strip, crisscrossed by two other runways, and a complex of hangars and administrative buildings and barracks. A small city in just two years. I squeezed his hand and then threw up into a waxy bag.

We had two weeks in Boston before Al shipped out. We got there in time for a combined party—welcome home for Al and me, farewell for Carmine and Jimmy. Our mothers cried; the boys got drunk; Cookie, with my two-year-old nephew Vincent and another baby on the way, sat at the table rocking her toddler and trying to hold back her tears.

The next morning Carmine and Jimmy got inducted at the

base in South Boston and were on their way to Fort Dix in New Jersey for basic training. Al and I had a chance to talk about where I'd live and what I'd do once he was gone. I told him it didn't make sense for me to rent an apartment just for myself. I'd move back in with my parents and get a job. After two years of working for the navy, I knew I had what it took to make a living. I was going to be okay, I assured him, remembering the haunted look on Cookie's face and vowing I wouldn't be a burden to anyone while Al was away.

We got back some of what we'd lost in those last months of exhaustion and worry on Trinidad. Spring was arriving in Boston and we made excuses to our families and took ourselves outside.

We walked all the way to the Esplanade on the Charles River.

"It's going to be different now, Rose."

"It's always been different for us, Al. And we've been apart before. I didn't forget what you looked like then. Or felt like." I grinned and put my hand on his chest, pushing him gently. I was trying so hard, you know, to let him go without worrying about me.

He grabbed my hand. "I'll never forget what you feel like, either."

I dressed in my best suit, put on stockings and high heels, gloves and a hat the day his ship sailed. I wanted Al's last memory of me to be special. I hadn't worn clothes like that since we'd left Boston two years before. The suit was a little snug, and I thought, That's what married life does to you— rounds you out. I stayed on the dock with the other wives as the ship left port, taking some comfort in our numbers. But I got on the trolley and went home very much alone.

I fought the loneliness by staying busy. I got a job right away at the Shawmut Bank, as a secretary to one of the vice presidents. When I took the typing and shorthand tests, I did the best of all the candidates. I'd learned a lot on Chaguaramas. You make opportunities where you find them. I put my hair up, knew how to address the higher-ups with respect and saw what I needed to do to make my boss look good. It wasn't long before the bank promoted me to office manager. I even had a nameplate on my desk—Mrs. Dante. I was twenty-one years old and felt as if I knew something.

In April I missed my period again and this time I didn't ignore it. But I was afraid to hope. I tried to put it out of my mind, busied myself with work so that I could bear the moment when, as always before, I'd start to bleed. But May arrived and I finally allowed myself to believe I might be pregnant. I kept my suspicions to myself until I saw the doctor, as if confiding in someone else might make it disappear. Generally I'm not a superstitious person. I don't go in for the *mal'occhia* that my mother's generation brought from the old country. But I did break down in Trinidad and let myself fall under the spell that despair sometimes drives us to, and I wasn't willing, just yet, to go back to being a totally rational person.

I found a doctor at Boston Lying-In Hospital. I didn't want to ask Cookie who her doctor was because I knew it would set off a chain reaction that would ripple through the family and only compound my grief if I was mistaken. I had to wait a few days for the answer. I didn't give the doctor my phone number because my mother might have answered. I made sure I was the one to pick up the mail from the box in the vestibule every morning. When the envelope finally came I stuck it in my apron pocket and brought everything else—a letter from Carmine and some bills—to the kitchen. I went to my bedroom, the same room I'd shared with my sister Bella as a girl, and sat down on the narrow bed. All my senses seemed sharper that morning—the feel of the chenille bed-spread against my bare legs, the rumble of city traffic on the elevated highway a few blocks away, the aroma of onions and garlic from Mama's cooking, the bitter taste of bile rising in my throat. I opened the letter and held my breath as I read the results of my pregnancy test. And then I cried.

The person I was when I'd left Boston for Trinidad was not the woman who returned. I thought at first that it was my pregnancy, the change in the weather and being without Al that made me feel so different. I heard all kinds of stories from aunts and cousins about the discomforts of carrying a baby, but for me, it wasn't that. My body felt strange—not my own, that was for sure. But the strangeness I felt had more to do with my head than my growing belly.

I was noticing things—about Boston, about life—that I hadn't seen before I'd lived in Trinidad. Now I didn't just stand on the wharf at the edge of my neighborhood staring out at the harbor, wondering what lay beyond the ocean's horizon. I'd sailed that ocean. Been out of sight of land and all that was familiar. Some people—a lot of people in the North End, I discovered—didn't even wonder or ask what lies outside the concrete and brick boundaries of their corner of the city. It was enough for them—the daily routine of waking up in their comfortable bed, drinking a cup of Maxwell House coffee with two sugars and cream, getting on the MTA with a pepper-and-egg sandwich in their lunch pail and keeping the circle of people they knew tight around them, not letting in anyone or anything new.

Maybe that was what Chaguaramas changed about me. I didn't have those routines to fall into. Sometimes on my days off, especially toward the end when Al was working nonstop to finish the air base, I climbed by myself to the top of the plateau past the housing compound. From there I could see the

Caribbean and forget myself in the endless vista of sea and sky. Close in, of course, were the battleships and tenders, an ominous reminder that we were at war. The harbor was as busy and congested as Boston. But if I looked up and off to the right, beyond the gray metal hulls and camouflage netting that disguised the glint of guns, I saw only open sea, and it opened up my heart.

I wished the rest of the world could feel this, instead of bombing cities.

There were other things I experienced at Chaguaramas. Imelda and her family, for instance. Her husband, Buddy, who played drums at a club in Port of Spain and delivered ice in his wooden wagon. Their daughters Jane and Margaret and their children, who ran around Imelda's garden and climbed into her ample lap.

I'd never been around black people before, had never seen them with their families. The first time Imelda offered me a cup of coffee, I have to admit I hesitated. A lot of the merchants in Port of Spain treated the navy people like invaders, intruders. But Imelda, up in her village—after her surprise at my sudden appearance the day I went looking for fresh vegetables—took an interest in me. Maybe I needed some mothering in those early months away from my family and she understood that. She didn't pressure me that first time, when she offered and I made an excuse not to stay and sit with her. But then I felt foolish. What was I afraid of? That someone would see and think I was doing something wrong? I usually don't care what other people think. So the next time she asked, I said yes.

Imelda's coffee was strong and sweet, like Mama's. Black coffee—espresso—was what Mama made for Papa after dinner. One demitasse with a shot of anisette and a twist of lemon peel is how he liked it. But in the afternoons, after she'd finished the laundry, the cleaning and the marketing and before she started dinner, Mama sat with her cup of "American coffee." She learned how to use the grinder at the A&P and brought home a bag that took her a month to use up. Sometimes she sat with her sister and visited. But more often than not, she enjoyed her coffee alone, listening to the radio.

At Imelda's table I felt like I was in my mother's kitchen. If I'd told anyone back home that, they would've thought I was crazy. Even the girls in the compound never went to the village.

"Rose, honey," Imelda would ask, "have you written to your mama lately? If Margaret or Jane and my grandbabies were so far away from me I don't think I could stand it." She fanned herself with an old catalog while she poured us both a cup.

Mama never learned to read, but I wrote her a letter every week. My brother Jimmy read them to her. She sent me photographs each month holding up one of my letters.

Her not being able to read made me realize how cut off she must've been from her own family when she left Italy. At least I knew we weren't going to be in Trinidad forever. But I wondered if I could've done what she did—leave everything and build a new life from nothing.

Motherhood

***

ALBERT DANTE, JR., was born on Thanksgiving Day at Boston Lying-In Hospital. It was Patsy, my maid of honor, who got me there, calling a taxi when my water broke and pain ripped through me. It hadn't been an easy pregnancy. I threw up for five months; I gained forty pounds and spent the last six weeks propped up at night with pillows because the heartburn was so bad. But I wrote none of that to Al. I wrote instead about the first time I felt the baby move, a flutter that felt like he was pushing off the inside of my belly as if it were the end of a swimming pool. I wrote about the shower the girls at the office gave me, the bassinet I'd found at Jordan Marsh that just fit in my room, the blanket Al's mother had crocheted. I didn't write about how terrified I was to give birth. Al had plenty of his own to be terrified about.

He was on a ship in the Pacific carrying marines. Like me, I think Al was holding back on describing the daily terrors of his life. I saw enough in the newsreels, read enough in the *Herald,* to know he was keeping the worst from me. And he was never one who liked to write a lot, so for him to fill one of those thin blue sheets every week with any news at all was a big deal.

He was bursting, of course, when I wrote him about my pregnancy, which I sat down and did minutes after I'd read the results of the pregnancy test. He worried that he wouldn't be with me when my time came. Honestly, I wrote him back, what man *was* when his wife was giving birth? He could pace the deck of his destroyer just as well as he could pace the waiting room of the maternity ward. He made me promise to send a telegram as soon as the baby was born.

I wasn't the only woman to have a baby alone while her husband was at war. But that doesn't help you much, I discovered, when you're scared and in pain and then in so much joy that no one else can share with you except your baby's father. I wanted Al with me so badly that first moment when the nurse put our son in my arms. I wanted to see Al's face light up; I wanted to watch him stroke the fine swirl of hair on his baby's head and kiss his cheek.

I wanted him to take us both in his arms.

Instead, I asked Patsy to take a photograph. She fixed my hair and made me put on some rouge and lipstick, and then presented me with a box wrapped in lilac paper.

"For the new mother. A little something to remind you that you're still a woman."

I opened it while she held the baby. Inside, buried in layers of tissue paper, was a peach-colored peignoir with a matching quilted silk jacket.

"You put this on, *then* we take the picture for Al. What better for a guy at war than a photo of his son in the arms of a woman worthy of being a pinup?"

So I changed and sat in the chair by the window, wrapped Al Jr. in the crocheted blanket from his grandmother and beamed at the camera.

Later, when the nurse took Al Jr. back to the nursery, my parents arrived with Thanksgiving dinner. With Carmine and

31

Jimmy overseas, my sisters and my brother Sal spending the holiday with their in-laws, and Cookie and her babies with her parents, Mama needed someone to feed, and I was it.

She made a turkey that she stuffed like a veal roast, with parsley, bread crumbs, sausage and hard-boiled eggs. She even put some *alice*—anchovies—in the stuffing, which she knew I liked but weren't a favorite with anyone else in the family. She had manicotti in her basket, as well, filled with her own ricotta. And she brought me a stuffed artichoke, overflowing with garlic and Parmigiano.

I leaned back and let her slice the meat and pile my plate with more than enough food. Papa, dressed in his Sunday suit, walked down the hall to peer at his new grandson and returned smiling.

"He looks like me. He's gonna be a good boy."

"Hah!" said Mama and handed him a plate of food.

It wasn't Al sitting there with me. God only knew when he'd see his son. But after I'd eaten the meal my mother had prepared for me, I was able to sleep. I wasn't alone.

When Al Jr. was four months old, my boss at Shawmut called. My replacement hadn't worked out; they wanted me back, if I was willing. With so many men called up in the war, the government was encouraging women, even mothers, to go to work. Because Mama offered to take care of Al Jr., I went back.

Mama had done piecework at home when we were kids. So the idea of a mother earning money, working at something outside the family, wasn't an issue for me. But I hadn't thought about what I'd do. I was so intent on giving birth, getting through what scared me the most, that anything afterward was still a dream. All during my pregnancy I prayed that the war would be over by the time the baby came, because I couldn't imagine being a family, being a mother, without Al.

But the war didn't end, and I brought Al Jr. home to the back bedroom in my parents' apartment. I sat on the edge of the bed and held him, and the fear I'd overcome by giving birth was replaced by the fear of having to be both mother and father to him. Once I had him in my arms, heard his cry, felt his heartbeat, I understood what I'd seen in Cookie's eyes the night before Carmine left. Because she was already a mother, she knew. The fierce need to protect our children, keep them safe from harm. It was such a monumental task. I asked myself how I was going to do it without Al, and knew I had to find a way.

The job—being able to provide for us—was part of how I survived the fear. I aired out my suits from the mothballs I'd stored them in, put on my stockings and heels and went back to work.

With so many men gone, there was too much for my boss to handle, and he turned to me. He gave me small jobs at first, but gradually he realized he could trust me with more. I took to numbers quickly. I liked the certainty; I liked the satisfaction of balancing debits and credits. I liked figuring out the worth of something and judging whether someone asking for a loan had the capacity to pay it back. Not just the dollars and cents, but the honor to make good on a promise.

I couldn't define the quality I was looking for when applicants came into the office. Maybe I was simply measuring them against Al, whom I knew to be true to his word, a man who'd face a challenge and meet it, despite the obstacles.

In the afternoons, when I got back from the bank, I changed into my housedress and fed Al Jr. his supper, stacked blocks with him, nuzzled and tickled him until he giggled and kicked his chubby legs. When I put him to bed, we kissed the photo of Al I kept on the dresser.

"Kiss Daddy good-night, sweetheart," I told him, long before he knew what a daddy was.

After he was asleep, I described everything he did in letters to Al. "Al Jr. took his first step today. Your mother held out a *biscott'* and he let go of the chair he was clutching and raced across the room to grab it." "He said 'Da-Da' tonight and pointed to your picture!" "He's out of diapers!" "He climbed the jungle gym in the park on Prince Street for the first time."

It never occurred to me that Al Jr. would be a little boy before he met his father.

I was helping Mama cook for Thanksgiving. We had celebrated Al Jr.'s second birthday on Sunday with his cousins, and Al had managed to send him a birthday card that arrived in time. Al was in the South Pacific. That was all I knew. The newsreels were full of images of planes dropping bombs and exploding battleships. All I could do was pray that one of them wasn't his.

I was up to my elbows in pastry dough for the pies. I'd convinced Mama that we should serve an American apple pie in addition to the sweet ricotta pie with ten eggs and grated orange peel she always made for the holidays—not only Thanksgiving, but Christmas and Easter, as well. I wanted Al Jr. to grow up an American. He spent the week with grandparents who only spoke Italian to him. But his father was an American serviceman, fighting for his country. The least we could do was teach Al Jr. to eat apple pie, sweet potatoes and cranberry sauce.

"You spend too much time with those Americans at the bank. What's wrong with what I cook for the holidays?"

"Nothing's wrong, Mama. It's delicious. But we're Americans, too! It's not such a bad thing. You and Papa chose to come here."

"I don't know how to make apple pie and I'm too old to learn. If you want your son to have apple pie, then you make it."

Which is why I was kneading dough when the doorbell rang. I wiped my hands on my apron and answered.

"Mrs. Dante?" The Western Union delivery boy stood in the doorway, a thin yellow envelope in one hand, a pen and receipt in the other. I blindly signed the form and took the envelope, my hand trembling and a silent voice screaming inside my head, *No! No! No!*

I sat down at the kitchen table and stared at the envelope, unable to move. Al Jr., who'd been playing with a toy truck on the floor, stopped and came up to me, tugging on my sleeve.

"Mommy, Mommy, what's that?"

Mama came in carrying a stack of shirts to iron.

"Rosa, who was at the door?" Then she saw the envelope, made the sign of the cross and kissed the crucifix that always hung around her neck.

"What does it say? Which one? Who?" she screamed at me.

I hadn't even thought of my brothers, God forgive me. But the envelope was addressed to me, not my parents. It could only be Al. But I couldn't answer. I was frozen.

Frantic, she grabbed the envelope and tore it open. She thrust it in front of my face.

"Read it to me!"

I didn't want to. Couldn't.

"Rosa, read it to me *now*. We have to know."

She spoke with the firmness of voice I'd learned to use with Al Jr., and I listened.

"'Mrs. Dante—We regret to inform you that your husband, Petty Officer Albert Fiore Dante, has been wounded in action in the Philippine Sea. The extent of his injuries is serious and he is awaiting transport to a hospital ship.'

"Oh, my God, he's alive! He's coming home." And I collapsed in tears in my mother's arms.

Reunion

———⟨⟨⟨ ⟩⟩⟩———

TWO MONTHS LATER, in January 1945, Al arrived at the navy hospital in Bethesda, Maryland. I got a few days off from the bank and took the train from South Station to Washington. It had been nearly three years since I'd seen him. When I walked into the ward on that gray day in January I scanned the line of beds looking for my husband and did not recognize him until the nurse pointed him out.

The tanned, robust man who'd left in the spring of 1942 had been replaced by a gaunt, pale shadow. In the intervening months since the telegram arrived, I'd learned that his back, leg and arm had been broken by the impact of an explosion. His body was riddled with shrapnel. Although many of the external scars had healed, he was still in a body cast and faced months of rehabilitation. The navy had informed me that his Seabee career was over. More than likely, he'd never work in construction again.

But he was alive, I repeated to myself. He was alive.

I moved to his bedside. I'd taken the time, when I got to Union Station, to change and put on some makeup. I was wearing his favorite perfume, and as I bent toward him I saw the flicker of recognition at my scent.

"Hey, baby," I murmured and kissed him on the lips.

"Hey, baby," he replied and, with his good arm, pulled me as close as I could get against his rigid cast. I exhaled. We were going to make it.

It would be another month before Al was transferred to the VA hospital in Boston. I couldn't stay with him in Bethesda—because of Al Jr., because of my job—but that first week. I barely left his side.

I fed him. I gave him ice chips to suck on and wiped his forehead when he got the sweats. I bathed the parts of his body not covered in plaster.

At first, he didn't want me to. Out of shame.

"C'mon, Al. I've touched every inch of your body. You think there's something I haven't seen? What did you do, get a tattoo with some other woman's name on it?"

I teased him.

"It's not the same," he protested. "I'm not the same."

"Neither am I. I wasn't a mother before you left. I have a few scars, too."

But it was more than our bodies, I knew, that we were thinking about. We weren't kids anymore. The war had seen to that. And we were strangers to each other. I'd kept so much from him in my letters, not wanting to trouble him with what he could do nothing about. He didn't know about the nights I'd spent walking the floor with Al Jr. when he had the croup and I was afraid it would turn into pneumonia. Or the fight I had with Mama about how to treat it—she with her witches' remedies and me wanting to take him to the doctor. He didn't know that I'd looked for an apartment during my lunch hour after that fight, ready to pack my bags and take my baby. Maybe I'd gotten too used to being on my own in Trinidad. Too much of me had been shaped into something Mama would never understand. There were nights I'd blamed Al for how I felt. If he'd been with me, not fighting the war, we'd have been a normal family with a place of our own. I never talked about this to anyone. I was so ashamed—how unpatriotic, when so many families were sacrificing even more.

I don't know how many times over the past three years I'd imagined Al's homecoming and what it would mean for us. He'd been gone longer than we'd been together and, in the grim, cold winters of Boston, with a sick baby and empty bed, I began to forget who he was. Our life together at Chaguaramas seemed like a fairy tale, a story that had happened to someone else, not Al and me. I wondered if we could ever be those two people again. I could only guess at the secrets Al kept from me during those years apart. Horror. Loneliness. Fear.

Don't get me wrong. Having him back, even broken as he was, was all I wanted. But I was scared. And I knew he was, too. It felt as though we'd have to start all over again, but this time with a child who didn't know his father, and parents—both his and mine—watching every move, listening to every word.

I wanted to scream.

Instead, I got back on the train to Boston at the end of the week, pulled a scrap of paper out of my purse and made a list of every positive aspect of our situation. There were so many women who didn't have half of what I had—no husbands, strangers or otherwise, to welcome back into their beds, no fathers to introduce to their children. They wouldn't even have graves to visit.

"Be grateful," I told myself. "God gave us a second chance."

As the train pulled into South Station late that night I'd calmed down. Al was in no condition to have me go all mopey. He needed me to be stronger now than all the years he'd been away. There'd be time for me to lean on him later.

Al spent two more months in the hospital, but once he was back in Boston, I could visit him every weekend and his mother learned how to take the trolley out to Jamaica Plain on Wednesdays so she could bring him food. We decided to wait until he was out of his cast before I brought Al Jr. to the hospital. It was the end of March by then and Al was able to sit up in a wheelchair. He was in the hospital solarium when we arrived. He'd shaved and gotten a haircut for the occasion and had even put on some weight since he'd been taken to Bethesda. I convinced myself that he looked close enough to the photograph Al Jr. knew as "Daddy" that he wouldn't be a total stranger to his son.

The whole ride out to the VA hospital I rehearsed with Al Jr. His little legs dangled over the edge of the trolley seat and he swung them back and forth. I'd shined his shoes the night before and pressed his pants and shirt. He looked well-cared for, content. I smiled at how much he was starting to resemble Al as he lost his baby face. I wondered if Al would see himself in his son's eyes.

"Remember, sweetie, we're going to see Daddy, the man in the picture. Just like Papa is my daddy, you have a daddy, too."

"Why doesn't he live with us, like Papa does?"

"Because he's been fighting far away. But he got hurt and now he's getting better so he can come home to us. But he misses you very much and wants to see you."

Al Jr. clung to my hand as we climbed the steps of the hospital, stealing glances along the hallway at bandaged men and briskly moving nurses. He squeezed my hand tighter. Maybe this wasn't such a good idea, I thought. Too much for a little boy to take in. But Al wanted so much not only to see his son, but to hold him, feel the weight of him in his arms.

At the end of the long hallway I bent down in front of the

door to the solarium. I took Al Jr.'s face in my hands and kissed him. "Your daddy is waiting for you and he loves you very much. I'm going to be right here with you."

Al was looking out the window when I opened the door. He turned, smiled first at me, then moved his gaze down to his son. His hands gripped the arms of his wheelchair and he pushed himself up onto his feet.

"Hello, son," he whispered. His eyes filled up.

Al Jr. grabbed my leg and hid behind me.

"He's not my daddy," he mumbled into my thigh.

A cloud moved over Al's face. He heaved himself back into the wheelchair.

I put my arm around Al Jr.

"It's okay, sweetie. He *is* your daddy. He just looks a little different from his picture. Remember the baby photo Aunt Patsy took of you the day you were born? You don't look like that anymore, do you?"

He shook his head, still keeping it hidden against me. "No. I'm growed up now."

"Right. And so is your daddy. He's grown up now, too."

He peeked out from his hiding place.

"What's his name?"

"Al. Just like yours. Can you say hi to him?"

He shook his head again.

I saw the disappointment in Al's eyes. And the hunger.

Give him time, I mouthed to Al.

"Well, Mommy's going to say hi, so you can stay here or come with me while I give him a kiss."

"Don't go!"

"I'm only going to Daddy. Not far."

I moved deliberately across the room to Al, but Al Jr. still clung to me, hiding behind me as I reached Al and leaned in to kiss him.

40

"Hi," I said, meeting his lips and lightly brushing his check, wet with tears.

"He's beautiful," he murmured.

"Like you," I answered.

"And stubborn."

"Also like you." I smiled, trying to ease his hurt with a little ribbing.

It was at that moment that Al Jr. let go of me and raced out the door.

I pulled back from Al and felt him stiffen.

"I have to go after him," I said, as if I needed to explain.

Then I followed Al Jr. down the hall, his legs pumping and his arms flailing as if he was running from a nightmare.

And I felt as if I was in the middle of one.

Stern nurses cast me disapproving looks as I chased after Al Jr., my high heels clicking against the linoleum. At the end of the hall an orderly saw him coming and scooped him up. He was sobbing and kicking by the time I got to him.

I thanked the orderly, apologized for my son's outburst with a very red face and took the tangle of beating arms and legs into my own arms.

"We're going outside, young man, while you calm down. Don't you *ever* run away from me again!"

I struggled between the words of a mother who wants to put the fear of God into a child to keep him safe and the words of a mother who understands her child's confusion and anger. I never for even a second felt like running away from Al but, sure as hell, there were moments I wanted to run away from how hard it was to see him the way he was now.

I took Al Jr. outside to a bench and held him on my lap until he stopped sobbing. I got out my handkerchief and wiped his face and made him blow his nose. I figured out I wasn't going to be able to explain to a two-and-a-half-year-old that in time he'd get to know the strange man in the wheelchair and understand how much that man loved him. But I wasn't above bribery and guilt.

"Daddy's feeling very sad because you ran away," I said. "I think we need to go back up and say, 'I'm sorry.'"

Al Jr. shook his head vehemently. "No! I don't want to go back."

"Well, if we go back and say, 'I'm sorry,' then we'd be able to stop at La Venezia on the way home and get a lemon ice."

When we returned to the solarium, Al was still there, thank God. I worried that he might have wheeled himself back to his room, and I couldn't bring myself to take Al Jr. in there. But the solarium overlooked the bench where Al Jr. and I had been sitting, and Al had watched us the whole time.

I carried our son into the room and sat on a chair with him on my lap, his head facing away from Al. I prompted him. "Al Jr. has something he wants to tell you."

It took him a few minutes, but the promise of a treat was enough to get the words out.

"Sorry I runned away."

"Okay, son. But don't ever do that again. Your mom and I want you to be safe. Hey. Now that you're here, do you want to see some pictures of my ship?"

Al pulled a small scrapbook out of the back of his chair and started turning the pages. At first, Al Jr. was wary, but his curiosity soon overcame his need to cling to me. He edged closer to Al and the photos—snapshots taken on the deck of his destroyer. But then he turned a page and Al Jr. recognized something.

"That's me!" He pointed to the photo Patsy had taken of the two of us the day he was born.

"Your mom sent that to me and I've always had it with me, right here." Al touched the pocket over his heart.

"I have a picture of you," Al Jr. said. "But you don't look like in the picture."

Al and I exchanged glances over his head.

"Pretty soon you won't need a picture of me. I'll be right there, home with you and your mom."

Homecoming

AL CAME HOME at the beginning of May, just before VE Day. He was on crutches and hobbled up the steps to my parents' apartment, his face as white as one of my aunt Carmella's bleached sheets that hung out on the line every Monday. The sweat was pouring from his face as he slumped into a chair in the living room.

I was glad we'd put off his welcome-home party until the following Sunday. I didn't want the rest of the family to see him like this—to take pity on him. And I sensed that he didn't want to be seen—by his brothers, his cousins—as less than the man who had left Boston so long ago. If I knew Al, it would only make him angry to have people feeling sorry for him.

And he was angry enough already. At the hand the war had dealt him; at the pain; at the gaping hole that was his future. What was he going to do with his life now that he couldn't build? Of course, he didn't tell me these things. I had to figure it out myself, lying alone in the middle of the night.

We didn't have room in my bedroom for a double bed, and Al was still recuperating, so he slept on a hospital bed we'd rented and put in the living room, and I stayed with Al Jr. in the bedroom. I was at my wits' end, longing for a moment alone with my husband. Not even to make love, mind you— I understood that was still months away. No, all I wanted was a blessed hour or two to eat a meal that I'd cooked and just the two of us ate, sitting across the table and talking to each other.

But my mother did all the cooking, with me still working at the bank—and thank God for that! Dinnertime was like a movie set for a Frank Capra extravaganza, with a cast of thousands. Al's parents came at least once a week, resentful that we weren't living with them, and we had to go to them on Sundays for dinner. Everybody wanted to see Al, wish him well, exult in the fact that he was alive.

I couldn't blame them. Just seeing him at the table in the kitchen reading the *Herald* when I came home from work was a comfort to me. A sign of normalcy.

But it wasn't enough. Not for me. And I knew that, soon, it wouldn't be enough for Al, either. I understood that we weren't going to have what we'd been blessed to experience on Trinidad at the beginning of our marriage. I'd accepted it. You can't go backward in life, not after you get hit with something as big as World War II. And not after you have kids.

But that doesn't mean you give up on having a decent life. I knew if we stayed too long with my parents, with Al out of work and sleeping in the living room, we'd slip into a pattern that would be too hard to pull away from.

That's why, on my way home from work one summer evening, I stopped in my tracks as I was walking down Salem Street. My feet were killing me; the heat had made them swell up and my pumps were too tight. All I wanted to do was get home and out of those shoes and my suit. I was rushing. And then I saw the sign in the window of Nardone's. It was a small pizza place on the corner of Salem and Stillman. They made a decent Neapolitan pizza and had a few basic dishes—meatballs, eggplant parmigiano—on the menu. I'd heard that old man Nardone had passed away in April.

The sign that made me stop said For Sale.

I stood on the sidewalk for a few minutes. The place was open and a few people were seated at tables. One of the things I'd learned in my time at the bank was the importance of location to a business, especially a business that served the public. I crossed the street and pretended to be looking into the Lu Ann dress shop, but I was actually watching the reflection in the shopwindow—watching the number of people walking past Nardone's.

Satisfied, I crossed back and pushed open the door to the restaurant. I sat down, ordered a cup of coffee and chatted with the waitress. I'd seen her now and then in the neighborhood. She'd been a few years ahead of me in high school, although I have to say she looked worn-out. Waitressing is the kind of job that can do that to you, on your feet all day, lifting heavy trays. Despite my too-tight pumps, I was grateful I'd had the training and the skills to get my job at the bank.

"Hey, Milly, I saw the sign in the window. How come the Nardones are selling the place?" I stirred my coffee as if I was just making idle conversation, not seriously interested.

"Anthony's convinced his mother to go to Miami with him. He wants to 'start a new life' and none of the other brothers care about the restaurant. He's champing at the bit to get outta Boston, but far as I know, nobody's biting. All I care is that whoever buys the place keeps me on. Hey, I hear Al's back. How's he doing? My brother was asking about him. Tell him Sonny said hi."

"Thanks, I'll do that."

When I got up, I left her a nice tip. She smiled and waved at me through the window when she went to clear the table.

The next day on my lunch hour I did some research on restaurant sales in the city. Not much was moving, since so many places got passed down to the next generation. I didn't know much about running a restaurant, but I knew food. I hadn't known anything about banking, either, when I'd started three years ago, and I'd learned fast enough. That night after I got Al Jr. settled in bed and Al was listening to the Red Sox game out on the stoop with his cousin, I sat down at the dining room table with my savings account book and my ledger. Al and I probably couldn't buy Nardone's on our own, but if my parents took a share and the bank was willing to give us a loan, we might be able to make an offer. I knew the Nardones owned the building, not just the restaurant, and there were three apartments above it. That meant Al and I could have a home of our own again, and we'd have the rent from the other apartments to help pay off the loan.

I went to bed with a sense of hope that night for the first time since Al had been wounded. I was pretty sure I could talk my boss into the loan—provided I promised to keep working for him and assured him I'd be handling the business end of the restaurant. And I was equally sure Mama and Papa would be willing to invest in and work at the restaurant. It was Al I needed to convince, Al I needed to inoculate with my hope.

I thought back to our early days, especially in our cottage at Chaguaramas, when we'd had nothing under that tin roof except each other, and I knew that, somehow, I had to find our way back there.

To get there, I lied.

I lied first to my boss. "I need to take Wednesday off, Mr. Coffin. An appointment for my husband's treatment, and I have to accompany him."

Next, I lied to Al. "I got a call from the hospital. They've scheduled a checkup for you, but not at the VA. They gave me an address in Marblehead."

"Marblehead? How'm I supposed to get there with these?" He waved his crutches at me. He was getting pretty good at using them as extensions of his emotions, but not so great at moving around with them.

"There's a bus that runs up 1A. I checked. And I'll go with you."

"You don't have to babysit me. What about your job?"

"I'm *supposed* to go with you. I think it's about some new treatment, and they want to teach me how to do it, be part of your recovery."

The thing is, I didn't feel I was lying with the words I was saying. I believed that the reason I was taking Al to Marblehead *was* going to help him recover.

I even lied to Mama.

"I'm not going to work on Wednesday, Mama, but I still need you to watch Al Jr. I can't take him with us to this appointment. It's too much for me with Al still on crutches."

The night before, I stayed up cooking. I made Al's favorite foods, not just Calabrese dishes, but one of the island specialties I'd learned to cook on Trinidad, fried bananas in a sweet rum sauce. I packed everything in a picnic basket the next morning and tucked our bathing suits and beach towels underneath the food. And I wore one of the sundresses I'd made that first year on Trinidad. It still fit, I'm pleased to say.

"You going to the doctor dressed like that?" my mother asked.

Mama let nothing escape her.

"It's a long bus ride, Mama, and it's hot. I've got a shawl to put over my shoulders when we get there."

"I think she looks great, Mama. The doctor will be jealous." Al was standing in the doorway. The look of appreciation on his face was the first spark of life I'd seen since he'd come home.

I twirled around in front of him, letting him catch a whiff of my perfume.

"You smell like you did on the island," he murmured.

I wanted to pull him into my bedroom right then and there. But with Mama standing in the kitchen, hands on her hips, and Al Jr. dawdling with his farina at the breakfast table, I knew that was a surefire way to extinguish the longing I'd just heard in Al's voice.

One step at a time, I told myself.

"Let's get going. We don't want to miss the bus." I grabbed the basket and brushed Al's hand to follow me.

I'd given us plenty of time to get to Haymarket Square and the bus stop. I didn't want Al to exhaust himself before we'd even started the trip. Our route took us past Nardone's. The For Sale sign was still in the window, but I didn't do anything as obvious as point it out.

Al was wearing his uniform, and everyone we passed made mention of it.

"Welcome home, son."

"God bless you."

"Thank you for your sacrifice."

I could see that Al was embarrassed by the attention.

"It's just their way of showing appreciation." I smiled at him, proud to be at his side.

"Yeah, but so many guys were braver than I was, and they're not here anymore."

"But your being alive doesn't make their sacrifice—or yours—any less." I stroked the side of his cheek.

"I know. But it's hard for me to believe that."

I fought the tears that were welling up in my eyes. I didn't want Al to think the conversation was upsetting me when, in fact, it was exactly what I'd wished for. Just the two of us, talking about things that were important.

We got on the bus and found seats near the front. Al stowed his crutches and the picnic basket in the rack above us and settled stiffly into the aisle seat with his leg stretched out. I saw the by-now familiar wince cross his face and heard the sharp intake of breath that was the only signal he allowed himself to indicate that he was in pain.

He would never have ventured this far, or been willing to risk the pain, if I'd told him where we were going. He would have refused and locked himself back in his empty silence in the living room.

But the twinge appeared to be fleeting this time, which I think surprised him. His face relaxed and I shifted my weight so that my thigh was pressed against his good leg through the thin yellow cotton of my dress. It was the closest we'd been physically since he'd returned, except when I was taking care of him, which didn't really count.

Little droplets of sweat were forming on my upper lip and also dripping down under my arms. I wasn't sure if it was the heat or my own nervousness. If I'd wanted to recreate the atmosphere on Trinidad, I'd gotten off to a good start. It was always hot there, and anytime Al and I had been close our bodies were slick with sweat.

Al reached up and wiped the sweat from my lip with his thumb.

"So where are we really going, Rose? Your mother was right. This dress is no outfit to wear to a VA doctor's office. I'd have to fight guys off with my crutches the minute anybody got a look at you!"

My face turned bright red.

"You knew? Are you angry with me?"

"I'm here on this crazy excursion, ain't I?"

"Well, then. We're going to the beach. Not Revere, where half the world knows us. I wanted us to get completely away.

50

And Marblehead has a bus that goes directly to the water. You won't have to walk very far."

"Why the beach? Why not a picnic on the Common?"

"Because I wanted us to remember Chaguaramas."

At that point, I couldn't hold my tears back. I wanted so much for him to remember.

"I remember Chaguaramas," he said softly. "I remember a beautiful woman in my bed, who made love to me in the rainy season, who swept away scorpions as if they were specks of dust, who kept my dinner warm and waited up for me."

"Oh, Al. I want that for us again."

"Me, too, Rose."

He put his arm around me and kissed me hard. And then he held me all the way to Marblehead.

When we got to the beach we found a spot that wasn't too far along the sand but also wasn't on top of other people. That's why I'd picked Wednesday, hoping it wouldn't be too crowded, like Revere on the weekends—which is fine when you're high school kids hanging out with your friends, but not when you're a couple of lost and lonely adults trying to find their way back to each other.

I spread the blanket on the sand near the shoreline. It wasn't the azure blue of the Caribbean, but the sun caught the water at just the right angle and broke up into thousands of pinpoints of light. It was as if my brother Jimmy's girlfriend, Marie, the Sicilian, had snagged one of her gaudy dresses and all the sequins had spilled across the ocean.

Al pulled me down next to him, and I swear, I would've done anything with him at that moment. But he whispered to me.

"I just want to hold you, Rose. Rest your head on my chest so I can breathe in your perfume."

We lay like that for a while, quiet, listening to one another breathe. I felt the weight of his arm draped over me and knew with certainty that's where I wanted to be.

When both our stomachs started growling, I stirred.

"How about some lunch?" I murmured.

"As long as you promise to lie down with me again after we eat."

I set out the dishes I'd prepared the night before: chicken salmi that had absorbed the flavors of wine vinegar and garlic and oregano overnight and that we ate with our fingers, the olive oil slick on our chins; string beans and potatoes with some chopped-up tomatoes from Uncle Annio's garden; and the fried bananas now soaked through with rum and brown sugar. I'd even managed to put a couple of bottles of beer in the basket.

"I used to dream of your cooking when I was sitting below deck opening up a can of C rations. Some of the guys in my unit swooned about their girls' hips or legs, the way they danced or kissed. But none of them could brag about the way their girls cooked, because you always had them beat."

"You talked about my food and not my looks? What, is *that* what you remembered about me?" I slapped him playfully, but hard, on the arm.

He laughed. "I kept those memories to myself. I didn't want to share with anybody else what you looked like coming out of the shower or stretched out next to me in bed. I could close my eyes and picture you asleep. Did you know I used to just watch you sleeping? Especially early in the morning when I left for work. Sometimes I sat on the edge of the bed and looked at your face. I couldn't believe someone as beautiful as you was my wife. I still don't."

I choked up a little at that. For a guy who'd been moping on the couch for two months without showing much interest in married life, he'd been holding back *a lot*.

"I'm glad you made us get away, Rose. The sun, the water. It's a little like old times."

"Let's go for a swim." I pulled at his hand. At first, he resisted. I don't think he wanted me or anyone else to see his scarred body. But it really was pretty deserted where we were. I made him hold a towel around me so I could change into my swimsuit, a two-piece from Port of Spain.

"I remember that suit. You still fill it out in all the right places."

He patted my backside. A good sign, I thought. I turned around and began to unbutton his shirt. He stopped my hand and shook his head.

"You go, and I'll admire you from the shore."

"I don't want to swim alone. Besides, it's just us on this part of the beach. I bet your doc would tell you swimming's great exercise. And if you swim, we don't have to lie about getting physical therapy today."

Reluctantly he agreed. But only if I'd glance away while he undressed and also walked ahead of him into the water.

"I don't care what your body looks like, Al. I just want to feel it close to mine."

But I plunged into the water and waited with my back to him until I felt his arms around me. I pressed myself against him and then wriggled free.

"Come on, swim with me."

I dived down under the water and took off. I hadn't been able to swim like this since we'd left Trinidad. The few times I'd taken Al Jr. to Revere Beach, I'd waded in the shallows while he splashed around.

I moved through the water, propelling myself with strong kicks and loving the sensation of slipping through the waves. I looked over my shoulder to see if Al was having as much fun as I was. He was behind me, stroking slowly and carefully, as if he was testing how far he could push himself before he started hurting. But his face was serene, not tight with pain or with the color drained out of him like he got when he hoisted himself up the stairs on his crutches. I think he was surprised.

I turned onto my back and floated, waiting for him to catch up.

When he swam up next to me, I threw my arms over his shoulders and wrapped my legs around him. Out of the water he could never have held me like this. But he cradled me and pulled me close, kissing me as the water lapped around us.

It's a good thing my face was wet and salty already, because it hid the tears.

We swam for about fifteen more minutes, then stretched out to dry on the blanket. Al put on his undershirt when we got out of the water. I turned away so he wasn't embarrassed. But I could see what six months in a body cast had done to the muscles in his chest. I bit my tongue to keep from saying anything, from letting him hear any pity in my voice.

We slept for a little while, relaxed from the swim and the sun in ways that the daily grind didn't allow us. When I felt him stirring, I chose my moment.

"Al?"

"Mmm?"

"Thank you for coming with me today."

"I wouldn't have missed it for the world."

"Me, neither. It's what I dreamed we'd have, all through the time you were away. It's what I dream we'll always have. I've got another dream, Al. A new one. You want to hear about it?"

He turned his body to me, so that we were facing each other.

"Fire away."

I told him about the restaurant for sale, the apartment above it. What I thought we could do with the place. A home of our own. Our own business. I started to get excited, describing the potential I saw on that street.

"Whoa, Rose." He raised his hand to stop my babbling. "How are we going to pay for this?"

He was well aware that I knew to the penny how much money we had in the bank and coming in every month from my paycheck and his navy pension. His question wasn't a challenging or incredulous one. I felt like he believed in me, believed that what I was describing wasn't a pipe dream but was really within our reach.

I sat up, enumerating on my fingers each of the sources I'd thought of. He listened to me.

"Have you talked to your folks yet, or the bank?"

"No, of course not! Not until I'd talked to you. I want this to be *our* future. But only if you want it, too."

"Aw, Rose. What do I know about running a restaurant? My ma did the cooking. All I know is how to hammer a nail and level a two-by-four. And now I can't even do that."

He started to slip back into his shell and I had to grab him before all the goodness from this day in the sun got wiped out by the darkness of his self-pity.

"Al Dante! I've never known you to give up, so don't go giving up on yourself right now. There was a time in your life when you didn't know what a two-by-four *was,* and you learned. You're a smart guy and a brave guy. And I can't believe you'd turn away from something just because you didn't know how to do it. If you have no *interest* in running a restaurant, or think it's a bad decision, then I'll listen to you. But if you're going to say no to every idea I present you with because you feel like you *can't* do it, then you're not the Al I love!"

"I need to take care of my family. I don't want you to feel you have to do it all."

"That's why I got excited when I saw the sign in Nardone's

55

window. I thought we could do it together. And live right above the shop, so I wouldn't have to go off to work every day and be away from you and Al Jr. I want us to have a chance, Al. Whether it's the restaurant or something else."

"You really didn't talk to anyone else about this?"

"No. And I won't until you give me the go-ahead. This is between you and me, Al. I know other girls bring their families into the middle of things, pit themselves against their husbands sometimes. But you and I had a different start than other couples because of Chaguaramas. We only had each other. And all the time you were away and I was living alone with my folks, I never once forgot that I was your wife first. I'm still your wife first, a daughter second. I believe in you, Al. I believe in us—that we have a future together. We're luckier than most. I know you look at yourself and don't see that yet. But you will. Believe in us, Al."

I hadn't intended to get so worked up. I'd meant to be rational and businesslike, to show Al what good sense it made for us to buy the restaurant. Instead, I was becoming dramatic. I had his hands in mine and held them tight, as if to transfer to him all the faith I had that we would make it.

Maybe it was the difference between men and women, or maybe it was the difference between being in the middle of battle and being on the homefront. I'd had fears, but bombs weren't exploding next to my bed; nobody'd pointed a gun at my head or at my baby. If that's what it was, we were always going to have that gulf between us—our separate experience of the past three years. And I'd have to be the one who fought for us to have faith in ourselves and our future.

That's what I grasped that afternoon on the beach, and why I poured my heart and soul into convincing Al that we had to have the courage to take the next step in our lives— even if that step seemed to be off the side of a cliff. I needed to let him know that I was holding the release cord on the parachute and I wouldn't let us fall.

"You really want this, don't you, Rose?"

"Yeah, I do. But not for me. For *us*—you, me and Al Jr."

"Then I'm okay with it."

It was all I could ask for right then—that he was okay with the idea. I understood he was still too scared and too tired to imagine himself strong enough to take on anything more than getting himself up the stairs on his own. But I didn't ever want him to think he wasn't strong enough to take care of his family.

I threw my arms around him. "Oh, thank you, Al!"

I kissed him hard and he pulled me close.

That night, Al came to my bed after my parents had gone to sleep.

"I need to hold you. I can't give you anything else right now. But lying next to you on the beach I realized how much I miss having you in my arms."

I lifted the sheet in welcome and he slid his sunburned body next to mine. I nestled my behind against his belly; he wrapped his arms around me and we settled into the best night's sleep either of us had had in years.

Paradiso

A MONTH LATER, the Japanese surrendered. The war was over. And the Dante and Vitale families bought a restaurant.

After Al had agreed to my idea on the beach at Marblehead, we sat down with my parents and asked them to put money into the restaurant. And as I'd expected, they said yes—not only to the money, but to helping us out, Papa with the renovations, Mama in the kitchen.

It took us three months to clean the place up. No wonder Anthony Nardone's brothers wanted nothing to do with it. It was a pigsty. One of the first things I did was get a cat to take care of the rats.

On nights and weekends I scrubbed and bleached and scoured. Al started tinkering with the equipment, and even though his right arm was too damaged to wield heavy tools, he found he could still do the delicate work with small parts that took a sharp eye and a slow, careful hand. He could've been a surgeon, I told him. Thanks to Al, we didn't have to scrap the stove or the refrigerator.

We hoisted a new sign over the windows just before Thanksgiving. *Paradiso.* It was red and black with gold leaf around the edges of the letters. Everybody got dressed up and we took a photo out front—Al and me, Al Jr., my parents and Al's parents. Then we went inside and toasted with a bottle of Papa's Chianti.

We held Thanksgiving dinner in the restaurant that year, shortly before we opened to the public. Everybody came. My brothers Carmine and Jimmy had made it back safe from Italy. My sister Bella traveled from Albany with her husband and three kids. My brother Sal, the butcher, who lived up the street, my sister Lillian, who'd moved out to the country when her husband got a job at the General Radio factory, my sister Ida, the nurse, who worked at Mass General, Al's folks, his brothers and their wives—they all trooped down to Salem Street. The first snow had fallen and everyone arrived with red cheeks and cold feet, hungry and looking for warmth and a good meal.

We didn't disappoint. We'd pushed all the tables together to fit the thirty of us. While the three turkeys roasted, Mama and I spent the morning arranging platters of antipasto with her pickled eggplant, olives, fennel, roasted red peppers, vinegar peppers, marinated mushrooms, tuna, provolone, salami, prosciutto and *soprasatto*. After the antipasto, we served escarole soup with little meatballs, then Mama's handmade manicotti and, finally, the turkey along with candied yams and broccoli and cauliflower that we'd battered and fried the way Mama did zucchini flowers in the summer. For dessert, Mama made her sweet ricotta pie and I, of course, baked the apple pies.

We ate for four hours. To have everyone together, especially the boys home from the war, was a gift. But not everyone was happy for us about the restaurant. I put it down to jealousy and lack of imagination. I felt resentment from my brother Sal's wife, who until then had been able to feel like the queen of the manor because her husband owned his own business.

My brother Jimmy worried that Mama and Papa were in

over their heads financially. Because I was the baby of the family, he thought my parents were spoiling me, doing for me what the others had to do for themselves.

So there was this undercurrent of tension at dinner. I saw the eyes of appraisal as people came into the dining room. It wasn't fancy, but it wasn't cheap-looking, either. We had curtains on the windows that I'd sewn and cloth tablecloths and napkins. The linoleum on the floor had been stripped and waxed and buffed, so it looked like new.

I knew the value of appearances. You had to look like a winner for people to believe you were a winner. But some of my family thought I was putting on airs, trying to be better than they were.

And they were right. I *did* want to do better. I didn't want to spend the rest of my life in a back bedroom overlooking the alley. I wanted my son and the rest of my children, God willing, to have more than we had growing up in the Depression.

Don't get me wrong. Most of them at the table that day wished us well.

"Salute," they said. *"Buona fortuna!"*

But those with small minds and jealous hearts only knew how to be naysayers, full of doom and gloom.

"What do any of you know about running a restaurant?" they sniffed.

"Do you know how many restaurants go under in the first year?"

"How much in hock are you—and Mama and Papa—for this place?"

At one point, I had to get up from the table and go into the kitchen to keep from shooting my mouth off and throwing the whole family into turmoil.

Al followed and found me furiously slicing bread, tears ruining my makeup.

"Hey, babe," he said quietly, putting his arms around me. "I miss you out there."

"They make me so mad! I was afraid I'd say something I'd regret and upset Mama."

"They can all go to hell. Especially after we show them what a success this place will be. Just ignore them. Let them stuff their bellies with your delicious food and then go home, mad that they didn't think of it themselves."

He kissed me on the neck. I wiped my face and brought the basket of bread to the table with my head held high.

I worked at the bank another whole year while we got on our feet with Paradiso. Al and I moved with Al Jr. into the space directly above the restaurant; we'd kept the tenants in the other two apartments—the Boscos, who had no children, in the smaller one on the top floor, and the Agostinos, who'd been in America about three years, right below them. Both families were good people who paid the rent on time and were happy with the change in landlords.

Paradiso survived that first year with all of us working hard. When I came home at three o'clock, I changed into my cooking clothes and headed downstairs to help Mama and Al. We served pizza and sandwiches—meatball, sausage and peppers, cold cuts—for lunch. At five o'clock we started serving dinner. We kept Milly on as a waitress, and when it got busy, I waited tables, as well. Al had been cautious in the kitchen when we first opened, deferring to Mama and doing whatever she instructed him to do, which wasn't much beyond adding ingredients to pots she'd already started. But when our volume began building, he saw for himself that he needed to take on more. He conquered pizza, mastered a kneading technique that only required one hand, and worked out a smooth assembly process that got the pies in the oven in record time.

From there, he started taking on other dishes with gusto, watching Mama downstairs at Paradiso or me on Sundays in the kitchen upstairs. He'd slip his arms around my waist and, in between nuzzling my neck, watch and sniff as the garlic and basil hit the olive oil in the pan.

"I figured it out the other night, Rose. Cooking in a restaurant kitchen and building bridges on a South Pacific island in the middle of conflict are a lot alike."

The business grew. At the end of our first year we'd more than kept up with our loan payments. When I finished doing the books in November 1946, just before Thanksgiving and Al Jr.'s fourth birthday, I got up from the kitchen table and found Al downstairs in the cellar taking inventory. He was counting jars of tomatoes that Mama and I had put up in August.

I leaned against the shelf and studied him. He wasn't as washed out and scrawny as he'd been the summer before, and the haunted look that had been his constant expression only broke through now and then when he wasn't busy. When you saw him from his left side, as I was doing, you didn't notice how withered his right arm was. It was more than having filled out on good Italian cooking. He looked sturdy and purposeful, a man who knew he was doing useful work. The more confident he became, the more he'd taken on in the kitchen. Pretty soon he'd moved from being Mama's apprentice to becoming our primary chef. I smiled to myself. He was still handsome.

"What?" He'd finished counting, wrote the total on his clipboard, then glanced at me with curiosity.

"Can't a girl admire her man once in a while, especially in a dark corner when no one else is watching?"

"You didn't come down here to flirt. What's up? Did you find a problem with the books?"

"Just the opposite. We've cleared enough in the past three months to cover my salary at the bank. I wanted to talk to you about my quitting and working full-time at the restaurant."

"You sure that's what you want? Your job at the bank's important to you. You're so smart. Is this going to be enough?"

He was really asking, *Am I going to be enough?* Sometimes the man could be so blind to how much I loved him and it drove me crazy that he thought my job was more important than him and our life together.... So I played it out a little to show him how ridiculous that was.

"Maybe you're right. Maybe I should forget about the restaurant altogether and stick with banking. I'll become a businesswoman and give up everything—my child, the man I love—for my almighty career. On my deathbed I'll pat the pile of money I've accumulated, 'cause that'll be all I've got, and tell myself it was worth it."

I stuck my tongue out at him. "Jeez, Al. I don't know where you get these ideas."

He put down the clipboard and took me in his arms.

"If you want to quit the bank and you think we can manage, then go ahead."

ROSE
1947–55

Miami

I HANDED IN my resignation on the Monday after Thanksgiving and by Christmas had packed up my desk in a Hood milk crate and headed out the door. Mr. Coffin was a gentleman about it, but we both knew there were five guys back from the war waiting in line to take my job.

I was also two months pregnant, which I found out on New Year's Eve. I hadn't experienced any of the throwing up or exhaustion I'd had with Al Jr., so it was a surprise. But not an "Oh, no, what am I going to do now?" surprise. I'd seen some women react like that, women with too many mouths to feed and a husband still trying to put the war behind him and get on with life.

Ours was a joyful surprise. You'd have thought Al had played the numbers and won big when I told him. He whooped and danced me around the restaurant. Later that night in bed, he lifted my nightgown and kissed my belly.

Our son Michael was born in July of 1947 and spent his infancy in a bassinet in the restaurant kitchen, falling asleep to the Frank Sinatra records we played and the sizzle of bracciola frying in olive oil. Our daughter was born in 1950. We followed tradition and named her after Al's mother, Antonella, but like many things my generation was doing differently from our parents, we called her Toni. That wasn't on her baptismal certificate, of course, but I don't think I ever called her Antonella. Even when I was yelling at her and stringing together all her names for effect, I always said, "Toni Marie Dante! You stop that right now."

My generation was different from our parents when it came to having kids. I don't know how my mother managed with seven. Yes, I do. She depended on the older ones to watch out for the younger ones; she laid down the law, expecting us to abide by it, and she pretty much left us to amuse ourselves while she cooked, cleaned, washed clothes and did piecework. She didn't worry the way I did about my kids.

By the time I had three, I was done in. One Saturday night in 1952, right after I'd nursed all three kids through two weeks of the measles, we cooked for a private party for an engaged couple—five courses, one hundred people and enough wine to give them all headaches the next day. I finished up in the kitchen, sent the extra help home with their pay and their tips and locked up. I crawled upstairs, checked on the kids asleep in their beds and collapsed in my own. It was more than physical fatigue. I was over the edge. I'd yelled all day: "Where was the extra wine we'd ordered?" "Who took delivery on the veal, because there wasn't enough?" "Why aren't the tables set?" "Do I have to do everything myself?" You get the idea. I'd been so wrapped up in making sure my kids didn't go blind from the measles or—God forbid—die from it, that I'd neglected the details downstairs and paid for it in a massive case of *agita*.

I must have slept for almost twenty hours after that. We closed the restaurant on Sundays back then, so my mind simply shut down. Al made the kids some pastina with beaten egg and let them play. They were just well enough to feel bored with being cooped up in dark rooms for two weeks and were getting on one another's nerves. How Al kept them away from me, I don't know, but he did.

When I finally woke up on Sunday evening, groggy and with my mouth as dry as my aunt Zita's almond cookies, Al already had the kids bathed and in bed.

"You need a rest, Rose. And I mean more than a long sleep like you just had. Why don't we close the restaurant for a couple of weeks after Christmas, ask Carmine and Cookie to watch the kids, and you and I drive to Miami?"

"How can I do that? What if they get sick again?"

"Then we come back. But you should've seen them today. They're full of energy. If you don't take some time off, you'll be the one to get sick, and then where'll we be?"

And that's how we started going to Florida every winter. It was a mixed blessing. Something I don't talk about, because Florida was how Al met Estella.

Despite my reluctance and reservations about leaving the kids, Florida was just what I needed that year. We stayed in Miami Beach at the Casablanca; after 1954, it was always the Fontainebleau, which was right on the ocean. Al, who always had a good eye for what looked good on me, had put a stack of boxes under the tree at Christmas, each one holding a beautiful outfit for me to wear in Miami: cocktail dresses in aqua-blue lace and wine-red satin; jersey halter dresses with plunging necklines and cinched waists to show off the figure I'd gotten back after Toni's birth; two Jantzen bathing suits, one a maillot and one a two-piece floral print that reminded me of the suit I'd worn years before on the beach at Marblehead; silk and cashmere wraps for the evenings. At the top of the stack was a tiny box with a pair of diamond earrings.

We had a ball. We went out dancing every evening, at the

Copa or the Napoleon Ballroom at the Deauville Beach. Then we slept till noon, ate lunch on the pool patio and walked on the beach in the afternoon. I swam laps in the pool or body-surfed in the waves.

One afternoon at lunch Al slipped an envelope across the table.

"What's this?"

"Two Pan Am tickets."

"Are we going to fly home? Has something happened to one of the kids?" I could feel my heart start to race.

Al grinned. "Everybody's fine, Rose. This is a little surprise. One of the guys I played cards with the other afternoon recommended a side trip to Havana—the casino, the nightlife. I thought we should give it a try, spend a night. It'll be like the old days, the island life."

So the next day we flew on a little puddle jumper to Havana, along with men my banking experience told me had a lot of cash to throw around. I made Al promise me he'd only take one hundred dollars in chips at the casino, and when that was gone, we'd spend the rest of the time dancing.

Havana was really something in those days, at least the Havana that we saw. Cadillac convertibles cruising the streets, pastel buildings filled with shops and restaurants, the casino ablaze with crystal chandeliers and open all night long. If Fidel Castro and Che Guevara were up in the hills then, nobody at the roulette table was giving it a second thought. Like most gamblers, they assumed their winning streak would last forever.

And the women at the casino were gorgeous. Elegant and sophisticated. You could tell that most of them were mistresses, not wives. The jewelry was too ostentatious—the consolation prizes for not having the diamond and the wedding band the wives back in the States were wearing. And I imagine that some of those beautiful women were sitting by the sides of men they might not have come with but hoped to leave with.

It was an experience. I wore the burgundy strapless number Al had given me for Christmas and I'd had my hair and nails done in the hotel salon. I'd pulled my hair back from my face so you could see the diamonds in my ears.

While I was getting dressed, Al kissed my neck.

"If I win big tonight, I'll buy you a necklace to match the earrings."

"If you win big tonight, we're putting the money in the bank for the kids, but I'll always remember you wanted to give me a necklace," I told him with a kiss.

I knew Al was proud of me when we walked into the casino. He had his arm around my waist like a caress. I spent the evening perched on a stool next to him at the blackjack table, my leg pressed against his through the satin. Every now and then he'd gently squeeze my thigh.

"You bring me luck, Rose. Throughout my life."

When he hit a thousand dollars, I leaned over and whispered in his ear. "Let's finish this stroke of good fortune in the bedroom."

With a smile, he gathered up his chips, cashed them in and followed me to our hotel room. Through the louvered shutters on the windows I could hear the waves and the music of Sinatra wafting from somebody's radio.

Two winters later, Al's cousin Mario and his wife, Vera, were down in Miami at the same time. Mario had heard Al go on about Havana and wanted to fly over for a couple of days at the casino. Vera didn't want to go. She was deathly afraid of flying and begged me to stay with her and keep her company while Al and Mario went. Against my better instincts, I agreed.

Al and Mario were gone longer than they planned. Like a fool, I initially assumed it was because they were winning. Al wasn't much of a gambler, but he liked to go to the track now and then. He must've been winning big. I pictured him tapping the cards with his good left hand and keeping his right arm resting on his lap. I'd tailored the white jacket of his tux to fit him. By the time he and Mario went to Havana he already had a nice tan. I could understand that in Havana's high-stakes, booming culture, a guy could get caught up in the excitement. With his slicked-back dark hair and penetrating eyes, I'm sure he was on every unattached woman's radar the minute he strolled into the casino.

There's a heat to the Caribbean that we both knew—a heat that has nothing to do with the temperature. It's in the music, the dancing, the way people—especially women—just walk down the street. When you're near someone, you see the sweat glistening on her skin and you smell her perfume mingled with her own distinctive fragrance.

My imagination was taking me places I really didn't want to go. By the end of three days of playing canasta with Vera and drinking too many daiquiris at the bar before dinner, I was ready to get on a plane myself and drag Al back. He hadn't even called.

He and Mario finally showed up on the fourth day, rumpled, unshaven, but with wide grins, big cigars and a lot of cash. Vera and I were on the patio having coffee and Danishes, so I wasn't going to make a scene in public, but I was seething.

They went upstairs to shower and sleep.

Vera shrugged. "Boys will be boys."

"Al's not a boy," I said sharply. "He's got three kids and a wife who loves him. He should know better."

I let Al sleep it off for a few hours. I considered going through his pockets, but decided not to stoop so low. Instead, I took a long walk on the beach without Vera, who was really annoying me. In my head I enumerated all the reasons I should give Al the benefit of the doubt. He'd always been faithful, never even looked at another woman. He took tender care of me; suggesting that we spend time in Florida at all had been for my benefit. He adored the kids. He worked hard. So what if he spent an extra couple of days throwing money around? He'd come back, hadn't he? I thought I could forgive him. But I promised myself I'd go to Havana with him from now on.

When I got back to the hotel room Al was getting dressed. You could see why a woman would be drawn to him.

I sat down on the edge of the bed. "You want to talk about why you stayed in Havana so long without even a phone call? For all I knew, someone had rolled you and left you in an alley somewhere."

"I'm sorry, Rose. We were playing so hard we lost track of time. We got into a card game—you don't just walk away down there."

"Since when do you gamble like that, Al? I've never known you to be so obsessed." Maybe it wasn't a woman.

"I'm not. But Mario, he's reckless. I felt I needed to keep an eye on him. My mother and my aunt Philomena would never forgive me if I let him get in over his head. Like I said, I'm sorry."

I stared hard at him, trying to see the truth in his eyes. It scared me that I doubted him. He'd never let me down. I decided I needed to give him this one. And I didn't ask him if he'd been with a woman.

"Okay," I said.

He lifted me from the bed and kissed me. He smelled of the hotel's fancy soap, Prell shampoo and his Old Spice aftershave.

But Cuba still clung to him.

I tried to shake the scent—and the suspicion. I didn't want

to be weighed down with it. I didn't want to ruin our last night in Florida.

I put a smile on my face, changed into my sexiest dress and went down to dinner with Al. But it was still there in the far-off look in his eyes every now and then, as if he'd remembered something. It was still there in my own watchfulness.

That night in bed we didn't reach out for one another—me because I couldn't bring myself to touch him, Al because he fell into a profound sleep minutes after hitting the pillow.

A Piece Missing

‹ ❦ ›

WE STARTED THE DRIVE back to Boston the next day and didn't speak about Havana again. By the time we arrived in the North End, to kids who'd missed us despite having a ball with their cousins, and a restaurant stove that needed to be fired up again, I was too busy to deal with whatever Al had done in Cuba.

Oh, my wariness was still there. I felt like I had antennae constantly rotating, trying to pick up a signal: an unexplained phone call, a letter with a Havana postmark, a receipt for a piece of jewelry that wasn't sitting in *my* jewelry box or a dress that wasn't hanging in *my* closet. I was on pins and needles. I didn't know what I'd do if I found any of those signs—after crying my eyes out, that is. I didn't find anything, nor did I want to. But I realized that didn't prove that nothing had happened.

As you can imagine, I was on edge those first weeks back. Florida was supposed to be our R & R, and instead, it had turned me into a bundle of nerves. On top of that, Al Jr. was having trouble in school. There was a note from Reverend Mother, asking me to come in for a meeting as soon as we were back.

I've never done well with nuns. The ones I'd had to deal with growing up always made me feel like a tramp. My skirt was too short or my sweater was too tight or I had on too much makeup. I took pains when I kept my appointment with Reverend Mother to wear a suit and not one of the outfits Al had bought for me. But I was still nervous.

When I walked into the school I could feel my stomach churn. The smell of whatever they used on the floors—disinfectant, wax—lurched me right back to when I'd been in seventh grade at St. John's, heading down the hall to be chastised for talking back to Sister Alphonsus when she'd wrongly accused Vinny Tosi, an immigrant boy who'd arrived from Avellino only a few months before. She always assumed the worst of the Italian kids, especially the boys.

Reverend Mother's office was stuffy and dark, with the blinds drawn instead of open to the playground where the children were at recess. Hanging behind her desk was a large crucifix with Christ in agony.

"Thank you for coming, Mrs. Dante. I was surprised when you didn't respond to my note, but Albert told me you and your husband were in Miami. We don't see many parents taking a vacation in the wintertime and leaving their children."

"My children were with their aunt and uncle while we were away." This woman was already making me bristle.

"Yes, well. Perhaps it was because you were gone that Albert thought he could get away with his behavior."

"Exactly what did he do?"

"He's disrespectful, Mrs. Dante. A back talker. We also have reason to believe he's being influenced by older, public-school boys. I brought you in to let you know that we don't tolerate insolence at St. John's. If you don't put a tighter rein on him, we may ask him to leave."

"I'll talk to him about his mouth and what he's picking up from the older boys. I don't expect to have to come back."

I got up and held my back straight the whole way down

that highly polished corridor. But instead of turning for home, I went in the opposite direction toward the waterfront. Some of the piers weren't the best place for a woman to walk, even in broad daylight, but there was a short stretch near Lewis Wharf where I could sit on a stone wall and see and smell the ocean. It was where I went when I needed to collect my thoughts.

I hated the way I felt just then. Small. A failure as a mother. Oh, I'd have my words with Al Jr. when he got home from school, especially about the older boys he was supposedly spending time with. The neighborhood was changing, not that there hadn't always been tough guys hanging out on the corners. But it wasn't what I intended for my own kids.

I felt as if my hold on Al Jr. was slipping, loosening far sooner than I knew a mother ought to let go. It wasn't just that Al and I had gone to Florida for a couple of weeks. I was being pulled in too many directions—the kids, the restaurant, the strain between Al and me since Havana—and I wasn't giving enough attention to any of them.

I was falling apart. I felt like I had a piece missing, something important that the people I loved needed from me and that I couldn't give. That I didn't have. Which was why Al had gone looking for it elsewhere in Havana, and Al Jr. had tried to find it by seeking out boys he thought were big shots in the neighborhood.

The wind off the harbor and my tears stung my cheeks. I felt frozen to the stone wall, unable to move, not knowing how I was going to fill this empty space inside me. But the afternoon was wearing on. Soon enough, Mike and Al Jr. would be home from school and Toni would wake from her nap. Mama and Al were already in the kitchen prepping for the evening meal. They were all expecting me.

But I didn't move. It scared me that I wasn't picking myself up and getting on with what I recognized as my responsibilities. I didn't think a conversation with a nun—even a Reverend Mother—could push me over the edge like this. But I knew it wasn't just the judgment that I was a poor mother.

I knew I'd bottled up my anger and kept my mouth shut about Havana because to all outward appearances nothing had happened there. I had grown up watching women of my mother's generation look the other way when their husbands had an *amante*—a mistress—on the side, as long as he put food on the table and kept up the appearance of a marriage. I just had never understood the cost.

Al had slipped back into our Boston routines without a hitch. But he'd never said to me, "I swear, Rose, I wasn't with another woman." Because I'd never asked him. What I realized now, sitting on this cold rock and shivering as the sun set behind me, was that I needed to ask him. I wouldn't be able to let go of the doubts that were eating away at my insides. And if he said yes, I needed to know why he'd been unfaithful.

Sometimes it's hard to look at yourself and face the truth. I really wanted to bury in some remote corner of my heart whatever Al had done in Havana. But no matter how many layers I tried to muffle it with, I could still feel it—like the pounding of the telltale heart in Poe's story. Well, I wasn't going to let this make me crazy.

Wrapping my coat tightly around me, I stood. The streetlights had come on. My feet were frozen, but I got the circulation back in them as I started walking. About halfway down Atlantic Avenue I saw a figure coming toward me. It was Al. I could see the white edges of his chef's jacket flapping beneath the hem of his old navy peacoat.

"Rose! Rose! Where the hell have you been all afternoon? I called Cookie and Patsy. Nobody had seen you. When it got dark, I thought maybe you had an accident! I couldn't stay in the restaurant not knowing where you were. I was pacing like a madman. First, I was furious with you for not showing up or even calling, then I was just worried. The kids are upset. What happened to you?"

"I got lost, Al. In my thoughts. I was upset after meeting with Reverend Mother about Al Jr. and we need to talk about that, but later. I went down to the water to think."

"How long does it take to think?"

I could sense Al's frustration and anger. Maybe this wasn't the best time and place to have this conversation, but I'd spent the last month finding too many reasons not to have it at all.

"Long enough to consider not coming home at all."

"What are you talking about, Rose? What did the nun say that would make you not come home? What did Al Jr. do?

"It's not Al Jr. But what happened at my meeting made me ask myself how I was living my life, and the answer is that I've been avoiding the truth."

"What are you talking about?"

"I've been hiding my anger. From you. From myself."

"Anger about what?"

I took a deep breath. "Havana."

I thought he'd start again about babysitting his cousin in the casino. But he didn't.

"What do you want to know, Rose?"

"I want to know if you had an affair in Havana."

The cold moisture that had been blowing in off the harbor all afternoon was turning to an icy rain. But the discomfort I saw in Al's face had nothing to do with the weather.

"I don't want to hurt you with my answer."

"You'll hurt me more if you lie."

"Her name was Estella. I spent one night with her. That's all. I swear to God. I'm sorry, Rose."

I felt a different kind of chill than what I'd been sitting through all afternoon on the pier. It spread from inside me, filling my belly with such pain that I thought I wouldn't be able to walk. Was this really better than the gnawing doubt?

"Why, Al?" I could barely say the words. "Am I not enough anymore?"

"It's nothing you did or didn't do. I was a jerk. Caught up in the high-rolling, anything-goes atmosphere of the casino. Telling myself that after all I went through in the war, all the struggle to recover from my wounds, all the work to make the business a success, I deserved it. It was…like I was outside my life, and that whatever I did wouldn't touch you or the kids. But after that I could tell something was wrong between us. You may think I don't notice but, Rose, I know—maybe sometimes even before you do—when something's bothering you. That's why I came looking for you tonight, when I realized you weren't with anybody and hadn't told us where you were. I knew I had to find you. I knew I didn't want to lose you. What I did was stupid and selfish."

I didn't want to lose him, either. But the pain of his betrayal was too fresh. The knowledge I had now had ended my doubts. I certainly didn't have to wonder anymore. But what I knew didn't give me any comfort. It didn't show me what to do next.

"I have no idea what to say to you right now, Al. I can't even think, I hurt so much. Let's just go home. If the kids are upset I need to be there."

We trudged silently. When we started to cross Hanover Street he took my elbow protectively and I flinched.

I had never felt so alone, not even when he was overseas.

When we got back to Salem Street, Al headed to the kitchen door of the restaurant and I went straight upstairs. Papa was with the kids. I could see from the dishes in the sink that they'd eaten macaroni.

Al Jr. was in the bedroom he shared with Mike and didn't come out. He knew I'd gone to see Reverend Mother and had probably put two and two together. Toni was lying on the couch fingering her blanket next to Papa, whose idea of babysitting is to read *Il Progresso*. He figures that as long as he's in the apartment, the kids can find him if they need him. Mike was sitting at the kitchen table with newspapers spread out, gluing together a model of a navy destroyer.

When I came in, Papa put the newspaper down. *"Dove eri tu?"*

His English is passable, but if he doesn't want the kids to know what he's talking about, he uses Italian.

"I had things to take care of. Important things. Thank you for watching the kids."

He shrugged, folded the paper and got up to leave.

"They need their mother," he mumbled.

Toni scrambled into my arms. "Where were you, Mommy? I woked up and you weren't there."

"I had a meeting, baby. But I'm home now. Let's go have a bath."

I stuck my head in the kitchen. "Mike, do you have any homework?"

He looked up sheepishly from his model.

"Just some arithmetic. I have to memorize the nine times table."

"Come and sit by the bathroom door while I give Toni her bath and go over them with me."

It was eight o'clock before I got Toni to bed and Mike had recited his multiplication table often enough to have it stick. I let him go back to his model and then went in to talk to Al Jr. Al was still downstairs in the restaurant but at that moment I didn't want him with me.

Those first couple of years of Al Jr.'s life, when we only had each other, we grew close. I could read in his face, without his saying anything, if something was wrong.

The lights were out and he was in bed. Now, this was a kid who thought he was too old for a regular bedtime, a kid who considered himself beyond the rules I set for his little brother and sister.

I flicked on the light and sat on the edge of his bed. "I know you're not asleep, A.J. Sit up, because I need to talk to you."

He turned his back to me and pulled the covers over his head. I had no patience for this tonight.

"Sit up right now, young man. Unless you want to have this conversation with the back of my hand."

That got him upright.

"Reverend Mother tells me you're being disrespectful at school and acting like those smart alecks down on Prince Street who do nothing but hang out on corners and smoke cigarettes. Is this true?"

It seemed to me I was asking for a lot of truth from the men in my life that day.

"They gave me a quarter for running errands for them."

"What kind of errands?"

"I got their cigarettes."

Oh, my God. Fireworks were going off in my brain. "You didn't *steal* those cigarettes, did you?"

"*No!* They gave me the cash and I ran down to the news store to get them."

"So, you're their errand boy, and for that privilege they let you hang around with them?"

"I'm the only one they talk to. The other guys in my class are such babies. I'm not a baby anymore."

He was going to be twelve in six months. Now, in my book, that's not a baby, but it's not a man, either. He was all arms and legs, not even peach fuzz over his lip.

"No, you're not a baby. You're a boy. Who ought to know better than to answer back or treat a teacher without respect. No matter what those morons on the corner do or say. Did it ever occur to you that the reason they're hanging out is because they have nothing in their heads? No dreams to strive for. No respect for themselves, let alone their teachers or parents. I don't want you running any more errands for them. If you're looking for more work and more quarters, I've got plenty for you to do downstairs. And I want nothing but 'Yes, Sister' from you at school. I never want to be called into Reverend Mother's office again. Do you understand?"

"Yes, Mom."

I hoped that would be the end of it. He had two more years to get through at St. John's, and I didn't need more of Reverend Mother's withering judgment or, God forbid, Al Jr. getting into trouble outside school with mischief that crossed the line into petty crime.

I was exhausted. I yelled at Mike to clean up the mess on the kitchen table and get to bed. I couldn't even give him a hug when I saw the tears well up in his eyes. What had he done wrong? It was his brother who'd gotten into trouble and his mother who'd been gone all afternoon.

I left the dirty dishes in the sink and went to bed, but I couldn't sleep. Too many pieces of my life were falling apart. I'd always felt rock-solid, been the one to make decisions and carry them out. For the first time, I didn't know what to do.

I couldn't stay in bed tossing and turning alone. Maybe it would've been worse if Al had been there, maybe not. I wasn't sure I could stand having him beside me, knowing he'd shared a bed with the Cuban. But I wasn't sure if I could stand *never* having him in my bed again, either.

I got up, put on my robe and slippers and went to the kitchen to heat myself some milk and a little brandy. I washed the dishes, figuring I'd only have a hardened crust of tomatoes to deal with in the morning if I left them.

The next morning was St. Joseph's Day. I'd forgotten. A day to invite people in off the street to a feast at the St. Joseph Table. A couple of years ago we'd begun to invite the neighborhood charitable societies for a free lunch in the restaurant.

Usually I spent the day before St. Joseph's baking cream puffs. I hurried out to the back landing off the kitchen where we keep our extra refrigerator. Inside it were the eggs and fresh ricotta I'd had delivered in the morning, which meant Mama hadn't gone ahead and made the puffs when I didn't come back this afternoon.

I lugged everything out of the refrigerator, rolled up my sleeves and put on my apron. I have to admit, furiously beating the eggs into the flour to make the cream puff dough was a lot better use of my *agita* than struggling to fall asleep.

By the time Al came upstairs from the restaurant I had three racks cooling on the kitchen table, another two dozen puffs in the oven and I was whipping sugar into the ricotta for the filling.

He didn't say anything. I could feel the muscles of my back stiffen, and my fingers clenched the whisk in my hand. But I kept my hand moving. I heard a sigh that sounded like relief to me. That I hadn't packed my bags—or his. That I was standing in my nightgown in the kitchen with a smudge of flour on my cheek, doing what I always did on the day before the feast of St. Joseph.

He went to the drawer and pulled out a knife and a pastry bag and started slitting the cooling puff shells. I finished preparing the ricotta cream and removed the last of the shells from the oven. He filled the pastry bag with the ricotta and began piping it into the puffs.

After that, I placed them on trays, wrapped them and set them in the refrigerator.

Neither of us had said a word.

Al was filling the sink with soapy water as I closed the refrigerator door on the last tray of cream puffs. He washed; I dried.

When we had nothing left to do in the kitchen, the thread that had been holding us together snapped. In the kitchen, we'd done what we'd always done; we hadn't had to make any choices or ask any questions.

But now, faced with moving from kitchen to bedroom, one question loomed over us.

It was Al who broke the silence.

"Do you want me to sleep on the couch?" he asked, standing in front of the linen closet.

Did I want him out of our bed? No. But the way I saw it, he'd taken himself out of it by his own action.

"Yes," I said. I handed him bedding from the closet. I went into our bedroom and shut the door. No night I'd spent without him during the war was lonelier or harder than that night.

In the morning, despite how late we'd been up making the cream puffs, he was awake before the kids and had put away the sheets. He had a pot of coffee going and was reading the *Globe* in the kitchen when the boys stumbled to the table. Like the night before, we slipped into a wordless routine. He poured milk into cereal bowls I filled with Rice Krispies. I signed school papers while he made sure the boys put on their hats and mittens.

We lived like this for a week, speaking to each other only the bare essentials, sleeping separately, working side by side without even an accidental brushing of hands. We both had darkening circles under our eyes. I was barely eating.

Mama, who never misses anything, commented on what was hanging on my clothesline the morning I did the laundry.

"You got too many sheets this week. You got company? Or is somebody in your house acting like a stranger?"

I didn't want to listen to her simplistic advice about not going to bed angry, and I definitely didn't want to discuss why Al was sleeping on the couch.

"It's nothing, Ma. Al's back was bothering him so he tried sleeping on a different bed."

That week was when the gift arrived. Oh, I'm not talking about anything lavish. I didn't feel as if he was trying to buy his way back into my bed. But one afternoon after I'd put Toni down for a nap I walked into the bedroom and found a single stem of Chaconia in a vase. It was the flower that grew all around our bungalow in Trinidad. I don't know how he'd managed to find one in Boston, in March. Propped up against the vase was a snapshot of me in a sundress leaning against our porch railing with one of the deep crimson flowers tucked behind my ear. I was smiling.

You know, it caught me off guard. The memory of that time in our lives—before the war, before Al's injuries, before *this* tearing us apart.

I took the flower out of the vase, put it in my hair and went downstairs to the restaurant. When Al saw me, I watched the light come back into his eyes.

After we closed the restaurant that night and Al came upstairs, he retrieved the sheets for the couch as usual. But I put them back in the closet.

He stood in the bedroom doorway.

"Do you forgive me, Rose?"

I looked at him and saw the pain and longing in his face. I also saw the man who'd had fought to get back on his feet after the war, the man who was the father of my beautiful children, who adored those children and who worked sixteen hours a day to make sure they had what they needed.

And I saw a man I knew loved me.

He'd made a mistake. But I wasn't going to force him—or all of us—to pay for it the rest of his life. I'd seen marriages like that. The North End is like a small town; everybody knows everybody else's business. I knew women filled with bitterness. They had the things their husbands provided but they didn't have love. They never let go of whatever pain had been inflicted on them thirty years ago. I didn't want to be one of those women.

"I forgive you, Al."

And I took him back into our bed.

It wasn't like our wedding night, or the night after the war when he was finally whole again. But it was new. I don't know how to explain it. We were like strangers and old lovers at the same time. We had added new layers over the core of knowledge we had about each other. My layer was something I'd learned about myself; I understood the price of honesty in a marriage and knew I was willing to pay it. Al's layer was taking responsibility for what he did.

We came to each other with a twinge of sadness and a great hunger. The coldness and loneliness of the past weeks needed to be put behind us. And I was the one who'd raised the barriers with my silence. I just had to be sure I was taking Al back for the right reasons. Al seemed to understand that, by being so patient and by putting up with that lumpy couch as if it were penance Father Lombardi had doled out after confession.

I never asked Al if he'd confessed to the priest about Estella. It was none of my business. He had confessed to me, and that was all that mattered. And I never questioned him again about her, never wanted to know any more than he'd already told me.

"I've missed holding you," he murmured to me as he

wrapped himself around me that first night back in our bed. And then his hands moved over my body as if he were learning it for the first time.

ROSE

1961–66

The Last Full Table

THE WOUNDS INFLICTED by Cuba healed, and like the physical scars Al bore from the Pacific and I from childbirth, we were stronger because of it. Forgiveness is a balm, for the one doing the forgiving as well as the forgiven. We were both released from the burden of mistrust and able to lean on each other again, for ourselves and for our family. God knows, they needed our attention.

Al Jr. was a smart boy. Thank God Reverend Mother had picked up on the bad influences when he was still in sixth grade; after that, I watched him like a hawk. Straight home after school—homework, then chores in the restaurant. He got a scholarship to Boston College High and the Jesuits took over riding his tail to keep him out of trouble. They also taught him how to use that smart-aleck mouth of his for good and put him on the debate team. I wasn't pleased at first that he was going all the way to Dorchester for high school, which took him so far from the neighborhood and its watchful eyes. But when he kept bringing home good report cards, I couldn't complain.

One thing Al regretted was that he'd never taken advantage of the G.I. Bill after the war and gotten an education. He was certainly intelligent enough. But it wasn't something Italian men of his generation did. There was no question for him about Al Jr. going to college. He was going. Period. We expected him to graduate from BC High and go right on to Boston College, even though there were a lot of O'Reillys and Kellys and not many names from our part of the city.

But Al Jr. had other plans. Oh, he still intended to go to college, but when he told us where, I could see Al's mouth get that tight line...

Pennsylvania. He wanted to go to Villanova. At least it was Catholic. But for both Al and me, it was like he was going to the moon. This was a first for our family. Cookie and Carmine's sons, Vincent and Anthony, hadn't gone to college; and Bella's kids were at St. Rose of Lima in Albany, where they lived.

I couldn't imagine Al Jr. not home every night and not at the table every Sunday afternoon for dinner. But I also understood his wanting to get away from the neighborhood, and I gently reminded Al that we'd done the same thing at his age when we left for Trinidad. So grudgingly, in the fall of 1961, Al and I packed up the Ford station wagon and drove Al Jr. to Pennsylvania.

It was a time of change, not only for us, but for the country. The year before, a Catholic had been elected president. Even though he was Irish, we considered John F. Kennedy one of our own. His mother, Rose, had been born in the North End a few blocks away from Paradiso. Al Jr., after reading Kennedy's *Profiles in Courage* during high school, had worked on his campaign, knocking on doors in the neighborhood to distribute flyers. It was the highlight of Al Jr.'s adolescence when Kennedy stopped by the campaign headquarters on Hanover Street to shake hands and thank the kids who were working so hard to get him elected. Kennedy's inspiring words had set

Al Jr. on the path he was following—to leadership, to accomplish something important in his life.

Like anyone who's old enough to remember, I can tell you exactly where I was that afternoon in November of 1963 when Kennedy was assassinated. The lunch crowd in Paradiso was thinning out and I was reviewing the reservations for that night, a Friday. The radio was on and I was only half listening. But when the words had sunk in, I went into the kitchen and found Al. We held on to each other in disbelief. Outside on the street, normally hectic as the weekend approached, all was still. All I could think to do was pray, so I put on my hat and coat and walked down to St. Leonard's. I wasn't alone. The church filled up with Catholics and non-Catholics alike, all seeking some solace for the incomprehensible.

That night, Al Jr. called us from Villanova. He was going to Washington for the funeral. We were all stunned, of course. But for young people like Al Jr., Kennedy's assassination was an anguished turning point. Some of his college friends reacted by becoming cynical and bitter. But not our son. If anything, he became more committed to the challenge Kennedy had thrown out to that generation with his inaugural speech. We were so proud of him. He joined the navy ROTC, which couldn't have made Al any prouder. Senior year he came home for Thanksgiving in uniform; when he walked into the restaurant, every head turned. He looked so much like Al.

I hold on to the memory of that Thanksgiving as though it's etched in stone. That was the first time Al Jr. had ever brought a girl home. It wasn't like in the old days when Al and I were keeping company and you couldn't even go to the movies without the boy coming into the house to meet your parents. With him in Pennsylvania during the school year, who knew if he was even dating, let alone who the girl was. In the summers, when he came home and helped out in the restaurant, there'd never been anyone special. If it hadn't been for ROTC, I'd have thought he was headed for the seminary.

So it was a big deal that he invited Marianne, a girl from New Jersey who went to Rosemont, the girls' college down the road from Villanova. I liked her right away. She came into the kitchen, told me it smelled just like her mother's and asked what she could do to help.

I put her to work peeling and chopping garlic for the stuffed mushrooms and artichokes and then had her rolling prosciutto and salami for the antipasto. I liked the way she joked with Al Jr. and took some of the wind out of his sails when he started talking like a senator instead of a college boy. And she was nice to Toni, who at fourteen was still a kid who looked up to her big brother.

I watched as Al Jr. brushed her fingertips when he passed her the breadbasket at the table, or put his hand on the small of her back when he slid past her in the kitchen. Just like his father.

When I had him alone for a few minutes behind the bar opening wine bottles for me, I asked him straight out. "So, is she the one?"

"The one what?" He was keeping his eyes on the corkscrew, not looking at me.

"You know what I mean."

The cork slid out of the bottle of Ruffino—not Papa's wine anymore. The younger generation, even though they'd grown up on his Chianti, mixed with water, wanted imported wine from Martignetti's at the corner instead of our own cellar.

"I guess that's up to her."

"And you want her to say yes?"

"What is this, Ma, the Spanish Inquisition?"

I lifted my hands. "I won't ask any more questions. But if she *is* the one, you've made a good choice."

I kissed him and went back to the thirty-four people sitting around the table, a wine bottle in each hand and a smile on my face.

What can I say? For a mother to see her son grown into a handsome, thoughtful young man in love with a woman she likes and approves of—what more could I ask?

I could ask that they be allowed to enjoy a life together, like Al and me. I could ask that a war on the other side of the world not cast its bombs and flames in the middle of my restaurant and my family. But I didn't know that then.

By the fall of 1964, with Al Jr.'s graduation only a few months away in the spring, the nightly news was sprinkled with reports from Vietnam. We had a TV in the bar now, and you couldn't avoid hearing Walter Cronkite every night. But I didn't understand until Al Jr. mentioned his commission at the dinner table that Thanksgiving.

"Looks like I'll get my papers in July, about a month after I graduate."

It wasn't like it had been for Al and me, when the whole country mobilized after Pearl Harbor. Unless you had a son in the service, Vietnam wasn't on your mind.

I thought of all the times I'd let Al Jr. go, sometimes sooner than I was ready for. I can still remember the ache in my heart when he stepped into his kindergarten class that first day, and certainly the moment Al and I drove away from Villanova in his freshman year. I cried the whole length of the Jersey Turnpike.

But I never dreamed I'd ever have to watch my son go to war. Not after the war his father had fought. Not when he had a life of promise ahead of him.

Until November 1964, only a handful of Americans had been killed in Vietnam—advisers to the South Vietnamese army, pilots flying bombing missions. But just before Election

Day an air base near Saigon had been shelled and seventy-six young Americans were wounded. I heard that as I was making a batch of meatballs. I stood there in the kitchen, my hands deep in one of our big stainless-steel bowls. I mix the meatballs by hand, and I use dried bread that I've softened in water and squeezed out—again by hand—instead of bread crumbs like some of the bigger places in the neighborhood do. I don't skimp when it comes to the quality of the food I serve. I also use ground round, not chuck, for my meatballs. They're tender and moist, not dense or heavy. That night, listening to the news as I cooked, I completely lost track of what I was doing. My hands came to a standstill and no meatballs took shape.

I thought of Al and all he'd suffered and could not believe we were once again putting our young men in harm's way. But it wasn't until Thanksgiving dinner, with Al Jr. sitting there in his uniform next to Marianne, that I began to understand what was at risk. My son. My firstborn.

The food and wine were as abundant as they'd always been at our table. You wouldn't have known we were at war. We still had everyone there, with us. My parents and Al's, in their places of honor, their bodies shrunken and wrinkled but their minds and tongues still sharp. My sister-in-law Cookie balancing her youngest grandchild on her lap while she ate.

"I don't want to let her go," she protested when her son Vincent offered to hold the baby so she could eat her soup.

My son Mike, a senior in high school, freshly showered after his football game, basking in the aftermath of a victory he'd secured with his field-goal kick and devouring every course—piling his plate high with manicotti after the antipasto and the escarole soup, followed by two servings of turkey and sweet potatoes. Al, his face flushed from the morning in the kitchen and then two hours on the football field, but his back straight and his eyes clear as he took in the scene. Even Toni, taking tiny bites because her braces hurt—how stupid of the ortho-dontist to put them in right before Thanksgiving—was making an effort to enjoy the meal and the family.

I describe them all now because it's important to me to remember that meal and that moment when we were all together and didn't yet know what was ahead for our family, for our country. Because by the next Thanksgiving, two places at the table would be empty.

Loss

MAMA WENT FIRST. She was seventy-seven, coping with the diabetes that Dr. Tucci had diagnosed the year before. I had learned how to give her insulin shots and went over to my parents' place every morning after Mike and Toni left for school. Usually she was sitting at the kitchen table waiting for me. Like most of the old women I knew, she was up at the crack of dawn, had the apartment cleaned and the laundry hung on the line by the time the rest of the world was turning off the alarm clock.

But one morning in January, when I let myself in the apartment, she wasn't in her chair. The coffeepot was empty instead of perking gently. I walked down the hall to her bedroom and peeked in the half-open door. Papa was on his back, snoring loudly, which was no surprise. He often slept late. But it wasn't like Mama to still be in bed, and it also wasn't good for her blood sugar if she had her shot late. I tiptoed into the room and reached for her.

As soon as I touched her I knew she wasn't going to open her eyes. I couldn't find a pulse. Still, I called to her, the daughter in me, the wishful thinker, not wanting to accept what my hand on her cold and stiffening cheek was telling me.

My cry of "Mama! Mama!" woke Papa.

"Que fa?" he asked, confused, his eyes cloudy with cataracts, his brain registering the unusual situation—me in their bedroom, his wife not yet up—but he hadn't quite connected what it all meant.

"It's okay, Papa," I found the strength to say to him, then slipped out of the room. They didn't have a phone in the bedroom, which was just as well. I didn't want him to hear what I was going to be saying, or how upset I was.

My hand and my voice were shaking as I dialed the operator and asked for an ambulance. I tried to explain, without breaking down, but it was all I could do not to wail.

I phoned Al and asked him to call my brothers and sisters. Then I went back to Papa.

He was sitting on the side of the bed next to Mama, stroking her hair and rocking back and forth, muttering a low litany.

The ambulance came just as Al and Carmine ran up the steps. Helplessly, we watched the futile efforts of the emergency crew.

"I'm sorry," one of them said, turning to me. "From the state of rigor mortis, she probably passed away during the night."

The remaining hours of that day were a blur, as the rest of my family arrived, the doctor came to sign the death certificate and we called my father's cousin Severino, the undertaker.

Somehow I held myself together, the way I always do in a crisis. I was most worried about Papa, who seemed paralyzed. I made him eat something, but I practically had to spoon it into him, as if he were a baby. He finally pushed the spoon away and just sat in his chair, staring out the window.

We closed the restaurant for the week and hung black bunting on the windows. Al Jr. took the train up from Philadelphia to attend the wake and the funeral. I thought about keeping Toni away from the funeral parlor. I didn't know if she'd be ready for an open casket. I had bad memories of when I was a kid and the wakes were held at home, with the body in the living room, and didn't want to inflict that on my baby. But she made a fuss, as only a teenager can, about *not* being a baby anymore. If her brothers were going to the wake, then she was, too. Frankly I was too exhausted to argue with her. I'd slept, badly, at Papa's the first night, not wanting to leave him alone. I don't know, maybe I was afraid I'd wake up to find him gone, too. I'd heard that sometimes happened— people dying of a broken heart when their wife or husband passes away. Mostly it was in dramatic stories from the old country—the kind of superstitious fable you had to take with a grain of salt. I remember one that Mama and my aunt Cecilia used to bring up about a distant cousin, Lucia, who had been barren. She'd once turned down a proposal of marriage because she had fallen in love with someone else. The mother of the rejected suitor had gone into the village piazza, bared her breasts and cursed Lucia, calling down upon her "a life full of misery." Given the sad state of Lucia's existence after that, Mama and Aunt Cecilia were convinced the curse had been the reason.

"Watch out who you harm with your choices" had been their warning.

As far as I knew, no one had placed a curse on either of my parents. But nevertheless, I made sure Papa took his blood pressure medicine and I checked on him several times during the night.

My sisters-in-law, God bless them, took over the kitchen at Paradiso during the week of the wake and the funeral and had a meal ready for us at five o'clock every day between the afternoon and evening calling hours. Cookie knew best what the family needed, especially Papa, and had pots of soup and some simple chicken—nothing heavy—simmering on the back burner as we came back from Severino's to take a break. Everybody was numb. Such a shock, we all said. One minute Mama was there—with her wisdom and her energy and her cut-through-the-bullshit observations—and then she was gone, without warning or a chance to say goodbye.

It was hardest on my sisters Bella and Lillian, who no longer lived close enough to see her every day, the way those of us still in the neighborhood had. They hadn't seen her since Christmas, and who knows what their last words with her had been. Everyone has regrets, the "woulda, shoulda, coulda, if I'd only known" kind of thoughts. It's why I still hug and kiss my kids, my Al, every time they walk out the door.

For me, besides the shock of finding her that morning, the pain was the empty place in the kitchen. The knives hanging unused instead of wielded by gnarled fingers chopping two dozen cloves of garlic or five bunches of parsley. The dwindling supply of mason jars on my cellar shelves that wouldn't be replenished come August when the tomatoes and eggplants were ripe and she, churning with industry, would've been canning for the winter.

We buried her in the lilac dress we'd bought for her to wear to my nephew Vincent's wedding. It broke my heart that she didn't live to see Al Jr. graduate from Villanova, but he stood with his cousins as pallbearer alongside her coffin at St. Leonard's. When he hoisted that box on his shoulder, with his white gloves and navy uniform—that's when I finally fell apart. Al held on to me as we followed behind the casket.

But Mama's funeral was a dress rehearsal for what was to follow.

Broken Glass

AL JR. GRADUATED from Villanova with honors in June of 1965. We retraced the journey we'd made four years earlier, this time with Mike, Toni and Papa along. After Mama's funeral, my brothers and sisters and I had realized that leaving Papa to live alone wasn't a good idea. He was eighty years old and had worked hard all his life shaping rough stone from Vermont quarries into the polished granite blocks of Boston's churches and banks and office buildings. But he could barely boil an egg and had probably never turned on the washing machine. More than his unfamiliarity with housework was our fear that he'd slide into a depression so deep he wouldn't come back out. As it was, he'd barely spoken or eaten since the morning of Mama's death.

I'd like to tell you I was the noble one in the family discussion, immediately offering to take him into my home. After all, I lived just down the street, and Mama had been working at the restaurant with us for twenty years. But I didn't. I held back. It's not that we didn't have the room. With Al Jr. about to go into the navy and Mike heading off to Holy Cross in September, we could've easily taken Papa in. But a piece of me selfishly thought it was time for Al and me to have a break—from responsibility and worry. But that wasn't going to happen. My brothers and sisters elected me, for all the right reasons, and I didn't argue.

We moved Papa in during the two weeks we would normally have gone to Florida. I fixed up a back room in the apartment for him with his favorite chair and his own TV. It was on the quiet side of the building, away from the bustle of Salem Street.

I made sure he got out to his social club, the St. Anthony Society, to play cards twice a week. In the evenings, sometimes, he'd sit downstairs at the bar in the restaurant. One night, when we were really busy, I asked him to pour a few drinks. He got behind the bar and surprised me. Despite his grumbling that nobody knew how to make a good Bellini, it was the first time since Mama died that he'd done anything with enthusiasm. It may have been the women waiting for their table who were enjoying his gusto in putting the cocktails together. He was good enough with his fractured English banter to get them to order a second round.

The next evening, I saw him put on a clean shirt and shave before he came downstairs.

"You want some help at the bar tonight?" he said to me after he finished his pasta fazool.

"Sure, Papa. That would be a big help."

By the time we all drove down to Pennsylvania for Al Jr.'s graduation, Papa was getting up in the morning like a man with a purpose. He even had a group of regulars who came in every evening to debate the latest news in *Il Progresso* and have a glass of grappa after their dish of spaghetti.

The graduation at Villanova was interesting. I didn't want us to look like a group of *cavonne* coming down from the tenements to the ritzy Philadelphia Main Line. I'd seen both *The Philadelphia Story* and *High Society,* so I knew what we might find here. I was no Grace Kelly, but I know how to shop to look classy. I put my hair in a French twist, wore the rose-colored mock Chanel suit I'd found at Filene's Basement and a double strand of cultured pearls. I made both Al and Mike get new suits, to much grumbling. Toni was more difficult to outfit. At fifteen, she was beautiful but not in a conventional way, so she didn't see it yet. I prayed that someday she'd come to recognize how attractive she was, but at that moment it was all I could do to keep myself from marching her in front of a mirror and yelling, "Look at yourself! You're gorgeous!"

But we were at that stage in the mother-daughter dance when nothing I said was considered worthy of attention. I still bought her clothes, however, and I combed through the junior sections in both Filene's and Jordan Marsh to find her something she'd wear without making all of us suffer because she hated it or thought it made her look ugly. I settled on an adorable yellow pique sheath with a bolero jacket that had daisy buttons. When she put it on, she could've been one of those *High Society* wedding guests. "Okay," she muttered, examining herself from side to side in the mirror. "Can I get yellow heels to go with it?"

So there we were that morning in Villanova, PA, trying not to look or sound like the urban version of *The Beverly Hillbillies*. I adjusted Mike's tie and, as we got out of the car, tucked a stray curl of Toni's hair—as black as Al's—behind her ear. She wore the tiny gold studs I'd finally allowed her to pierce her ears with. I smoothed Al's collar and kissed him on the lips.

"Big day," I said.

"You look like Elizabeth Taylor," he said.

"I was trying for Jackie Kennedy."

"You're much prettier. And you've got a better ass."

I didn't like him to talk like that in front of the kids, but they were ahead of us, and I shot him a look of mock disapproval mixed with appreciation. I was forty-four, with a teenage daughter who was driving me crazy and two sons stepping into new stages of their lives.

Every time one of my kids passed a milestone—first day of school, first communion, confirmation, graduation—it was like giving birth all over again. I felt as though life was changing for me, too. *When this day is over,* I thought to myself, *I'll be the mother of a college graduate and a navy ensign.* How did I get here so fast? One minute I'm sewing myself maternity clothes and the next I'm sitting on a folding chair in the sun, watching a tall, handsome young man march past. I was on the aisle. As he moved by me, he squeezed me on the shoulder. Just like Al. Letting me know it was going to be all right.

When we got back to Boston, we held a family party for him at the restaurant. It was a big deal, a college graduate in the North End. Most of his buddies from St. John's were working in the trades. Some of them were no doubt as smart as Al Jr., but nobody had expected as much from them as I had from him. I didn't regret for a minute that I pushed him hard. I'd always had ambitions. Seeing to it that my kids got educated was one of them.

What a party! We received permission from the city to use the vacant lot behind the building. We strung Christmas lights and hired a band to play live music. Al's cousin welded some oil drums together and made us big grills to cook the sausage and peppers. We had all of Al Jr.'s favorite foods—lasagne, eggplant parm, *sfogliatelle,* even big tubs of lemon ice from Mike's Pastry Shop. You'd have thought it was one of the feast days, except there was no Madonna on a wagon draped with ribbons pinned with dollar bills.

The kids danced. My aunts sat on their plastic beach chairs, fanning themselves and pinching Al Jr.'s cheeks as if he were still a little boy. Papa and my uncles sat at a back table playing pinochle.

"*Come sei buono!*" How good you are!

"God bless."

My friend Patsy came over and put her arm around me. "You did a good job. I remember the day he was born, and you scared to death about raising him alone. Be proud of him, but be proud of yourself, too."

We toasted him many times and teased him about running for mayor, finally giving us an Italian in the new city hall just on the other side of the expressway. He laughed, but I could tell it wasn't such a far-fetched idea to him. It was 2:00 a.m. before we doused the lights and folded up the tables and chairs.

And then he was gone.

He took the train to Virginia, where he trained as a medic. By October he was in Vietnam. I never questioned for a minute that he should do his duty. But sending a son to war was the hardest thing I'd ever done.

Because he'd joined ROTC at Villanova, Al Jr. had volunteered, not been drafted. It was still early in the draft, so not too many boys from the North End had been called up yet, although they would be soon enough, especially since so few of them were in college. There were no other women to share my fears with—in the family or in the neighborhood— facing the day as I did every morning, turning on the *Today Show* the minute I got out of bed, watching Walter Cronkite every evening as I cooked in the restaurant.

"You're making yourself crazy, listening to this garbage every day, Rose," Al said to me one night, flicking off the TV as a draft dodger burned his draft card in front of a courthouse.

"I *need* the news, Al. I need to see what he's seeing."

"He's on an aircraft carrier, Rose. He sees planes taking off and landing. And when someone in one of those planes comes off on a stretcher, he's ready with an IV and bandages. He's going to be fine, Rose."

Al and I each found separate ways to get through the day. Al's was to believe that Vietnam wasn't the navy's war, and that Al Jr. wasn't reliving his father's nightmare of twenty years before. But every now and then he'd come up against the war in unexpected places, despite his deliberate refusal to watch the evening news.

One afternoon he ran over to Haymarket when we were short on our order of broccoli rabe. He knew a couple of guys with stalls who were willing to give him a wholesale price.

An antiwar rally was going on in City Hall Plaza, a shallow sloping bowl of paved brick built to mimic Siena's Piazza del Campo. Two of Al's cousins were masons who had worked on it.

Al could hear the loudspeakers and the chants of the crowd and wandered over to the fringes with his shopping bags full of greens. What he saw and heard disgusted him.

"Goddamn freaks," he said as he slammed the bags on the stainless-steel counter in the kitchen. "Bunch of unwashed cowards. And the police just stood on the sidelines, letting them rant and rave!"

"This is America, Pop. They're allowed to rant and rave." Mike was helping out on a weekend home from Holy Cross.

"Is that what your Jesuits are teaching you? What about your brother, fighting so these morons can spout their disrespect-ful drivel."

"He'd be the first to tell you they've got the right."

"Are you turning into one of these antiwar nuts?"

Mike shut up. There was no point arguing with Al when he was so single-minded.

I don't know how I would've felt if I'd been face-to-face with the protesters as Al had been. If they were dishonoring my son and his sacrifice, I'd probably have slapped them across their mouths. It was one thing to question whether the government had made the wrong decision, but another to blame the young men laying down their lives.

It had been so different when Al and I were young. The country was united. We knew we were doing the right thing. A family had been proud to hang a blue star in the window when they had a son in the service.

Nowadays there were no stars. Maybe people were afraid their windows would be broken. I felt lonely as the mother of a serviceman. Al poured his concern for Al Jr. into anger at the war protesters. I had no comfort there—not from Al and not from my own mixed feelings.

Thanksgiving 1965 was a quiet one, our first without Mama, of course, but Al Jr. was eating his turkey on a ship in the South Vietnam Sea. I'd sent a package of canned goods—anchovies, roasted peppers, marinated mushrooms and olives—and I double-baked the peppery hard biscuits Papa liked to dip in his wine. I figured they'd keep in transit. I put in hard salami and a round of provolone coated with wax. It wasn't lasagne or fresh mozzarella and bruschetta, but I knew he'd appreciate the taste of home. We got a letter just before the holidays and I read parts of it out loud at dinner so everyone could hear his voice coming through in that smart way he had with words.

"Give everyone around the table my love and remind them how good life is. The guys in my battalion, when I describe our Thanksgiving to them, can't believe what goes into it. I'll be thinking of you all. I'll imagine the aroma of the turkey wafting up the stairs; the lasagne bubbling as it comes out of the oven; the artistry of the antipasto platter that I'm sure Toni has arranged so the colors are as vivid as the taste; Mom bursting with pride when everything's finally on the table; Dad standing like a samurai with his carving knife ready to slice. I miss you all. God bless."

We didn't know that he'd been transferred from the carrier to a river operation. The navy had started building up its inland forces with small boat patrols. But the nightly news wasn't carrying stories about them. Like Al, I began to be lulled by the thought that since he wasn't a pilot and wasn't in the infantry, he was safer than most. But we were mistaken.

When the two navy officers walked into the restaurant one night in April, I assumed they were customers. Toni offered to seat them, and then I saw the puzzled look on her face. She came to the kitchen door. "Mom, Daddy, the captain is asking for you." Al took off his chef's cap and wiped his hands. We exchanged a look and he grasped my hand as we went out to them.

"Is there a private place we can speak with you?" They glanced around at the busy dining room. People were starting to notice them. I was beginning to shake. Al had the presence of mind to lead them to the office. I heard a glass break in the stillness that had descended on the usually hectic kitchen.

Al closed the door and held me as we listened to the report of our son's death, the medal he would receive posthumously, the date we could expect the plane carrying his body home.

A pain pierced my heart at that moment, leaving a hole that has never been filled.

I lost two children that night and I almost lost Al. Toni, reeling from a world gone suddenly and horribly wrong, needed a mother who could be a refuge and a role model. Someone who could show her how to put one foot in front of the other even when she didn't know where she was headed or why.

But I failed her. The tension between us that had been simmering in her early teens exploded after Al Jr. died. She was sixteen and we could barely speak to each other without yelling and tears. She pulled away from me, one small step after another, and in my own grief I didn't realize that until it was too late.

I felt I was the last person in the world she wanted to be like. I was someone to be ashamed of, someone who couldn't possibly understand her.

She'd always been artistic as a kid. She'd keep busy for hours in the restaurant during the early days, as long as you gave her a stack of paper and some crayons. You'd think she'd been given a pot of gold the day she got a box of 96 Crayolas.

Before the funeral she grabbed the photo albums I'd been keeping for each of the kids and picked out several pictures of Al Jr. She spent hours alone in her room listening to Joan Baez.

I didn't make her go to school that week. I could hardly get out of bed myself. Cookie made sure we had food in the kitchen, but who could eat?

One night, Al peeked in Toni's room after she'd fallen asleep. Taped all around the walls were big sheets of black paper with pastel portraits of her brother—as a little boy, a teenager, a navy officer. The last one was sketched from a photo taken the night of his graduation party. She'd captured each moment with excruciating accuracy.

Al made me get out of bed to see what she'd done. Her fingertips were smudged with the colored chalk, and the dark circles under her eyes looked as if she'd drawn them herself. What she'd created was as much a shrine as Mama's painting of St. Anthony that she'd kept on her dresser with a flickering red votive candle.

I sat on the floor for a couple of hours, surrounded by the images, rocking myself and crying silently. I didn't want to wake Toni. I crept out around midnight.

Al coaxed Toni into letting us frame the sketches and hang them at the wake. He'd explained to her that we wouldn't have an open casket like we did for Mama. Those drawings brought people to a standstill, like they were at St. Peter's in Rome in front of Michelangelo's *Pietà*.

Throughout the wake Toni sat in one of Severino's wing chairs in a black suit that looked too old for her. I hadn't wanted her to wear black at Mama's funeral and I couldn't bring myself to shop with her for this one. Patsy had taken her downtown and let her pick out something at Ann Taylor. She looked like a career girl, not my baby, but I kept my mouth shut for a change. Not out of common sense or understanding that my daughter was growing up, especially after a tragedy like Al Jr.'s death. I was just too locked inside my own pain to care.

And maybe that's what happened to Toni and me. She thought I didn't care about what she did or who she was anymore, so she stopped trying to tell me.

Somehow we got through the funeral. St. Leonard's was full to overflowing. Family, Al Jr.'s classmates from BC High and Villanova, friends of Mike's and Toni's, people from the neighborhood. Al Jr. was the first boy from the North End to be killed in Vietnam, so even the politicians showed up. Marianne, the girl Al Jr. had brought to Thanksgiving dinner in 1964, had driven from New Jersey. She'd sat with me at the wake for a while the night before, both of us in silence. There was nothing we could say to each other, but she held my hand—the hand that should have blessed them on their wedding day and held their babies.

I thought I'd already emptied myself of tears, but I cried through the whole Mass. At the cemetery, when the young navy officer handed me the flag that had been draped over Al Jr.'s coffin, I hugged it like an infant.

This isn't supposed to happen, that a child goes before a parent. It's unnatural. We are left not knowing how to go on.

Al and I faced our son's death in totally different ways. Al was still angry, but he turned his anger into activity. He started renovating the restaurant, throwing himself into a marathon every day so he wouldn't have time to think about his lost son. And me, I thought about A.J. constantly and stopped living. I sat at the kitchen table in the mornings after Toni had gone to school and didn't move, my coffee grown cold in its cup, the plain toast I thought I could stomach lying uneaten and dried out on my plate.

At noontime Papa would come in and ask, "Where's lunch?" and I'd make him some peppers and eggs or open up a can of Progresso soup. Al grabbed himself some cheese and prosciutto in the restaurant kitchen and didn't bother coming upstairs.

After I fed Papa, I went to bed. I was usually sleeping when Toni got home from school. She did her homework and went downstairs to wait tables for the supper crowd. Al let me disappear like that for a couple of weeks. He crawled into bed around 1:00 a.m. and fell asleep from exhaustion. And because I'd been sleeping all day, that's when I woke up. I tried to stay in bed with him, but I tossed and turned and eventually gave up. I wandered around the apartment. Sometimes I sat in the bedroom Al Jr. and Mike had shared, still full of books and sports equipment and LP albums. I smoothed the bedspread. I opened the closet and tried to breathe in the scent of my boy, but like a good housewife, I'd hung mothballs to protect the unused coats and jackets that he'd hung there before he left.

"Rose, you need to see a doctor," Al said to me one morning. "You can't continue like this. *We* can't continue like this."

But the doctor didn't solve my problem. He gave me Valium, which numbed the pain and let me get some sleep at night, but made me care even less about everything falling apart around me.

Al was spending too much money on fixing up the restaurant at a time when business in the neighborhood was turning bad. We'd managed to weather the ups and downs over the years because I'd watched our costs, and kept our waste to a minimum. Like Mama, I'd learned to make do in times of scarcity and put by in times of abundance. But now I just wasn't there. Al wasn't paying attention to that part of the business because he'd never had to. The financial end of things had always been my responsibility. At the same time, Toni was hiding in her room whenever she was in the apartment. She didn't seem to have any friends. She was a bookworm, like Al Jr., and when she wasn't reading she was drawing. I was relieved, frankly, that she didn't have a boyfriend at sixteen, as I had when I started dating Al. She was going to Sacred Heart, an all-girl Catholic school, so she didn't have much opportunity to get herself involved. God only knows what might have happened if there'd been boys around. We had nieces on both sides of the family who'd gotten pregnant as teenagers. Oh, the boys married them, but what a way to begin a life together.

One night Al came upstairs with mail that had accumulated in the mailbox. I was so out of it I wasn't going downstairs more than once or twice a week.

"When's the last time you paid the bills or did the books?" he demanded, slamming a pile of overdue notices on the dining room table.

I looked at him blankly.

"Rose, wake up! You can't keep living like this, ignoring everything around you. Including me. Don't you care anymore?"

How do you say to the man who's been by your side for almost thirty years, who'd overcome incredible pain and survived, who adored you, that you didn't care about anything? I was speechless. The pills made me so weepy that all I could do was cry.

Al stomped into the bedroom and grabbed the pill bottle off the dresser, then pulled me into the bathroom.

"I want you to watch." And he dumped every last pill down the toilet. "I'm calling the drugstore and the doctor and telling them not to renew your prescription."

I was scared and horrified. I didn't think I could face what I knew was coming if I didn't have the Valium to take away the pain.

"We need you, Rose. All of us, but especially me. You're the life of this family, and without you we're dying, just as surely as Al Jr. died.

"Take care of yourself, Rose. Take care of us. And pay the damned bills!"

He went back downstairs, where he'd been spending most of his time.

I fought the urge to find something to replace the pills— a glass of Scotch on the rocks, anything. I looked in the bathroom mirror. I was a mess. My hair was like a rat's nest, pulled back with a rubber band. My skin was rough and without any makeup. My neck was dirty. I didn't recognize myself.

I turned on the shower, hoping to drown my tears and wash away the scum I felt had accumulated all over me. I scrubbed and scrubbed. When I finished, I spent half an hour combing the tangles out of my hair. I filed my nails, which were chipped. I put on a clean pair of slacks and a blouse. I admitted there might be some wisdom in the busywork of my mother's generation. If you kept moving, working, you might not have time to feel the pain.

So I cleaned the house, starting with the bathroom. I pulled down curtains, gathered up the throw rug and the toilet seat cover and got everything in the washing machine. I dusted and polished and vacuumed. When I reached the dining room I saw the pile of bills and remembered.

I put away my dust rags and mop. I found my checkbook and sat down. I was overwhelmed by what I saw—charges for work I had no idea was going on; prices from our suppliers that I didn't remember negotiating; orders for items that were well beyond what the receipts showed we needed.

I sorted through everything, trying to decide what to pay first, what to question Al about. When I added it all up, my stomach was churning. For the first time since Al Jr.'s death, I was feeling something other than emptiness. I was angry, and I was staring at our survival—as a business, as a family.

It was past midnight when I finished organizing everything and knew exactly how much we owed and how much we didn't have. I'd made a list of what I had to do in the morning—who I had to call, orders I needed to reduce, a loan I'd try to arrange to get us back on our feet. I had to put the fire out before I could figure out how to rebuild what was so clearly falling apart.

I was furious with Al, of course, for throwing away money we didn't have. But I was more furious with myself for throwing away what I'd worked so hard for.

When he came upstairs, it was with the usual expectations—a wife somewhere in la-la land, dirty dishes in the sink, a daughter hiding from us. At least I was able to surprise him on the first two counts. He saw that both the house and I were clean. He saw the neat stack of stamped envelopes on the counter. He saw the old Rose in my eyes—not the dull and clouded haze of indifference.

"It's bad, Al. We've got a lot to talk about in the morning. But I'm back."

After a couple of yelling matches—of the "How could you do that?" variety—over the next few weeks, we settled into a partnership that we knew would be our only chance of survival.

We were lucky to be heading into summer. The tourist business picks up, and even though we're not on Hanover Street, we get enough foot traffic to pull people in. But we needed more than a steady stream of customers to stay afloat. I canceled some of the work Al had scheduled for the renovations and I took a hard look at the menu, what people were ordering and what it was costing us to prepare some of those dishes. It was one thing to offer regional specialties that we'd grown up with, but did we have to put *everything* on the menu? I cut back on the variety. And I returned to work in the kitchen so I could keep an eye on the little things, like how much food they were putting on the plate, only to scrape it into the garbage later.

I even managed to get us a loan. Somehow we made it through that year. Our economic survival was paramount, but I also hoped that my renewed energy sent a subtle message to Toni. She never commented on the change, but it was enough for me if she absorbed the lesson that change was possible.

It wasn't easy. I didn't crawl back into my bed, afraid that everything I'd worked for would be gone when I woke up. That fear overshadowed my grief. In that way, I became more like Al, driving everything I was feeling into work.

ROSE

1969

Emanuel

BY THE WINTER of 1968 we'd turned a corner. We were paying the bills, the dining room was full and we were no longer in the red. Although Al was head chef, I continued to have a hand in the cooking and experimented with dishes I thought we could add to the menu. Business had improved enough for us to add staff that year, as well. In addition to family, we still had Milly, who'd been waitressing for us for more than twenty years. One of the Agostino boys, who lived in the apartment above ours, bussed tables and washed dishes. Over time, we'd had waitstaff come and go. I had high expectations for the people I hired; some of them worked hard to meet my standards and others couldn't be bothered, so I showed them the door.

At Christmas, Al put four plane tickets to Miami under the tree and right after New Year's we took Mike and Toni to the Fontainebleau. It was Toni's last year of high school; Mike had one more year at Holy Cross. Because he was the only surviving son he wasn't going to lose his deferment after he graduated from college if, God forbid, the war was still on.

I hadn't realized how much in his brother's shadow Mike had felt. I'd never had much interest in child psychology books—written by men who had no kids, if you asked me. I let my kids know how much I loved them, I came down on them hard when they messed up and I always forgave them. I also made sure I knew where they were, who they were with and what they liked to eat. They understood that when they felt lousy they could come into Mom's kitchen and get filled up—with attention, with linguine and white clam sauce, torta Milanese, zabaglione…whatever they wanted. I'll admit I found it easier with the boys than with Toni.

It was good to take time off with the kids. Toni spent her days at the pool in a two-piece bathing suit slathering herself with baby oil and burying her face in a book. She'd never had a steady boyfriend—or even many dates—and I had mixed feelings about that. I didn't have to worry the way some mothers did about their daughters, but I also regretted that she hadn't had someone special in these past few years of so much loss. I worried, too, that she'd be going off to college with so little experience of men. She was almost too naive. I didn't think she'd even been kissed. Who knew? Maybe she was going to be a nun. I wasn't crazy about that idea; in my opinion, you give up too much as a woman—the love of a man, children, a home. She wanted to go to art school. Mother Bede, the art teacher at Sacred Heart, had allowed her free rein in the studio and she'd produced a mighty portfolio that she'd carted around to art schools in Providence and Boston and Portland, Maine. Two people in her life were not happy with her choices: Mother Bede, who wanted her to go to *Catholic* schools, and Al, who didn't want her to go to art school at all.

"What kind of work can you get with an art degree?" he demanded. "Are you going to wind up decorating store windows at Filene's? Why can't you go to school for nursing or teaching or accounting? Something practical."

Al finally relented when she pointed out that she could

always teach art when she finished. All her applications were done by the time we got to Florida, so I expected her to relax and enjoy herself.

"I *am* enjoying myself, Mom," she insisted when I told her she didn't seem to be having a good time, stuck on a chaise lounge while the other young people at the hotel had found one another.

"They're jerks. I'd rather read my book."

So I kept my mouth shut. We'd gone shopping a couple of times, but I couldn't interest her in a haircut or a manicure when I went to the salon. She said she didn't want "old lady" hair. She'd grown hers long and wore it parted in the middle like all the folk singers whose albums she collected. I thought the hairstyle didn't flatter her at all—it made her nose look big. But I could tell her that until I was blue in the face and she'd still wear it that way. What did I know?

"Relax and let her be, Rose." Al didn't get caught up in the struggle. But at least a few times I was able to shrug it off and leave her at the pool. She was almost eighteen, not much younger than I'd been when I married Al. I had to believe she'd figure out what she wanted, even if it was just a quiet afternoon reading a book and getting a tan.

Mike, on the other hand, was out from morning till night with a group of college kids he'd met on the beach. He made it to dinner with us every evening because we insisted, but then he was off to the clubs. He was a little reckless, that one, not the solid citizen of his older brother or the bookworm, dreamy artist of his sister. But I couldn't complain. They were both good kids and they were all I had.

So that vacation was as much of a family trip as you could expect with two nearly grown children. Until it became something else entirely.

Before we'd left Boston, Al had gotten a letter from an old

friend of his from the neighborhood, Dominic Morelli. They'd gone to St. John's together as boys, but after high school, when Al went into the navy, Dom had entered the seminary and become a priest. We'd lost touch with him when his order, the Franciscans, sent him to Delaware. But the letter came from Florida. Father Dom was working with Cuban refugees at a parish in Miami's Little Havana. He asked Al to give him a call when we were down so they could get together, but Al let it slip.

Al played cards most afternoons in one of the lounges. When the game was over, the waiter who'd been serving the drinks stopped him.

"Mr. Dante?" Al had signed the check, so the waiter was aware of his name. He was Cuban, one of the refugees who'd come over in the December 1965 airlift, he told Al. And he knew Father Dom.

"Father Dom said to tell you there's something you should know," he said. "Someone you should meet."

Al didn't want to listen to him. But he called Dom that night and asked him what it was all about.

"Let's have breakfast tomorrow. We've got a lot of catching up to do."

The next day, Dom joined Al and me on the patio around ten. Thank God the kids were sleeping late.

He wasn't alone. Antonio, the waiter, was with him, and a boy about thirteen.

"I want you to meet Emanuel," Dom said.

And we looked into the dark, somber eyes of a boy who could've been Al Jr. or Al at that age.

It took my breath away.

I watched Al struggle with himself, ready to leap up from the table and run away from the past—or reach out and touch it.

"Shall we take a walk?" I said. I didn't want this played out in front of strangers.

We went down to the beach, the five of us.

"Antonio and Manny are cousins," Dom went on. "Manny's mother died of emphysema when he was ten. Before she died, she told Antonio about Manny's father and she gave him his name and this photograph." He handed Al a faded Koda-chrome that looked like it had been handled many times. It was one of those pictures nightclub camera girls used to take. Al, tanned and handsome in his white dinner jacket, with his arm around a honeyed blonde in an orange chiffon dress.

Al turned to me.

"I didn't know."

"I believe you."

Antonio nodded vigorously. "My aunt never told Mr. Dante. She never saw him again. She wanted me to get Manny to America. When she got so sick, she made me promise to get Manny out of Cuba and find you."

"One evening when I was shooting hoops with the kids," Dom interjected, "I mentioned how I'd played on an asphalt court in my neighborhood in Boston. Antonio heard the word *Boston* and remembered what little his aunt knew about Manny's father. He brought the photograph to me. That's when I wrote you the letter, Al. I had to tell you in person, not long-distance."

All this time Manny stood on the edge of the conversation, saying nothing but not taking his eyes off Al. He was a skinny little thing, not yet grown into his body. I wasn't sure he understood English or, if he did, whether he knew what his sudden presence in Al's life meant for Al—and for me.

I could only imagine what was going through Al's mind. But after the initial shock and disbelief—how could this be? I asked myself—something happened to me that I can't really explain.

Al and I had managed to lock up the whole Cuban episode in some hidden place in our hearts years ago. We never spoke of it after that painful winter, and I never threw it in his face when we fought. The jagged tear in our marriage that his affair with the Cuban had caused had been stitched back together over the years. Sure, if you ran your fingers over it you could tell it was a repair job. But like the fine, tight stitches of Mama's darning, it had held, maybe even more strongly than before.

Until that day on the beach. When I saw the photograph of her and Al, that wound just split wide-open. I didn't think I could bear the evidence that he had loved someone else. But that moment, when I felt as if my insides were spilling into the ocean swirling around my feet, I looked into the eyes of that boy—hungry, haunted—and knew what I had to do.

"What is it you want?" Al was asking Antonio, like he was negotiating with a union steward to prevent a strike. "Money?"

"He doesn't want money," I said to Al. "He wants a father. He needs a father."

"How am I going to do that?" Al glanced from me to Manny.

"I don't know yet. But we'll figure it out. Dom, Al and I need to talk about this. We'd like to take you out to dinner tonight. Can you meet us back at the hotel at six?"

Antonio seemed reluctant to let us go now that he'd found Al. I wondered how long he'd been looking for him.

"Don't worry, we won't disappear." I dug into the straw bag I'd taken with me and pulled out a pen and a scrap of paper.

"Here. This is our restaurant in Boston, so you'll always know where to find us. And Father Dom knows our address, too. But we'll be here tonight. Okay?"

That seemed to calm him down. He nodded and shook Al's hand. Manny put his hand out, as well, and Al pulled him close with a hug. When he released him, I could see the tears in his eyes.

The boys and Dom turned back toward the hotel. The beach was growing crowded. The early-morning fly fishermen were reeling in their lines as the cabana boys set up lounges and umbrellas.

"You want to walk or you want to sit?" I asked Al, who, despite his tan, looked stricken.

He answered me by heaving himself into one of the beach chairs. He leaned back, eyes closed. I sat at the edge of the chair, facing him, and took his hands in mine.

"Oh, my God! Oh, my God, Rose. I never for a minute even suspected. What am I going to do?"

"You're going to do the right thing, Al, like you always do. The boy is motherless and fatherless at probably the moment in his life when he most needs a parent."

"This must be killing you. After all these years."

"I thought back there that it would. But something happened to me. I saw the boy, not the sin that created the boy. I know this is going to sound like my cousin Nancy who spends too much time lighting candles and saying novenas, but I feel God put that boy in our lives for a reason. Did you notice how much—"

"—he looks like Al Jr." Al finished my sentence in a whisper.

"We can't see him as a replacement, a substitute. We need to love him for himself." I said it out loud to remind both of us.

"Love him? How can you do this, Rose?"

"It's not like you kept a woman on the side for years, Al, taking away from me and the family. It was one night. And it made me mad as hell, don't be mistaken. But that child is a consequence of that one night. And I've never known you to walk away from the consequences of what you do."

"I won't walk away. But I can't ask you to take this on."

"You're not asking. I'm taking it on because I see a child who needs to be fed and loved and guided, and I think I've got a good track record in that department. Particularly with boys."

"You don't have to do this. We could send a check every month, make sure he gets an education."

"Living with a twenty-year-old cousin in a city that's all glitz and booze and fast women? That's like asking Mike to raise a child right now. We can do this, Al. Together."

He leaned toward me and stroked my face.

"You're remarkable, Rose."

"So are you, Al."

We walked back to the hotel arm in arm, working out how much to tell the kids about who Manny was and what we intended to do. In the end, we decided it was too soon to tell them anything at all. We asked Mike to take Toni out to eat and didn't include them at dinner with Dom and Manny and Antonio. The next afternoon, Al asked Dom to help us find a local lawyer.

By the time we flew back to Boston we'd started the paperwork to adopt Manny and get him citizenship papers. Once his adoption was final we'd bring him home. We thought that would give us a chance to prepare the kids and the rest of the family.

We decided that no one, not even Mike and Toni, needed to know that Al was Manny's father. We told everyone we'd heard about some Cuban orphans through Al's priest friend in Miami. It wasn't too much of a lie, since it was through Dom that Antonio had been able to connect with Al. We said to the family that although Mike and Toni were almost grown, we weren't quite ready to give up taking care of kids.

A few eyebrows went up, but most of my women friends

understood, especially those who'd recently watched their youngest get married and move out. I didn't want anybody to think I was a saint and put me on a pedestal or, worse, think I was crazy and pathetic for taking my husband's illegitimate child into my home. I wanted them to believe that I was adopting a child to fill my own need as well as the child's. And I was.

In March, Al and I drove back to Miami to complete the adoption and bring Manny home. When we left Miami he called us Mr. and Mrs. Dante and sat silently in the backseat hunched against the door and staring out the window. We took our time getting back, stopping along the way at South of the Border. Manny and Al played Skee-Ball and tried to grab a stuffed animal with one of those claws. We ate too many fried onions, had our picture taken with huge sombreros on our heads and picked up some fireworks to save for the Fourth of July.

By the time we got to Baltimore, Manny and I had switched places in the car. He sat in front beside Al, joking with him and playing with the radio. When we stopped to eat, Al said, "Manny, we're your family now, your parents. Strangers you call Mr. and Mrs., but your parents are Mom and Dad."

I didn't think it would be difficult for Manny to call Al Dad. After all, he'd been looking for his father ever since he'd arrived in Miami. But I was a different story. I was pretty sure his memories of his mother were strong enough that he'd somehow feel he'd be dishonoring her if he called me Mom.

"You can call me Rose, honey, if it's too hard to say Mom. I understand."

"I never called my mother Mom," he said. "She was Mami. Maybe I could call you Mama Rose."

And that is who I became.

Good Friday

ONCE BACK IN BOSTON we got Manny settled into seventh grade at St. John's and talked to Father Collins at BC High about enrolling him there for high school when the time came. We wanted him to have the same advantages his older brothers had been given. But we also had the same expectations. He had chores in the restaurant, bussing tables at dinner after he'd done his homework. We discovered he liked baseball, and Mike took him to opening day at Fenway to see the Red Sox play the Yankees, and then found him a Little League team in the neighborhood. Mike even offered to coach a summer team when he finished at Holy Cross.

Both Mike and Toni were more than great about our taking Manny into our family. Both of them got a kick out of having a little brother. And both of them were such do-gooders, always lecturing us about "social justice," that they felt some of their ideas had finally rubbed off on us. They were proud of us. We'd surprised them, they said, by doing something "cool."

"Maybe we should tell Toni and Mike the truth," I said to Al one night soon after we'd gotten back. "I worry about them finding out some other way. And I think it's hard on Manny to ask him to keep a secret like this when he's so young."

"What if the kids turn on me, lose respect for me, because of this? Especially Toni. You've had fourteen years. Remember how you felt when you first found out? I thought you'd never forgive me. Let them get used to Manny before we tell them he really is their brother."

I understood Al's fear. He'd given so much to our kids. But more than their respect, I think he feared losing their love.

"They'll be angrier that we lied to them than that you're taking care of your own son," I countered. "They're also smart, Al. If you and I saw the resemblance the moment we laid eyes on Manny, how long do you suppose it'll take them to wonder why he looks so much like Al Jr.?" I knew I was pushing him, but I was listening to my heart on this one, just as I had that day at the beach.

"Let me think about it."

It took a few more weeks of my gently bringing it up, usually late at night when we were getting ready for bed and I had his undivided attention. Manny was starting to fill out on my cooking and I predicted a growth spurt as I watched him wolf down plates of baked ziti and linguine with stuffed squid. I dug out some of my recipes from Trinidad, thinking I might hit on a few dishes that were similar to what Manny had grown up with in Cuba. That gesture, plus the attention he was getting from Toni, who joked with him and helped him with his English homework and sat on the bleachers during his baseball games, made him seem more comfortable in his own skin.

He was becoming such a part of us that we'd begun to forget he hadn't always been a member of the family. For me, his taking his place at our table was a blessing, a miracle filling me up.

"Did you see the kids tonight after closing, working together to clean up? They were laughing and fooling around as if they'd being doing it forever. Toni's not going to turn her back on you, Al, for bringing Manny into the family."

"Okay, I hear you. How do you want to do this? Talk to them together when Mike comes home for Easter?"

I put my arms around him and kissed him. "That's a great idea."

On Good Friday we always closed the restaurant. Papa was going to a fish fry at the St. Anthony Society after the Stations of the Cross, so that's when we decided to sit down with the kids to explain why we'd adopted Manny. They'd have a couple of days to absorb what we expected would be a bombshell before the rest of the family descended upon us for Easter Sunday.

I made a simple meal: filet of sole baked with garlic, parsley and bread crumbs and an artichoke-heart pie made with mozzarella and Bisquick. Toni sliced some tomatoes and Bermuda onions and I sent Manny down the street to pick up a loaf of Campobasso bread.

Mike caught the early bus from Worcester and arrived just as we were setting the table.

When everybody was seated, I rested my hand on Al's.

"Daddy and I want to talk to you all about something important, something that needs to stay in this house."

Toni and Mike looked across the table at each other.

"What's wrong? Is one of you sick?" Toni's voice was agitated. She'd always been the worrier in the family.

"Nothing's wrong. It's just something we want to keep in the family."

Everyone waited. I squeezed Al's hand. This had to be his show, not mine. He cleared his throat.

"A long time ago, I made a mistake and hurt your mother. She had the goodness to forgive me then, and we thought we'd put it behind us."

Even with that limited information, I could see the understanding of what his father meant spread across Mike's face. I prayed he'd keep his mouth shut and let Al finish.

"We found out this winter that my mistake had greater consequences than the pain I caused your mother. The woman I'd been with—yes, Toni, that's what I'm talking about—had a child. My child. I didn't know that till Father Dom told me in Miami."

Al stopped for a minute. He'd kept his eyes down and his voice was almost a whisper.

Toni started to speak, but Al held up his hand.

"Not only did I find out I had a child, a son," he went on. "I also learned that he'd lost his mother. He was an orphan."

I put my arm around Manny, who was sitting next to me, as Toni and Mike understood what Al was telling them.

"Your mother, God bless her, knew before I did what we needed to do for this boy, and that's why we adopted him. We want you to know that Manny isn't just your adopted brother. He's your *brother*. I'm his father."

The table was silent.

Toni's face crumpled as she tried to suppress tears. I could read her like a book even though she thought I didn't understand her, and I knew she was fighting back disbelief that her daddy could have done what he'd just described. I held my breath, praying that she'd weigh the evidence of all that she knew of her father's goodness against this one fall from grace, as I had done. But she couldn't see beyond the betrayal. She threw down her napkin, pushed back her chair and bolted from the room. We heard her door slam.

Mike turned to Manny, who was shaken by Toni's departure.

"Hey, squirt. I *knew* there was a reason you were such a good athlete! Welcome again to the family." And he high-fived him.

"Do you want me to talk to her?" I asked Al.

"No. I've got to do it myself. I was afraid of this." He stood from the table, squeezing Manny's shoulder as he left the room. He was not a happy man.

"I'm sorry, Mama Rose. I shouldn't have come to Boston."

"No, honey. You don't have to say you're sorry. You belong here. Toni knows that. She just needs time to forgive her dad for not being perfect."

Nobody seemed interested in eating anymore. It was as though everything had been sucked out of the room—appetite, oxygen, conversation. I got up and began clearing the table, and Mike and Manny went into busboy mode, whisking all the dishes into the kitchen in record time. We all stayed busy, the boys rinsing and loading the dishwasher, me putting leftovers away.

At least Toni hadn't locked her door and had let Al in. I was afraid she was so hurt and angry that she'd refuse to speak to him. But from the low murmur coming from behind her door, I could tell she'd allowed him to say what he needed to say to her.

"Let's watch TV." Mike pulled Manny into the living room when the kitchen was back in order. I was relieved that Mike wasn't leaving to have a beer with his buddies the way he usually did on a Friday evening when he was home from Holy Cross. He seemed to understand that we needed to circle the wagons and pull ourselves together that night.

I went and sat with the boys while they watched *The Wild, Wild West,* but I was too distracted to follow the show. Had I been wrong? *Should* we have protected Toni with our lies? And what was going through Mike's head? He'd been kind to reach out to Manny, who was the innocent in all this, but would he do the same for his father?

My heart ached for Al, trying to do right by all his kids. And I worried that I had urged him to be honest. Maybe there were good reasons the old generation had handled things like this by sweeping everything under the rug, hiding the truth.

My head was pounding by the time Al came out of Toni's room. I got up and met him in the kitchen.

"How'd it go?" I bit my lip.

"She's pretty angry. I asked her if she would've wanted us to abandon Manny when we found out about him. And she said, no, she was glad we'd brought him home and into the family. So I asked her, should we have continued to lie about who he was, and again, she said no, that she needed to know he was really her brother. She said sometimes she sees flickers of Al Jr. in his eyes and his smile, and now she knows why."

"Those are all positive things."

"Yeah. But her disappointment in me, that's what I can't shake. 'How could you, Daddy?' is what she kept saying to me. I'm no longer my little girl's hero. I'm the bad guy. And I gotta tell you, Rose, it's killing me."

"Give her time, Al. Just like you gave me. She's too young to understand that everybody makes mistakes in their lives, does things they regret. She'll come to understand that what you're trying to do now is make it right again, not make it worse. What's she doing now?"

"She said she wants to be left alone. But I told her Manny could use a hug from her, and soon."

That's when we heard her door open and her footsteps go down the hall. I looked through the dining room and saw her slip down to the floor where Manny was sitting and throw her arms around him.

I thought that would be it, a quick squeeze and then back to her hiding place. But she stuck around and watched the rest of the show with her brothers.

I made Al and me cups of black coffee and put a shot of anisette and a strip of lemon peel in them.

"I'm proud of you, Al. You did a hard thing today, a brave thing. It's the end of innocence for Toni, but maybe that's not so bad. Someday she's going to look back on today and realize how important it was. And she's going to be grateful to you for telling her yourself. I'm glad she didn't hear it from some mean-spirited person who'd only be doing it to hurt our family."

"You're a dreamer, Rose. But I agree—in the long run, it was the right thing to do. But, man, it hurts like hell to see that look in her eyes. I wish I could rewind my life and do it over again."

"We all do, Al. But there's one thing I wouldn't change even if I got to relive my life."

"What's that?"

"Marrying you."

After that Easter, we settled into the ups and downs of family life with three kids. Manny, after his honeymoon period of welcome to the family, got himself into a few scrapes that required some strong words. He was a little too quick to use his fists on the playground and more than once came home with a bloody nose and a note from Reverend Mother—not the same one who'd been head of the school when Al Jr. was there, thank God.

We had two graduations that spring, Toni's from Sacred Heart and Mike's from Holy Cross. Manny got his first suit; he'd grown four inches since January. Toni was accepted into art schools in Portland, Maine, and Boston, and we told her we wanted her to stay in Boston and live at home. I didn't think she was ready to be on her own, especially in Boston in the late 1960s, where every time you turned around there was another demonstration against the war or, worse yet, a love-in in Franklin Park with girls dancing around wearing flowers in their ratty hair and next to nothing on while everyone smoked pot. And with Toni at art school, it was going to be hard enough for her to hold on to the way she'd been brought up without also having to fend off the pressures and temptations that come with living on your own. I'd already had too many of my cousins tell me about the birth control pills they'd found in their daughters' underwear drawers when they were putting laundry away. Maybe that was better than finding out your daughter was pregnant, but if you ask me, it was the fear of getting pregnant that kept most of my generation on the straight and narrow. Toni was still an innocent, too inexperienced and a prime target for getting hurt by the kind of freedom that was screaming at her from every corner and every television set.

She didn't like our decision one bit and cried and pleaded with us to let her rent an apartment down by the Museum School on Huntington Avenue. But we stood firm and lived through the silent treatment for a few weeks until she realized what a good deal she had—her own room, great food that she didn't have to shop for or cook and parents who thought she was doing wonderful work.

Mike came home from Worcester after graduation and got a job at the New England Merchants Bank. When we gathered for Thanksgiving that year we were a full house again. I added black beans and rice to the menu and learned how to make a mole sauce for the turkey.

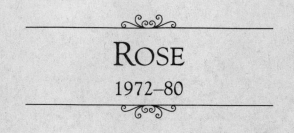

ROSE
1972–80

The Wedding

I SHOULD'VE BEEN a better judge of Bobby Templeton when I first met him. It wasn't at our home, where he should've come to meet us when he started going out with Toni. Instead, they'd meet at her art studio after school. I didn't even know about him until I ran into the two of them downtown. They were holding hands. After all my worries about her not having any experience with men, I was too thrilled to see she had a boyfriend. I just wished she'd felt comfortable enough to introduce him to us at home.

They were coming up out of the Park Street T station as I was on my way to go shopping.

"Hey, Mom! We're headed to Mike's Pastry to pick up some cannoli. This is Bobby. Bobby, my mother, Rose Dante."

He let go of Toni long enough to shake my hand.

"Hi, Mrs. Dante. Nice to meet you."

"Good to meet you, too, Bobby. Stop by the restaurant with Toni sometime and have dinner with us. In fact, if you two are going to the neighborhood, join us tonight."

"Can't, Mom. Sorry. My print class is throwing a birthday party for our instructor. I'm bringing the pastries."

"Are you in Toni's class, Bobby?"

"Who, me? No, I'm not an artist. I'm an engineer."

"Where do you go to school, then?"

"I'm out of school. I work over in Kendall Square in Cambridge."

"Shouldn't you be at work now?"

"I'm on my lunch break. Just volunteered to help Toni pick everything up. She seems to think the only place worthy of her patronage is on Hanover Street."

He shot her a wide grin, obviously humoring her. I don't know who I expected Toni to fall in love with, but in my wildest dreams, it wasn't somebody like Bobby Templeton. He was, let me put it bluntly, not like us. To begin with, he stood well over six feet, with blond hair and blue eyes. At least he wasn't one of those long-haired, guitar-playing, skinny artists sprawled all over the steps at the Museum School when we went to see Toni's exhibits. He was clean-cut; he had a job. He wasn't Italian, which was probably going to be a little difficult for Al. But the world was changing and, of all of us, Toni was the one out in front, finding her place in it.

I had mixed feelings, of course. On the one hand, I was excited to see her starting to figure out how talented she was. She'd begun to really blossom at the Museum School, bursting out of the narrow ideas the nuns had about art. I was no expert. Most of what I knew on the subject came from a book on Italian masterpieces Toni had given me one Christmas. But I did know that what she was painting came right out of her heart and stopped you dead in your tracks. The summer after her second year in art school, she'd painted a mural of the Bay of Naples on a wall in the restaurant. One of her classmates had sent her a postcard with a view from a hillside overlooking the harbor with Vesuvius in the distance. She studied that photograph and turned it into a work of love that brought tears to the eyes of the old-timers in the neighborhood. They'd probably stood on that very hillside—maybe just before they left Italy forever. I watched people at her exhibits at the Museum School get lost in her portraits, faces staring back at you and pulling you into their secrets.

I regretted that we'd sent her to Catholic high school. It was different for the boys with the Jesuits. They taught them to think on their own. But the nuns at Sacred Heart cared more about the length of the girls' skirts than the depth of their ideas. I hadn't realized how tightly they'd contained Toni until she started to paint in college. Also, putting her in an all-girl school meant she hadn't had a chance to get to know boys.

I think Bobby Templeton was the first boy to pay attention to her, and he swept her off her feet. He was the kind of person everyone stared at when he walked into a room. He commanded attention. Part of it was those all-American good looks. Not to my taste, mind you, but he had a quality like James Dean or Steve McQueen that made people, especially women, notice. So I guess Toni was flattered that somebody who was wanted by everyone else wanted *her*.

At first, like any mother, I worried that he'd hurt her. She was so crazy about him, although she wouldn't admit that to me for a minute.

Between her studio classes and the academic courses she was taking to get the teaching degree Al and I had insisted on, she wasn't home much. It made me nervous that she was often out late, but she spent every night at home. Other than school, Bobby Templeton was her whole life.

One night, I decided we needed to talk. They'd been going out for about a year. Their generation was starting to disregard the taboos ours had respected about sex. Couples were moving in with each other, setting up house, without a ring and the blessing of the priest. In my opinion, that was a recipe for disaster, especially for the girl. I didn't want that for my daughter.

So when I heard her key in the door, I was waiting in the kitchen with a pot of tea, which is what she's always liked to drink.

"Toni, have a cup with me. I don't get to see you enough, and this seems like the only time we're both home."

She set down her knapsack. I could see she was about to protest, beg off because she was tired. We'd never done well at this mother-daughter thing. Somehow, no matter how much I loved her, no matter how thrilled I was with the wonderful woman I saw her becoming, I managed to garble the message. She must have seen something in my face—a longing or a resistance to being put off—and she thought better of saying no.

She slipped reluctantly into a seat at the kitchen table and I poured her a cup of tea. We got through the "how was your day?" part of the conversation pretty quickly. Then I said what was on my mind.

"Toni, I know you and Bobby are getting serious—at least, that's how it appears to me. I need to talk to you, woman to woman. You know I'm not an openly religious person. I don't make a big show of going to Mass every day or lighting banks of candles. But I have to tell you, every night I pray to Jesus, Mary and Joseph that you are not having an affair with Bobby Templeton."

She almost spit out the tea she'd just sipped.

"Ma! An affair? An *affair* is something your generation has, something between two people who shouldn't be together— usually because one of them's married to someone else. It's sordid and secretive and bound to hurt somebody. I'm *not* having an affair." She didn't have to say out loud that her definition of an affair came straight out of her father's life.

"Well, *my* definition of an affair is sleeping with someone who isn't your husband. I don't care what the rest of the world is doing right now, casually jumping into bed with one another. You give up something precious, a part of yourself, when you make love to a man—and I'm not talking about your virginity. If you find out later he's not the man you want to marry—or he decides he's had what he wanted and moves on—you're setting yourself up for a terrible loss. I don't want you hurt, Toni."

She was bristling. But she pulled back whatever argument she'd planned to throw in my face.

"I know you want to protect me. Look, I'm twenty-one years old. I'm not going to do anything stupid. I'm not going to get myself pregnant, if that's what you're worried about."

"Oh, that's only part of it. I'm thinking more about you, not the family's reputation. I trusted your father, body and soul, when I put myself in his arms. I just want you to be sure that you can trust Bobby in the same way."

"I do, Ma, no less than you did when you placed your trust in Daddy."

I should've known that when she fell in love, she'd measure her experience against her memory of her father's betrayal.

"We're all imperfect, Toni. But I knew, because of what we'd been through together, that even when he stumbled, your father was a good man. If you can ask yourself and know in your heart that at the core of Bobby's imperfections, he's a good man, that's all I want for you. It's your life, honey, and I want you to have a happy one."

I didn't ask her straight out, *Are you sleeping with Bobby?* Because what was I going to do if she said yes? She'd move in with him if I tried to stop her. I wanted her to understand what the consequences were. Not to say "I told you so" if she got hurt in the end. Just to make her think about it and maybe get through the next part of her life with a little wisdom.

"Be careful," I said softly.

When Bobby asked her to meet his mother over Thanksgiving, I sensed it wouldn't be long before I wouldn't have to worry anymore about her having sex outside of marriage. And I was right.

She came into the restaurant kitchen one night just before Easter, breathless with laughter, Bobby at her side.

"Mom! Dad! Bobby asked me to marry him!"

She took her left hand out of her coat pocket and showed us the ring.

Al came up beside me and slid his arm around my waist.

We hugged and kissed her and let her bask in the excitement. Her face was flushed, not just from the heat of the stove but also from the emotion. I don't think I'd ever seen her in such an agitated state.

"I can't believe this is happening to me," she said as she whirled from one station to the next, receiving the congratulations of one after another of us. Manny teased her, humming the wedding march. Papa retrieved a bottle of champagne and poured glasses all around.

Then Al, pulling Toni and Bobby with him, went into the dining room, turned off the music and made an announcement to the guests sitting over various stages of their dinners. For a few minutes, forks went down and veal scallopine, chicken francese and spinach fettuccine with porcini sat idle.

"Ladies and gentlemen, please share in the good news with my family. My daughter, my princess, has just gotten engaged. Drinks all around, on the house!"

Glasses went up and *"Salute!"* echoed across the room.

People clapped, and someone tapped a spoon against a water glass. Toni, even more red-faced than before, uttered in exasperation, "Daddy!"

Bobby looked like a deer in the headlights, standing in the doorway and facing the raucous tumult.

"They're waiting for you to kiss her," I murmured to him, and he finally got the message.

A roar went up when he took her in his arms. Then Manny, as if to rescue his sister, put the Frank Sinatra album back on and people returned to their dinners.

"You should make the rounds," I told her. "A lot of people here tonight will want to congratulate you."

She took Bobby by the hand and moved from table to table, initiating him into the family business. He needed to know he was going to be on display for a few months, at least until the wedding was over.

The wedding, even I have to say, was an extravaganza. The restaurant was fine for an engagement party, which we threw for them a month after their announcement. The wedding itself we held elsewhere.

But we almost didn't make it to the wedding at all, or not in the way we'd expected.

I was surprised by Al's exuberance that night in the restaurant. The little time we'd spent with Bobby up to that point hadn't given us much comfort that we knew who our future son-in-law was. Later that night in bed, Al and I talked about it.

"You got carried away with your announcement tonight. What got into you?"

"It's been a long time since I've seen her so happy. If marrying this guy is what she wants, and it can lift her so high, then I *do* feel like celebrating. We're only going to get to do this once, so why not shout it from the rooftops—or at least from the kitchen door? Why? Did I embarrass you or something?"

"No, of course not! I think it's sweet that you got so excited for her. Some fathers might feel they were about to lose their daughters. It was kind of like the old days, watching you order drinks all around and make such a big deal. It's been ages since we've had reason to celebrate. I feel I've been too skeptical. You did the right thing tonight, Al. Thank you!"

"You know, it's a pretty important moment in our lives, too—the first of our kids to get married. It made me remember that Christmas I proposed to you."

"I thought of that, too. What kids we were! What did we know? I wanted to marry you so much."

"We've done okay, Rose, despite how blindly we went into it." He drew me close and kissed me.

"I only hope Toni and Bobby are as blessed as we were."

"You don't sound too sure."

"Oh, Al, I'm not trying to put a damper on things. I may just be reading into the situation something that isn't there."

"Like what? What am I missing?"

"He's not like you, Al. I want to know she's with someone who loves her for who she is, not who she might be someday. Someone who'll stand by her when they hit bumps in the road."

"You worry too much, Rose. We have to trust her that this is the guy who makes her happy. Did you see her looking at him tonight? The light in her eyes?"

"You're right. I should know by now we can't be sure of anything in this life. We have to take a leap of faith sometimes."

The next few weeks—as Toni and Bobby planned their wedding—tested both of us. Even Al, convinced as he was of Toni's happiness, had to fight with himself to accept some things he'd never imagined.

We knew we were on unfamiliar territory because Bobby wasn't Italian. Toni was the first of the cousins to marry someone who hadn't grown up with the same traditions, the same sense of family. When Bobby's mother, a widow, came east from Indiana for the engagement party, she put her best face on a situation we could see was not to her liking.

From what Toni had told me of her visit at Thanksgiving, Bobby lived in a fancy suburb. They were country-club people, who kept crystal decanters of bourbon and Scotch on a tray in the living room and served cocktails every evening before dinner. For all I knew, they had a black maid in a uniform who did the cooking and cleaning. Hazel Templeton struck me as the kind of woman who wasn't used to getting down on her hands and knees and scrubbing her own floors.

I'm proud of my home. I keep it spotless myself, just like I learned from Mama. And everything in it Al and I worked for. I suppose we could've moved the family to a house up the North Shore, to Lynn or Swampscott, but it would've meant running the business differently if we didn't live above the restaurant the way we always have. So, even after we were successful, we stayed put. Close to family. Close to the business. My kids never suffered for living in an old section of the city. They got good educations, understood the value of hard work to get where you wanted in life and looked out for one another and those who had less than they did.

But Hazel Templeton was clearly pained when she set foot in my home, wondering what her son was marrying into. She barely ate anything, drank only martinis and asked pointed questions of Toni about how she planned to decorate the home she and Bobby were buying.

That was actually the first time Al and I heard they were going to buy a house. Bobby had a new job out in Concord, so, without discussing it with us, they decided to look in the suburbs for a place to live rather than stay in Bobby's apartment in Cambridge. Instead of a fifteen-minute T ride from the North End, they'd be almost an hour away by car.

I know—Al and I went all the way to Trinidad when we got married. But we came back, as we always knew we would. Toni wasn't coming back. Along with the Templeton name she was going to be taking on a whole lot of other ideas that felt at odds with who we were.

It hurt. I can't deny it. And Al couldn't understand why they hadn't told us.

"Is she ashamed of us, of the home she grew up in, that she's taking off for Bedford without even telling us?" This was after Bobby and Hazel had left and we were getting ready for bed.

"I think she's seeing us through Bobby's eyes, not her own," I said, saddened that she was putting such distance between us.

The house was only the beginning. When they started talking about where they were going to be married, both Al and I hit the roof. Arlington Street Church. So many things about that choice felt like a slap in the face to us. To begin with, it wasn't Catholic. It wasn't even in the neighborhood. Back Bay instead of the North End. You have to understand, the North End is not simply a collection of streets. It's a village, just like all the ones our parents came from in Italy. And on top of everything, the Arlington Street Church was at the heart of the antiwar protests. A few years before, it was where young men had burned their draft cards.

I didn't think Al would even set foot in that church.

"What the hell is going on, Rose? Why can't they be married at St. Leonard's—where we got married, where she was baptized and made her first communion?"

148

We felt we had to get everything out in the open with them. No more surprises. I told Toni we would all sit down across the table and have dinner together on Sunday. Command performance. No excuses.

I did what I always do when we have something important to discuss. I put care into what we were going to eat. For the pasta course I made orecchiette with peas and ham in a cream sauce. It was one of Toni's favorites. For the main course I did a rolled breast of turkey, stuffing it with spinach and ricotta, and on the side, artichoke hearts sautéed with garlic and then baked with bread crumbs and Parmigiano. For dessert, I whipped up a frothy *zabaione*.

I wanted Bobby to see that Italian food is more than smothering everything in tomato sauce and melted mozzarella.

A wedding's supposed to be a time of joy for a family, not a reason for *agita*. Every day it seemed Al and I were tossing on a very stormy sea in a gondola designed to float on the Venice canals. Some days he had the oars, some days I did. We were taking turns calming each other down and trying to find our way.

"I want her to be happy, you know I do, Rose. But has she lost her mind? That night in the restaurant when she came bursting in with the ring, I breathed such a sigh of relief. She's always been a loner and an intellectual, and I worried she'd never find the kind of love you and I were lucky enough to have. I know she's different, not like her cousins. But not to get married in the Catholic church? That's going too far for me. As far as I'm concerned, they can call the wedding off. I'm *not* walking her down the aisle of a Protestant church."

"You know if you tell her that, they'll just go off and have their wedding without us. Neither of us wants that. We need a compromise."

I was asking a lot of Al to try to meet Toni halfway. When

he seizes on something, he doesn't often let go. Most of the time, that's been a good thing. His passion for me, for instance, hasn't cooled in all these years, and he never once wanted to throw in the towel on the restaurant, even in those early years when he was learning to do things he hadn't imagined would ever be part of his life.

"We can figure this out, Al, because we love her and want her to be happy. I'm not going to have her start her married life estranged from us."

Before the Sunday of that dinner arrived, Al decided to get help from Father Dom. Since bringing Manny to us he'd spent a few more years in Miami before being transferred back to Boston. He was working at a Spanish parish in the South End. Al invited him to lunch at the restaurant and we told him about Toni's decision.

"She said she and Bobby had considered St. Leonard's out of respect for us and had gone to Father Cavallo to talk about the wedding. But he'd berated them because Bobby isn't Catholic. She said he's opposed to mixed marriages and won't perform the ceremony. She was furious. I can't blame her. But I still want her to be married in the Church. Is there a way?"

"Some parish priests are more conservative than the orders. Let me talk to Toni and Bobby. If I'm satisfied that they're entering into marriage as a sacred act, I'd be happy to marry them. And as far as a church, what about the chapel at Boston College? With all your boys educated at BC High, you've got a connection. I can make the call."

Al and I looked at each other across the table.

"This works for me," he said. "Let's just hope it works for them. Dom, do us one more favor and come to dinner with them on Sunday. She'll listen to you directly better than hearing this from us. She's ready to leave the Church entirely."

After Father Dom left, I threw my arms around Al. "I know

it's not over yet because we still have to talk to them, but thank you for coming up with a way to solve this. You're the best!"

He kissed me hard. "I want this to work as much as you do, Rose. Married life is complicated enough without a problem like this casting its shadow on a couple."

Toni had always loved Father Dom, especially as she got older and understood the work he did with the poor. I knew she'd hear him out. What I didn't know was if Bobby had any idea how important it was to us—and if he loved her enough to give us this.

I tried to broach the subject as she and I set the table for Sunday dinner. We were using the good dishes, the silver and the embroidered tablecloth my aunt Cecilia had brought back from Italy as a twenty-fifth anniversary gift.

"Why are you going to so much trouble when it's just family? I mean, Bobby's part of the family now."

"I'm setting a nice table *because* it's family. I want this meal to be memorable for us all. A day we can look back on in years to come and say, 'We got it right.'"

"What do you mean? What's going on?"

"Your father and I are trying to give you the wedding you've dreamed of, but we also want you and Bobby to understand what's important to us. A wedding isn't just about the bride and groom. It's about joining two families. You hope the families agree that what matters is the happiness of their children and that everybody works together to start the couple off right."

"Do you think we're *not* working together?"

"I didn't say that. I just want to make sure that you and Bobby—especially Bobby—are open to listening to what your father and I have to say. We invited Father Dom to come, too."

"What's Father Dom got to do with it?"

"He wants to help us find a solution."

"If that solution involves St. Leonard's, I'm not interested."

"Don't worry. Daddy and I actually agree with you about St. Leonard's. It breaks my heart that you won't be married in the same church Daddy and I were, but that's not important in the bigger scheme of things."

"What *is* the bigger scheme?"

"I want you and Bobby to be willing to listen to our side today. Can you ask him to do that?"

"Of course."

At two o'clock I pulled Manny and Mike away from the TV and the Red Sox game. Bobby and Father Dom had arrived in front of the building at the same time and had walked upstairs together—Bobby in his tailored, handmade suit towering over Father Dom in the brown robe and sandals of the Franciscans.

Father Dom said grace; Mike poured everyone a glass of Asti Spumante and we made a toast to Toni and Bobby's future. Toni then surprised us by making another toast.

"To Mom and Daddy, for all they do for us and for bringing us together today. *Salute.*"

The first part of the meal was all small talk—Father Dom asking Manny about BC High, where he was already a junior and playing varsity baseball; Bobby complimenting me on the pasta and taking a second helping; Papa deciding to go have a nap after the salad.

When we'd finally cleared the table of the dinner dishes and were sitting with our coffee and biscotti, Father Dom turned to Toni and Bobby.

"I understand you're having some challenges finding a church that everyone's happy with?"

"No offense, Father, but if it weren't for the close minded-ness of the priest at St. Leonard's, we wouldn't even be having this conversation. Did he never hear of Vatican II?"

"Walking away from St. Leonard's doesn't have to mean walking away from the Church. I'm not one to promote cafeteria-style Catholicism, where you pick and choose what you want to believe. But there are some parts of the city where you might find a more welcoming reception."

"That's why we chose the Arlington Street Church," Bobby interjected.

I could see the color rising in Al's face and was about to jump into the conversation to steer it away from talking too soon about the one thing that could make him explode. But Father Dom turned to Bobby and spoke to him calmly but firmly.

"Bobby, the Arlington Street Church is a wonderful institution and has been a beacon of light and wisdom not only in the history of Boston but also of this country. I know the pastor well and he's carrying on the traditions that were established in the nineteenth century. Al and Rose have great respect for the Arlington Street Church. *But it's not their church.* The Dantes are Catholic. And unless I've missed something, Toni is still a Catholic."

He looked at Toni and she nodded, almost imperceptibly.

"The Dantes want you and Toni to start your marriage off well, and to them, that means treating it as a sacrament and being married by a priest. They aren't insisting on St. Leonard's, even though the family's history is tied to it. Toni and Bobby, I'd like you to consider being married by me, in a place that also has meaning for the family. The chapel at Boston College."

Toni, who'd been watchful and tense throughout the meal and now this conversation, seemed to relax a little, as if we weren't asking for more than she could give.

She turned to Bobby. "What do you think? This would work for me, if you'd be comfortable with it."

I held my breath and waited to see what Bobby would do. It was a test of how much he cared for my daughter and how willing he was to bend. In my eyes, you needed to be flexible to make a marriage work.

"I thought you had your heart set on Arlington Street—the Tiffany windows, the hand-rung bells."

"The beauty of the church is one thing, but if it causes my parents pain to have us marry there, I'm willing to go to BC."

Bobby shrugged. "Then I guess it's fine with me. However we do it, whatever prayers get said over our heads, it doesn't matter to me. What do we need to do to make it happen?"

"I'll want to spend a few moments talking to just the two of you. I'm still bound by the rules of the Church, but let's say I have a more open interpretation of Vatican II than Father Cavallo does."

Al and I and the boys left the three of them in the dining room and cleaned up in the kitchen with the door closed.

"God bless Dom. I think he's saved this family a lot of grief," I said to Al.

"Let's hope this is the end of it. The world's changing too fast for me."

He smiled at the boys. "Do us all a favor and marry Catholic girls when the time comes. I don't want to have to go through this again."

"Don't worry, Pop. I've already got one picked out." Manny grinned.

"And who might that be? That cute girl who always sits over by third base at your ball games?" Mike started in on him.

"You're just jealous 'cause nobody comes to watch you when you're sitting on a bar stool at the Rusty Scupper."

The two of them went at it, teasing each other while they dried the pots, and Al and I felt that life was getting back to normal.

★ ★ ★

With the decision about the church behind us, I felt like I could put my heart into making a beautiful wedding for Toni. She asked me to handle the details for her.

"I have so much to do between now and the end of school, Mom. If you'd organize everything, it would take such a load off me."

I was happy—no, overjoyed—to do it. She asked if she could wear my wedding dress; it needed hardly any alterations. She and Bobby picked out an invitation and I took care of getting them printed and addressed. The invitation list was huge—three hundred people. That's why we couldn't hold the reception at the restaurant. We wound up at Al's cousin's golf course in Chestnut Hill, near Boston College. I told him I didn't want any skimping on the meal, only the best, and he came through for us.

The ceremony itself, which we had struggled so much with, seemed to fulfill everyone's expectations. St. Mary's Chapel at Boston College didn't have the Italian flair of St. Leonard's, but the stained-glass window of the Madonna and the white marble altar made us feel right at home, and I could tell that the unadorned stone walls fit Toni's idea of beauty. They didn't have Mass or Holy Communion, but the service and the prayers were straight out of the Catholic missal. Bobby followed along without stumbling; Toni appreciated Dom's simplicity in the homily; Al and I were grateful for the familiar words of the blessing and for the dear friend who was raising his hand in the sign of the cross over their heads.

Like Toni, the ceremony had a quiet grace. The reception, on the other hand, was the kind of party Al and I know how to throw when we have something important to celebrate.

During the cocktail reception it took your breath away— two huge carved ice swans with their necks entwined like lovebirds. Hollowed out between their wings were jumbo shrimp, chunks of lobster, and clams and oysters on the half shell. The dinner was three courses. Pear and arugula salad with balsamic dressing; for the pasta course, spinach tortellini with pesto sauce; and for the entrée, filet mignon with green beans and roasted rosemary potatoes. The wedding cake came from La Venezia on Hanover Street.

Of the three hundred guests about two dozen came from Bobby's side. He had no family at all except his mother, his sister, Sandra, and her husband. Both his parents were only children, so no aunts or uncles, no cousins. I felt bad that, compared to them, we had so much in the way of family and tried to welcome them. Some of Hazel's friends made the trip from Indiana, and they seemed stunned by the celebration. I guess weddings in the Midwest were more subdued than the parties we were used to giving.

You should've seen the dining room just before we threw open the doors. I did everything in gold—the tablecloths and napkins, the cutlery and the rim around the cream-colored dishes. With all the candles lit, the room shimmered.

I watched Al on the dance floor with Toni as the band played "Daddy's Little Girl," and I remembered a handsome soldier who'd put his arm around my waist more than thirty years before as he led me in our first dance as a married couple.

I said a little prayer that my daughter was stepping into a marriage that would be as solid and as deeply loving as ours. I wished I could shake the feeling in my heart that, despite the gaiety and lightness surrounding her, she and Bobby had a long way to go and a lot to learn if they were going to make it.

I was starting to feel like my mother, God rest her soul, who saw things the rest of us missed or overlooked in our rush through life. She could cut through appearances and find the core of truth in a situation. My fear for Toni was that she'd wrapped herself in a gauze of illusions. Like my wedding veil, which had disintegrated in its box in the closet when we took it out, I was afraid her dreams for this marriage would crumble.

I hoped I was wrong.

Raising Sons

⸺ ❦ ⸺

I BECAME A GRANDMOTHER a little under a year later, when Toni gave birth to her son, Joseph Albert. I was both thrilled and relieved. I had no idea how overwhelmed I'd feel when I first took that baby in my arms. I understood then why my mother would hold up each of her grandchildren when they were presented to her and utter, *"Il mio sangue."* My blood.

You begin to feel immortal when you have a grandchild, like you'll live on in them.

I was relieved for two reasons. The first was that she had been married longer than nine months before Joey made his appearance. I didn't have to endure any more raised eyebrows or suspicions that she'd been pregnant when she walked down the aisle. As soon as she'd announced she was pregnant back in September, tongues had started to wag that one of Rose's "perfect" children wasn't so perfect. As it was, the family had wondered why they were in such a hurry to get married, only a few months after he gave her the ring. "Because they're in love," I told everybody. "Just like Al and me. Remember, we got married a *week* after he popped the question." Joe was born a full eleven months after the wedding, and that shut everyone up.

I was also relieved that she'd been able to get pregnant so quickly, instead of suffering as I had with doubts that I was barren. I wasn't sure she would've kept trying if it had been difficult for her—not because she gives up easily but because I'd worried that she might not want kids at all. Or rather, that Bobby might not want kids and Toni would go along with his decision.

Who knows? Maybe the pregnancy was an accident, a glitch in the carefully orchestrated life they'd laid out for themselves. But Toni adapted with grace. She had Joe close to the end of the school year, so she had the whole summer with him before she went back to teaching art at Bedford High School in September. If they'd lived closer I would have watched Joe for her, just as Mama had done for me after Al Jr. was born. But I couldn't leave the day-to-day needs of the restaurant or Papa, who, at eighty-nine and nearly blind, needed almost as much attention as an infant. And Toni felt it was too far to drive the baby to me in the city every morning before she went to school.

So she hired somebody, a stranger, to take care of her child. Oh, she had her interview checklists and talked to everybody's references before she made her decision. But to me, it was yet another sign of how far apart her generation and mine were. I accepted that times were changing. It was harder for Al.

"I don't understand why she can't take a few years off and stay home with her baby."

"Al! I worked when the kids were babies."

"Yeah, but that's because I was away at war and then in a VA hospital for a year. Her husband's an able-bodied guy with an engineering degree."

"She wants to work, Al. It's why she got an education, why we *paid* for that education."

"I knew if they moved out to Bedford it was going to be too easy for her to forget about her family."

As much as it hurt me that I didn't have them close, I'd learned long ago not to question the decisions made by my daughter and her husband.

While Toni was starting her life as a mother, I still had my own two boys at home to deal with. In Manny's junior year of high school, our bright student and star athlete slid into a funk after he broke his arm one afternoon horsing around stupidly with his buddies at the playground. One of them came running into the restaurant yelling, "Mrs. D! Mrs. D! Come quick. Manny's hurt himself."

Both Al and I raced down the street. Manny was writhing on the asphalt, badly scratched up, with his arm at an alarming angle and the bone sticking out.

Al blanched, terrible memories of his own damaged arm flooding back. I sent him home to call the ambulance while I stayed with Manny.

If only it had been a simple broken bone. But it was so badly shattered the orthopedist didn't think Manny would be able to pitch again, and certainly not with the skill and strength he'd shown. His dreams of getting a baseball scholarship to college and aiming for the major leagues began to unravel. He lost interest in everything—his schoolwork, the team, even helping out in the restaurant. We'd excused him from his regular duties downstairs for a couple of weeks to give his arm a chance to heal. The doctor at Mass General had told us no lifting, no unnecessary motion. The arm had to rest. But that inactivity cost Manny. He'd been such an active kid, always on the move. He had practically danced on the ball field. And when he was a base runner, the other team had to watch him constantly or he'd steal a base. He didn't know what to do with himself, cooped up in the apartment with Papa, who slept most of the afternoon. He was angry with himself and with his buddies and couldn't bring himself to suit up and sit on the bench to cheer his teammates on. I didn't realize soon enough exactly what was bothering him. By the time I did, he was locked in his room with headphones on, listening to the Grateful Dead and getting Fs on his papers because he wasn't handing them in.

When we got his midterm grades it was our turn to be angry. Al was beside himself.

"Do you think a broken arm is an excuse to become a bum? Where do you think I'd be if I let what happened to *this* determine my whole life." He pointed to his own arm.

"You don't understand." Manny pushed back. "Without baseball, I have nothing. I am nothing."

Later that night, after a fruitless discussion with Manny that resulted only in frayed tempers, Al and I tried to come up with a way to get through to him.

"Al, if anyone can reach him, you can. Put aside who you are now and remember the young man who was released from the VA hospital and could barely make it up the stairs. You'd lost hope. Everything you thought you'd do or be felt out of reach. If you can let Manny know that you've been where he is now, maybe it'll help."

"But, Rose, I managed to climb out of that hole because I had you. You showed me how. Made me believe I could be somebody despite my broken body."

"And now Manny has both of us, Al. But he's not going to listen to me. He assumes I won't understand what it means to him not to play baseball."

The next day we told Manny we expected him to return to work in the restaurant. He wouldn't be able to bus tables with one arm immobilized, so we put him on a salad station, arranging plates of ingredients that had already been cut. It was close to Al, who could keep an eye on him, but who also was

161

going about the complex work of cooking. Manny couldn't help seeing Al's swift movements, adapted over the years to compensate for his weak arm. Al said nothing for a couple of days, other than to let Manny know what needed to go on the plates, depending on what salad a diner had ordered.

"You can arrange the plate any way you want," he told Manny.

At first, it was all he could do to throw a handful of romaine, some sliced onions and a couple of carrot slices on a plate just to keep up with the orders. He was frustrated, but he was at least *doing* something instead of lying on his bed.

Most of the time as a busboy he'd been moving in and out of the kitchen so quickly he hadn't paid much attention to what was being created there. The plates he'd seen were the ones he was clearing off the tables, either wiped clean by a piece of bread to soak up the last bit of gravy or, worse, filled with picked-over remnants a diner had pushed around with a fork but not savored or enjoyed.

We wanted to keep him busy and have him absorb the silent message of Al's success. But we got something unexpected.

After a few days, Al noticed that when the kitchen was slow, the salads were looking less like a pile of greens dumped on the plate and more like the artist's palettes Toni had used at the Museum School. Manny was fanning the tomato or pear slices. Placing olives strategically like punctuation marks. Still, Al said nothing.

You can't force a message on someone who's not ready to hear it.

One night during a lull between the turnover period, when the early diners were eating their cannoli and tiramisu and before the next wave had arrived, Manny was on a break. He was rubbing his shoulder on the broken arm. I fought back the urge to let him off early. I knew he'd done his homework in the afternoon, so if I sent him upstairs, he'd retreat into his headphones. Not a good place, as far as I was concerned. He stood around, watching Al at the stove finishing off some rabbit with olives that had been simmering in wine.

"Dad, how'd you learn how to cook?"

"Mostly by doing and by watching Mama Rose and her mother."

"Was it what you always wanted to do?"

"Me? Nah. I was a builder before the war. I figured cooking was women's work. When I got out of the VA hospital I thought my life was over because I couldn't work at what I'd been trained to do. You can ask Mama Rose. I was one angry guy. Here, stir this a minute while I check on the lamb in the oven."

He handed Manny the wooden spoon and left him at the stove. I watched Manny plunge the spoon in the pot and imitate the scraping motion Al had been using to loosen bits of meat and onions from the bottom. He wasn't great at it, but he shoved the spoon around enough to keep the meat from sticking.

Al came back with an order slip in his hand. "Manny, we just got two orders for the rabbit. Plate them up with some potatoes and broccoli rabe." And then he walked away.

Manny took two plates from the warmer and spooned out a couple of pieces of rabbit onto each. One at a time he carried them over to the vegetable trays and arranged the potatoes and rabe, then put them under the infrared lamp for the waitstaff to pick up.

"You want me to plate anything else, Dad?" he called over to Al.

"Keep an eye on the orders as they come in. I've gotta go down to the cellar for some olive oil."

Now, I knew very well there were at least two gallons of oil in the cabinet. Al was deliberately leaving Manny on his own. I saw Manny straighten his shoulders. Whatever ache had bothered him earlier seemed to have disappeared. He pulled order slips off the shelf as they came in from the dining room and started arranging plates of linguine with shrimp scampi and eggplant parmigiano. By the time Al came back upstairs he'd plated six different orders.

He was fast and sometimes a little careless, but he looked as if he was enjoying what he was doing.

I nodded to Al as he came back into the kitchen. "I think you unlocked a tiger from his cage," I whispered.

Al smiled. "I can live with a few screwed-up orders if the kid finds himself."

Over the next few weeks Al kept giving Manny more responsibility in the kitchen. It wasn't always easy. Al could overlook a dropped plate of chicken piccata or a forgotten side of string beans, but he blasted Manny if he got lazy or didn't clean up any messes he made. Al wanted to do well by this boy to make up for all the years he hadn't known about him. But he wasn't going to spoil him or let him get away with anything.

Manny, for his part, would go into a sulk whenever Al caught him slacking off; he'd scowl and slam heads of lettuce on the counter until he cooled off. But little by little I could see Manny trying harder, picking up little tips Al gave him, taking on extra work when we got really busy.

You know, even though all three of our other kids had worked in the restaurant as teenagers, none of them had shown the slightest interest in the back of the house. They'd waited tables or bussed, did setup, ran the cash register. The other boys had been helpful with unloading deliveries. But nobody had ever stuck a spoon in a pot except to grab a taste of something for themselves.

I guess we should've seen it coming the day Manny said to us, "I don't want to go to college."

"What is this, you think college was just a place for you to play baseball? Of course you're going to college." As far as Al was concerned, there was no discussion.

"You're a smart boy, Manny. You got your grades back on track. Dad's right. Colleges are interested in your mind, not just your pitching arm."

"But you always said to us how important work is. Mike and Toni, they're doing jobs they needed to go to college for. The work I want to do, I don't need a college education."

"What do you want to do?" Al asked him, but we already knew the answer to that.

"Work in the business with you."

There was probably nothing that could have made Al prouder than to have his son say he wanted to join the business. But we both realized the world had changed since we'd started out. You needed a lot more than hard work and street smarts to survive in our business these days.

"You need an education, Manny." Al's voice was firm, but I knew Manny could hear the love underneath his gruff tone.

"Why not let him go to a college that offers restaurant management?" That was Mike's suggestion, trying to bridge the gulf between Manny and us. "He doesn't have to study medieval art or philosophy to get a college degree."

"He wants to cook."

"Then check out places that'll let him do both. He knows by now it's a business, not just a place for making a delicious veal scallopine. Let me look into it, ask around. I'll see if I can find out what the good schools are."

It was a big help to have Mike step in. Because he was still living with us, he understood his brother. He knew what baseball had meant to Manny. If Manny was willing to replace

165

that dream with being a chef, we didn't want him to be disappointed a second time. But not going to college was out of the question. To Al and me, it was like treating him as a second-class citizen compared to his siblings.

What if, God forbid, the restaurant failed? We'd survived our mistakes in the past, but who was to say the place would still be thriving for Manny to take over? No, he had to have something to fall back on. But you can't tell a seventeen-year-old, even one who'd made it out of Cuba, that you need to be prepared for anything life threw at you.

Al still wanted him to go to Villanova.

"You can't ask him to replace Al Jr.," I said to him. "We agreed when we adopted Manny that he's not a substitute for what we lost. He's having a hard enough time measuring up to his own dreams. Don't saddle him with that, as well."

By Thanksgiving of his senior year in high school, Manny's arm had healed sufficiently to let him prepare simple dishes in the restaurant, not just plating entrées and putting salads together. He cooked on Saturdays and was often downstairs before either Al or me, chopping onions and garlic and taking deliveries. He'd have trays of lasagne assembled and waiting in the refrigerator before Al and I had finished our first cup of coffee.

He worked side by side with Al and me that year to prepare the Thanksgiving meal for the family. The crowd had grown, with so many of my nieces and nephews getting married. We invited Hazel to join us. I didn't want to have Toni gone a second year in a row, but I felt bad if that meant Hazel would be alone for the holiday; Bobby's sister, Sandra, was going to her in-laws' with her husband. I thought she might say no, since she'd never seemed very comfortable at our place, but I guess the pull of being with Bobby and Toni, now that Toni was pregnant, was strong enough to give her a reason to accept.

She was older than Al and me, in her sixties. She'd married and had her children late in life. So the prospect of a grandchild was one she'd waited for a long time.

But I knew even she had questioned whether Bobby and Toni had rushed into marriage because Toni was pregnant. I guess she was looking for reasons her son had married someone as "unexpected" as Toni. I could never shake the feeling that Hazel thought Bobby had married into a family that was beneath him.

I'd hoped that Toni would get to the restaurant early to arrange the antipasto platters like she always did. But apparently Hazel had prepared one of Bobby's favorite breakfasts—pork tenderloin in cream gravy and cheese grits—and it was almost noon by the time they'd finished.

They walked in the door of the restaurant just before 2:00 p.m., Toni arriving like a guest instead of one of the family who contributes to putting the meal together.

"What's the matter, Rose?" Al had asked me when I realized Toni wasn't coming to assemble the antipasto. It wasn't that I resented the extra work. Most of the dishes had been prepared in the days before—cannellini beans marinated with garlic and parsley, tuna mixed with onions and capers, my own eggplant and mushrooms pickled in August. It was just my sense of a shift, a slight change that shouldn't have been a big deal to me, but was.

Al came up behind me and kissed my neck as I was rolling prosciutto to put around the edge of the platter.

"You're going to make the antipasto too salty," he murmured as I dabbed my tears with the handkerchief I kept in my apron pocket. "She's married now. She's got her mother-in-law staying with her. Give her a chance to be a good daughter-in-law, like you are."

Al had a way of easing me into a better frame of mind. He

knew he could soothe me with a nuzzle or a kiss. I was fifty years old but I felt like a teenager when he put his arms around me. And he was right. I remembered how I'd felt trying to adapt to Al's family when the difference was only the distance between Naples and Calabria—a few more hot peppers than I was used to. Toni had a lot more to cope with, and I had to stop myself from wishing time could stand still.

"She's coming to dinner, even if she isn't here in the kitchen," Al murmured.

When Manny had a free minute, he danced over to the counter and rolled a few dozen slices of Genoa salami before slicing the fennel and arranging it on platters with green and black olives.

"We'll get it done, Mama Rose."

And we did.

Manny whisked the turkey gravy at the last minute, freeing my hands to fry the batter-dipped broccoli and cauliflower in hot oil.

Al and Mike each carried out one of the thirty-pound turkeys we'd roasted; a third one we kept in the warmer for second helpings.

The place was pandemonium that year—so many kids. We had a children's table for the ones old enough to sit by themselves, although more than one of my nieces had to cut the turkey on their kids' plates. We had at least three in high chairs at the big table.

Hazel seemed overwhelmed at first by the noise and confusion, but I saw how attentive Toni was to her mother-in-law, introducing her to aunts and uncles, serving her graciously. And I have to admit, I watched to see if Hazel appreciated it— my daughter's care and our food. She ate like a bird, only putting little spoonfuls on her plate of the unfamiliar parts of the meal, but at least she tried things and didn't turn her nose up at the antipasto or manicotti before tasting them. And each bite seemed to soften her expression, widening the smile on her lips the more she ate.

After Thanksgiving, Mike sat on Manny to get his college applications done. He even drove him down to Rhode Island to see a school where he could get both the chef's training and the management courses he'd need. But while they were there, they heard from one of the other families visiting the school about the new Culinary Institute of America in Hyde Park, New York. Manny's attitude up to this point had been resignation. He knew we weren't willing to back down from insisting on college but his heart wasn't in it and he was just going through the motions.

He was ready to get in the car and go back to Boston, but Mike decided they should keep driving and take a look at the Culinary Institute.

"What have we got to lose, except a few hours?" he said to Manny. "Who knows, maybe this is the one."

And it was.

When Manny and Mike got back from New York, Manny couldn't shut up about what he'd seen and the people he'd talked to. He also realized how hard it was to get into and was suddenly on fire to put together the best application he could.

Al wasn't crazy about the fact that he was only going to get an associate's degree and I wasn't happy that the school was hours away in New York instead of just down the expressway in Providence. But Mike spoke up for Manny.

"I talked to some of my restaurant clients at the bank, and they all say this place is the best. If he's accepted, it's like going to the Harvard of the cooking world. If you make him go to a lesser school, even if it's close to home and he comes out with a bachelor's degree, he'll just be wasting his time. Look, we've finally got him excited about school. Let him try for this. To him, it's like being drafted for a Red Sox 'A' team."

When the acceptance letter arrived in the mail, I could hardly wait for him to come home from school. I propped the envelope up against a glass at the table. When he came into the kitchen for something to eat, he headed first for the refrigerator and grabbed some leftover *pasta e piselli*. He was going to eat it cold, but I took it from him.

"Sit and let me warm it up for you." I steered him to his chair and waited for him to see the envelope staring him in the face. He let out a whoop and then held it for a minute, weighing it in his hand.

"Okay. Time to face the music." His hands were shaking as he picked up a knife and slit open the envelope. Then he read out loud from the letter: "'Dear Mr. Dante, we regret to inform you…'"

My heart sank. It wasn't what I'd expected. Oh, boy, he was going to need a lot more than my pasta. And then I noticed the impish grin and the sparkle in his eyes.

"'…that we have turned down countless qualified candidates to make room for someone as brilliant and talented as you.'"

I flipped the dish towel in my hand at him. "That's not what it says!"

"You're right. It says, 'Congratulations! Now you're *really* going to work your ass off.'"

I hugged him and he got up from the table to dance me around the room.

"Go downstairs and tell your father. And call Mike!"

We sent Manny off to CIA in September and suddenly the house and the restaurant were too quiet. Mike and Papa were still with us, but Mike was almost never home, between his job

170

and the social life he had, which seemed, as it always had, to center around the bars that were flourishing down near the waterfront.

The run-down wharves on the edge of the neighborhood were being bought up and turned into offices and apartments right on the harbor. They drew a lot of young people and Mike, never one to miss an opportunity to make friends, had quite a circle that made the Rusty Scupper bar their home away from home. When they got hungry, he led them like the pied piper to Paradiso.

He was usually surrounded by friends but never seemed to have one special girl. I knew young people were taking more time than our generation had to settle down, but he was already twenty-six with no one in sight.

I asked him about it one night when he was actually home before midnight and he sat in the kitchen with me. It was a chance I didn't want to lose, and although I was bone-tired, I heated up some 'scarole soup with the little meatballs he'd loved as a kid.

"Ma, you don't have to feed me. I can do it myself. Why don't you go to bed?"

"It's okay, sweetheart. I don't see you much, even though you live under the same roof. How's work?" I started out with the easy stuff.

"It's fine. But I might make a change. I don't think banking is the right place for me."

"I have to tell you, Mike, knowing who the bankers were when I was at Shawmut, I didn't think you were cut from the same cloth. You like your good times too much."

"Is this going to be a lecture on my extracurricular activities?"

I threw up my hands. "Excuse me, I'm only your mother."

"Don't worry, Ma. I know you think I spend too much time

171

partying. I bet you want to ask me when I'm going to settle down. It's all I heard at Thanksgiving, not just from the aunts but also from my overly fertile cousins, who seem to believe it's their mission in life to triple the Italian-American population of Boston."

"I want you to be as happy as Daddy and me, that's all. I'd hate to see you go through life alone. Sometimes I wonder if you have it too good here at home. Not that I want you to leave. I can't believe I'm saying this, but I don't want you to become a mama's boy, so tied to my apron strings that you can't find a girl who lives up to your expectations. Like your father's brother Rocco, who still eats at your grandma Antonella's every night and never got married. If you ask me, he got trapped taking care of his mother twenty years ago and wound up feeding her cats instead of his own children. I'd kick you out in a minute if I thought you'd still be here when you're forty."

"I haven't found the right person yet, Ma."

"Do you honestly think the right person's going to be sitting next to you some night at the Scupper?"

I sighed; I could see we weren't getting far. "Change of subject," I said. "What did you mean earlier, about changing jobs?"

"One of my customers at the bank is looking for an accountant. We've been talking."

"What kind of business?"

"He runs a magazine in one of the converted buildings down on the waterfront. He's the smartest guy I've ever met, a real Renaissance man. He knows a lot—art, science, business. Like Leonardo da Vinci. I feel I could learn a lot from him."

"How long has he been in business?"

"About ten years. The magazine is solid, doing well. And he's thinking about expanding. That's why he's hiring."

"So what are you waiting for? You have any doubts about this?"

"I guess, despite my party-boy reputation, I'm still a numbers guy, and I want to run a few more before I make a commitment. I think I learned that from you, if I'm not mistaken." He smiled.

"I don't think you're asking for my advice—or are you?"

"You're a good businesswoman, Ma. Not just a great cook and mother. What do *you* think I should do?"

"Bring me a copy of this magazine. And invite him to dinner next week."

And so, instead of figuring out where Mike was headed in his love life, I got to pass inspection on his possible new boss. I wasn't sure what to expect from Mike's description. Was he going to be an egghead, talking over my head? I had subscriptions to *Life, Ladies' Home Journal* and a restaurant trade magazine. If I had time to sit down and read, it usually wasn't a magazine. So I couldn't really be helpful on that front. But I'd always been a pretty good judge of people. I knew I'd be able to tell if he'd do well by Mike.

I liked Graham Bennett the moment he looked me in the eye and shook my hand. He wasn't a big man physically, but he carried himself with confidence. His eyes behind his black-rimmed glasses were warm and direct. In spite of how smart Mike claimed he was, he wasn't showing off his intelligence at my table. He showed respect for Al and me, and seemed to understand what it took to run a successful restaurant. I wouldn't have been able to tell if his magazine ideas were going to work, but his answers to my questions about how he ran his business satisfied me.

I gave Mike my thumbs-up in the kitchen when he helped me get the coffee. Mike handed in his notice at the bank a week later and right after Christmas started working at the magazine.

If only finding him a steady girlfriend could be this easy, I thought.

173

Changes

PAPA PASSED AWAY in the spring of 1974. He was eighty-nine and it seemed as if he'd decided it was time to go. His failing eyesight had excluded him from the card games he loved to play at his club, and most of his *compares,* who for years had whiled away the afternoons with a demitasse of espresso and a cigar with him, had one by one slipped away. He was practically the last one left. Once again the whole family gathered for a funeral, ten years after Mama's death. The last month I'd spent almost constantly at his bedside, watching the life seep out of him. The little he spoke was in Italian, as if the closer he got to the end, the more his mind returned to his beginning, his childhood in Italy. With his passing, I was now the oldest generation. Both my mother and father were gone, and without them as anchors, we started to drift apart as a family.

Thanksgiving 1974 was the first time that all my sisters and brothers and their families didn't gather together at Paradiso.

"The family's getting too big and the kids are too wide-spread for us all to come to Boston," my sister Bella said, calling from Albany to excuse herself and her family.

My brother Sal and his wife decided to take a cruise since their kids were going to their in-laws.

It bothered me. It is not that I took it personally, that they suddenly weren't coming to *my* place. It was just how quickly, without Papa, they no longer considered it important for the family to be together. Maybe I should've seen it as less work for me and less *agita* all around. In a family as large as ours, somebody always had a beef; there was always a burning topic that people were never in agreement on—the Church, the president, the football game.

I should've appreciated the fact that it was going to be a quieter holiday than we'd had in many years. Even Toni, Bobby and the baby were going to Indiana. I knew I'd cook too much food. Nobody ate the way we used to. For days before, I was slamming cupboard doors and making and remaking lists as one family member or another called with his or her excuses.

"Rose, what's eating you?" Al asked me. "Is it too much to do Thanksgiving this year after Papa's death? You want somebody else to take it on?"

"No! That's the last thing I want. I'm disappointed, that's all. I feel like the family's splintering and I should be able to hold it together, like Mama did."

Al gave me a neck rub as I sat at the kitchen table refiguring quantities.

"Your sister Bella hit the nail on the head. The family is now so many families, with all the kids getting married and having babies. Maybe it's time for them to each have their own traditions."

"I know you're probably right, but I'm not ready. Thanksgiving to me is a room full of people, all talking at once and enjoying my food."

"So, let me get this straight. It's a room full of *people,* not necessarily *family?*"

"Well, if I can't have the family, I guess, yes, I'd still want a full house."

"Then let's fill the house. I bet Mike's got friends with no family in town. And I bet those classmates of Manny's from other parts of the country aren't going home."

And that's how we made up for my own family's absence that Thanksgiving and began to throw open the doors to friends who had nowhere else to go.

Mike's boss, Graham Bennett, came that year. It surprised me that he wasn't married, a successful man like him and nearly thirty-five. But I figured when you start a company, there's not much time for starting a family, too. Al and I were lucky that we were together and had already begun having kids when we opened Paradiso. I couldn't imagine not having a family.

The next few years were peaceful ones for us. To begin with, nobody died. Manny graduated from the Culinary Institute in 1976 and came home with his hair four inches longer and his head full of ideas. He and Al jostled each other so much for control of the stove that, for the sake of my sanity, I told them they had to work different shifts. It was time Al got a break, anyway.

In the winter of 1977 we took a whole month off for our trip to Florida. As Joey had gotten older and Toni got pregnant again, she was more willing to leave him with us so she could get some rest. And when her second son, Benjamin, was born, it seemed like the right moment to take Joey to Florida with us for his first excursion to Disney World. That gave Toni a chance to devote all her attention to Ben and us a chance to spoil our grandson.

Around this time, the neighborhood was changing, ever since the city had spruced up Quincy Market, a derelict collection of old warehouses, and turned it into shops and food stalls and restaurants. One of the restaurants was a high-end Italian place and the owners had a cooking show on public television. She was British and he was Italian, and frankly, she made him out to be a buffoon. She was supposedly explaining Italian food as if she were the expert and he'd get all emotional over the seasoning in the meatballs. It was embarrassing. I also went to eat at their restaurant and it wasn't so good. They were trying too hard to make the food elegant instead of satisfying.

But Quincy Market turned out to be good for our business. It attracted a lot of tourists following the Freedom Trail, which guided people around all the historical sights in Boston. Even though Quincy Market was on the other side of the expressway, people would come over to the North End to find Paul Revere's house and the Old North Church and then stay for dinner.

Manny should've had a cooking show. He had a flair in the kitchen and was a lot better looking than Luigi and his snotty wife.

Manny had learned growing up in the restaurant that we treated our customers like family. Al always came out from the kitchen during the evening to see how people were enjoying their meals, especially if they were regulars. Manny started doing that on the nights he was cooking. Some of the old-timers remembered when he'd been a busboy. He had an excellent memory and would greet people by name the second time they came to eat.

He also began to attract a new clientele for us—young, very pretty women. Once word got out about the good-looking chef at Paradiso, the girls from the offices and banks along the waterfront started to flock to the restaurant on their lunch hour or on Friday nights.

The place was packed. When we heard the building next

door was going up for sale, Al and I both had the same idea. We could break down the wall on the first floor and expand. We'd hesitated to do it before; the original restaurant had been all we thought we could handle. But with Manny, who was eager to do more—enlarge the menu, open up the kitchen so diners could see the meal prepared as it if were a show—we decided it was the right time.

Manny joked about naming the new section the Inferno and having an open-hearth brick oven in the front of the house to bake pizzas. But Al nixed that idea.

"Not everybody will get the joke, and I don't want people saying, 'I'm going to Hell,' when somebody asks where they're eating dinner."

It took more than a year to get everything done once we'd made the decision. Permits, loans, an architect who cost an arm and a leg but who came recommended by one of Manny's teachers at CIA. The whole thing was a headache for me, especially acting as a buffer and a go-between for Al and Manny. Al liked the tried-and-true, the traditional, comfortable place we'd built from nothing over thirty years. Manny, a little too full of himself and his education, kept pushing for this or that.

"Everything has a cost. Show me how we make them up at the cash register, your fancy ideas. We're not Stella Mare down on the waterfront. We're on Salem Street."

In the end, we compromised. We deferred the brick oven but put a half wall in the back of the new section so people could watch the grill; we also added more Northern Italian to the menu.

When we finally had the grand reopening Al and Manny were speaking to each other again, Toni was pregnant for the third time and Mike, at twenty-nine still wasn't married.

He did, however, decide to move out. He just went upstairs. The Boscos, who'd rented the apartment on the top floor for forty years, decided after the blizzard of 1978 that they'd had enough of Boston winters and bought a mobile home in Palm Beach Gardens.

Mike jumped at the place when I started worrying about finding someone to rent it.

"Let me take it, Ma, and pay the rent. You said yourself you don't want me still living with you when I'm forty."

"I *meant* that you should be living in your own home with a *wife*."

But I gave in. He needed his own place, married or not, and if he didn't go upstairs, sooner or later he'd move, maybe out of the neighborhood. I half expected Manny to want to go with him, but Mike was pretty quick to quash that idea, and we wouldn't have let him, anyway. He was too young, too headstrong and there were already too many beautiful girls chasing after him at the restaurant. I didn't need them trooping up the stairs, too.

For our fortieth wedding anniversary, Al took me to Italy. I didn't think he'd be willing to leave the restaurant for that long, but Manny was proving himself, even at twenty-four. What a trip! We treated ourselves to *la dolce vita,* staying at first-class hotels and eating at the best restaurants in Rome and Florence and Venice. Al and I made mental notes on the dishes, comparing them to what we offered at Paradiso.

"They're using rosemary in this bean dish."

"I like what they did with the prosciutto and figs. We could do it in the summer."

After a whirlwind tour through the famous sites, we relaxed on Capri for a weekend. I'd bought a new maillot swimsuit for the beach but I felt like an old woman when I saw everyone else, even women my age, in bikinis. Al noticed, too.

"You could be wearing one of those, Rose. You've still got the body for it."

At lunchtime, when we walked back up from the beach, he stopped at a shop that had bathing suits displayed in the window and pulled me in.

He flipped through the rack and pulled out a couple of colorful bikinis, all in shades of aqua and green. I tried each of them on and watched Al's face light up in admiration. We bought one of the suits and then strolled back to the hotel arm in arm. The Italians have the right idea about siesta. There's nothing more relaxing than going to bed in the middle of the afternoon with the sound of the sea outside your window and a ceiling fan rotating slowly above your head.

I couldn't remember when Al and I had last been able to enjoy lovemaking with such disregard for everything else in our lives. We had no responsibilities. Not an aging and ill father or kids struggling through one crisis or another on the way to adulthood or a business that demanded so much of our energy and attention. That was the true luxury of this vacation, not the fancy hotels or the celebrated restaurants. We'd been so busy swallowing up as much of Italy as we could that we'd forgotten to take the time just to enjoy each other. But Capri changed that.

Al couldn't wait to get me back to the hotel. He took me in his arms as soon as we were inside the door.

"Do you have any idea how good you looked to me back in the store?"

"I think so." I smiled through the kisses.

We pulled back the covers on the bed and stretched out. That delicious first contact of skin on skin sent ripples through me. Even though I knew every muscle, every line and scar on his body, it still felt thrilling to me. I hoped we'd never tire of this, because in many ways it was what had helped us survive. We were crazy about each other. In all the years of our marriage, through all the ups and downs, Al's arms wrapped around me, holding me close, always reminded me what was important.

In the final days of the trip we rented a little Fiat and drove to Calabria to visit cousins of Al's on his father's side. They didn't have much, a small farm in an out-of-the-way village. The women, my age or younger, looked years older, worn out by the hard work and their large families. I saw old women in the marketplace who could have been my mother, their heads wrapped in the kind of kerchief Mama wore when she was cleaning the house. They were bent with age but still moving with purpose, haggling over the price of a sack of onions or half a pound of tripe.

If Mama and Papa hadn't left for America, this was the life she would've led. Who am I kidding? This was the life *I* would've led. I shook my head at the poverty in the village. Most of the houses didn't have toilets. Al's cousin at least had plumbing in his house and even a washing machine, but it was like the tub and wringer Mama had used forty years ago. I felt that Italy was two countries—the postcard country of the Sistine Chapel and gondolas, and this forgotten place in the hills of the south, where time seemed to have stopped a hundred years ago. Some people might think it was romantic, like the hippies in America living in communes. But I thought it was horrifying.

When Al and I were getting ready to leave, I felt we needed to do something for his cousins, who, despite how little they had, willingly shared it all with us.

"Do you think they'd be insulted if we gave them money as a gift? They need so much, I don't know where to begin to help them."

"Tino has his pride. I'm sure he'd refuse it if we tried to give him an envelope."

"What if I gave it to his wife? Or we put it on the dresser

with a thank-you note? I remember when my aunt Cecilia came back to visit her sister, she told Mama she felt she couldn't go without leaving some cash, even though she'd brought gifts for everybody."

We wound up tucking several hundred-thousand lire notes in a card I'd picked up at St. Peter's in Rome. Maybe all I was doing was easing my conscience, since we were the lucky ones, the ones who'd made it in America. But I can remember my parents sending money to Italy when we were young. When Papa came home every week with his pay, Mama would parcel it out into envelopes—so much for rent, so much for food, so much for those left behind in Italy. It was what you did for family.

ROSE
1980–81

Disintegration

THE SPRING AFTER we returned from Italy, our grand-daughter, Vanessa, was born. I went up to Bedford and stayed with the boys while Toni was in the hospital. Joey was already in first grade and Ben was in nursery school, and Toni didn't want them to miss any days.

We had fun, the boys and I. We baked cookies and built Lego space stations and I even got them to sit still for a couple of Tomie dePaola stories that I found on the bookshelf in their room. I liked that Toni had Italian stories for the boys. *Strega Nona* made me laugh, reminding me of the old women in the neighborhood with moles on their chins and bowls of water and olive oil for warding off the evil eye. They used to scare me to death when I was a kid. But *The Clown of God* was my favorite. One of the nuns at St. John's had told us the story one day in church, in front of the statue of the Madonna with the Christ Child on her lap holding the golden ball. After I heard that story as a seven-year-old, I used to sneak into church to see if He ever played with the ball the juggler in the story had tossed Him.

"Did you ever see Him throw the ball, Nana?" Joey asked me, wide-eyed when I told him about the statue in St.

Leonard's. I wasn't sure these kids had even been in a church after their baptisms.

What *wasn't* fun was spending time with my son-in-law. I thought he'd get home to have supper with his boys, or at least kiss them good-night. But it was almost ten before he walked in the door the night after Vanessa was born. Okay, I thought, he's been spending the evening with Toni and Vanessa at the hospital. I didn't find out till later that he'd barely made an appearance at Mt. Auburn's maternity ward after Toni gave birth.

I was crocheting in the family room, wearing my nightgown and robe, when he got home.

"You want something to eat, Bobby? I made veal cutlets and string beans tonight."

"No, thanks, Rose. I'm not hungry. I'm just going to have a drink."

He poured himself some bourbon from one of those big jugs people get at the New Hampshire state liquor store across the border in Hampton. It was already half-empty, and from the size of the glass he poured for himself, it probably hadn't taken him long to get it there.

He couldn't sit still, jumping from one thing to the next. He flipped through the mail, tossing aside what looked like bills without even opening them, grabbing *Newsweek* and turning a few pages before leaving it open on the counter.

Despite telling me he wasn't hungry, he rummaged through the fridge and cabinets for junk food—Cheetos, ice cream with fudge sauce, a bag of peanuts whose empty shells he left scattered across the coffee table while he watched the Celtics game.

He didn't say anything about how Toni and the baby were doing until I asked, and he didn't seem to care how the boys had spent the afternoon.

He finally grabbed his drink and went down to the garage

where he tinkered with his motorcycle until two in the morning. I went to bed around eleven but when I got up to go to the bathroom, I heard him still down there.

In the morning he was gone before the boys and I were up. I didn't know how he was managing to work with so little sleep and so much whiskey. Maybe he was just coming to terms with the fact that he'd fathered three kids in eight years. Maybe he saw these few days while I was taking care of the boys and Toni was in the hospital as his last opportunity to have a break before the reality of what he was shouldering set in. I tried to tell myself he was acting normally. But I was truly frightened for my daughter and my grandchildren if this was what life with him was going to be.

"I'd like to stay for a few more days after Toni gets home," I told Al. "You and Manny will have to manage without me. I'm worried, Al. I get this sinking feeling that Bobby doesn't care a damn about those children. I don't even know if he still loves Toni." My voice broke at the prospect of something so terribly wrong in my daughter's marriage. When your children hurt, you hurt, maybe even more than they do.

"You want me to come up there and talk to the son of a bitch?"

"Let's wait it out. I don't want her to feel we're butting in, and it's better if they can work it out themselves. I just figure if I'm here to take care of the kids, she'll have some time to give to her marriage. Who knows, maybe that's all it is—that she's been so tied up with the boys and teaching and this pregnancy that he's feeling like a neglected husband."

I wished that was the answer. When I told Toni I'd stay another week until she got back on her feet she started to protest.

"It's not necessary, Mom. Vanessa's a good baby and I got lots of rest in the hospital. We'll be fine."

"My experience is they're always good for the nurses in the hospital, and as soon as they get home they have you walking the floor all night long. I can keep the boys occupied, get them to school and put up some meals for you in the freezer. It's not a burden. I'm happy to stay."

I thought she might put up more of a fight. She'd always been so private with her emotions that I knew it was hard for her to have me smack in the middle of her life. But I was *not* going home. Neither of us mentioned Bobby. She didn't say to me *Bobby will help* or *I'm not alone.* And I didn't ask, because I already knew.

In the next week I did my best to stay out of the way when Bobby came home to give them time together. But it seemed that he was doing everything possible to avoid Toni. He wasn't even sleeping with her, on the grounds that Vanessa was keeping him awake. Toni was breast-feeding and had Vanessa sleeping in a cradle next to her side of the bed.

Although she can't have sex for six weeks or so after she gives birth, a woman still needs to be held and cherished in bed. That Toni was being denied this comfort really bothered me.

"Do you think he's got another woman?" Al asked me during one of our daily phone calls.

"I don't know. But it seems like more than that. He ignores the boys, too. And I don't think I've even seen him pick Vanessa up. Not that I'd want him to after he's been drinking all night. He's completely disconnected. In another world. Toni's putting on a brave face, but I don't think I can keep my mouth shut any longer."

"I'm coming up there. We'll talk to her when he's not around and the boys are in school."

Al came for lunch that afternoon. I made some pasta fazool, one of those comfort foods I knew Toni loved.

She greeted Al with a hug. "Daddy! What brings you here in the middle of the day?"

"I missed your mother," he said, sweeping me into his arms for a kiss. It was something the kids had grown up witnessing, Al and me always greeting each other with a passionate kiss. But I caught a glimpse of pain on Toni's face as she watched us, a question forming in her head—Why don't Bobby and I have this?

"But I also wanted to see you. Your mother and I are worried about you, honey. We want to help you if you'll let us."

"But you *are* helping me. Mom's been great. My house hasn't been this clean since before I had kids, and I've got enough meals in the freezer to feed my family for a year."

Her mouth was set in a forced smile.

"We think you need more than a cleaning and catering service. How are things between you and Bobby?"

She looked from Al to me. At first she threw me a "What have you been telling him?" glance of irritation, as if I'd betrayed some secret of hers. But she hadn't confided any secrets to me, and it began to dawn on her that what she was going through was only too clear to somebody who loved her.

The phony smile was gone. "Bobby's sick."

"You don't have to make excuses for him, Toni."

"I'm not. He's mentally ill. He's seeing a psychiatrist. He's supposed to be taking medication, but I think he stopped."

"He's medicating himself with a bottle of bourbon."

"He's always had more to drink than you've been comfortable with, Mom. It's part of his culture."

"He has no culture," Al muttered.

"That's not fair, Daddy."

"What do you want to do, Toni?" I asked softly.

"His moods go in cycles. He's just in a down phase right now. I've weathered this before."

"How long has it been going on?" Al was having difficulty believing that she'd been able to keep something like this from us.

"A couple of years. It started around the time Ben was born."

"Why didn't you tell us?"

"Because I knew it would upset you, like it's doing now. And because it was under control. There wasn't anything you could do, anyway. You can't cure what he has by having a man-to-man talk about his responsibilities to his family."

"Why the hell did you have another baby?"

"Al!" I was shocked he'd said that to her.

"Its fine, Mom. Legitimate question. We were actually doing reasonably well last year. And my idea of a family has always been three kids. We weren't really trying, but we thought if it happens, great. If it doesn't, that's okay, too."

"But it wasn't okay."

"He started to slide about two months ago and I braced myself. Look, I've made my bed, as you've so often told me. You two didn't give up on each other when things got tough. Especially you, Mom."

"How can we help you?"

"By understanding that this is something I've learned to cope with, as painful as it is. Don't push me to leave him."

"But what about the kids? It can't be good for them to see their father like this."

"They know that when Daddy gets very sad, it's not their fault. And I give them extra attention."

"I think you're asking too much of them and yourself."

"I'm doing the best I can, Daddy."

Vanessa woke up at that moment and Toni went to get her.

"How are we going to talk some sense into her, Rose?"

"Would you have listened to your parents at her age? Everybody thinks nobody else could possibly understand what they're going through, especially when it comes to marriage. We're on the outside, Al. If she doesn't want to hear what we have to say, there's nothing we can do, except be ready when everything comes crashing down."

"And it will."

"I know. I know."

Al, as usual, was angry that he couldn't protect Toni. And I was hurt that she wouldn't let us do more. I even wondered if I was making the situation harder by staying, but I couldn't bring myself to leave when I saw how much she had on her shoulders. I tried to keep in the background whenever Bobby was home, which, frankly, wasn't often. During the day, I found myself as busy as Mama had been—grocery shopping, cleaning, laundry, cooking. Anything that would take pressure off Toni. At night, I stayed in the guest room and watched TV on the little portable set, trying to block out my worries.

I finally went home when Vanessa was two weeks old. I could see I was adding more stress than I was alleviating. I felt she was putting on an act to convince me that everything was fine. I didn't want to make things worse by having her worry about what I thought of her marriage and her choices.

I left her with a full freezer, a spotless house and a sweater set for the baby. If only that had been enough.

Just before Thanksgiving, as I was peeling sweet potatoes, Toni called. Her voice was flat.

"Mom? I just wanted you and Daddy to know that Bobby's left."

"Left? As in moved out? Do you want us to come? What do you need?"

"I'm okay. If you want to know the truth, I'm relieved. It's over. I can stop trying to save him."

Toni had stood by Bobby during his depressed state, but when he came out of it he decided he needed to move on. He'd quit his job without telling Toni, sold his car and taken off on his motorcycle. Al was ready to go after him and strangle him.

"Let him go, Al. If you ask me, it's a blessing that he's gone. Maybe now she can get on with her life."

All Toni would tell us was that she'd come home from school after picking up the kids to find Bobby in the bedroom packing a suitcase. She thought he had a business trip. He'd been jumpy the past couple of weeks. The slow-moving guy who'd ignored everyone when Vanessa was born had been replaced by someone so full of nervous energy that he couldn't sleep.

She sat on the edge of the bed nursing Vanessa while Bobby moved from closet to dresser to suitcase, talking a mile a minute while he threw things into his bag. He claimed he had a job offer in Boulder, Colorado, the opportunity of a lifetime. He was leaving immediately on his motorcycle.

She made him say goodbye to the boys. She told us she wondered whether she'd even have gotten the meager explanation he'd given her if she'd stopped at the Star Market to pick up groceries on her way home. If she and the kids had been later, would he have waited? Or would he have left without saying goodbye, his empty side of the closet the only indication that he was gone?

She didn't know.

She made supper for the kids and put them to bed like any other night. She called us the next day.

Al wanted her to come home.

"How are you going to manage on your own with three kids way out there?"

"Daddy, I've been living here for over seven years. And most of the time I *have* been on my own, even when Bobby was here. We're fine. We'll see you at Thanksgiving. I'll stay over so you can spend more time with the kids."

We didn't tell anybody else at Thanksgiving dinner about what had happened, except Mike and Manny, of course. Like their father, they couldn't believe what Bobby had done to their sister. It was beyond understanding.

When aunts or cousins asked about Bobby, we just said he was away. Toni didn't want the whole family discussing her life or making comments, especially in front of the kids.

I thought she'd be on the edge of a nervous breakdown, but I have to hand it to her—she held herself together. She came in with the kids on Wednesday afternoon and plunged right in to help. She even put the boys to work, setting the kids' table. She had Vanessa in one of those baby carriers that hold a baby on a mother's chest, close to her heartbeat. It left her hands free and I was impressed by how much she could get done in the kitchen. And Vanessa didn't fuss.

"I wish they'd invented that thing when you kids were small! Keeping you happy while I was in the kitchen used to run me ragged."

I noticed things over those five days they stayed with us. Toni was calmer than I'd seen her in ages, and the dark circles under eyes were disappearing. Maybe it was that Vanessa was starting to sleep through the night or that Toni no longer stayed up worrying about Bobby. She laughed with her brothers. She moved around the table at Thanksgiving, spending time with her aunts and uncles and cousins, introducing herself to Mike and Manny's friends—time she hadn't spent in years because she always seemed distracted by making sure Bobby was comfortable. They'd always just come for dinner in the past and had often been the first to leave, as if Toni had extracted from him the compromise of attending the meal and nothing else.

In spite of the uncertainty of her future, she seemed to be enjoying herself. She seemed to *be* herself.

I was glad she had those days surrounded by family and activity. Mike took the boys to the Museum of Science. I took them to the new Disney movie. We sat around the dining room table at night and played cards.

I felt like I had my daughter back. I hated that the price to be paid for that was the breakup of her marriage. But if those early days were any indication, it might have been the best thing that had happened to her.

I don't mean to downplay how difficult the next year was for Toni, dealing with the messy details of Bobby's abandonment of his family. More than once, she thought about taking him back, even moving out to Colorado. Apparently she'd been talking to him.

"Are you nuts?" I said to her when she told me she was considering it.

"He's the father of my children."

"And he *abandoned* them. Look at how well they're doing! How good a mother you are. If you go out there, knowing no one, who'll be there for you when it all falls apart again? Because it will."

Thank God she had friends who told her the same thing. Everybody could see the change in her for the better. And no one wanted her to go back. She finally accepted that it was a fool's mission. She'd bought a plane ticket to go to Boulder for the weekend, "just to talk," she said. She was taking Vanessa because she was still nursing her but realized it would be too hard on the boys. She also didn't know what condition she'd find Bobby in, or even how he was living. But when she got to Logan a massive storm system was moving across the country and flights were being delayed left and right. She waited with Vanessa for five hours. Mike went into the airport to have supper with her and it's a good thing he did. The flight was cancelled at 11:00 p.m. She called Bobby to let him know, and from what Mike could tell, Bobby didn't seem to care one way or the other if she came—that weekend or ever. She wavered about rebooking for the next day, but Mike said, "I think this cancellation is a message. You're not supposed to go, Toni. If Bobby wants his family back, let him come to you."

She burst into tears, but she knew her brother was right. She got into a cab with him and they returned to our place. She never talked about following Bobby to Colorado again.

She got a lawyer after that, somebody Graham Bennett recommended, and started divorce proceedings.

When we heard she was selling the house, Al urged her to move back to the neighborhood.

"Let us help you, Toni."

"Daddy, it's wonderful of you to offer. I can't tell you how important it's been these past few months to have you all around me. But I need to be on my own for a while. Besides, with my job at the high school, living here in the city would be too far to commute. I'll find a place to rent that I can manage financially, and I promise to be here every week for dinner with the kids."

She stood her ground. As much as she'd become one of us again since Bobby had left, she held on to that private part of herself that I knew had always been there.

"She doesn't want to be smothered, Pop," Mike explained to Al after he'd tried again to convince her to take an apartment in one of our buildings.

"She's a thirty-year-old woman. What does she think, that we're going to treat her like a teenager?"

"Wait till she starts dating again. I guarantee you, you'd be watching who goes up the stairs, and whether or not he comes back down."

"Don't be smart!"

"Pop, you don't want to know everything that's going on in our lives. Trust me!"

I reminded Al what a difference it had made when we'd gotten our own place after living with my parents.

"Don't you remember what it was like? Mama, no matter how much I tried to keep our problems from her, saw and heard everything! And had an opinion about it."

"Yeah, but you've said yourself you wish the family wasn't so spread out. The farther people move from the neighborhood, the looser the bonds that keep us together. Look at what happened after your father passed away. I just want her close enough to protect her. If we'd known sooner what was going on when she was married to that jerk, maybe things would've turned out differently."

"I want her close, too, Al. I hurt for her in ways I didn't know were possible. Let's give it time. Look how much more often she's with us. She's not keeping us at arm's length like before. If it makes sense for her to stay in the suburbs, let her be."

Toni was the first one on either side of our family to get a divorce. She wouldn't be the only one, but in 1980 it was still cause for shame and disapproval. People who didn't know what they were talking about and who had no business saying anything saw fit to criticize my daughter. Someone even had the nerve to suggest that Toni was at fault.

"Who'd walk away from his children unless he thought they weren't his?" That was one of the outrageous comments that got back to me. Of course, nobody dared say anything like that to my face. But the phone lines were humming the minute after Toni told my niece Annette, the cousin she was closest to. Naturally Annette told her mother, my sister Ida. By the time word got to Bella in Albany, I was bracing myself for the questions and advice.

"Is she going to get an annulment? Tell her to talk to the priest. If she doesn't, she'll be cut off from the Church. How's she going to raise those children if she can't receive communion?"

I didn't bother to tell my sister that Toni probably hadn't taken communion in years, and that I didn't think a little wafer would make any difference in how well she brought up her kids. She was already doing a fantastic job.

I have to admit the idea of divorce was unthinkable to me, too—until it happened to my own. You see the world changing all around you but you don't believe it'll reach in and grab *your* family. I used to think that people who couldn't keep their marriages together were weak, quitters, selfish. But after what I saw in my daughter's house and how she struggled to make peace with her situation, I began to understand why, for some families, it's the only choice.

Accepting Toni's divorce, as painful as it was, made me realize that sometimes the ideas we've believed for a lifetime get shaken up and tossed in the air—like clowns on one of those round nets at Ringling Brothers. When those ideas come back down, they're slightly lopsided.

I thought I'd made enough adjustments in what I expected to see in my children's lives. The little things, like Manny's taste in music or the length of his hair—a ponytail! Let me tell you, Al was not happy. The bigger things, like Mike's lack of a girlfriend. But nothing prepared me for the blow that seemed to come out of nowhere one day in June 1981.

I never go to Beacon Hill. My friends don't live there. The stores on Charles Street charge prices that might impress the people who shop there, the kind of people who like to carry around the fancy shopping bags proclaiming that they're rich enough to afford the baubles inside the bags. But on this particular day I was down there to pick up a small painting Toni had taken to be framed at Boston Art & Framing. I didn't know it was a parade route. Lots of people were milling around on the sidewalk and, in spite of gray clouds that were spitting rain now and then, people in apartments and offices on the upper floors had their windows open and were looking up the street. I got caught in the press of people and couldn't make it across, so I waited along with everyone else.

"What's going on?" I asked the woman next to me.

"Gay Pride Parade," she said, as if I were an idiot. That's what I mean about Beacon Hill. Am I somehow stupid because I live on the other side of the expressway? Do I have *Italian from the North End* tattooed on my forehead?

I inched my way to the curb, curious to see why the parade was attracting so much attention. I could hear the strains of music approaching and then a wave of applause from the onlookers lined up along Charles Street. Men and women passed by in lavender T-shirts and carrying banners—*Harvard*, *BU*, *UMass* were the ones I could read. They didn't all look like college kids, though. Some were older. Behind them came more groups, some without signs. They didn't seem to mind the rain; they were waving and dancing to the beat of the music coming over a loudspeaker on a van. And then my heart stopped.

Approaching the corner, in the middle of a small group, was Michael. Next to him was Graham Bennett, and they had their arms around each other. He was smiling.

I slipped back into the crowd and almost dropped the package with Toni's painting. You think you know your children, understand their heart's desires.

I walked slowly back home, the sounds of the music and the cheering from the parade growing fainter as I put more distance between myself and Charles Street. I tried to figure out how I'd missed that Mike was gay. Maybe he wasn't, I told myself. Maybe he was just marching to support gay people, the way he'd protested for civil rights when he was at Holy Cross. But I reminded myself that he'd never been serious about a girl. Other than that, he didn't fit the idea I'd always had of gay men.

I didn't consider myself a naive woman. I read the *Globe;* I went to the movies. I knew there was something called a "gay subculture," especially in cities. I just never imagined that my son was part of it.

I didn't really know what to do with what I'd learned about Mike. He'd been keeping it a secret from us. Did he think we wouldn't understand? Did he think we'd be angry with him for not meeting our expectations?

My heart ached with the knowledge. I knew it couldn't be easy for him to be a gay man in our neighborhood. There's always been too much emphasis on being a "tough guy" in the North End. No wonder he'd spent so much time at the bars on the waterfront that attracted an outside crowd of more sophisticated young people. I'd assumed it was because he was more educated than a lot of the boys he grew up with. The ones who did well had become cops and firemen. The ones who didn't went in the other direction. He didn't have much in common with either group.

I couldn't sleep that night. I couldn't bring myself to tell Al or Mike what I'd seen on Charles Street. How many secrets do mothers hold in their hearts? I remember Mama telling me she never stopped worrying about us, even after we were adults.

"*Especially* after you were adults," she said. "The hurts when you were small were easy to fix. When you grew up, I couldn't fix anymore."

I thought I was spiraling into despair. A daughter abandoned with three children; a son leading a double life. I felt betrayed by motherhood. I wanted to crawl into bed and pull the covers over my head. I wanted to blame somebody and call curses down on them. But then I remembered the last time I'd felt like this. I *had* hidden in the stupor of pain and forgetfulness after Al Jr. was killed in Vietnam.

The next day, I drove out to the cemetery. I spent about an hour weeding and cleaning up in front of Al Jr.'s headstone and I planted an azalea bush, a purple one. By the time I was done, sweat was running down my forehead and my fingernails were caked with dirt. I sat back on my heels and cried.

And I said to myself, Toni and Mike are *alive*. Toni's children may not have a father, but they have a loving mother and grandparents and uncles who adore them.

I picked myself up and went home.

I didn't ask Mike about the parade. I decided when he was ready, he would tell us. In the meantime, I welcomed Graham like another son and stopped pressing Mike to find a girlfriend and get married. As well as I could, I started preparing Al so that he'd be ready to hear what Mike had to say. I began by telling him about my trip to the cemetery and the peace I found there, grateful for what we had in Mike and Toni and Manny and the grandchildren.

And I let Toni take her time figuring out what was best for her family.

TONI
1980–98

Safety

I GAVE UP TRYING to live on my own with my kids after my apartment was broken into. I walked into the front hall with six-month-old Vanessa asleep in her car seat. The boys, thank God, were at school.

I heard clattering at the back of the house and thought one of the neighborhood cats or, worse, one of the brats from upstairs had somehow gotten into the pantry.

"Hey!" I yelled and marched over there in a fury to chase away the nuisance.

But as I moved through the dining room into the kitchen, my eye caught the disarray. The drawers of the built-in china cabinet were pulled open and the Venetian lace tablecloths I'd received as wedding presents and never used were strewn about the floor. The glass door above the drawers hung ajar, swinging gently on its hinges as if someone had just pulled it open.

I was still furious, thinking the kids had done more mischief than I'd imagined they would dare. When I got to the kitchen and saw that my bedroom door was open I thought they'd hidden in there. In an instant of recognition, though, coupled with a sickening sensation in my stomach, I realized it couldn't have been cats or kids. The contents of all my drawers had been dumped on the bed. My jewelry box was wide-open and empty. The pillowcase had been stripped from one of the pillows and was missing. Like the teenagers in the neighborhood who marched around on Halloween with pillowcases as their trick-or-treat bags, the intruder had taken one of mine and filled it with everything valuable in my crummy apartment.

It made me want to throw up. Some stranger's hands going through my underwear, fingering the pieces of jewelry my ex-husband, Bobby, had given me, back when he was still in love with me. Even my diaphragm case had been opened.

I turned from the chaos and saw where the door to the porch had been jimmied open. Still seething, I ran out onto the porch, but all I saw was the rustle of leaves on the lilac bush where the thief had probably jumped the fence.

Vanessa started to whimper.

I picked her up and dialed 9-1-1. Then I called my brother Mike.

"Don't tell Mom and Daddy yet. But I need somebody here tonight. I don't want to be alone and I don't want to scare the kids. Can you come?"

I knew I could turn to Mike. We'd always had each other's back—he, the big brother who'd defended my independence when my parents thought I was defying them; I, the sympathetic and accepting listener when he revealed to me that he was gay. I knew it hadn't been easy for him, growing up in a neighborhood like ours with its macho culture. I'd hurt for him, knowing how unhappy he was at not being able to be himself. But then he met Graham Bennett, and their relationship evolved from colleagues turning out a hip magazine to life partners who loved and cared deeply about each other. Although they hadn't come out to my parents, Rose and Al treated Graham like another son. Both men were wonderful uncles to my kids.

Having him with me that afternoon was a solace.

When he arrived he found a board in the basement and nailed it across the back door. The police weren't hopeful of tracking down the thief.

"Probably some addict just grabbing enough easily fenced stuff to buy his next fix. You got insurance?"

I pulled myself together and cleaned up the dining room, where the thief had emptied my silver chest. Everything was gone, including the baby spoons my three kids had received at their baptisms. I couldn't deal with my room or even think of sleeping in my bed that night. The only thing I did was bundle up the sheets with my clothes piled in the middle and carry it to the washing machine in the basement.

Mike met my boys, Joe and Ben, at school and told them we were going to Friendly's for dinner. They ate their burgers and fries, then listened solemnly and wide-eyed as I told them what had happened.

"Did the robber take my Transformers?" asked eight-year-old Joe.

"No, honey. He didn't touch any of the stuff in your room. He only wanted jewelry."

"Why would a robber want jewelry? He couldn't wear it, could he?"

"That would be pretty silly, wouldn't it? No, he took it to sell so he could get money."

"Mommy, is he going to come back and take more stuff?" It was six-year-old Ben, who worried enough for us all.

"No, Ben. He's not coming back."

I answered him with conviction, keeping my voice calm and my eyes focused on his, willing myself to see his innocence and absolute trust in me instead of my pink bra dangling over the edge of my bed, my stockings spilled in a crumpled pile on the floor.

I had to protect them from my fears as well as their own. It had been easy to sweep away the monsters under their beds, even after Bobby left me and the kids. He'd stopped taking his meds and decided he needed his freedom.

When he left for Colorado, I felt only relief. I believed I could hold my family together. While Bobby was disintegrating in front of my eyes, it took all my strength, all my energy. After he was gone, I no longer had to take care of him *and* the kids. I wasn't waiting up at night till three in the morning, listening for his car in the driveway or the phone call from the police telling me he'd driven into a tree. I didn't have to bite my tongue to hold back the accusations and doubts that had already spilled into every crevice of our lives together. After he was gone, I took a deep breath, gathered my kids around me and promised to be their strength and protection.

Now, faced with my shattered back door and equally shattered confidence, I faltered.

"You know what?" I said to them to gain some time. "Let's have a slumber party tonight! We'll all sleep in the same room with our sleeping bags."

"Even Uncle Mike?" Joe looked at Mike hopefully.

"Yeah, squirt. Even me." Mike smiled at him.

We made a big deal out of pulling mattresses onto the floor in the boys' room and shaking out sleeping bags that had been rolled up in the closet since before Bobby left. He'd gotten excited about introducing the boys to the "wild" outdoors during one of his manic phases and ordered a pile of gear from L.L. Bean that, like many originally enticing objects, he quickly lost interest in. I had neither the time nor the desire to take the kids camping. I was a city girl, whose entire experience of nature growing up had been class trips to the Boston Public Garden.

Joe and Ben whooped, jumping from one mattress to the next, as Vanessa watched, propped up in her infant seat, sucking on her binky.

I finally got them settled enough to listen to a story and they crowded around me, sprawling across my lap, giddy with the novelty of sleeping on the floor. I read several chapters of *The Chronicles of Narnia,* not wanting to dispel the lulled mood that came over them as they listened. I was grateful they'd become lost in the story instead of caught up in remembering that an intruder had violated our home.

Ben nodded off first, his head heavy and damp on my thigh. Joe asked for one more chapter and I acquiesced. He was asleep before I finished.

I eased myself out from the tangle of their limbs and checked on Vanessa, asleep, as well—at least for a few more hours.

Mike was in the living room, sipping a beer he'd found in the back of my fridge and watching TV.

"Do you think you're going to want to stay here— long-term, I mean?"

I hadn't really thought about it yet. I'd moved to the duplex in Arlington two months before, after I'd sold the Bedford house Bobby and I lived in for the seven years of our marriage. I'd never been comfortable there, a brand-new house in a suburban development with no sidewalks. But Bobby, a WASP from Indiana, had this vision of what home was supposed to be. I remember the first time he brought me to meet his widowed mother. It was for Thanksgiving in my last year of college. I was an art student at the School of the Museum of Fine Arts in Boston, studying printmaking. I'd met Bobby at a bar in Kenmore Square one night after a Red Sox game. He'd been at the game with a bunch of his buddies. I'd stopped for a beer after working late at the studio to finish a project. My cousin Annette worked as a bartender there and we often took the Green Line home together late at night.

I had paint in my hair and was wearing one of Mike's discarded work shirts, spattered with the inks and chemicals I used. Apparently Bobby found me intriguing and struck up a conversation with me at the bar, where I was listening to Annette complain about her mother, my mother's sister Ida. He bought me another beer; we talked. There was no way I was going to leave with him that night, not with Annette watching and ready to take whatever she saw straight back to the neighborhood. But I agreed to meet him for supper and a movie later in the week.

We saw *The African Queen* at the Brattle Theater in Harvard Square and afterward ate roast-beef sandwiches with Russian dressing at the Wursthaus. It always astounded me, this kitschy German restaurant, complete with leaded glass windows and flower boxes filled with geraniums to look like some Bavarian village inn, serving bratwurst and schnitzel, and it was owned by Italians.

Bobby astounded me, too, back then. He was so American, so unhampered by the snarled web of family that seemed to enmesh me anywhere I went in Boston. He was exuberant, curious, full of boundless energy—and interested in me. I assumed his fascination with me had to do with what must have appeared to him as my exoticism. I was an artist, ethnic and urban. He was a six-foot-six blond engineer from a Midwestern suburb whose mother belonged to a garden club. But he continued to pursue me, and I was both flattered and curious myself. What I didn't realize until later—much later— was that his exuberance and intense interest in me had more to do with the manic phase of his illness than it had to do with loving me. But as I said, that was later.

When he invited me to Belle Arbor, Indiana, for Thanksgiving, I said yes. My mother, however, voiced her objections.

"What do you mean you're going to Indiana for Thanksgiving! Thanksgiving is here, with the family, like always."

"He wants me to meet *his* family, Ma. Please let me go."

"When a man takes a woman to meet his family, it means something. He's looking for their approval of someone he sees as more than a movie date. You ready for that?"

"You read too much into things, Ma. He's just doing what Americans do—invite guests for Thanksgiving."

"Hah! Don't be blind *and* stubborn, Toni. Are you ready for him to ask you to marry him? Because that's what this trip to Indiana is all about."

"So are you going to let me go?"

"Tell him to have his mother call me. Then I'll decide."

After my mother talked to Bobby's mother, she discussed the invitation with my aunt Cookie, my godmother Patsy and finally my father. The women had concurred. I was old enough and Bobby serious enough about his intentions; I would be allowed to go. My father, faced with these three women and their conviction, threw up his hands and gave his approval. I hugged him.

My mother, in the midst of preparing Thanksgiving dinner for the family, made extra for me to take to Belle Arbor. We were driving with Bobby's sister, Sandra, and her husband, who lived in Portsmouth. My mother made a lasagne with the handmade fennel sausage that she got from my uncle Sal, the butcher who supplied the restaurant.

"I froze it so it'll keep in the cooler while you're driving. Tell Bobby's mother, one hour at three hundred and fifty degrees and keep it covered with tin foil till the last ten minutes."

She also put together a basket of her own preserves—a quart of plum tomatoes with whole basil leaves floating among them; eggplant strips pickled in olive oil, wine vinegar and hot pepper flakes; marinated wild mushrooms she'd picked herself in some secret pocket of the urban landscape she'd discovered years ago.

Belle Arbor, Indiana, is a long way from the North End. I should have recognized what that trip foreshadowed about my marriage to Bobby.

Hazel, Bobby's mother, while politely grateful for the provisions I had brought, clearly had never encountered anything like them and didn't know what to do with them. Out of deference to me she did actually bake the lasagne and we ate it for supper on Saturday night—not as a preturkey course on Thanksgiving Day as my own family did.

The meal we sat down to in Hazel's elegantly decorated dining room, with monogrammed silver on the table and striped silk upholstery on the Chippendale chairs, resembled nothing I had ever eaten, except for the turkey itself. She served scalloped oysters, which, I discovered, consisted mostly of crushed soda crackers and lots of cream and butter; succotash with corn, lima beans and an ample amount of paprika; corn bread stuffing—which Hazel called "dressing"—and an aspic made with V8 juice that had stuffed olives, celery and green peppers suspended in its shimmering middle.

The rest of my stay in Belle Arbor featured equally unfamiliar meals as Bobby, Hazel, Sandra, her husband and I were invited to the homes of one after another of Hazel's social circle. I was fed breakfasts of cheese grits and scrapple, lunches of Smithfield ham salad coated in homemade mayonnaise and dinners of pork tenderloins smothered in cream gravy. I consumed more dairy products in four days than I'd tasted in four months back in Boston.

The culinary journey wasn't the only revelation. I noticed that everyone in Belle Arbor—at least, everyone Hazel knew—had a green living room. Various shades and textures of green, to be sure, but all green. Refined, subdued, punctuated by bowls of freshly cut flowers and untouched coffee-table books about the Silk Road or the Great Barrier Reef. The bookcases were filled with books and not overflowing with family photographs. I encountered no flocked velvet wallpaper or white-and-gold furniture upholstered in wine-red brocade—the staples of my mother's and aunts' living rooms.

Throughout the visit I felt as if I were on display, like Pocahontas in London. The strange native of the Eastern city who had captivated Bobby and turned his head from the daughters of Belle Arbor, who were waiting with their Tupperware containers full of tuna casserole and braised short ribs—if only he'd sit at their tastefully decorated tables.

We returned to Boston with a slab of Smithfield ham and a container of Quaker grits to which Hazel had thoughtfully taped the recipe for cheese grits. For Christmas, she sent me a copy of the *Joy of Cooking* with all of Bobby's favorite dishes carefully bookmarked. It was the first cookbook I'd ever used. I grew up watching my mother cook with no recipes at all except what was in her head. She would taste and adjust, with a handful of chopped parsley or a fragment of cheese hand-grated and tossed into the pot. I used to think she'd been born with the knowledge of how to cook, something she'd absorbed in the womb.

Following a cookbook was a new experience for me, but I threw myself into learning how to produce the dishes Bobby had grown up with. Once a week I took the T to his apartment in Kendall Square near MIT, carrying a shopping bag filled with ingredients I'd never seen in my mother's pantry. I made pot roast with carrots and potatoes, Cornish hens stuffed with rice and onions, and pork chops with sauerkraut.

After I started to cook for him, Bobby and I became lovers. We'd leave the dishes on the drop-leaf table, a hand-me-down from Hazel, and slide into his narrow bed. I never spent the night. I lived at home and there was no way my mother and father would have condoned or understood such behavior. They didn't even know I was cooking for him, because they would've disapproved of my being alone in his apartment.

On the nights I did cook, I told them we were going out to dinner.

"Why do you always go to strangers to eat?" asked my mother one night. "What's wrong with bringing him to Paradiso once in a while?"

I rolled my eyes, memories of the dining rooms in Belle Arbor rising up alongside the dusky interior of Paradiso, its mural of the Bay of Naples stretching like a fresco across the rear wall, the bud vases of silk flowers on each table, its antipasto table covered with platters of provolone and soprasatto, olives, anchovies and cherry peppers. I had a hard time envisioning Bobby finding something he'd want to eat on the menu.

I slipped further from my family and my neighborhood with each recipe I mastered in the *Joy of Cooking*. I made buttermilk pancakes from scratch, separating the eggs and beating the whites into lofty peaks. I made hors d'oeuvres. Hors d'oeuvres! A nonexistent concept in my family, along with the daily Belle Arbor ritual of cocktail hour. My mother and father didn't drink before dinner. They were too busy cooking it. But I learned how to pile crabmeat and cocktail sauce on cream cheese and surround the platter with Triscuits. I hard-boiled eggs and deviled them with Hellmann's and paprika and mustard. I wrapped bacon around water chestnuts and chicken livers to make rumaki.

Bobby ate it all, reveling in each dish. When the weather got warmer, I prepared foods we could take on picnics. He bought a Kawasaki motorcycle in April and on Sunday afternoons, when Paradiso was closed and I didn't have to waitress, we headed out Route 2 to Walden Pond or Mount Wachusett and ate homemade biscuits stuffed with ham salad and sweet pickles and drank iced tea laced with mint.

Bobby was brilliant and funny and wild about me. I sketched him as he leaned against a tree, his leather-clad legs stretched out, his calf nestled against my hip as I quickly moved my charcoal across the page. He smiled as he watched me, his blue eyes intently following the movement of my hand.

"Have you thought about what you'll do when you graduate?"

"I've applied for teaching jobs. If that falls through, I can always increase my hours at Paradiso. My parents would be happy to see more of me." I spoke those words dryly. As much as they were true—that my mother and father wanted me close to home and in the business—Paradiso was the last place I intended to spend my future.

"I just got a job offer out here in Concord. I was thinking about moving out of Cambridge, finding an apartment closer to work."

"That would certainly alter our pattern. I can't exactly hop on the T and get out here."

"Actually, I was thinking you could move in with me."

"Right. Over Rose's dead body, as my mother so colorfully likes to emphasize when one of her kids wants to do something she regards as outrageous."

"Would she say that if I were to marry you first?"

I stopped sketching and looked up, into his face, at the smile twitching at the corners of his mouth.

He leaned forward and pulled me into him, crushing the sketch pad between us, blurring the lines of the face on the page.

"Will you marry me, Toni?"

And I said yes, for all the reasons, right and wrong, that we say yes when we're twenty-two and the future looks vast and lonely. Did I love him? Yes, in that sense of wonder and awe I had for this gorgeous man who knew how to make me feel alive and beautiful. Did I acknowledge to myself that he was my escape route from the confines of Salem Street and all it represented? I knew deep in my heart that the only way my parents would let me go would be in marriage. My memory of the twinkle in my mother's eye and her conviction—that the only reason a boy invites a girl home for Thanksgiving is because he wants to marry her—was floating in my brain. I had resisted the idea back in November, hadn't really considered marriage for myself—with Bobby or anyone else—despite the fact that girlfriends and cousins were busy getting fitted for bridal gowns and asking casts of thousands to be in their wedding parties.

I had vague plans to develop my craft as a printmaker. My master teacher at the Museum School, Peter Ricci, sat with me one night while I waited for an acid bath to complete the etching on a plate I'd finally finished—a portrait of a wild-haired man I'd sketched one afternoon at the Boston Public Library.

"You have to make a commitment." Peter was frustrated by what he saw as my divided loyalties. He knew I was taking courses to get my teacher certification and he thought it was pulling me away from my true work, diluting my art.

"You have talent, Toni. But you're not putting time and energy into developing it. I thought you were serious about your art, but this last year you've become—I don't know—conventional, predictable."

He threw up his hands, weathered, nicotine-stained, bearing fine white scars where gouging tools had slipped.

"Go be a teacher, if that's what you want. Find some nice

middle school in Lexington where you can demonstrate the color wheel and show them how to do collages of their favorite sports or animals. Don't take risks or experiment. Because that's where you're heading, and you'll never be an artist if you think you can straddle both worlds."

I recoiled emotionally as if he'd struck me. I loved the work I did in the print studio. It was in the basement of the school, a warren of rooms lit by hanging lamps that cast pools of warm light on the scarred wooden workbenches and left pockets of dim shadow in the corners that reminded me of the chiaroscuro of Caravaggio's *Christ at Emmaus.* The play of light and dark, illuminating and obscuring. Even the smells were familiar and comforting—the bite of the hydrochloric acid in the shallow tubs that lined the wall; the metallic taint of the inks; the distinctive odor of the hard rubber rollers I used to ink my plates. We were a secret society, we printmakers. Unlike the painters who craved the light, we were a clan of cave dwellers working in the dark because of the light-sensitive films we used on our silk screens. We were pale, our eyes attuned to seeing what others often missed.

The hours I spent in that basement were precious to me. A hiding place. But I knew I couldn't stay there permanently. For one thing, my parents had imbued me with a work ethic. You had a duty, a responsibility—to your family, to yourself—to put food on the table, keep a roof over your head. We all worked in the restaurant—me, my brothers Mike and Manny, even my grandparents.

My parents were proud that I had gone to college, but as far as they were concerned, there was a straight line—unbroken—from graduation to a job. Printmaking was not a job. My father called art "a casino," a gamble as tenuous as sitting at a blackjack table in Vegas.

"I don't care how beautiful your work is. If it's not bringing in a steady paycheck, it's not work."

"You could teach, Toni. A girl as smart as you. Look at Marie Filizolla. She gets the summers off. You could help out in the restaurant during the tourist season."

Little by little, I felt my mother shaping my unfinished parts, rounding me out to fit the mold of Italian womanhood. Slightly updated, of course, for the education she had never attained. Marriage, a teaching job and beautiful hand-printed Christmas cards that she could hang in Paradiso and boast about to customers. "My daughter's artwork. She's the one who painted the mural on the wall."

Let's face it. I was too scared of the unknown, too unsure of my own talent to embrace Peter's view of my possible future as an artist. I got the teaching job. I married Bobby. I knew what I was doing. I was staying safe.

Return to the Neighborhood

I SHOULD HAVE UNDERSTOOD that safety is an illusion, especially after reading C. S. Lewis and Madeleine L'Engle stories to my children. Heroes and heroines don't hide from danger and the unknown. They plunge into it, even though they're terrified, and come out the other side scarred but wiser and in possession of whatever is necessary to save the world.

All I wanted to save was my children, and at first, after Bobby left me, I thought I had to do it on my own. I felt like the cliché of my generation—educated professional woman, single mother, in possession of half the wedding gifts. I got the Cuisinart and the vacuum cleaner. He got the stereo system and the color TV. Bobby traveled light when he left on his Kawasaki, but his lawyer made sure his share of the household goods were shipped to Colorado, along with half the proceeds from the sale of our raised ranch when the time came.

The loneliness and exhaustion were nothing new to me. Bobby had been emotionally missing from our lives long before he walked out the door. I joined a single-parent group that had just formed in Cambridge, people who were exploring the idea of living communally, or at least matching up fragmented families. It was like "let's see if my jagged edges fit into your empty spaces." I met with three different people and their kids—a tortured dad who seemed to have self-pity oozing out of his pores, a British woman, several years older than I, whose main interest in the arrangement was to find a live-in babysitter, and a woman about my age whom I liked well enough but whose child drove me bananas. With three children of my own, including an infant, I wasn't considered a prime catch. I made a list for myself, one of those two-column charts, placing in the plus or minus column the issues I'd identified in each household. Some were as simple as "not enough bedrooms," while others were more complicated, like "doesn't believe in setting limits." I had almost nothing in the plus columns for any of them.

The kids and I went to Sunday dinner at my parents' shortly after the robbery. My mother got down on the floor with Vanessa and played finger games with her. Manny and Mike taught the boys how to play Pong. The sweet aroma of Mom's chicken salmi wafted into the living room from the kitchen. Outside the windows the sun was shining and the street was bustling. The plus column was getting crowded. After we ate, I spoke to my parents.

"Mom, Dad, when did you say that apartment would be vacant?"

We waited until the school year was finished, and then the kids and I moved in over the summer. I enrolled Ben and Joe at St. John's and kept my job at Bedford High. I spent July and August showing the boys the neighborhood—how to cross the street safely, where the playgrounds were, who had the best lemon ice.

When Mom sent Joe on his first errand, to walk down to Giuffre's fish market on the corner and pick up an order of octopus and squid, he started out looking over this shoulder as he passed each doorway while Mom stood on the stoop at Paradiso, smiling and waving at him. He finally ducked into the store and out of sight.

Mom remained in the doorway, her eyes glistening with tears.

"How many times have you stood here, watching one of us walk down the street?"

She picked up the corner of her apron and wiped her eyes. "I'll never tire of it. It's the first taste of independence any of you got. And you always knew I'd be waiting for you right on this spot when you came home."

A few minutes later Joe strode down the sidewalk carrying a bag that was almost as big as he was. He was bursting with what he'd seen.

"Big bloody buckets of fish heads the guy was chopping off, and spiky things with slippery insides and black ropy things he said were eels. It was really gross!"

For a kid who'd grown up in a subdivision with three different models of houses repeated endlessly along winding streets with names like Meadowlark and Robin and Cardinal, Joe adapted to city life with unbridled gusto. Sharing a playground with a bunch of other kids—especially one on the edge of the harbor—was far superior to playing with his kid brother on his own swing set.

Ben, on the other hand, was slower to warm to all the changes in his life. No longer the baby, not quite understanding where his daddy had gone and having to sleep in a strange room for the second time in a few months, all took their toll. He didn't want to go to the playground. He would only eat pasta with butter and cheese. He would've been quite happy to spend the whole day in front of the TV playing Pong if I'd let him.

"Give him time," Mom said. "Once he goes to school in September and makes some friends in the neighborhood, he'll be a changed boy."

I wanted to believe in my mother's simple conviction that the rhythm and patterns of life in her familiar and close-knit world would heal us. But I knew enough about Bobby's mental illness to be aware that his children were more likely to develop it than children who didn't have a parent who was manic depressive. In her own way, though, my mother was right. Biology wasn't the only determinant. I was most concerned about Ben, but I was determined to give all three of my children the love and stability that coming back to the neighborhood represented.

I kept them occupied with treks to the aquarium and the Children's Museum, the children's room at the library, the wading pool in the Boston Common. We put Vanessa in her stroller and set out on foot with juice boxes and animal crackers. If nothing else, the excursions exhausted them and they fell asleep without complaint at the end of the day. If I'd learned anything growing up in my mother's house, it was that keeping busy dispelled, or at least disguised, sadness. I raised the activity level for Ben's sake, but I was doing it for myself, as well. I didn't want to sit still for too long, because that gave me time to think about my life.

When the kids were in bed I painted the apartment, made curtains, refinished old dressers and, as summer neared its end, organized my lesson plans and arranged field trips for the fall.

Now that I was living in Boston, I decided to meet with the educational program directors of the museums in person and coax them into special tours and behind-the-scenes visits for my students.

I asked Mom to watch the kids the day I scheduled appointments along the Fenway at the Museum of Fine Arts and the Isabella Stewart Gardner Museum. The last time I'd been at either one I'd been shepherding a raucous group of students who saw the trip as a day off from the classroom. Very few had appreciated what they'd seen. The rest had only paid enough attention to fill out the worksheet I'd distributed on the bus.

I'd given myself time when scheduling the appointments to wander through my favorite galleries. When I was done, my mission at both museums accomplished, I came out the side door of the MFA. Across the street was the Museum School. I hadn't been back since I'd graduated. It wasn't the sort of place that invited alumni back for reunions.

I was curious enough to make my way into the building. I told myself I was gathering information from the admissions office for my few serious students who were thinking about applying to art school.

But if I'd been honest, I'd have realized that I was looking for a lost part of myself. I felt like an interloper, an impostor, when I walked into the building. The school had a summer session and was swarming with students—intense, paint spattered, arrayed in a wild panoply of colorful, mismatched, funky clothing.

I was so out of place. I'd dressed as the suburban mother of three and schoolteacher that I was for the meetings at the museums. The Toni who'd once roamed these halls cringed at the Toni now stepping carefully into the lobby. And not just because of how I looked.

I almost turned around and left. But I followed my nose and my memories down the stairs to the print studio, not quite sure what I was seeking. I hesitated before opening the door.

You don't belong here anymore, a voice inside my head scolded. *You gave this up a long time ago. You can't go back. You can't undo that decision. Stop before you make a fool of yourself.*

I took my hand off the doorknob, ready to listen to the cautionary voice. But someone on the other side of the door pushed it open and rushed through, knapsack flying. She didn't close the door behind her and I found myself standing in the hallway looking into my past.

The late-afternoon light slanted across the floor through windows as dirty as they had been years before. The few people in the room were bent over workbenches and didn't bother to glance up at the stranger in their midst. I took a deep breath and crossed over the threshold into the studio.

"Excuse me." I addressed no one in particular. "Do you mind if I look around? I'm an alum, an art teacher."

The student nearest me shrugged. "Go ahead."

I started moving around the room. Prints were hanging from wires strung across the middle of the space above the worktables. Many of the pieces were striking. Dramatic abstract images. Nothing at all like the work I had done, which had been very personal—figures revealing stories. All that work had been packed away in portfolios for years.

I could hear voices coming from the pressroom beyond the studio and the sound of one of the larger presses being cranked. Not wanting to disturb what was under way, I began to walk back to the entrance of the studio. Then I heard my name.

"Toni?" The questioner's tone was a combination of surprise and disbelief.

I turned in response to see Peter Ricci standing by the pressroom and felt his eyes sweep over me in appraisal and instant judgment. I expected that he was congratulating himself on his accurate prediction. The talent he'd once recognized and tried to nurture had been diluted by years in a suburban high school. I stood there in my gray linen suit and my Capezio pumps, my hair pulled neatly in a ponytail, and regretted that I'd even gone into the building.

Peter moved toward me, his hand outstretched in greeting, formal and without warmth.

"What a surprise! What brings you back? In town for a day of the arts?"

I couldn't blame him for thinking I was a "lady who lunched." Someone who came into Boston for a few hours to do some shopping in Copley Square, have lunch at the Ritz and take in the latest exhibit at the MFA. "I live in Boston now. I had appointments to set up field trips for my students and I thought I'd stop at the school to pick up admissions information. I couldn't resist the opportunity to poke my head in and see the state of the art. Despite the age-old methods, your students are doing some very modern stuff."

"It never gets old to me. These kids continually find new ways to express themselves. So you're still teaching? Did you continue your printmaking?"

I shook my head. "Life took over after I graduated."

"That's a shame. A waste, actually. You were one of the most remarkable artists to come through here."

"Thanks, I'm honored that you thought so, but what I see here today is far beyond what I was doing back then."

"If you'd continued, who knows where you'd be today."

The longer we talked, the more uncomfortable I became. I wasn't willing to have my choices questioned or to be reminded of lost opportunities. I had a family to support. My father had been right; art was a gamble, one I couldn't afford.

I looked at my watch and made my apologies.

"I'm so sorry. I've got to get back to my family. It's been good to see you."

"Come again, Toni. Bring your class next time."

"Thanks. I'm sure they'd love it."

And I escaped. I felt claustrophobic. Riding back to Government Center on the Green Line I wished I hadn't gone down to the print studio. It had unsettled me and raised painful questions about how much I'd changed. The talented artist

Peter had recognized no longer existed. We both knew that, and I didn't know which one of us regretted it more.

School started, and in October I brought my seniors into town for their field trip to the MFA. I decided not to take Peter up on his invitation to his class. The last place I wanted to be was the studio.

Hazel wrote, asking me to bring the kids to Belle Arbor for Thanksgiving. I suspected she might be trying to bring Bobby and me together. I'd heard from Sandra that her mother had been distraught about the divorce. What she didn't tell me seeped back to me from friends of mine who also knew Sandra. Hazel found it incomprehensible that Bobby would leave his family. She was convinced I'd done something so unforgivable he had no choice but to leave. More than likely, she thought, Vanessa wasn't his daughter.

I was hurt and outraged that she'd even entertain such a thought. Throughout my marriage I'd tried to be a good daughter-in-law.

"She's an old woman whose faith in her son has been shattered. She's grasping at any explanation to feel better about him. Let it go. But don't go to Indiana." This was the advice from my brother Mike, who, in the months since we'd moved back to the neighborhood, had become my confidant.

I sent a letter and pictures of the kids, the subtle message of their blond hair and blue eyes underscoring that they were decidedly Templetons. Even though it had been more than a year since Bobby left, I still felt raw and vulnerable.

A few days after Thanksgiving, just before Paradiso was booked solid for office Christmas parties, Mom tripped on the cellar stairs and broke her ankle. She was effectively off her feet until Christmas.

"Toni, I've got a deal for you," she told me that afternoon

when I got home from school. Her foot was propped up on a kitchen chair. "I'll watch the kids in the evenings if you'll take over hostessing downstairs."

I wanted to ask who would do my lesson plans and grading, but I knew I'd fit them in somehow.

Considering everything my mother had done for me, I could spell her for a few weeks in the restaurant.

"Put some makeup on and find something a little softer to wear than those suits of yours."

I'd grown up watching my mother open boxes from my father every year on her birthday and Christmas, boxes filled with gorgeous dresses, cashmere sweaters, diamond bracelets. I thought that's what all men did, but I'd learned otherwise. I didn't have a thing in my closet that would meet my mother's requirement for how the Paradiso hostess should dress.

I enlisted my cousin Annette to go shopping with me.

"How tarty do you want to look?"

"My mother doesn't dress like a tart!"

"She dresses like a movie star from the 1960s. Think Sophia Loren. Gina Lollobrigida. Elizabeth Taylor in *Butterfield 8*."

"Do you think I can pull it off?"

"Toni! You've got my uncle Al's smoldering bedroom eyes and jet-black hair, and my aunt Rose's figure. We are not talking Audrey Hepburn here, although the black dress from *Breakfast at Tiffany's* wouldn't be a bad start."

Annette poked through racks and threw things over the dressing room door. In the end, I settled on a short black skirt and a couple of sweaters, "sexy but elegant" in Annette's assessment, and a red dress for the catered parties.

"You're a 'winter,'" she told me, based on some *Cosmo* article that categorized flattering colors by the season. She also made me buy a pair of stiletto heels.

"I wore nurses' shoes when I waitressed during college," I protested.

"You're not a waitress anymore. You're the woman with the power to banish someone to the hell of a table near the restrooms or bestow upon them the gift of a seat by the window, where anyone walking by can see how favored they are. You may not be the queen Aunt Rose is, but you are the princess and you should look the part. Besides, you never know who might walk into Paradiso tomorrow night and be struck dumb by your beauty."

"I'm not ready for that."

"You never will be if you continue to dress like you're going to a PTA meeting. Our next stop is the lingerie department. You need sheer black stockings and a push-up bra. You know, Toni, I don't remember you dressing so conservatively when we were kids. You were a lot more of a free spirit. It's good to have you back in the neighborhood, cuz."

She put her arm around me, guided me through intimate apparel and then marched me to the cosmetics department.

"My friend Elaine works for Lancôme. She'll set us up with what you need."

The next afternoon, after getting home from school, giving the boys a snack and making sure they'd done their homework, I got dressed in the new clothes. I herded the kids downstairs to my mother's apartment at four-thirty.

"Turn around—I want the whole effect," she said when I walked into the kitchen. Vanessa, who'd been with my mother all day, was clamoring for a hug and a kiss. I scooped her up, nuzzled her and then let her squirm out of my arms to toddle over to her brothers, who were on their way to the TV.

"Don't let them watch too much," I said.

"Don't worry. Manny is sending up some ziti in about an hour and then we'll play cards. Let me see you! Nice. Very nice. Eventually a haircut would be a good idea. Enough with the hippie folksinger look. But on the whole, you look enticing."

"Gee, thanks, Ma. Glad you approve."

"Now go downstairs before your father starts getting *agita* that there's nobody in the front of the house."

And so began my new role as the hostess of Paradiso. I'd like to say my performance that first night was as successful as my appearance, but it took me a while to learn how to balance the flow and recognize who should get the best tables. It had always looked so effortless when Mom had done it. I was exhausted by the time I got upstairs.

The kids were sound asleep. Mom and I had already talked about having them spend the nights with her and Daddy, so I slipped off my heels and padded up the stairs to my own place alone. I washed off the unfamiliar makeup and went to bed.

I was into my second week when Peter Ricci came in for dinner. I don't think he recognized me at first, especially since I'd taken the plunge and had my hair styled, again with Annette by my side. We went to a salon on Newberry Street, where I paid a fortune, but came out with a look that was all tumbling waves.

Both Manny and Mike gave me the thumbs-up sign, which was a relief. Mom thought it was a little too tousled. "Bed hair," she called it. But she agreed it was better than the Joan Baez look. I'd never had so much attention paid to my appearance.

It finally dawned on Peter who I was as I handed him his menu.

"Toni? What are you doing here? I thought you were teaching."

"I am. This is my family's place. I'm helping out for a few weeks. Enjoy your meal."

I sent over a small antipasto on the house for him and his date.

I wasn't crazy about seeing Peter Ricci again. It was too much of a reminder of how sharp a turn my life had taken. Unfortunately Peter didn't realize how unwelcome his presence was, and he actually got up from his table and asked me to come over and meet the woman he was dining with.

"I've been telling her about you."

Great, I thought. A cautionary tale of unfulfilled potential. Watch out, or you, too, could become a lapsed artist, fallen away from your calling to show slides of the *Mona Lisa* and Michelangelo's *David* to bored teenagers.

"Maybe you know her work," he said as we walked back to their table. "She's Diane Rocheleau."

Of course I knew her work. She'd emerged in the late sixties and had several shows in New York that had garnered critical acclaim. The last I'd heard, the Whitney had held an exhibition of her work. She was a printmaker.

"What's she doing in Boston?" I'd begun to wish I'd seated them at a better table.

"She's a guest lecturer at the school for a couple of weeks. Why don't you come down to one of the evening classes next week? That is, if you can get away."

Good. He'd given me an out. "It's hard to do. This is a busy season for us. I'll try to make it, but no promises. Thanks for the invite."

Diane was gracious, and even though I tried to detect a note of condescension, she was genuine and down-to-earth. I was grateful that neither one of them asked me what I was currently working on. How would I have answered? Finding the right shade of yellow for my daughter's bedroom?

"The meal was wonderful," Diane said. "Our compliments to the chef."

228

"Thanks, I'll let him know. My brother's cooking tonight. It's always a little spicier when he's in the kitchen."

After they left I tried to brush away the glimmer of re-awakening longing that had surfaced. Now, more than ever, I told myself, I don't have what it takes to be an artist. I picked up a stack of menus and turned up the wattage on my smile as I saw the mayor's chief of staff walk in the door.

Peter Ricci's invitation wasn't an idle one. He stopped by the restaurant two days later, not to eat but to give me the schedule of Diane's demonstration classes.

"You look great, by the way. Different than you did this summer. City life seems to be agreeing with you."

"My mother's influence. She thinks the sizzle shouldn't just be in the frying pan if you're going to run a successful restaurant."

He laughed. "You know, I've eaten here many times and never realized this was your family's place. I bought a loft down on Union Wharf a few years ago and have adopted this neighborhood. It reminds me so much of where my grandparents lived in New York." He paused. "I just had a thought. I started a neighborhood art program last year at the community center. I scrounge whatever supplies I can for the kids, and I've twisted a few arms among the faculty at the Museum School to get them to come down here and teach a class or two. You've probably got your hands full with your own teaching load and the restaurant, but if you were interested, I could use someone with your talent and experience."

It was my turn to laugh.

"Besides my teaching and the restaurant, I also have three children I occasionally try to see, Peter. I wish I could help you, and I'm flattered that you asked. I think it's wonderful of you to be doing this. But at this point in my life, it would be impossible. For the same reasons, I know I can't make it to one of Diane's classes. But thank you."

I hoped that the wall I was erecting around me was high enough not to be breached. I wanted to say to him, *Stop trying to reclaim the Toni who was your star pupil. She doesn't exist anymore.*

"Okay. I understand. I didn't realize you had kids. But if you change your mind, give me a call. Here's my card."

I stuck the card in my pocket, but I didn't intend to use it.

I had spent too many years allowing someone else to define who I was. My parents. The nuns at Sacred Heart. Bobby. Even Peter, who thought he knew who I was when I'd been his student. I'd returned to the neighborhood for the sake of my children, so they could grow up surrounded by love. But I was determined not to go back to the old definitions of myself. I was trying to shed masks I'd accumulated over the years, masks that had come at great cost to the original Toni, whoever she was.

In the final year of my marriage to Bobby I'd been in hell, caretaker to his disintegrating personality as my own identity disappeared. After he left I found myself in a kind of limbo. Neither pain nor joy made its way onto that neutral shore. The weekend my plane to Colorado was canceled, I'd abandoned the ridiculous notion that Bobby and I might reconcile, eliminating the opportunity to even open the discussion. Mike had been at the airport with me and Vanessa, and rather than read me the riot act, he was very quiet and thoughtful. His comforting presence forced me to think through what I really wanted, and I knew it wasn't resuming my life with Bobby, in Colorado or anywhere.

But I hadn't a clue yet what I *did* want. At night, after my kids were settled in bed and my work organized for school the next day, I sometimes sat in my darkened bedroom looking out at the city. My room was in the front of the building now.

Like the old ladies on the street who know everyone's business
because they sit at their windows all day watching the neighborhood as if it were a soap opera, I sat and watched late at
night. The street had an emptiness then that echoed my own
loneliness. The few people out and about were moving quickly
in the cold, their footsteps and muffled voices bouncing off
the brick facades of the buildings. I wondered if they were
hurrying home or racing to the arms of a lover.

I was not moving at all. Frozen. Rooted. Behind a wall not
of brick, but of ice.

Annette, emboldened by the success of the makeover she'd
engineered, decided to push on to higher stakes. I thought
she'd be content when she managed to entice me into getting
a manicure regularly.

"The first thing people see will be your hands as you distribute their menus. Well-manicured nails reflect on the quality
of the house. If you don't believe me, ask your mother, who
never misses an appointment with Bernadette up the street."

I got my nails done—just a shaping and a coat of clear
polish. But for Christmas, I picked out a deep burgundy to go
with the velvet dress I was wearing to Christmas Eve dinner,
and I stayed with that shade.

But Annette wasn't satisfied.

"Now that you have a new look, it's time for a new man."

"No, it isn't. I told you, I'm *not* ready."

"Not ready to get married again, with that I concur. But
you are certainly ready to enjoy life a little."

"I enjoy my children. I enjoy my family. I enjoy my work."

"That's wonderful. Commendable for the Italian mother
and daughter you are. But why, if I happen to be looking out
my window late at night and glance across the street, do I see
my cousin pensive and sad at her own window?"

"Are you spying on me?"

"Don't deflect from the point I'm trying to make. Enjoying family life in its many Dante forms is all well and good. But there's a piece missing from your life. Whether you believe this or not, Toni, you deserve the attention of a man. And it's my next mission in life to find you one."

"Don't, Annette."

"Nonsense. We're not talking about *the* man. You're right about that. It's too soon. You're too miserable to attract him."

"Thanks a lot!"

"I am talking about injecting some lighthearted fun into your overly responsible existence. A movie date. Dinner at some place other than Paradiso with somebody whose meat you don't have to cut."

Annette reached out to her network and started setting me up on blind dates. The son of one of her father's customers, who took me to Pier 4 for lobster and popovers and then expected a nightcap of sex while my children slept down the hall. I left him firmly at the door. A minor-league hockey player who appeared to have been rammed against the side-boards a few too many times and had difficulty carrying on a conversation that consisted of more than two or three words.

"Annette, I'm an art teacher. I read books. My idea of a good time is an exhibit at the MFA or a play at the Colony Theater."

"Okay. I'm working on it."

She found me an accountant and a stockbroker, both educated and well-groomed and totally boring. One talked only about himself, without a single question to me. *Am I invisible?* I asked myself. *Or just a mirror reflecting back his glowing opinion of himself?* The other was too inquisitive. I felt as if he had a mental checklist for the ideal woman as he questioned me about my life. When we got to how I felt about kids and

I started describing the wonder and delight and physical exhaustion of being a mother to three unique beings, the questions stopped. It was clear he had no idea I'd been married before and had children; his eyes glazed over.

"I thought this was supposed to be a fun-filled romp for me, Annette. Frankly I'd rather have all my wisdom teeth pulled than go out on another date. I'm done. This is worse than being lonely."

My mother had gotten back on her feet after Christmas and no longer needed me to do nightly hostessing at Paradiso, but I found I missed it. Manny had talked my parents into keeping the restaurant open when they went to Florida in January and he asked me if I'd fill in again. A few more weeks of turning outward instead of inward, on my feet and chatting with customers instead of sitting morosely by my window at night, sounded more than appealing. My cousin Vito's teenage daughter Mira came over to watch the kids and I went back downstairs.

I discovered during my stint as hostess that I enjoyed the theatrical aspects of the restaurant business. Manny had understood that we were putting on a show every night and had been making changes at Paradiso ever since he got back from school. My parents had established the reputation of Paradiso with the quality of the food, but Manny was generating attention that was starting to draw a hipper crowd. It used to be rare for a neighborhood place like Paradiso to be significant enough for a restaurant critic to notice. I think most of the Boston food writers dismissed North End restaurants as nothing but tourist traps offering a list of standards—meatballs, sausage, eggplant parmigiano and lasagne—smothered in red sauce. We'd always presented a more varied menu, and our regulars knew that. Manny was finding ways to attract new customers who were looking for something adventurous. So word spread, the critics started coming around, and Manny and I wanted to put on a good show. I flirted with the men; I complimented the women.

"I love your earrings! They really set off your face."

"Welcome to Paradiso! As Beatrice said to Dante, come sit awhile at my table. Enjoy your meal!"

I started bringing each table a small plate of tidbits to nibble on while they read the menu—olives, celery stuffed with Gorgonzola that had been mashed with olive oil and lemon juice, a couple of anchovies rolled around capers. On weekends, when the place was busiest and guests often had to wait, I brought them spiced nuts and chatted with them to make the time pass more quickly. I roamed the floor, making sure everyone was content. I'd grown up watching my mother welcome guests to the restaurant as if it were her dining room upstairs. She'd put her hand on someone's shoulder as she stopped at a table. If she knew the people, she'd ask about the family. If she didn't, she'd tell them they'd made a good choice in whatever they were eating.

"My favorite," she'd say. "My mother's recipe."

One night, Peter Ricci showed up. I hadn't seen him since I'd turned down his request to help at the community center.

I felt myself stiffening, the defenses going up, but I put on my hostess face and welcomed him.

"Happy New Year, Peter! How many in your party tonight?"

I continued my usual performance as the evening wore on, trying not to notice that Peter was watching me as I moved around the room. Probably sharing with his fellow guests, none of whom I recognized, the sad tale of my wasted potential. I forced myself to return to his table as their meal was winding down. I was gracious. I recommended the panna cotta for dessert. I kept talking so he couldn't bring up art.

When they were leaving, he told his companions to go ahead, he'd catch up with them, and then he turned back to me.

Here it comes, I thought. He hasn't given up yet, has he?

"It was great to see you tonight, Toni. I missed you the last time I was in. Uh, this may sound a little off the wall, but do you enjoy dance?"

Dance? Not, Have you created any lithographic images lately or etched a sheet of copper?

"What kind of dance?"

"Modern. I've got two tickets for the Nederlands Dans Theater at the Metropolitan Center next Thursday. Would you like to join me? I saw them in Europe last summer and found them compelling. I thought you might…"

I wasn't quite sure where he was headed with his invitation. Warning bells deep in my brain were signaling that any contact with Peter Ricci, no matter how unrelated to my lost talent, would not be a good thing for me. But instead of the self-assured master teacher, the in-your-face, knowledgeable professor, what I was seeing was a vulnerable adolescent asking me out on a date. To do something that actually appealed to me.

I said yes. My brother Mike agreed to host for me; my cousin Annette watched the kids.

The dance company was as compelling as Peter had promised—dramatic and thought-provoking. We walked back to the neighborhood after the performance, so caught up in conversation about what we'd seen that we ignored the cold.

When we got to Salem Street I noticed how red his nose was.

"Can I offer you a warm drink? I'm sure Manny still has some espresso or cappuccino in the kitchen."

He accepted, and we went into the restaurant. The last

table was being cleared and Mike had already gone upstairs to relieve Annette. I led Peter to a booth, then walked into the kitchen to get us some coffee.

Manny was sipping a glass of wine and about to dig into a plate of linguine carbonara. He was always famished at the end of the evening.

"How was your date with the art teacher?"

"Intriguing. Fine. Why do you ask?"

He smiled. "The guy's been waiting for you for months. Every time he came in for dinner he asked about you. Showing up last week wasn't a coincidence. I'd mentioned that you'd be working when Mom and Pop went to Florida."

I threw a sugar packet at him. "You don't need to be my matchmaker."

"You had a good time, right?"

I left the kitchen with the coffee and a plate of biscotti.

Peter smiled as I slipped into the other side of the booth. I didn't know what to do with the knowledge that his invitation hadn't been spontaneous.

It had been years since I'd felt someone genuinely interested in me. For once, I took Annette's advice and decided to enjoy it. Peter and I talked until the coffee grew cold, not about art but about life. His growing up in Rochester, New York, with a father who worked at the Kodak plant and a mother who was a hairdresser. The inspiration provided by a high school teacher that had propelled him to the Rhode Island School of Design.

I shared with him a condensed version of my life since graduating, sparing him the melodrama of the collapse of my marriage. I was still wary of tainting new friendships with my own misery.

"I was an asshole ten years ago to have criticized you for becoming a teacher," he said.

That was unexpected. He went on.

"I'm a product myself of a wonderful teacher. I think I equated what I saw happening to you, your art, with your decision to teach. But, in fact, it was something else, not the teaching. You were shutting down emotionally. I don't know what it was—and you don't have to tell me—but it was still there when you came into the studio this summer.

"But you've changed since then. Not just physically—although, believe me, that's been striking. I've watched you here at the restaurant. You're vibrant. You cast a spell on people."

That was when he leaned across the table to kiss me. It was soft and inviting and filled with longing. When he stopped, he looked at me, cupping my face in his hands.

"You're an amazing woman, Toni."

The lights went off in the kitchen. It was late. I reluctantly said good-night to Peter.

"I had a wonderful time. Especially our conversation."

"Shall we continue it tomorrow?"

"I'm hostessing again. Why don't you come by near closing time. I'll ask Manny to whip us up a late supper."

He kissed me in the vestibule before I went upstairs.

Mike was watching the *Tonight Show* on the couch with Vanessa sprawled across his chest. I gathered her gently into my arms and settled her in her crib, but she woke up. I wound up walking the floor with her to get her back to sleep, wondering what I'd been thinking when I opened myself up to Peter. I couldn't afford to let a man into my life the way Peter Ricci seemed to want. The intimacy of our conversation that evening, despite my reticence, had been both satisfying and draining. I couldn't imagine being able to sustain that. Not with everything that was pulling at me for attention—my children, my teaching, my responsibilities to my family.

When I finally got Vanessa to sleep, I crawled into bed and wrapped the comforter around me for warmth. I longed to have Peter beside me, holding me, making love to me. But at one in the morning, exhausted and already anticipating the start of another day—with kids to rouse and feed and get off to school, traffic to face, classes to teach—I realized that wasn't going to be possible. Better to accept that now rather than make a mess later. I was afraid I'd be doing all the taking from Peter and have nothing to give in return.

The phone rang. I answered quickly so Vanessa wouldn't wake up again.

"It's Peter. I'm sorry if I woke you."

"You didn't. I just got to bed."

"I couldn't sleep. I feel as if I left things unfinished."

"Peter…" I wanted to stop him.

"I'm in a phone booth down the street. Can I come up?"

I sat up in bed. I told myself I should say no. I should say I can't go any further.

"Yes."

In the few minutes it took him to reach the building I opened the drawer in my night table and took out the new diaphragm Annette had encouraged me to get as part of my transformation. As with her other suggestions, I had protested at first. But my hand trembled when I took it out of the case. I felt both relieved to have it and in a state of joyful disbelief that I might actually need it. When the intercom rang, I tiptoed down the hall and buzzed him in, listening to his footsteps as he climbed the stairs.

He stepped inside the apartment, picked me up and carried me down the hall to my bedroom.

Bobby had stopped making love to me months before Vanessa was born. And before that, our lovemaking had been sporadic and more a physical release than an expression of love or even desire. I didn't realize how much of my pleasure in sex had been deadened, wrapped in layers of neglect and abandonment. I'd forgotten what it felt like to be caressed and cherished. I thought I could live without passion. That night with Peter threw me off balance, opening a rift in the shell of protection I'd constructed. It exposed a need so raw and hungry that it frightened me.

He was an extraordinarily tender lover. When we got to the bedroom he sat on the side of the bed and I sat with my legs wrapped around him. At first, we simply rocked to a lullaby that emerged from our kisses and sighs. His kisses moved from my lips down my neck to the opening at the top of my nightgown. His hands moved down my back and slid the fabric up over my head. Once free, I lifted my arms to unzip his jacket and unbutton his shirt. I forgot about the chill in the room as he pulled me down and we lay facing each other, his bare chest against mine. I somehow managed to get the rest of his clothes off in a blur of movement, my mouth continuing to kiss him as my fingers released the five buttons on his jeans. Peter was nearly forty, but his body was lean and strong, cradling me with a fierce warmth. I responded to his exploration of my body with a ferocity of my own. It wasn't a sweet reawakening of my long-dormant sexuality. Instead, it was explosive, driven, frenzied. We both seemed to be in a state of want that only the other could fill.

I didn't know myself.

We finally collapsed, hearts beating wildly against each other, our breathing gradually subsiding into a steady, synchronized rhythm. We hadn't spoken a single word since the phone call hours before. Talking had been superfluous. Our means of communication was tactile, the responses unfiltered by judgment or caution. Our lovemaking had been intemperate. Insatiable. And we clung to each other afterward, unable or unwilling to break the connection. I was trembling, and he held me tighter, gathering the covers around us as I had earlier, when I thought I'd come to terms with my loneliness.

We slept. Around five, the tenuous thread connecting us broke when Vanessa began to cry. I groped for the nightgown shed with everything else I thought I knew about myself and went to my daughter. It was still dark. By the time I settled Vanessa, Peter was up and pulling on his jeans. We looked at each other across the room, an acknowledgment passing between us that what had happened during the night had been inexplicable, arising out of some unfulfilled hidden need neither of us had understood. Then we moved toward each other in an embrace.

"Thank you." We both murmured it at the same time.

As much as we'd taken from the other, we'd also given.

And then he was gone.

I stood at the window and saw him cross the street and round the corner, heading toward the harbor.

I got through the first part of the day on autopilot, filling bowls with Cheerios, making peanut butter and banana sandwiches, packing Vanessa's diaper bag and leaving her with Manny to drop off at my aunt Ida's later in the morning. My makeup disguised the dark circles under my eyes, but not the haunted expression in my eyes.

"You look like hell."

"Thanks, dear brother. Vanessa was up a couple of times during the night. She'll probably sleep for a couple of hours now. I've got to get to work. See you tonight."

I drifted more than once at school, feeling like an adolescent caught in the hazy euphoria of remembered passion. No wonder I'd sealed myself off from sex. It rendered me dysfunctional.

When I got back to the neighborhood I met the boys at

their school and walked them to Aunt Ida's. She was watching them for this last night before my parents got back from Florida.

"You don't mind keeping them overnight? Fridays are always late for us."

"It's not a bother, honey. They're good kids. We have fun, don't we, guys?"

I kissed them all and walked down the street to my place to shower and change. I pulled out the red dress I'd bought in the fall with Annette. I put my hair up to accentuate the neckline of the dress, which bared my shoulders.

I was downstairs by four-thirty, reviewing the reservations and taking calls. It was going to be a busy night.

"You're looking better," Manny said when I poked my head in the kitchen. "You want a bite to eat before we open the doors?"

"No, thanks. Not hungry." I didn't tell him I hadn't been able to eat all day.

I kept things moving, not rushing people, but mindful of those waiting for tables. I started watching the door around ten o'clock. I didn't know when to expect Peter and tried not to panic with each passing quarter hour. The euphoria I'd experienced during the day was draining out of my veins, reminding me of the cost of a night like the one I'd had.

By eleven I was convinced he'd fled, overcome with regret or self-loathing. He had a wife and had decided to go back to her. He was lying in an emergency room somewhere paralyzed, as Deborah Kerr had been in *An Affair to Remember,* unable to keep her assignation. I thought I was going to be sick to my stomach. I was blowing out candles when I felt two familiar hands around my waist and heard my name whispered in my ear. I turned to face him. He kissed me, urgently. The taste of last night lingered in the familiar softness of his mouth on mine.

241

"How was your day?" he murmured, planting a second kiss on my bare shoulder.

"Distracting. I felt like I was underwater most of the day."

"Me, too. When will you be done here?"

I nodded toward the two tables still occupied. "Not until they leave. Are you hungry? Manny made roast pork in almond sauce tonight."

"I've had no appetite at all today. It's as if I have no room for anything else except you."

"I've been the same way. Is this what addiction feels like?"

The last of the guests finally left. I spent another thirty minutes supervising the breakdown of the dining room, then said goodnight to Manny. He didn't miss the fact that Peter was with me.

"Have fun." He grinned.

I took Peter by the hand and walked upstairs with him.

"I've been thinking about slipping the rest of this dress off you ever since I walked into the restaurant tonight and saw your shoulders. They set off such a wave of memory of your body." He was already unzipping the dress. It fell to the floor and I stepped out of it.

We made love for hours, as hungry as we'd been the night before but with a deepening awareness of each other's needs. And we broke the silence. In moments of repose, as our bodies came back down from their heightened states where nothing existed except pleasure, we spoke to each other.

"The minute you walked into the studio in August I felt a jolt of recognition. I thought the pain I was feeling was that of a failed teacher who'd lost his star pupil. I saw what I *thought* you'd become—a comfortable suburban matron who 'appreciated' art but no longer created it herself."

"And you've been trying to save me ever since?" I was propped up on my elbow facing him, stroking him gently with my free hand as if I were sculpting clay.

"I tried. But you were remarkably resistant to saving. I began to see a strength in you that I hadn't perceived before."

I frowned. "Is this seduction just one more way of convincing me to return to art?" My hand stopped sculpting.

He grabbed the stilled hand and kissed it.

"God, no! I asked you out because I realized my interest was no longer that of a teacher for a student, but a man for a woman. I was probably drawn to you ten years ago and unable to admit that my anger with you for giving up on your talent was muddied by my jealousy."

"I knew back then that your disapproval was intense. I even felt it in August. It never occurred to me that it was so personal."

"I was a selfish jerk. Forgive me."

"Forgiving you is easy. Despite your blurred intentions, you were encouraging me do to what I loved. Forgiving myself is a lot harder. I've made a real mess of my life because I didn't trust my own talent. And I'm afraid that by coming back here, I'll slip into another kind of complacency."

"At least in coming back, you've reentered *my* life." He smiled, then continued. "Don't beat yourself up about returning home. First of all, you need to heal and be taken care of, and it seems that your family—especially your brothers—are more than willing to do that. Second, and more important, this place, this life, is the root of your talent. It's what nurtured you. Tap into it again."

"I don't know if it's there anymore."

"Is that doubt enough to stop you? That doesn't sound like the Toni I've seen emerging over the past several months. Or the Toni who's made love to me the past two nights."

I felt my face redden. "I don't know that Toni. She's a revelation to me."

"Then get to know her. Even if it's just to let her move

your hand sketching—the way she's been moving your hand over my body."

"You're talking like a teacher again."

"No. I'm talking like a man who's in love with you."

When we woke in each other's arms the next morning, the lovemaking was languorous and unhurried, gentler than the night's quenching of an endless thirst.

"Let me cook for you," I said when we finally stirred, the winter sunlight cutting across the bed and the sounds of the street rising up—metal shutters clattering open at the green-grocer's and my uncle Sal's butcher shop, delivery trucks backing into narrow alleyways.

I surveyed my refrigerator, filled with provisions for feeding three children—yogurt cups and peanut butter and applesauce, leftover meatballs and fusilli. Not much for entertaining a lover. But I found some eggs and day-old bread and cinnamon. I didn't have any vanilla left, the bottle emptied the last time I'd made chocolate-chip cookies. I dug around under the cabinet in my pantry and unearthed an old bottle of Drambuie. I splashed a dollop into the beaten eggs and presented Peter with a platter of French toast garnished with my mother's peach preserves.

I set the table in the dining room and used my good dishes, not the sturdy but scarred pottery that had withstood years of children. I felt as if I were creating a bubble, insulated from the rest of my life, where for one more hour it was only Peter and I, sipping coffee and holding hands in the midst of warmth and sweetness and nourishment.

"What are you doing today?"

"Picking up the kids at my aunt's. Grocery shopping for me and my parents, who get back from Florida this afternoon. Spending time with the kids. Saturdays they know they have me to themselves."

"Do you want to bring them over to the community center later? We're holding an open house. The kids can get their hands dirty—finger painting for Vanessa, clay and woodworking for the boys."

"Is this a ploy to get me to volunteer?"

"No expectations. I know how much you have on your plate. I just thought it might be fun for the kids."

"Okay. We'll try to stop in."

"I should leave and let you get on with your day. I know this is a tough question, with your parents returning, but when can I see you again?"

I looked at him. There was nothing I wanted more at that moment than to have him back in my bed, in my body. And there was also nothing I feared more, to be as consumed as we had been by each other.

I kissed him. "We'll find the time, when it's right."

When he left, I stripped the bed and put the sheets in the washing machine, grabbed my coat and went across the street to bring my children home.

We *did* go to the community center after lunch. Joe was the least enthusiastic. He would much rather have gone to the rink and played hockey, and dismissed the art studio as stuff for babies. But when we got there, he gravitated to a table where some older boys were making monster masks and he stopped moping that we only did things that were fun for Ben. I knew Ben liked to draw. Much as I did as a child, he'd use any blank space as a drawing tablet—the margins of his notebook, the backs of envelopes. He could go through a pad of newsprint in an afternoon, sketching rocket ships and imaginary space creatures. The teachers at the community center had wrapped an entire wall in paper and handed kids multicolored markers when they walked in. Ben chose a corner, sat cross-legged on the floor in front of it and began a meticulously detailed air battle.

Vanessa, as Peter had predicted, found her calling at the finger-painting table.

The room was humming with color and activity. A Raffi album played in the background. I looked around for Peter but didn't see him, which was both disappointing and something of a relief. My reaction to being near him was still too visceral and I didn't trust myself to disguise my pleasure. There were too many people from the neighborhood here, parents from St. John's, customers who ate at Paradiso. I wasn't quite ready for it to be so clear that Toni Dante Templeton had a boyfriend.

Vanessa was growing bored with the finger painting and starting to make a mess. I cleaned her up and collected the boys to go home. One of the volunteers, a student from the Museum School, snipped Ben's drawing off the wall and rolled it up for him. Joe put his mask on. Vanessa's painting was still wet, so the student hung it on a clothesline strung across the room and I promised I'd stop by on Monday to pick it up. She handed me a sheet of paper with the studio hours and class schedule.

"Please come again!" She was cheerful and efficient and the kind of person I'd be happy to have working with my children. We trooped home and I asked the boys if they'd like to go to the studio again. When they both answered in the affirmative I began to see a way to spend time with them *and* offer help to the program.

We welcomed my parents home from Florida late in the afternoon and the kids spent the evening with my mother as she unpacked and I worked the Saturday dinner shift. As the late diners started dessert, I hurried upstairs to retrieve the kids. My mother went down to set up for the next day.

I carried Vanessa to her crib, ushered the boys to their bunk beds and retreated to my room. The bed was still bare, not yet made up. The light on my answering machine was blinking.

I listened to Peter's voice, apologizing for not being at the studio. He'd been called to the Museum School because of a burst pipe that had left several inches of water in the press room. No damage to anyone's work, but a mess to clean up.

"I know you need to spend time with your parents. I won't disturb you this evening. But give me a call when you get in if you want to talk."

I hauled the sheets out of the dryer and made the bed before climbing into it and calling Peter.

"Where are you?"

"In bed. I thought it wouldn't seem so empty if I settled in with at least your voice close to me."

We talked for two hours.

The next week I started volunteering one afternoon a week at the community center. After facing the indifference of high school students, the exuberance of the children was infectious. They played with their art unselfconsciously, and their playfulness became one more source of encouragement, one more incursion into the wall of restraint I'd built around myself.

The Sketchbook

PETER GAVE ME A gift for my birthday. A small bound sketchbook and a set of charcoal pencils.

"Carry it with you. Use it like a journal and record what you see, only for yourself."

"Thanks, Teach." I was ready, I realized, to resume what had been a daily practice for me before I'd married Bobby. The book was beautiful, with heavy pages of pale cream that beckoned to be filled. I put it in my knapsack. The first time I used it I was pushing Vanessa in her stroller through the square to Old North Church. It was an unseasonably warm day and the old men were out on the benches arguing with one another and punctuating the air with their gestures.

Vanessa had dozed off, so I parked the stroller and pulled the notebook out of my backpack. I quickly sketched two of the men, one using his cane as an extension of his arm, the other shading his eyes from the sun with a rolled up copy of the *Herald*. It took me just ten minutes, and then we were on our way again.

Within a month I had filled the notebook. It surprised me. But I had trained my eye to see small squares of life. Some were as minute as a gnarled hand grasping a plum tomato from the basket on the sidewalk in front of the greengrocer's. Others were more expansive, like the shanks of prosciutto hanging from hooks in the window of my uncle Sal's shop or the cityscape framed by my bedroom window.

One night after the kids were in bed, I sat with the book and examined the pages. Some were better than others, but on the whole I'd captured a substantial number of images I was pleased with. The next day I went downtown and bought myself some sheets of watercolor paper, inks, brushes.

I chose one of the images in the notebook and recreated it in pen and ink with a soft wash of color.

It was on my dresser drying when Peter saw it there. We'd found a rhythm to being together that seemed to balance feeding the hunger we had for each other with the demands of everything else in our lives—especially my children's hunger for me.

I had introduced Peter to my parents a week after they returned from Florida by inviting him to the Sunday dinner my mother continued to prepare; it was how she got us all to sit down at the same table at least once a week. Bringing him to that meal was my way of hiding him in plain sight. He had a number of labels attached to him—former teacher, current colleague, neighbor, Paradiso regular. Enough to distract and deflect from the primary roles he played in my life, those of lover and friend. Even though most thirty-two-year-old divorced mothers of three probably had sex lives, to my parents sex remained something reserved for the marriage bed. I assumed Manny, who was still living under their roof, fulfilled that side of his life away from home in the beds of any of the lovelies who were ratcheting up the popularity of Paradiso. For me to spend even a couple of hours away from home in Peter's bed was nearly impossible. Too many questions. Too much judgment. But bringing Peter in the front door, making him a very visible presence, actually reduced speculation.

He got to know my boys at the community center and turned out to be an adept craftsman who was helping them collaborate on a scale model of a spaceship Ben had designed and Joe was constructing in their bedroom. When the children were around, Peter and I exchanged penetrating looks full of the promise of things to come. Once they were asleep, we shared a few hours made more pleasurable by the anticipation.

It was late spring when Peter saw the pen-and-ink wash on the dresser. He hadn't noticed it when he'd first come into the room because we'd been too intent on getting each other out of our clothes. But afterward, as he was dressing in the soft light, he saw it and picked it up. I hadn't shown him the notebook. As he'd promised when he gave it to me, it was mine alone. Not an assignment. Not an expectation. He turned to me with the sheet outstretched.

"It's wonderful."

That was all. No questions about how I felt to be creating again. No suggestions about what to do now that I'd plunged back in. He let me be, which was an even greater gift than the notebook itself.

I knew the piece was wonderful. I'd once found a quotation from the author James Dickey when I was a student that I kept tacked to my bulletin board—about the moment of revelation when, as a writer, you realize what you've created is "damn good." I'd had that moment. And I wanted more of them.

I bought another sketchbook. And filled it with more images from my life, my neighborhood. Manny hovering over a saucepan, the veins in his arms tracing a path of intensity as he stirs and then lifts the spoon to his mouth to taste; my parents sitting side by side at Joe's fourth-grade concert, my mother's diamond-bedecked fingers entwined with my father's withered hand.

I kept going.

In August 1983, my parents rented a place down on the Cape for a couple of weeks and offered to take the children.

"You need a break. Have some fun. Make plans with your girlfriends," my mother said.

Peter took me out to dinner the first night they were gone.

"I have something important I want to talk to you about." He didn't elaborate until we were seated on an outdoor terrace. We'd driven all the way to Gloucester.

"Hear me out," he said when I asked him to stop keeping me in suspense. "Don't respond until I tell you everything."

"Walt Bergeron has decided to retire."

Walt was Peter's colleague on the faculty, a printmaker like himself.

"He's ill and wants to spend whatever time he's got left making art instead of teaching."

"I'm so sorry for him."

"I am, too. He's a good friend as well as a colleague. And I understand why he'd up and leave. But it also creates a huge gap in the department just before term begins. Which is why I wanted to talk to you."

I started to speak, but he reached up with two fingers and touched my lips gently.

"Please wait. I want to offer you the chance to join the faculty, teach printmaking. You're more than qualified, especially with the ten years you've taught in Bedford."

The prospect of having students who *wanted* to be learning, the opportunity to be back in a studio… It was tantalizing. But I saw one major obstacle.

"How can I take the job when I'm your lover? You'd be my boss, right? That sounds like a situation the school would frown on."

"But if you weren't my lover anymore, they'd have no reason to complain."

251

I felt tears rising. "Are you asking me to choose?" I was incredulous.

"No, Toni. I'm asking you to marry me."

He took my trembling hands in his. Now he was the one with tears in his eyes.

"Please say yes."

Peter and I were married on Thanksgiving Day in the courtyard of the Isabella Stewart Gardner Museum. It wasn't a church and we didn't have a priest, but my parents put aside their expectations, recognizing that even with those blessings there were no guarantees that a marriage would flourish.

My mother was anxious that I was marrying again "too soon."

"Mom, it's more than three years since Bobby left. Peter and I have spent two years learning about and loving each other, and we had four years before that, as well. I'm sure of him, Mom. He makes me happy. And I know I do the same for him."

We held the reception at Paradiso. Faculty members from the Museum School with their funky hairstyles and shabby-chic clothes mingled with our Italian relatives—mine from the neighborhood and Peter's from Rochester—in their beaded dresses and flashy sports jackets. My boys got their first suits for the wedding, and Vanessa was old enough to be a flower girl. My mother went overboard and got her a dress from Priscilla of Boston, the shop that created Grace Kelly's wedding dress.

On my mother's dresser was a photograph of her in Trinidad that had been there for as long as I could remember. In it, her back is to the camera, her arms outstretched touching the frame of the open doorway in which she's standing, and her head is turned over her shoulder. She is wearing a Japanese kimono, embroidered in flowers.

"Where is the kimono now?" I asked her one afternoon before the wedding. "Do you still have it?"

She did, packed away with other mementos of Trinidad. It was exquisite—navy blue silk with a riot of color spilling down the back. I asked her if I could wear it for the wedding.

"Are you sure?" she asked, recalling that I'd worn her gown for my first wedding.

"This is something else, Mom. Daddy gave it to you, right?"

We agreed that a gift of love, like the kimono, could only be a good omen, and that is what I wore.

Manny created the menu. Because of the larger crowd than we normally fed at Thanksgiving, he decided to make rolled turkey breasts instead of roasting whole turkeys. He flattened the breasts and layered a mixture of sausage, cheese and eggs with fresh sage leaves and slices of mortadella, then rolled the breasts up and roasted them, basting them with white wine. We had the usual accompaniments of sweet potatoes, stuffed mushrooms and broccoli and cauliflower florets sautéed in olive oil with garlic and lemon peel.

Between courses Peter and I circled the room to greet our guests. He kept his hand on the small of my back, a point of connection that he didn't break. It was a source of energy for me, propelling me, warming me, protecting me, as I stepped into the next stage of my life. One of the first things I did was let go of the Templeton name and take back Dante.

We decided to keep both our homes. Peter moved into my apartment when we married. It was large enough for all of us and didn't disrupt the kids' lives. We kept Peter's loft on Union Wharf as a studio for both of us—a place to retreat and to work.

I kept filling sketchbooks and began turning my pen-and-ink interpretations into prints. I experimented with etchings and lithographs until I found a process that conveyed what I was trying to achieve. I held my first show as part of the faculty exhibition at the school.

I loved teaching at the Museum School. The atmosphere was so charged and the ideas so explosive that I was continually challenged by my students about the definition of art. Peter and I started a tradition of dinners at our home for our students; they often evolved into spirited debates that went on into the early hours of the morning.

Peter embraced my children and gave them time to accept him as their stepfather. We tried to have another child, but it wasn't meant to be. Instead, we became surrogate parents to our students and the friends of our children who gravitated to our home.

After the exhibition of my work at the faculty show, I was invited to participate in shows at Smith College and Brandeis. A publisher of art books saw my work at the Smith gallery and approached me to do a collection of prints entitled "Faces of the North End."

In fifteen years of marriage, the passion that had brought us together that first cold winter night continued to burn. We never grew tired of each other or bored in bed. We were bound together, our connection forged in the soul-baring heat of our lovemaking.

We weathered the challenges any marriage faces—the adolescent traumas of the children, the aging of our parents, upheaval at work. My worries that any of the children might inherit Bobby's bipolar disorder faded as they reached adulthood.

We were content. When Vanessa graduated from high school and started her freshman year at Harvard, we had dinner alone and toasted each other. We thought we'd not only survived, but flourished. That we'd made it up the steep side of the mountain and had earned a glimpse from the summit. But we were wrong.

VANESSA

1998

Freshman

———✦———

I GREW UP ABOVE my grandparents' restaurant—Paradiso on Salem Street in the North End of Boston, the city's Little Italy. My grandparents, Rose and Al Dante, live on the second floor of the four-story brick building; my mother and father, my two brothers and I on the third; and my uncle Mike on the fourth.

My earliest memories are redolent with the aroma of Grandma Rose's gravy. Huge vats of her Neapolitan marinara bubbled softly on the back of the range in the restaurant kitchen. If I was hungry before dinner she tore off a chunk of crusty Campobasso bread full of air pockets and skimmed it across the top of the pot, where the pockets filled up with tomatoes and basil and garlic. She put the bread on a saucer and handed it to me.

"*Mangia,* sweetheart. But not too much or you won't have room for macaroni later."

When I was ten, I helped Grandma Rose fill the lidded bowls of grated Parmigiano on every table. When I was fourteen, I folded the napkins that came in every morning from the laundry. Grandma Rose didn't believe in paper napkins. When I was sixteen, I waited on tables on the weekends.

My mother, Toni, is Paradiso's weekend hostess. During the

day she usually wears jeans and a Cape Cod sweatshirt picked up in Orleans during the two weeks in summer when the restaurant closes and we all go down the Cape to the same cottage we've rented since I was a baby. But in the evenings, when Paradiso opens for dinner, my mother puts on a black V-necked sequined sweater, a tight-fitting black skirt, high heels and makeup.

Watching my mother get dressed late every Friday afternoon was my first lesson in transformation. She might've been scrubbing the toilet or making my brother Joe sit at the kitchen table and do his algebra homework, but once she puts on those clothes, her mascara and her Estée Lauder #148 Hot Kiss lipstick and goes downstairs, she's like an actress stepping out of a limousine onto the red carpet.

She's the first impression people have when they walk into Paradiso. She greets everyone with a voice that flows over them and makes them feel like she's been waiting all night for them to arrive and she saved the best table just for them.

I haven't figured out how to do that yet.

My mother was okay with my waitressing at Paradiso—after all, the whole family is involved in the business. But she wanted more for me and my brothers.

"You're too smart to go to the nuns for high school," she declared the summer before I went to eighth grade. High school was a whole year away, but everybody in the neighborhood went to Catholic high school when it was time.

"I want you to study for the entrance exam to Boston Latin," she said. And that was that. I studied. I got in. While my girlfriends at St. John's were buying their uniforms for Cathedral, I was at the library checking out books on the summer reading list. Chaucer. Milton. Emerson. Aristotle. Even Dante.

My grandfather Al liked to tell us how the family got its

name when his father landed on Ellis Island from Calabria. His name was Bernardo Alighieri. The immigration clerk couldn't pronounce or spell it.

"Like Dante!" my great-grandfather exclaimed in exasperation. And that's what the clerk wrote down on his papers.

I did my summer reading sitting at a corner table in the restaurant before the dinner crowd showed up. Some people think my mother pushed me during high school, like I was her last hope. My two brothers, Ben and Joe, are five and seven years older than I am. Ben was a sophomore at Northeastern studying computer science when I started Boston Latin. Joe had gone to Bunker Hill Community College, but stopped there. My mother's uncle Carmine got him an apprenticeship in the electricians' union and he's happy enough.

But people who think it was my mother's thwarted ambitions rather than my own that propelled me out of the North End would be wrong. It wasn't just the gap in our ages that made me different from my brothers; we have different memories because of that gap.

Joe and Ben remember our biological father, for example, and I don't. A month after I was born, Bobby Templeton quit his job, emptied his closet in our suburban raised ranch in Bedford and took off for Boulder, Colorado. Joe and Ben remember a daddy who occasionally played catch with them in a backyard that had a sandbox and a wading pool. But they also remember a household that was cast in the shadows of our father's mental illness—or lack of moral compass, depending on which member of the family is describing it.

I have none of that. I don't even remember the apartment in Arlington that my mother rented after she couldn't afford to keep the house in Bedford. Where she tried to be independent and strong and hold our fragile family together.

My memories and my boundaries are tightly defined by the

bricks and mortar of Salem Street, by the demands of a family restaurant, by the enveloping and, yeah, sometimes smothering love of my Italian family.

Going to Boston Latin, even though it was only across the city, blew open my world. Some people might think it didn't lead me far. After all, I'm only across the river now in Cambridge. But let me tell you, Harvard Yard's a world away from the North End.

It's a little weird, being a freshman at Harvard when you've grown up in an enclave like the North End. It's especially a disconnect because people don't get that I'm Italian. Not only do I have Bobby's quintessentially Middle-American last name, but I also have his blond hair and blue eyes. So all the private-school, country-club kids believe I'm one of them and don't understand why I'm not flying to Jackson Hole or Saint Kitts for Thanksgiving break. And all the gritty, urban, ethnic kids who wear their heritage on their hard-working, rolled-up sleeves believe I'm some privileged legacy, with a long line of alumni in my family preceding me.

But frankly, I'm working too hard to worry about it. Boston Latin was a piece of cake compared to this. My mother was right: I'm a smart kid, but so is everybody else here. I hole up in Widener Library until it closes, my yellow highlighter furiously moving back and forth across the pages of my plant physiology textbook. I AP'ed out of bio, chem and American history, so I'm taking 200-level courses. Grandma Rose fusses that I don't come home often enough.

"What could it hurt to get on the T and come for a good meal now and then, Vaness'?" she asked me when she'd called me one Sunday afternoon.

"Tell me when you're coming and I'll make your favorites—the ravioli with the porcini mushrooms and a torta Milanese with spinach and red peppers." Rose accepted my being a vegetarian, unlike my brothers, whose idea of a balanced meal is a steak and a beer.

"I can't, Grandma. I've got two papers due this week and a midterm. I'll be home for Thanksgiving."

"Okay, sweetheart. I'll see if I can find that fake turkey you told me about. What's it called again?"

"Tofurkey, Grandma. Hey, thanks. Gotta go—my study group's meeting before supper. I'll see you soon."

"Vaness', before you go. You know if you've got any friends that have nowhere to go for Thanksgiving, you invite them here, you understand?"

"Yeah, Grandma. Thanks. I'll do that."

I didn't think about Thanksgiving again for another week. Too much to do, to worry about, like keeping my scholarship. When the Monday before Thanksgiving rolled around, I was in the dining hall with my dorm mates. I live in Canaday, an anomaly—architecturally speaking—in Harvard Yard. If you're thinking ivy-covered, eighteenth-century, high ceilings and fireplaces in the common rooms, you'd be totally wrong. Canaday was built in the 1970s and, although it's brick, that's the only resemblance it has to anything else on this hallowed ground. It's all sharp angles and flat roofs, with six separate pods, each possessing its own utilitarian entrance cluttered with bikes and an overflowing bulletin board. The floors alternate male-female, something my mother and I mutually agreed not to share with my grandparents. Mom was cool about it, though. I feel she's come to terms with the ramifications of pushing me out of the nest at such a high altitude.

So I was at dinner in Annenberg Hall with the other girls on my floor—my roommate, Megana, who comes from Roslyn on Long Island, but whose parents are from Mumbai; Sonja, from Minnesota, who grew up in a town exactly like Garrison Keillor's Lake Woebegon; Elise, from Savannah via

Miss Porter's School; Kelly, a hockey player from Buffalo; Naomi, from the Bronx High School of Science, another urban exam school, like Latin; Jessica, from Salt Lake City and the first Mormon I'd ever met; and Raquelle, from San Antonio, who had once regaled us with the extravagance of her *Quinceañera*. Harvard Dining Services, like every other institutional dining room in the Boston area, seemed to think that students needed more than one Thanksgiving dinner that week. Turkey with all the trimmings—sweet potatoes, gravy, corn, cranberry sauce—was arrayed on the steam tables of the cafeteria line. They had thoughtfully provided tofu burgers for us vegetarians.

The menu, of course, got us talking about the holiday—plans for trips home, families we missed or could live without. Everybody was babbling away except for Sonja, who seemed focused on her plate.

After the meal, walking back to the dorm, I caught up with her.

"Hey, are you heading back to PBSville on Wednesday?"

She shook her head. "I'm hanging out here. Don't really have time to go back." She didn't seem to want to expand on the reasons.

I remembered Grandma Rose's directive and considered asking Sonja to come home with me. I hesitated, surprised by my own ambivalence about opening a window into the life I'd left in the North End when I was trying to figure out my new life here at Harvard. I didn't want to acknowledge that I was feeling slightly embarrassed by my family. There were just too many of them to control. But I also thought about how, despite their rough edges, it was hard to feel lonely or unloved in their midst. And Sonja looked truly adrift at the prospect of spending five long, empty days in the dorm. I pushed aside my reservations and plunged in.

"My grandmother has issued an open invitation to her Thanksgiving feast. She doesn't believe in eating alone, no matter what the occasion. Why don't you come across the river to Grandmother's house with me? It's not exactly through the woods, but I can promise you a meal better than you got tonight."

She wavered for a minute, the Norwegian martyr—"Oh, no, I couldn't trouble you. Just let me eat my bread and water here by myself"—trying to emerge. But then I told her it would be a favor to me if she came. It would put my family on their best behavior with a stranger at the table.

She said yes. I gave her the address, but told her I'd meet her at the Park Street T station if she wanted me to. She seemed grateful for that, not having ventured very far beyond the environs of Harvard Square in her three months.

I warned her. "My grandparents shut down Paradiso for the day and cook for the family. Um, that means there'll be about forty people—aunts, uncles, cousins, in-laws. Just so you don't think it's going to be a nuclear family event. It's an ever-changing guest list that shows up at Paradiso on Thanksgiving."

I didn't want to frighten her away or overwhelm her. It probably would've been better for both of us if I'd said, Hey, I'll stay here, too, and we can go eat Indian or Chinese and watch movies. But that would've been an impossible choice for me, incomprehensible to Grandma Rose and unacceptable to my mother. So Wednesday afternoon I packed up my knapsack, pulled on my Harvard sweatshirt and went back to the neighborhood.

Dangerous Games

PETER RICCI HAS BEEN the only father I've known. He taught me how to roller-skate, suffered through my piano recitals and made me apologize to my mother when I was thirteen and the daughter from hell, slamming doors and yelling, "You're ruining my life!" because she wouldn't let me hang out at Waterfront Park after dark. He adores my mother and resides only a notch below my grandpa Al in the eyes of Grandma Rose.

"Peter is cut from the same cloth as my Al. He gives with his whole heart. Take my word for it, Vaness'. When it's time for you to choose a man, compare him to your father to see if he measures up."

In spite of everything Peter had done and been for me, in spite of how much I loved him, I found myself one dreary winter afternoon in Widener Library looking for Robert Templeton on the Internet. I was mildly curious. What becomes of a man who decides to reinvent himself, freed of familial responsibilities? What did he look like?

Any photos my mother had of the early years of her marriage to Bobby had been put away by the time I had memory. When I was sixteen I found their wedding album among some old boxes in the basement and had turned the stiff and yellowing pages in secret, trying to see in Bobby Templeton's eyes some reflection of the demons that had driven him away from us. But he looked content, optimistic and a lot like me. Maybe that's why I let the seed grow inside my brain, why I allowed myself to wonder where he was, what had become of him.

Although Grandma Rose has preferred to wipe his existence from our family history, my mother has been relatively comfortable with it, considering. Her attitude is, "Hey, this happened and it sucked. We can let it eat away at us, or we can thumb our nose at it and move on." Until my other grandmother, Hazel, passed away, my mother kept in touch with her. She always ordered extra copies of our school pictures and had us make cards for her on Mother's Day and her birthday.

My brothers wrote Bobby Templeton off a long time ago, especially Joe, who seems to have absorbed my grandmother's philosophy of "He's dead to me." Ben is more closed about his internal life. If he cares at all about who Bobby Templeton is, he doesn't share it with any of us.

I think I was just bored that first time I typed Bobby's name into a search engine. I was in the procrastination phase of writing a paper on Nabakov for my Comp. Lit. class and *any* diversion was welcome. Robert Templeton is a fairly common name, I discovered. The search bounced back fifty-nine references. I clicked on a few, entertaining myself with the possibility of our Bobby Templeton being a physics professor at Gonzaga University or a state senator in Louisiana or a late-night radio jock in Lincoln, Nebraska. Then I got sensible, preferring not to be up until 4:00 a.m. writing my paper, and stopped playing on the computer.

It really was just a game to me at first, my own version of *Where's Waldo?* I didn't mean for it to become anything more than clever stories to entertain my dorm mates. It was nothing. Until it became something. It kind of took over, feeding some need in me that was more than curiosity.

This must be what adoptees feel like, trying to find their birth parents, I told myself. I tried to justify it on medical grounds. What if he's a diabetic? What if he's passed on some genetic disease that's a ticking time bomb? But it was more than that. I wanted to look Bobby Templeton in the eye, not in an aging photograph but in person, and understand who he was. And who I was.

I found him when I stumbled across a photograph online, one of those stiff, formal company portraits, the corporate equivalent of yearbook pictures. Well, at least he wasn't a homeless derelict living in a cardboard box, which is the fate I think my grandmother had envisioned. He lived in Nashville, Tennessee.

I e-mailed him. I didn't have the money or the nerve just to show up on his doorstep, like one of those movies where the adorable little girl drops into the life of the confirmed bachelor, throwing his carefully established routines into chaos and ultimately winning his heart. I'm not adorable. I'm what my friends charitably call "edgy" and what my brothers define as a pain in the butt. I'm either direct or brutally honest, depending on your perspective. I tend not to sugarcoat things.

I somehow thought he'd jump at the chance to know his daughter once she presented herself. It didn't occur to me that he'd known where I was for eighteen years and could have made my acquaintance at anytime. But didn't.

It will come as no surprise that he did not respond. However, I chose to ignore his silence and began sending him regular updates—dispatches from a college freshman.

And then, on my birthday, he sent me a card. Not one of those sappy "To a Dear Daughter" confections you find in the racks at CVS, but a hilarious Far Side cartoon. The guy had a sense of humor.

I sent him a thank-you note and we then began a regular exchange, via e-mail.

Does your mother know you've contacted me? he asked, like a responsible adult.

I thought about blurring my answer. But I reluctantly admitted to myself that keeping my relationship with Bobby a secret from my mother and, yes, father was probably a stupid idea. Hey, I go to Harvard. And even though my grandfather suspects that my classmates were born with high intelligence and low common sense, I'd spent enough time in the world before Harvard to know that reaching across the rift to Bobby was bringing him not only into my life, but into everybody else's, as well.

So I told my mother.

We were in the pantry between the kitchen and the dining room. She leaned back against the counter with her arms folded across her chest.

"Why didn't you tell me you were interested in finding Bobby? I could have saved you the search."

"You knew where he was?"

"He wasn't hiding."

"You're not mad at me?"

"No, sweetie. Dad and I expected that sooner or later you'd want to know something about him. Just…well, don't expect too much. I don't want you to be hurt."

Okay. That went better than I'd expected. She didn't jump on me, yelling, What were you *thinking?* If she had, I couldn't have answered her. I don't know why I wanted to find Bobby. I don't know what I wanted *from* Bobby. An apology? An explanation?

I was going to find out. He'd told me he had a business trip to New York. Close enough to rent a car and drive up to Boston. He offered to buy me dinner in Harvard Square.

He took me to Upstairs at the Pudding, the sort of place where families treat their offspring to graduation dinner. The place takes reservations months in advance.

"A fancy dinner is not going to compensate me for nineteen years of desertion," I said during the appetizer.

I asked what he'd been doing while he was gone. He told me. He'd remarried, had two kids, gotten divorced.

"Do they know about us?"

"My ex-wife, yes. The kids, no."

"Why did you send me the birthday card?"

"It was your birthday."

I made a face. "That doesn't answer the question."

"I wanted to know who you were. And let you know I hadn't forgotten that I left a family behind."

"You left a wreckage."

"I'm sorry."

"That's supposed to make up for what you did?"

"I was young. I was sick."

"I'm young, but I know you don't do that to your wife and kids. No matter how bad a shape you're in or how hard life is."

"If you're so angry with me, why did you try to find me?"

"I wanted to know what kind of man you are. I didn't contact you to forgive you. I contacted you so I could figure out who *I* am, where I came from."

"You look like me."

"Duh."

"Other than the superficial traits I seem to have passed on to you, I don't think I had much to do with the young woman you've become."

"Are you happy?"

"I have two failed marriages, four of my five children are not speaking to me and I'm a prime candidate for a heart attack. You tell me."

"What do you want, Bobby?"

"Redemption."

"I can't help you with that. I was a baby when you walked. I can't restore you to the self you were before you deserted us because I don't remember you. Did you even hold me before you left?"

"In the delivery room."

"After that?"

"No. I couldn't. It hurt too much. I knew I was going to leave. I was in hell, Vanessa."

"It sounds to me like you still are. Look, I'm a kid. I may have scored 1580 on my SATs, but I'm not smart enough to figure out what you need."

"Do you think your mother would see me?"

"I can't answer that. She knows you're in town. I told her."

That was when I really began to understand what I'd done by bringing Bobby back. Dumb. Dumb. Dumb. I started to cry.

"Don't you dare wreck our lives again!" I got up from the table without finishing my crème brûlée and ran back to my dorm. He didn't try to stop me.

When I got to my room the phone was ringing. I didn't answer it and let it go to voice mail. It was my mother.

"Hi, sweetie. I just called to see how you were doing after your dinner with Bobby."

I picked up the phone.

"Oh, Mom, I'm so sorry! I wish I'd never found him."

"What happened, Vanessa? Are you okay?" I could hear the rising note of anger tinged with hysteria that was the signature of the women on my grandmother's side of the family.

My mother, normally a reasonable and even-tempered woman well in control of her emotions, could be pushed over the edge if she thought one of her kids had been hurt.

"I'm okay. I'm just so stupid. He doesn't care about me. He's using me to get to you."

The other end of the phone was silent.

"Mom?"

"I'm sorry, Vanessa. I'm sorry he's hurt you. Do you want me to come over?"

I'm not much of a mama's girl. Ordinarily I would've turned to one of the girls in the dorm to calm down. But I didn't think any of them would understand. And I was worried about my mother. I felt I needed to inoculate her against Bobby. I didn't think I could stop him from getting in touch with her. But she needed to know what a loser he was.

"Yes, please, Mom. Thanks."

"I'll be there in twenty minutes."

When she got to Canaday I made some tea and we sat curled up on my couch. I'd stopped crying, but I was still upset I'd been such a fool.

"Don't beat yourself up, sweetie. There was nothing wrong in your wanting to know what had become of Bobby. But seeking knowledge like that has its costs. The important thing to remember is that, despite Bobby's absence from your life, you've turned out great! You're an impressive, resilient young woman, and I'm so proud of you!"

"Your life's turned out great, too, Mom. Don't let him drag *you* down. He's miserable. I felt contaminated by his unhappiness."

"Don't worry about me. I've got a hazmat suit on when it comes to Bobby Templeton."

By the time she left I felt reasonably certain she could kick Bobby's ass if he came groveling at her door. I imagined her in her hostess regalia, sequins flashing, long red fingernails tapping the table list as she sized him up as an out-of-town nobody she could stick at the worst table in the dining room.

Bobby disappeared from Boston without contacting my mother, and my systems backed down from high alert. Unfortunately he was only regrouping.

My mother had an exhibition of her prints at a gallery in New York a couple of months later. I took a day off from school and joined her for the opening reception. My father was in Italy with a group of students on an exchange program.

Everything was going well. Some hotshot critic from the *New York Times* had shown up and my mother, in addition to having mounted a brilliant show, looked her ravishing, Italian-actress best. My aunt Annette had done it again. I keep telling her she ought to launch a new career as a stylist.

My mother was entertaining the critic, champagne flute in one hand, the other flowing through the air as if she were conducting an orchestra.

The critic was nodding; Miles, the gallery director, was beaming and I wandered off to watch the crowd milling around the prints. I liked to eavesdrop on what they were saying about her.

I had my back to one cluster of people, trying not to be obvious that I was listening.

I heard one of the men say he thought this was her best work yet.

"I've been following her career since she began," he said. "In fact, I own several of her prints."

"You sound like a devoted fan," a woman responded.

"I am. As far as I'm concerned, no one else comes close."

My pulse was screaming in my ears when I recognized that the voice speaking so passionately about my mother's art belonged to Bobby Templeton.

I slid away from the group, hoping he hadn't seen me. I wanted to warn my mother, but she was still talking with the critic. I retreated to the bar, where I grabbed another glass of Apollinaris and had a pretty good view of the room.

As soon as the critic moved on I headed toward my mother. But I was too late. To my horror, Bobby slipped up next to her. I saw a flicker of surprise on my mother's face. Her hand holding the champagne flute was trembling.

"Don't kiss him!" I almost shouted out loud. The evening had been filled with far too much of that phony art-world kiss-kiss. But she didn't. I watched her stand, listening to whatever he was telling her, trying to decipher from her face what she was thinking. I should have gone up and interrupted them, broken whatever connection he was trying to reestablish. But I didn't want to talk to him. And apparently he had no desire to talk to me, either. His attention was totally focused on my mother.

The conversation only lasted a few minutes. Other guests wanted a piece of my mother. She'd shaken her head a few times, then finally nodded. I could read her lips well enough to see that she'd mouthed the word *okay.* As he moved away from her, he brushed her hand. My mother turned to the others with her warm hostess smile. "I'm so happy you could make it!" But I could see, even from a distance, that there were tears in her eyes.

Bobby left the gallery after that. I was relieved until things were winding down and my mother approached me.

"Vanessa, I'm sorry to do this to you, but Miles wants me to go to dinner with a client. His assistant has offered to take you out for something to eat. I'll meet you back at the hotel."

I wanted to protest. To tell her that I knew the "client" was Bobby. I was so pissed with her for doing this, and didn't want to admit I was the one who'd set this whole mess in motion.

"I thought this was supposed to be time for us to spend together."

"I know, sweetie. I really *am* sorry. Look, we'll go to the Tavern on the Green tomorrow for brunch and then go shopping. Okay?"

"Fine." I found the anorexic assistant, assuming she'd watch me while I ate, and left my mother to lose her soul.

TONI

The Commission

I WAS UNPREPARED for the sight of Bobby approaching me in the gallery. Miles had told me that some avid collector had arrived, eager to meet me and interested in discussing a commission with me. When I saw it was Bobby, I thought, *What a line!* But then he launched into how moved he was by my work and how happy he was that my talent had been realized. He told me which of my prints he owned and why he'd selected them. What meaning they'd had in his life.

Every fiber of my will was stretched taut with the effort of resisting the emotional depths he was pulling me toward. I wished I hadn't had the two glasses of champagne I'd been blithely sipping as I greeted guests. I should've known better. I was working this exhibit, not just the celebrated guest. Bobby's tale was as compelling as it had ever been. It stunned me that after almost twenty years he could suck me back into his troubled world. He made my heart ache for him, as futile as I knew that was.

It seemed he truly did want to commission me.

"I'm asking you to capture the image of my children in print. I don't know of any other way to hold on to them."

"Which children?" I asked. I knew I was being brutal.

"All of them."

"No. I won't give you mine. They are no longer your children. You abandoned them. You didn't even pay child support."

He stepped back as if I'd slapped him.

"Okay." He acquiesced. It wasn't like him to accept less than he had asked for. I was wary. This was probably not the end of it.

"There are other people here waiting to talk to me. You can talk to Miles about the details."

"When the reception is over can we talk some more? Let me take you to dinner."

"I can't. I have plans."

"Please, Toni. Just hear me out this one time. That's all I'm asking."

I saw the pain in his eyes and reluctantly said yes. I knew Vanessa had been watching our exchange, and my heart sank. She wasn't going to understand. No one was going to understand.

When I got back to the hotel Vanessa was still up studying. She didn't speak to me.

I went into the bathroom to get ready for bed. I looked terrible, pale with dark circles under my eyes. The conversation with Bobby had drained me. I took a shower, trying to relax my tensed muscles and wash away the residue of his guilt and remorse and sense of being misunderstood that had settled on me like ash from a newly awakened Vesuvius.

When I came out of the bathroom Vanessa was waiting by the door.

"I know you were with Bobby."

"Yes, I was."

"What are you going to do?"

I wanted to reassure her, to tell her it was going to be all right, that his presence tonight was not going to disrupt our lives. But I couldn't. It was too late. The disruption had already occurred, and at that moment I was furious with her for triggering such an upheaval by bringing him back into my life in the first place.

Her face twisted in anger and fear, and with clenched fists she pounded on my chest. "You can't! You can't let him in! Don't do this to us!"

She went into the bathroom and locked the door.

"Vanessa!" I didn't have the energy or the will to deal with her at that moment.

"Go to hell."

She finally crept out and climbed into her bed about an hour later, her eyes red and swollen from crying.

I turned out the light.

In the morning she got dressed in silence and only spoke to me as she picked up her knapsack.

"I'm taking the train back to Boston."

I checked out of the hotel and went downtown to the gallery to wrap up some paperwork with Miles. He told me Bobby had bought two of my most expensive prints.

"That guy from Nashville seems obsessed with your work. He told me he owns eleven of your prints. Are you going to do the commissioned piece for him?"

"I don't know yet. It's complicated." I didn't want to explain to Miles what I could hardly explain to myself—that I was both repelled by Bobby's intrusion into my life and compelled by his need to provide what little solace I could with my art. He'd made me feel powerful, as if I could give him something he so desperately wanted, and that power was seductive.

I was exhausted. From being on my guard with Bobby, from

the fight with Vanessa, from the energy I'd poured into mounting the show and schmoozing the guests at the reception. I climbed into my car around noontime and drove back to Boston.

When I got home all I wanted to do was crawl into bed. But I checked the mail and phone messages first. Peter had sent a postcard from Pisa, an image of one of my favorite frescoes from the Camposanto Monumentale of a woman holding a falcon. The message was detailed, written in Peter's rapid, angular hand, full of the minutiae of shepherding a group of wide-eyed students on their maiden voyage to Italy. I missed him. I wished he'd been with me at the gallery, an anchor holding me fast against the turbulent storm that had blown in from Tennessee. I propped the card on my night table and picked up the phone to retrieve my voice mail.

The second message was from Peter. His voice was tight, cold.

"Toni, what the hell is going on? Vanessa called me, hysterical, that you'd abandoned her in New York to be with Bobby Templeton. Call me."

I started to shake. I'd done nothing the night before except listen to Bobby, but I'd underestimated how out of control Vanessa was in her reaction. That she'd called Peter and instilled in him a sense of betrayal chilled me. I didn't know how I could have a conversation with him without revealing my own confusion about my reaction to Bobby—and to Bobby's interjection of himself into my life. Why would I create a work of such personal meaning for him?

I looked at the clock, hoping it would be too late to call. Almost four o'clock in the afternoon, ten in the evening in Italy. Peter had left the number of his hotel in the message and I dialed it.

"Peter, it's Toni. I just got home and picked up your message. I'm sorry Vanessa was so upset."

"What happened?"

"I asked Miles's assistant to take her to dinner so I could discuss a commissioned piece with Bobby."

"He shows up after nearly twenty years and wants you to paint a picture?" Peter's voice was incredulous. "Is that all? If that's what he's telling you, I don't believe him."

"I'm not naive. I know this isn't an ordinary commission."

"Then why are you even considering it? I don't understand why you'd give him anything as precious as your talent. Do you really want that? Because if you do, you're not the woman I thought you were."

I didn't have an answer.

"I can't talk about this over the phone, Peter. I haven't agreed to anything. When you get home on Friday we can discuss it. I need your help to sort it out, but you're no help if you're going to prejudge me."

"Do you have any idea how angry this makes me? Not for *me,* but for what it could do to you. Don't let him pull you back to where you were emotionally after he left you."

I didn't tell Peter that I was dangerously close to being there already. I was a wreck. And for the first time in our marriage, I felt he didn't understand me.

"I'll see you in a few days. I hope the rest of the trip goes well." And I hung up.

I was too agitated to sleep.

I grabbed the keys to the studio and walked to the harbor. Once inside the studio I sat by the windows for a while just looking out to sea. I love the light that comes in through the floor-to-ceiling expanse of glass on the eastern wall. I watched as night descended on the ocean, the sky deepening from lavender to violet to indigo. When it was too dark to see the water I got up and turned on the lights.

I made myself a pot of tea—Sleepytime. It was the only tea I drank when I was nursing and, after nineteen years, its aroma brought me right back to that time when I was the sole source of nourishment for my children. It had been so simple to meet their needs then. Hold them close, suckle them, rock them, sing to them. Vanessa's favorite song had been "Somewhere over the Rainbow," and I'd sung it to her constantly—in the car stuck in traffic, walking the floor with her at night.

What could I sing to her now to reassure her?

I paced the floor with my mug for a few minutes and then went to the bookshelf where I kept my sketchbooks. They were arranged chronologically, so it was easy to pick out the early years. I pulled two books off the shelves and sat at my workbench on a high stool, slowly turning the pages I'd created before my marriage to Bobby. I was looking for a reminder, a sign, of who I'd been back then.

Like most of my work, the sketches were intimate portraits, attempting to capture the essence of the individuals in the lines and contours of their faces. I was startled to see how many of the sketches were of Bobby. I'd forgotten that I'd often used him as my subject. In some, his face was ravaged; the eyes staring out at me were blank. In others, he was looking away, unaware that I was sketching him, and he had a softness about his lips and his eyes, almost as if he was asleep. Perhaps he had been. When I first met him, I'd been swallowed up by his physical presence. I used to watch him, the way he moved with the confidence of a man used to being admired, his long, lean body proportioned like one of Michelangelo's sculptures.

It disturbed me that I still found him so physically powerful. When our marriage had begun to dissolve, his withdrawal from my bed—long before he swung his leg over his motorcycle and rode away—had been wrenching. To have that primal need reawakened was frightening.

A chill had drifted into the studio after the sun had set; despite their modernization these old buildings were drafty, their cavernous spaces quickly dissipating the heat. Rather than turn up the thermostat, I opened the potbellied stove, built a nest of crumpled newsprint and twigs and lit a fire. We still had a small supply of logs left after the winter. With the fire going and a second cup of tea in my hand, I continued to turn the pages of my notebooks. But it wasn't just Bobby's face, in all its variations of mood, that I was seeking. It was the artist herself. I'd become someone else in the years since Bobby had left. The woman who'd been muffled and silenced during my marriage, constrained first by Bobby's expectations and then by Bobby's needs, had finally emerged after his abandonment. Why would I risk losing her?

I finally fell asleep on the daybed, too tired to walk back home, too unsettled to resume my domestic life. I was startled by a ringing sound early in the morning and it took my groggy brain a few seconds to grasp that it was a telephone, not the alarm clock I was unsuccessfully groping for. I shivered as I put my bare feet on the floor and wrapped the quilt around me. I picked up the phone on the counter.

"Hello?"

"Toni? Oh, thank God that's where you are! I worried all night when Joe told me you weren't back."

"Sorry, Ma. I came over to the studio to do some work and was too exhausted to go home late at night. Didn't mean to have you worry."

"Are you alone?" Her voice was sharp, expecting the worst.

"Of course. Who else would be here?"

"I talked to Vanessa last night when you didn't come home. I thought maybe you'd stayed in New York with her. She told me Bobby Templeton showed up at the gallery."

"And you thought I was spending the night with him while

my husband was away?" I was incredulous that my mother would imply such a betrayal.

"You're angry with me, but from what Vanessa told me you're treading on very thin ice, Toni. Are you crazy to be jeopardizing everything you hold precious in your life?"

"Ma, I'm not sleeping with him. I'm not even remotely considering the *possibility* of sleeping with him. It's a business transaction, nothing more."

"Don't be a fool, Toni. And don't ruin your life. Come home, take a shower and remember who you are now." And she hung up the phone.

I wondered who else would berate me as word spread across the family that the devil himself had returned.

I cleaned up the studio and left for home. It was only seven in the morning. Maybe my mother was right. If I got back into the rhythm of my life I'd be able to calm the storm Bobby had created in my mind. I hoped so.

I threw myself into the frenzy of activity that I'd watched my mother and grandmother engage in when I was a girl. When trouble hits, clean and cook. I put on my jeans, pinned up my hair and prepared the house for Peter's return, vacuuming and dusting and polishing to keep from brooding on the mess my willingness to listen to Bobby Templeton had generated.

After I finished cleaning, I went down the street and picked up ingredients for Peter's favorite meal—fennel and onions from the greengrocer's, salmon filets from Giuffre's fish market and white wine from Martignetti's. One bottle to cook with and one bottle to drink.

I was carrying my shopping bags up the stairs when my mother opened her door. Her arms were folded across her chest.

"I'm happy to see you back."

"Just to let you know, I had every intention of coming home."

"Have you talked to Vanessa since you got back from New York?"

"Vanessa isn't speaking to me right now, although apparently she's had no problem airing my life to anyone who'll listen. Who else knows? Aunt Bella in Albany? Father Dom?"

"Toni! She's your daughter, and this escapade of yours affects her, too!"

"It's not an escapade! Look, I've got to get the fish in the refrigerator. If you still need to tell me how terrible I am, then come upstairs instead of yelling at me on the landing."

"I'm not yelling at you. And I don't think you're a terrible person." She was following me up the stairs, taking one of my bags.

In my kitchen she helped put things away.

"You've been cleaning."

"Thanks for noticing. I learned it from my mother." I tried to smile.

"How about a cup of tea?" She already had the kettle in her hand.

I was going to refuse, tell her I had work to do. But I knew that sooner or later she'd manage to have this conversation with me. My mother was indefatigable. She gave up on nothing and no one.

"Sure," I said, and let her bustle around getting cups and tea bags.

"Listen, sweetheart, I'm only trying to tell you what I see happening to you and what I've learned from what's happened to me. I'm so proud of you! Look at what you've accomplished in your life. You've raised three wonderful children, married a man who adores you and made a name for yourself with your beautiful artwork. I see all this, the Toni sitting here at the table with me, and I compare you to the Toni of nineteen years ago, weighed down by the burdens of marriage to a selfish, immature man who didn't love you."

I opened my mouth to protest, but she held up her hand.

"Don't tell me he loved you. A man who loves doesn't do what he did. That's why I cannot understand why you would even listen to him, let alone do 'business' with him, as you put it. He has no right to even ask you!"

I didn't know how to answer my mother. I saw so many shades of gray where she only saw black and white. I couldn't explain to her what I was feeling because I didn't understand it myself. The memories of the Bobby who'd once drawn me into his orbit were jumbled together with those of the Bobby who, as my mother so accurately and painfully described, had not loved me, and the Bobby who was so deeply troubled by his mental illness and addiction to alcohol.

"I feel pity for him."

"You can't save him, Toni. You tried before. All it did was drag you down. Why do you think you can help him now? Believe me, this will bring you heartache. And it will drive a wedge between you and Peter. Even if it's only a stupid picture. Because that won't be enough. He'll keep taking more. Please, sweetheart."

She stretched across the table to squeeze my hand.

"I hear you, Ma. I know you're speaking your heart, and I understand in my head what you're saying. I'll think about it. I promise."

"I've got to get downstairs. Why don't you eat with us tonight? I'm making tuna and olives with polenta."

"Thanks, Ma. But my stomach's upset. I'm just going to have some chicken soup and try to get a good night's sleep. The daybed in the studio isn't the most comfortable place to spend the night."

"Okay. I'm not surprised you don't feel good. But listen, before you go to bed, call Vanessa. You may think she doesn't want to talk to you, but she needs to hear from you."

She kissed me and left me alone in my darkening kitchen.

When the phone rang, I thought it would be Peter or Vanessa and steeled myself for more lectures and outrage. But when I heard the voice on the other end, I broke into a sweat.

It was Bobby. And he'd been drinking.

"Toni. I needed to hear your voice. Ever since I saw you in New York you've been on my mind."

"Bobby, don't start." I didn't want to hear this.

"You're the best thing that ever happened to me. It took me a long time to understand that, but now I know. I'm not asking you to take me back into your life, but I really need you to listen to me just this once. Just for tonight."

"Bobby, that's what you said the other night. I can't give you what you're looking for. If you were Catholic I'd tell you to go to a priest for absolution. But I can't, I *won't*, absolve you."

He started to sob.

"Where are you? Can I call someone to help you?" I was concerned that he was alone, in despair.

"I'm in Boston."

I went rigid. *Don't go to him,* all the voices in my brain were screaming. If you step out your door, you're stepping into hell. *Do I abandon him, the way he abandoned me and the kids?* I answered back. *He needs help.*

And then I knew what I had to do.

"Where in Boston?"

"I'm at the Langham Hotel."

"Meet me at the bar in half an hour."

I hung up the phone. But instead of leaving for the hotel I dialed Mike's number, praying he was home. He and Graham had bought and renovated a town house in the South End before gentrification—one of the many collaborations they'd successfully pulled off over their years together.

I was relieved when he answered.

"I need an enormous favor from you," I said.

"You sound like you've seen Nana's ghost on the stairs. What's the matter?"

"Come with me on an errand. An errand of mercy. I need your moral support and I need you to help me keep my resolve."

"I've already got my jacket on. Where should I meet you?"

I walked quietly down the stairs. I didn't want to explain myself to my mother. Once on the street I headed toward the financial district and the hotel. When Mike arrived, I told him what I intended to do.

"And my role in this drama?"

"Keep me in sight and make sure I walk away when I'm finished."

"Do you think he might hurt you? Because if you do, I'm not letting you near him."

"No, he's not dangerous in that sense. But he can suck me into his suffering—he has already—and I have to put an end to his ability to do that."

"Good for you. I know you've been getting it from all sides of the family about this. But you had to come to this decision on your own. I've got your back, Toni. If you start to waver, just look across the room."

"Thanks, Mike. I knew I could count on you. And thanks for not adding to the chorus telling me what to do. Thanks for trusting me."

When we got to the Langham, I went to the bar first. Mike followed a few minutes later and took a seat where he could see me and Bobby couldn't see him.

Bobby was grasping an old-fashioned glass filled with bourbon when I slipped into the seat across from him. He looked as if he hadn't slept since I'd left him in New York.

He grabbed my hand as soon as I sat down.

"You don't know how much this means to me, that you've come. You haven't given up on me, like everyone else in my life."

"Bobby, I'm not *in* your life. I haven't been part of your life for nineteen years. More, if you consider how isolated we were from each other at the end."

"But you're here now."

"I'm here now to tell you what you need to hear. Not to forgive you or save you from whatever demons are clawing at your soul. Including that one." And I pointed to his glass. "The only person who can do that is you."

"But I can't do it on my own."

"You're right, Bobby."

"I knew you'd understand."

"Bobby, I understand that you need help. I understand that you're in pain. And I came here tonight to tell you that. You need help. But not from me. My artwork isn't going to change your life. My listening to you and comforting you isn't what you need."

"But you've already helped me, just by coming."

"Bobby, you need something I can't give you. You're an alcoholic. You suffer from depression. The forgiveness you're seeking has to come from yourself. Get into a program. Find a doctor. You are sick. And I can't heal you. I couldn't when we were married and I certainly can't now."

"I need you, Toni."

"No, Bobby. I'm not what you need. I might be a Band-Aid for some minor cut, but you're bleeding out. Look at yourself in the mirror tonight. And then get on a plane and go home."

I pushed my chair back and stood.

"Don't go! Please."

"No. I've said what I came to say. Anything more is point-less. Listen to me. Go back to Tennessee and do whatever you must to get well."

"Will you do the portraits?"

"No. Untangle your relationships with your kids in Ten-nessee instead of trying to preserve their images."

"What can I say to change your mind?"

"Nothing."

"Will you write? Can I call you?"

"No. No. When I walk out of here tonight I'm walking out of your life. I don't belong in it. And you don't belong in mine. Goodbye, Bobby."

I was on my feet and moving toward Mike.

"Toni, stop! I love you."

I kept walking. Mike put himself between Bobby and me, and we headed home.

We got to Salem Street and climbed the stairs arm in arm, as quietly as we had when we left. At the door to my place, Mike kissed me.

"Are you okay, sis, or do you want some company?"

"I'm fine. Set free, actually. Thanks. You're the best."

"I'm just returning the favor you did for me by accepting me when I came out." He smiled that sweet, embracing smile of his that's always made the world seem right, and went on down the stairs.

I called Vanessa as soon as I was in the door. The adrena-line that had propelled me to the Langham and through the conversation with Bobby was rapidly ebbing. I wasn't sure I had enough left to break through Vanessa's resistance *and* keep my own anger in abeyance at the complications she'd precip-itated by bringing everyone in the family into this mess. She answered on the second ring, and the brightness in her voice disappeared the moment I spoke.

"I don't have anything to say to you."

"I'm not asking you to. Just listen for a few minutes."

"I don't want to hear your explanations. I'll never understand how you can do this to us, so don't bother trying."

"No explanations, and no expectations. I just wanted to tell you that I told Bobby no tonight. No to the commission, no to his intrusion into my life. I won't let him back in."

Silence at the other end of the phone. I waited.

"Mom? I'm so sorry I opened the door to let him in!" She was crying.

"Oh, honey. This wasn't your fault!"

"But if I hadn't contacted him, he'd never have—"

"He'd have found another way. You did nothing to cause this, Vanessa. And now it's over."

"Really?"

"I promise."

"I'm so relieved. I was so scared you were going to leave us and go back to him."

"I will never leave you, Vanessa. Ever."

"Okay."

"I love you, sweetie. And now I've got to get some sleep."

The next morning I sat by the window in my bedroom, the eastern light illuminating the open page of the sketchbook in my hand. It'd been several months since I'd drawn anything new. Preparing for the show at Miles's gallery had involved translating the rough work of my notebooks into finished etchings and lithographs, and I'd put aside the daily discipline of the sketchbook. But my night of introspection at the studio had reminded me how important a record my sketches were—like a writer's journal.

My hand moved quickly on the page, the soft charcoal

pencil leaving traces that revealed the shape of my brother's arm draped protectively around my shoulders; my mother reaching across the table to stroke my hand. And then, emerging under my strokes, a face. Strong, chiseled, with eyes whose gaze was direct, open, vibrant. Peter's face.

An Open Book

WHENEVER PETER AND I traveled separately we didn't
see each other off or welcome the other back at the airport.
The North End was just on the other side of the tunnel from
Logan and it made more sense for the traveler to hop in a cab
and be home in ten or fifteen minutes. But this time I decided
I couldn't wait at home for the sound of his key in the door.
I wanted to see Peter's face when he walked out of customs
and throw my arms around him.

I was nervous. We hadn't spoken since the afternoon I'd
gotten back from New York, when he was so angry. I stood
with at least fifty other people clustered around the international arrivals gate. I realized that many of them were probably
the parents of the students Peter had been shepherding.

Finally, passengers began trickling out of customs trundling
their suitcases, weary from the long flight. Peter didn't see me
when he first emerged. Unlike the others who were scanning
faces for family or friend or lover, Peter was focused on getting
out of the building.

I called out to him and he turned. I didn't trust myself to
read the expression on his face. Was it relief that I was there

and hadn't run off with Bobby? Or questioning and suspicious that I'd shown up at the airport?

I moved toward him, needing to close the distance between us. An urgency fueled me. I was moving so swiftly that my knapsack was flying behind me. I hadn't closed it securely, and as I reached Peter my sketchbook fell out and landed open at his feet.

We both bent to pick it up. He touched it first and, as he started to close it, glanced at the open page. His own image.

His fingers traced the charcoal on the page. My fingers traced his face itself.

He closed the book, tucked it back in my knapsack and took me in his arms.

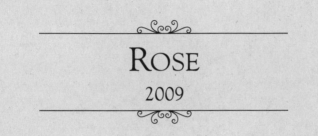

ROSE

2009

Epilogue

I DON'T THINK OF myself as an old woman. In my heart, I'm still the young bride sweeping out her first home on the bluff at Chaguaramas and setting out Thanksgiving dinner on plank tables in the sunlight.

I can't even count anymore how many Thanksgiving dinners I've cooked for my family. Some have been more memorable than others. This year was especially so. We had much to celebrate. Toni and Peter's anniversary. Al's survival from cancer. The christening of my first great-granddaughter. Even a trip to Washington to visit Marianne, Al Jr.'s old girl-friend, who lives there now with her family. I found Al Jr.'s name on the wall at the Vietnam Memorial, close to the beginning, and ran my fingers over the letters.

Manny went crazy with the food for Thanksgiving dinner. There's a reason *Boston Magazine* named him chef of the year and the *Globe* has given Paradiso four stars. It *was* paradise to eat that meal. Al and I sat at the head of the table, taking turns holding Olivia, Vanessa's baby. After she graduated from Harvard she went to Italy for two years and got a master's degree in Italian. We teased her about meeting an Italian boy and falling in love, and sure enough, that's what she did. It kills me that she's so far away, but she and Marcello come to Boston every year. Now, of course, with the baby we want to see them more often.

Al, thank God, got the best treatment at Dana–Farber, and beat kidney cancer five years ago. That's when we decided to make the most of what time we had left. We turned Paradiso over to the kids and moved to Bal Harbour in Florida. He still plays cards every afternoon and we go dancing on Saturday nights.

Toni and Peter are as much in love as ever. He retired in June and my bet is Toni will follow soon, now that Olivia has arrived. They've been talking about buying a place in Umbria to be near Vanessa, and I don't blame them.

Joey and Ben also got married. Joey to a nurse he met when Al was in the hospital; Ben to Jennifer Conti, who was in his fifth grade class at St. John's and has been his best friend ever since. Each couple has a son—Joey's Al, and Ben's Matthew.

Mike "came out" to the family a few years ago. Like me, most of them had figured it out. Even Al. I have to hand it to Al. Of all of us, it was hardest for him to accept. But the cancer changed him. Made him recognize what was precious in life. When Mike told us he and Graham were committed to each other, we both said they had our blessing.

We were surrounded by all of them at the table and, after grace, raised our glasses.

"Salute!" we said. "To life."

★ ★ ★ ★ ★

LINDA CARDILLO

Dancing on Sunday Afternoons

A Graziuccia *e* Federigo Cardillo
Per la vita!

Acknowledgments

I am so grateful, first of all, to the members of my family who were the caretakers of Graziuccia's and Federigo's letters: my parents, Lena and Fritzie Cardillo, and Aunt Susie Lauricella—as well as Aunt JoAnn Petrillo, whose kitchen-table conversations nourished my imagination.

I am blessed with a wonderful, supportive family: my husband, Stephan, who does countless loads of laundry and washes piles of dishes so that I can hole up in a library and write; my children, Luke, Nicola and Mark, who have been my champions, my techies, my fashion consultants and my photographers.

I am also indebted to my circle of Italian ladies in Springfield, Massachusetts—Christina Manzi, her daughter Rosa Anna Ronca and the assorted aunts, cousins and friends who fed me eggplant and meatballs and helped me translate many of the letters.

I thank my writing friends—Adele Bozza, Julie Winberg and Sharon Wright—who read, advised and encouraged me through many drafts and who asked the tough questions; and my agent Maura Kye-Casella, whose unfailing enthusiasm and insightful comments sustained and mentored me.

And finally, my deepest appreciation for my editor, Paula Eykelhof, who guided me through a rigorous process, mined the manuscript for the best material and helped me shape a compelling story.

Prologue

Two Husbands
Giulia D'Orazio
1983

I HAD TWO HUSBANDS—Paolo and Salvatore.

Salvatore and I were married for thirty-two years. I still live in the house he bought for us; I still sleep in our bed. All around me are the signs of our life together. My bedroom window looks out over the garden he planted. In the middle of the city, he coaxed tomatoes, peppers, zucchini—even grapes for his wine—out of the ground. On weekends, he used to drive up to his cousin's farm in Waterbury and bring back manure. In the winter, he wrapped the peach tree and the fig tree with rags and black rubber hoses against the cold, his massive, coarse hands gentling those trees as if they were his fragile-skinned babies. My neighbor, Dominic Grazza, does that for me now. My boys have no time for the garden.

In the front of the house, Salvatore planted roses. The roses I take care of myself. They are giant, cream-colored, fragrant. In the afternoons, I like to sit out on the porch with my coffee, protected from the eyes of the neighborhood by that curtain of flowers.

Salvatore died in this house thirty-five years ago. In the last months, he lay on the sofa in the parlor so he could be in the middle of everything. Except for the two oldest boys, all the children were still at home and we ate together every evening. Salvatore could see the dining-room table from the sofa, and he could hear everything that was said. "I'm not dead, yet," he told me. "I want to know what's going on."

When my first grandchild, Cara, was born, we brought her to him, and he held her on his chest, stroking her tiny head. Sometimes they fell asleep together.

Over on the radiator cover in the corner of the parlor is the portrait Salvatore and I had taken on our twenty-fifth anniversary. This brooch I'm wearing today, with the diamonds— I'm wearing it in the photograph also—Salvatore gave it to me that day. Upstairs on my dresser is a jewelry box, filled with necklaces and bracelets and earrings. All from Salvatore.

I am surrounded by the things Salvatore gave me, or did for me. But, God forgive me, as I lie alone now in my bed, it is Paolo I remember.

Paolo left me nothing. Nothing, that is, that my family, especially my sisters, thought had any value. No house. No diamonds. Not even a photograph.

But after he was gone, and I could catch my breath from the pain, I knew that I still had something. In the middle of the night, I sat alone and held them in my hands, reading the words over and over until I heard his voice in my head. I had Paolo's letters.

Chapter 1

The Cigar Box
Cara Serafini Dedrick
1983

THE PHONE CALL didn't come at two in the morning, but it might as well have. I was on my way out the door of my office at four, hoping to catch an early train out of Penn Station and make it home to New Jersey for an early start to my vacation. I run a catering company in Manhattan called Artichoke and in the last weeks of August my clients have retreated to their summer homes, giving me and my staff a breather before fall. Celeste, my secretary, waved to get my attention, receiver nestled between her ear and her capable shoulder.

"It's your mother."

"Tell her I'll call when I get home—got to make the 4:25."

"She says it can't wait. A family emergency."

My body stiffened and I could feel the color drain from my face. My mother was not the kind of woman who called with reports of every hospitalization or divorce or out-of-wedlock pregnancy in our large extended family. With eighteen aunts and uncles and twenty-nine first cousins, plus both grand-mothers, there was ample opportunity for a family emergency. But I trusted my mother's sense of what was urgent and what was merely news, and knew she wouldn't insist on talking to me now if it wasn't someone close. Had my father gone into diabetic shock? Was my brother in a car accident?

I turned back to my desk and picked up the phone. "Mom?"

"Cara, thank God you're still there! It's Nana."

My father's mother, Giulia, was a robust woman in her nineties who ran circles around most of us. Three weeks before, against the wishes of all eight of her children, she'd flown to Italy to be at the bedside of her dying older sister. Zia Letitia—we used the Italian form to refer to the aunts of my grandmother's generation—Zia Letitia had graciously managed to wait until Nana arrived before taking her last breath. After she died, Nana had assumed the task of arrang-ing her funeral and organizing her financial affairs. Zia Letitia had been a widow and her only son had died many years before, so there was no one left in the family to wrap up the loose ends of her long life except for Nana. As far as I knew, those tasks were almost finished and she was expected back early the next week.

"What's happened?" I couldn't imagine what could have dis-rupted my grandmother's determined and vigorous grasp on life.

"She fell last night. It was in Zia Letitia's house. She was alone, and no one found her until this morning. Emma, the woman who looked after Zia Letitia, called to let us know."

"Oh, my God! Is she all right? Where is she now?"

"They got her to a hospital in Avellino, but apparently she's broken her hip. She needs surgery. We thought we could fly her home, but the doctors there said it was too dangerous—

the risk of an embolism's too high. Which is why I'm calling you." So it was more than just to inform me of my grandmother's accident.

"What do you mean?"

"We don't want her to go through this alone. It was one thing for her to go off by herself to hold her sister's hand, but now it's simply out of the question. I'd go, but with Daddy needing dialysis every three days, there's no way I can leave him. Nobody else in the family has ever been to Italy—I don't think they even have passports.

"Honey, you've lived in Italy, you speak Italian, and she'd listen to you sooner than one of her children, anyway. I need you to say *yes* about this, especially for Daddy's sake. He's angry with her for going in the first place, angry with himself for letting her go, and now he's feeling helpless—although he won't admit it—because he can't go and rescue his mother. Will you do this, Cara?"

"Do you realize what you're asking me to do?" I groaned. I thought of the two weeks left of summer that I'd planned on spending with my kids. A week at the shore, then a week getting ready for school.

"If you're worried about the kids, I can look after them for a few days, and Paul and Jeannie offered to take them to her mother's house at the lake. There really is no one else who can do this, Cara. I know you think of Nana as formidable and indestructible, but she's in a precarious state."

I listened in silence, watching the minutes pass on the clock on my desk. I'd already missed any chance of making my train. I was both dismayed at my grandmother's situation and frustrated that the competence and independence I had developed in my life apart from my family were now the very things pulling me back. I did not want to go. But I knew I would. I fought the resentment that I was the one my mother had turned to—me, with a very full plate of full-time job and four children—when she could have asked my sister or my cousin, both younger, freer, teachers with summers off and no children. But I was also proud that she'd called on me, knowing she was right when she said I was the only one who could do this.

"I'll need to talk to Andrew and sort everything out with the kids. I'll ask Celeste to book me on a flight to Rome tomorrow and I'll take the train from there to Avellino. Do you have some contact information for me—the hospital, Emma?"

I heard my mother exhale in relief.

"Thank you, honey. I knew I could count on you. I've got all the numbers right here. Let me read them off to you."

I spent the next half hour writing down the information provided by my mother, phoning my husband and giving Celeste the task of getting me to Italy within the next forty-eight hours. I finally collapsed in a seat in the second-to-last car on the 5:43 to Princeton, scribbling lists to myself and trying to remember a language I had not spoken regularly in seventeen years.

The next afternoon, with my husband and children heading off to Beach Haven, my bag packed and my passport in my purse, I drove up to my parents' house in Mount Vernon, just outside New York City. When my mother had called Giulia that morning to tell her I was coming, Giulia had dictated a list for me—things to do, things to bring. I picked up the list and the key to Giulia's house from my parents and said my goodbyes, recognizing the gratitude in my father's eyes despite his gruff warnings about watching out for both my grandmother and myself.

I left my parents' neighborhood of manicured lawns and stately colonials and drove south to the neighborhood my grandmother had lived in since she'd arrived in America. I climbed the steep steps to Giulia's front porch, past the rose garden her husband Salvatore—my father's stepfather—had planted for her in the middle years of their marriage, well before I was born. With Giulia in Italy for the last three weeks, many of the blooms were long past their peak. Had Giulia been here, I know she would've trimmed the flopping, untidy heads.

I let myself in the front door, but not before glancing up and down this so-familiar street. To my right, a row of pale stucco houses, many of which Giulia owned. To my left, the beginnings of commerce—the butcher, the barber, Skippy's Bar & Grill—and on the corner, Our Lady of Victory elementary school. I remembered how one frigid November morning, when I was in kindergarten, I had dutifully exited in a silent, straight line as we'd been trained by the nuns to do when the fire alarm sounded. I'd been careful to line up along the side of the building, trying to keep still in the cold. It had been at that moment that Giulia had emerged from Lauricella's grocery store across the street and observed the shivering children and the sisters bundled in their black shawls.

"Where is your coat? How could that nun let you outside in this weather without your coat?" Giulia stood on the sidewalk and scolded me from across the street.

She was making a spectacle and I was mortified. The only modestly saving grace was that she was speaking in Italian, but her gesturing and agitation were clearly understood by the nuns and my classmates.

"Go back inside this minute and get your coat!"

I wanted to explain to her that this was a fire drill, but was afraid to speak, afraid to break the rules so dramatically presented to us by Sister Agatha as a matter of life and death. Six hundred children had burned to death at Our Lady of the Angels in Chicago because they hadn't followed the rules.

My grandmother knew none of this. She knew only that her grandchild was shivering and the woman responsible for her was ignoring that.

I had watched in horror as Giulia crossed the street, removing her own coat and ready to wrap it around me, when the bell rang and we began to retrace our steps back into the building.

Now, inside Giulia's house, I adjusted to the dim light of the long front hall. The portrait of the Sacred Heart, his hands spreading his cloak to reveal his throbbing scarlet heart, still hung in its place of honor above the radiator.

The house smelled of ammonia and wax and lemon oil. I was sure Giulia had scrubbed and polished meticulously before she left, leaving the house spotless, reflecting her own sense of order.

My sandaled feet echoed in the silent house as I walked down the hall. Although what I'd come for was upstairs in Giulia' s bedroom, I went first to the kitchen.

Check the sink, the freezer, the pilot light on the stove, she had instructed. Make sure the back door is secured. Dominic Grazza, her neighbor who was supposed to be watching the house, wasn't as reliable as she would like.

But all was as it should be. I drew myself a glass of water and sat in the red vinyl chair at the small table tucked into the alcove formed by the chimney wall. The table was only large enough for two. Through an archway was the larger table where supper was served, but at noon, when it had only been my grandmother and me, it was at this small table that we'd eaten together. I attended the morning session of kindergarten and came to her house every school day for lunch and to spend the afternoon. She always had ready a warm bowl of her homemade chicken soup or *pasta e fagioli*.

After lunch, when the dishes were dried and put away, I had remained at the table, my back against the warm wall, and watched and listened as women from the neighborhood came for my grandmother's magic.

We called it the "eyes"—her spells to ward off headaches and stomach cramps; to bring on a late period; to counteract whatever curse had been set upon the suffering soul knocking at my grandmother's back door.

It wasn't just the immigrants who came. My own mother, my aunts, women who worked in banks and offices and got dressed in suits and stockings and high heels every day, made their way to her kitchen. There she'd lay her hands on them and dispel the pain with her incantations. When I was sick, the fever and nausea and loneliness flew from my troubled body into my grandmother's open and welcoming arms.

Later in the afternoon, she always went upstairs to sleep, exhausted and without words.

I would retreat to the living room, knowing it was time to be quiet, and watch "The Mickey Mouse Club" until my father came to pick me up at the end of the day.

My afternoons with Giulia were an arrangement put in place because my own neighborhood had no Catholic school. Sending me to kindergarten in a public school was not an option in our family, so I spent the first year of my education in Giulia's parish until my family moved uptown. Everyone seemed happy with the solution, especially my mother, home with two younger children and relieved of the burden of getting me to and from school every day.

I finished my water, carefully rinsed and dried my glass and replaced it in the cupboard. My responsibilities in the kitchen were fulfilled, and I walked slowly up the stairs to the back of the house, where Giulia's bedroom overlooked the backyard and the garden. On her dresser were propped more images of saints. In front of them were three small red glass pots holding votive candles. It was the first time I'd been in the house when Giulia wasn't there, and it was a disturbing reminder of her absence that the candles were unlit. I pulled out Giulia's list and began to open drawers, tugging at the wood swollen with August humidity. Her checkbook and accounts ledger were in the top drawer, as expected. I had to hunt for the sweater she thought she'd need now that the evening air in the mountains was beginning to chill with the approach of September. A few more small articles of clothing were easier to find. The last item on the list was identified simply as a "cigar box" that was supposed to be in the bottom drawer under some bed linens. I was expecting another set of the flower-sprigged percale sheets and pillowcases that were on her neatly made bed, but these bed linens were heavy white cotton, elaborately tucked and embroidered with Giulia's large and graceful monogram. I had never seen them on her bed. Small packets of cedar were scattered in the drawer and the pungent smell indicated to me that the drawer had not been opened in a long time. I lifted the linens and found a boxlike shape wrapped in another embroidered cloth. When I unwrapped the cloth, I saw that I had indeed found the cigar box.

It was papered in garish yellow and brown with the portrait of some nineteenth-century barrel-chested tobacco mogul on the cover, and a Spanish label. The box had once held Cuban cigars, but I was sure it wasn't cigars I was bringing to Giulia.

I sat on the floor and carefully lifted the cover. Inside the box were stacks of letters on pale blue notepaper, each stack tied with a thin strand of satin ribbon. I could see that the letters had been written in a flowing hand in Italian and signed *Paolo,* the father my father had been too young to know, the grandfather whose red hair I had inherited.

I closed the box, feeling I'd already gone too far, that I had violated the privacy of a very private woman. Why she would want me to remove these letters from what appeared to be a hiding place and carry them across the Atlantic to her was both perplexing and intriguing. The woman who was asking me to do this was not the woman I knew my grandmother to be— the matriarch of our very large family, who had not only her sons and daughters, but her nieces and nephews, grown men and women in their fifties and sixties, listening to her and deferring to her as if they were still children; the businesswoman who'd asked me to collect her mail as well as her checkbook so she could manage her real-estate investments from her hospital bed; the woman who could be counted on to have a sharp opinion and directive about everything that touched the lives of her children and grandchildren.

Perhaps because I'd been a baby when her husband Salvatore had died and I had only known Giulia as a widow, I could not fathom her ever being in love. I knew, of course, that she'd been married before Salvatore to Paolo Serafini. But that had been long ago, and whatever traces of him remaining in her memory were well hidden. We did not even have a photograph of Paolo.

Giulia had never seemed to have much use for love. She had warned me away from romantic entanglements more than once when I was a teenager.

"Stay away from Joey Costello," she told me one evening as we were shelling peas on her front porch. I was thirteen; Joey lived next door to her. He was a year older, full of the swagger and bravado of the good-looking Italian teenage boy. But he had noticed me and was paying attention to me in ways that I, bookish and reserved, found thrilling.

"He's nothing but trouble. You don't need to be hanging around the likes of him. At the very least, you'll get a reputation, like that *putana* of a sister he has. And at the worst, he'll break your heart as soon as somebody who can sway her hips better than you walks by him. You're too smart, Cara *mia*. Don't waste your time on boys like that."

Later, when I was sixteen and spending a week with her while my parents were away, I developed a crush on a neighbor who lived nearby, one of her tenants. He was married and in his twenties, with two small children. But he did chores for Giulia around the garden and the house, so he was around to talk to as he fixed a faucet or dug up some rosebushes she wanted to transplant. He was cute and funny and attentive and, in the short time I'd been there, it seemed to me he was finding quite a few things to do for Giulia. When his wife went to visit her mother with the kids, I suggested to my grandmother that we invite him to Sunday dinner.

"Phil's all alone today. Wouldn't it be nice to ask him to eat with us?" I was trying to sound like the gracious lady of the manor, bestowing kindness on the hired help, rather than the infatuated teenager I was, looking for any reason to be in his presence. I was nonchalant, mentioning it as an afterthought as she and I cleaned up after breakfast.

Giulia looked me in the eye, put her hands on her hips, and said, "Absolutely not. Don't think I don't know what's going on in your head. He's a married man. He stays in his house and eats what his wife left for him, and you put your daydreams in the garbage where they belong."

And that was that. I spent the day sulking at the lost opportunity and marveling at Giulia's ability to sense even the most subtle vibrations of sexual attraction. She was the watchdog at the gates of my virginity, the impenetrable shield that would keep me from becoming a tramp.

Now I gathered up Giulia's possessions and stowed them in the zippered tote bag I planned to take onboard the plane.

After a final glance around the room, I shut the door and headed down the stairs and out to my car. I pulled away from the curb and the memories and headed for the airport and Italy.

Chapter 2

Journey to the Mezzogiorno

THE CACOPHONY OF THE Naples train station assaulted me as soon as I stepped off the express train from Rome. Announcements of departing trains reverberated across the vaulted space; mothers scolded misbehaving children; whistles shrieked; a group of yellow-shirted boys kicked a soccer ball near the far end of Platform 22.

As I adjusted the strap of my bag, I also adjusted my mental state—from efficient New York manager and organized mother of four—to Italian. It was more than recalling the lyrical language that had surrounded me in Giulia's house. I knew I had to pour myself quickly into the fluid, staccato pace of Campania in August or I would be trampled—by the surging population, the Vespas leaping curbs, the suspicion of strangers and by my own sense of oppression.

I knew this because I'd been here seventeen years before, a bright-eyed high-school art student who'd spent the summer in the rarefied atmosphere of Florence, living in a *cinquecento* villa, painting in the Uffizi on Mondays when it was closed to the hordes of summer tourists, reading Dante and Boccaccio. I had believed that I knew Italy. But then I had come south, to visit Zia Letitia.

I had traveled by rail then as well, through Rome to Naples. A stifling heat had encroached on the overcrowded train as it journeyed farther south, toward an Italy that I didn't recognize. The blue-greens and purples of the Tuscan landscape, warmed by a honeyed light, had given way to an unrelenting sunshine that had seared the earth to an ocher barrenness.

Everything I saw seemed to be the same color—the rough-hewn cliffs, the crumbling houses, the worn faces.

When I'd arrived at midday in Naples—sweaty and cranky—I felt myself to be in a foreign country. For the first time in my life, I had felt menaced—by the drivers in minuscule Fiats who ignored traffic signals, by the barricaded expressions of the people massing and knotting around me, by the heat and clamor and stench that had so unraveled the beauty and civility of this once-splendid city. The life of Naples was in the streets—raw, intemperate, flamboyant— and to the eyes of strangers, emotionally closed and hostile.

That day seventeen years ago, I had escaped on the two o'clock bus to Avellino, arriving two hours later in front of a bar named the Arcobaleno. In contrast to the press of humanity in Naples, a melancholy emptiness greeted me here. In the bar, where I bought a Coke and sought a telephone, I was the only woman. Two old men in the corner interrupted their card game to stare openly; the younger men, playing pinball, were more surreptitious but watched just as closely.

I called a phone number given to me by Giulia to make arrangements with a distant relative who could take me to Letitia. But the woman who answered was irritable. She had no time and could not help me. I would have to manage on my own. Take the bus, she barked. Just tell the driver you need to go to Venticano. And she hung up.

Shaken and feeling increasingly alone, I'd found a bus that could take me up the mountain. Later than I'd hoped, the driver cranked the door closed and began the laborious climb out of the valley. He'd brought the bus to a halt in a deserted piazza and thrust his chin at the door to announce my destination. Within seconds I stood alone in the road, facing shuttered houses and an overwhelming sense of abandonment. Why had I even considered making this journey? I had naively traversed half the length of Italy expecting to be welcomed in my ancestral home, but instead the doors were locked and no one was willing to acknowledge me as their own.

With only Zia Letitia's name—no address—I had approached a woman darning in the doorway of a nearby house, whose wary eyes had been upon me since I'd descended from the bus.

"I am looking for Signora Letitia Rassina," I had explained, proud of my flawless High Italian, the only thing that stood between me and panic.

"You come from the north." It was a statement, spat out in distrust and contempt, not a question requiring confirmation.

"I studied in Firenze, but I come from America. I am the granddaughter of Signora Rassina's sister." Unwittingly, I had uttered the magic formula.

The guardedness and suspicion fled from her face. She took me by the arm.

"Come, I'll show you where the *signora* lives."

As we turned to walk down the hill, I saw faces appearing at suddenly unshuttered windows and heard voices calling out to the woman. Within minutes, nearly thirty people crowded around us, jostling for a glimpse of the Americana as we arrived at Letitia's house.

The house—ancient, once elegant—presented facade to the tumult in the street below. No one respo our energetic knocks and shouts.

"She must be sleeping. Giorgio, go around and get Emma."

"Emma takes care of your aunt, and she has a key to the house," she explained to me.

A few minutes later, smoothing down what seemed to be a hastily donned black dress, a middle-aged woman had hustled breathlessly after Giorgio with a key ring in her hand.

"No one sent me word from America that someone was coming!" She was both suspicious and injured to have been left out of the preparations for my visit.

Horrified that I'd been allowed by my family to travel alone, she was nevertheless satisfied that I was indeed Giulia's grand-daughter. With a shriek of pleasure, she inserted an iron key into the massive arched doorway of the house.

Inside was a musty vestibule, lit by the late-afternoon sun streaming through a window on the rear wall where a stone staircase led to a landing on the second floor. Emma led me up the stairs. Behind us came the rest of the villagers.

Once again, our knocks were met by silence. Emma called out Letitia's name in a loud voice. "She's old. She doesn't hear so well anymore," she murmured to me.

Finally, the door opened and a woman appeared, her face marked by confusion. She stared uncomprehending into my face. I stared back at a woman who could have been my grand-mother's twin. Letitia's confusion receded as she listened to me identify myself, ignoring the commotion that surrounded her. Then she reached out and stroked the opal hanging from my ear. It was Giulia's, and she'd given it to me on my sixteenth birthday. I'd been wearing the earrings all summer, and they had become so much a part of me that I'd forgotten their origins.

"Giulia's earrings," she whispered. "You are my blood."

Letitia had pulled me into the apartment, embracing me with the mingled old-woman aromas of garlic and anise and must. She sent Emma down to the shop to purchase ingredients for dinner and told the villagers lining the stairs to go home to their own kitchens. Alone together, we sat with a glass of very strong wine as she hung on every word I brought her of her distant family.

After dinner a group of young women from the village had arrived at the door to take me for the evening *passeggiata*—a walk around the village. Letitia had shooed me away with them. Severia, the young woman who'd been my tour guide, was the schoolteacher in the village. I was stunned when she told me she was only twenty. Like Emma, and nearly every other woman in the village, she was dressed in a severe black dress that extended below her knees. She wore her hair in the style of my mother's generation.

The village was a grid of two or three streets clinging to the side of the mountain. Only the main road from Avellino that continued farther up the mountain was paved. Few of the stone buildings had electricity, and all of them showed the ravages of centuries of wind and earthquake. Dust swirled at our feet as we crossed the meager piazza, shared with a goatherd leading his scraggly flock back to a lean-to for the evening. Severia had pointed out with pride the small schoolroom where she taught from first through sixth grade. If parents wanted more schooling for their children, they had to send them down the mountain to Avellino.

I had recognized that what I was seeing and the lives that were enclosed here were little different from what Giulia had experienced as a girl. In that instant, I had understood that it might have been my life, as well.

"Thank God," I had whispered to myself. "Thank God that my grandmother got out."

The next morning I left, as I had come, on a dusty bus that had stopped when Emma flagged it down. She'd packed me a cloth-wrapped sandwich of bread and pungent cheese, with some tomatoes and figs from the garden behind Letitia's stone house. She had clucked and worried about the long trip ahead of me to Milan and my flight home and had given me stern instructions to speak to no one on the way to Naples.

"Girls alone disappear," she had said.

As the bus pulled away, I had looked out the window. Letitia stood waving from her balcony. She had changed from her morning housecoat to a green silk dress. In her hand was a lace-trimmed handkerchief that she dabbed at her eyes.

I stood now in the rotunda of the Naples *Stazione Centrale,* about to make the same journey. This time, instead of depending on SITA buses to get me up to the mountains, I had reserved a car. But before picking it up, I detoured to the flower shop, hoping to find something that would survive until I reached Avellino. The saleswoman recommended a potted hydrangea and wrapped it extravagantly in layers of purple cellophane and a massive bow, wishing my grandmother *buona sante* as she handed me the gift with a nod of approval.

Armed with a map and directions outlined for me by the clerk at Avis, I located my Fiat in the parking lot, took a deep breath and plunged into the late Sunday afternoon traffic, keeping an eye out for the Autostrada symbol and signs for the A16, the east-west highway that connected Naples with Bari on the Adriatic. About a quarter of the way across the ankle of Italy's boot, I knew I'd leave the highway and head south into the mountains and Avellino.

I was tired and hungry. My jet lag was catching up with me. A part of me longed to stop at the Agip motel on the broad avenue leading toward the entrance ramp of the Autostrada.

Its familiar sign, a black, six-legged, fire-breathing mythical creature on a yellow background, beckoned like a McDonald's Golden Arch, promising a cheap, clean room. But Giulia was expecting me at the hospital Sunday evening, and even though there'd be little I could do for her at that time—no surgeon to confer with, only a night nurse on duty—I pushed myself past the fatigue to be at my grandmother's side.

The highway had not existed seventeen years ago, and I was astounded that I was able to cover the hundred kilometers to Avellino in under an hour, compared to the nearly three hours it had taken the bus on my last trip. When I exited the highway, a sign welcomed me in four different languages.

When I drove onto the grounds of the hospital of San Giuseppe Moscati, the doctor saint of Naples, it was nearly sunset.

I grabbed the hydrangea and my tote bag from the backseat and headed into the hospital, moving from the brilliance and shimmer of light and heat that had surrounded me all day into shadowed dimness. Everything in the lobby was in shades of brown, like the sepia tones Renaissance artists used to create the sinopia, the preliminary sketch under a fresco. The highly polished linoleum, the wooden paneling that climbed three-quarters of the way up the whitewashed walls, the tattered seats in the waiting room, even the habit of the Franciscan nun sitting at the reception desk, created an aura of subdued and quiet sanctuary.

She looked up as I approached. When I asked for my grandmother, she jumped up.

"Oh, we've been expecting you! The *signora* was telling everyone that you were coming. Let me call Reverend Mother. She can explain your grandmother's condition before you go up to see her."

Within minutes, Reverend Mother, an energetic and ageless

woman and the director of the hospital, swooped into the lobby and kissed me on both cheeks.

"Can I get you some tea, my dear, while we talk about your grandmother? Come, let's go to my office."

I sank into the chair she offered and gratefully accepted the hot cup of tea that she produced within a minute.

On her desk was a file on which I could read my grandmother's name. I was beginning to feel—with some relief, given my fatigue—that Giulia had things under control here, if she had the hospital so well prepared for my arrival.

"Your grandmother is quite a formidable woman, as I'm sure you know. She was very busy the last two days keeping us all informed of your coming. I believe she feels a need to protect and watch out for you. But I must tell you, my dear, she needs *you* to watch over *her,* although she'd be the last to admit it. She's in a weakened state because of the night she spent alone after her fall—we've been replenishing her fluids with an IV, but at her age, even twelve hours of dehydration can be damaging. She was disoriented when she got here. She has recovered her faculties enough to issue edicts and lists, I understand, but I have to caution you that your grandmother has a long road ahead to recover from this fall. In many cases, with patients of this age, we would not even be considering a hip replacement."

I absorbed Reverend Mother's report in silence, gradually comprehending the gravity of my grandmother's condition.

"I hadn't realized how serious this fall was," I murmured. "I naively believed I was asked to be here as a companion to her."

"I'm not trying to overwhelm you and burden you so soon after your arrival, but I felt it was important for you to understand the severity of her injury and to warn you before you see her. She's quite bruised and also very angry with herself for falling. We've also had to increase her morphine dosage because of the pain, so she may begin to drift.

"The surgeon will be in tomorrow morning at eight o'clock and can give you the details about her operation. More than likely he will operate on Tuesday morning."

I nodded, understanding that I would need to be an advocate for my grandmother.

"May I ask you if you've booked a place to stay? If not, I'd like to encourage you to stay here with your grandmother. We can have a cot set up in her room. In my opinion, it would be a blessing for her to have you so close."

I set down my teacup because my hand was shaking. With four children, I'd seen my share of emergency rooms, and my youngest had been hospitalized for four days with pneumonia, so I was no stranger to the emotional fragility caused by illness and the need for a family member to be close at hand. But despite my confidence in Giulia's ability to control even this situation, Reverend Mother had quickly and authoritatively set me straight.

I leaned my elbows on her desk and put my head in my hands. I felt the adrenaline of the last two days seeping out of me and tears of exhaustion and doubt well up. Reverend Mother came around her desk with a handkerchief and put an arm around me.

"Everything Signora D'Orazio has said about you convinces me that your family has sent the right person. Why don't I show you where you can wash your face and then let's go see your grandmother."

Once again, she whisked me down the hall, this time to the ladies' room. When I was ready, we took the elevator up to the orthopedic floor. As we passed open doors, I saw and heard clusters of people gathered around patients' beds, family members taking advantage of the Sunday-evening visiting hours, and was relieved that now Giulia would have someone at her bedside, too, even if what I could offer was simply a voice and a face from home.

Reverend Mother knocked at a partially opened door.

"Signora D'Orazio, she's here! Your granddaughter is here!"

I willed a smile to my face and walked into the room.

"Nana," I said. "It's me, Cara."

She turned toward the door and reached out her hand. I was glad Reverend Mother had prepared me, but even so, her bruised and swollen face and the black-and-blue marks on her arm appalled me. She looked as if someone had beaten her, and then I remembered the stone steps in Letitia's house.

I went to her, put the hydrangea on the floor and threw my arms around her, careful of the IV and reluctant to hold her too tightly for fear of hurting her sore body.

"How good you are to be here!" she whispered.

I sat on the side of her bed and she stroked my hair, by now flying out of its ponytail. She rubbed my bare arms, as if assuring herself that I was truly there.

Reverend Mother left us, letting me know that she was going to order the cot.

Shortly afterward, Giulia's supper tray arrived. When the nun bringing the food saw that I was there, she said she'd call down to the kitchen and have them send something for me. In the meantime, I busied myself with cutting meat and buttering bread for Giulia. She waved me away when I lifted a spoonful of soup to her mouth.

"I didn't break my arm, for God's sake. Just help me sit up a little higher so I don't dribble all over myself."

This was the Giulia I knew, and it was a relief to have her scold me.

By the time we'd both eaten, an aide had delivered a cot, sheets and pillows and made up a bed by Giulia's side. I went down to my car and retrieved my suitcase and then stole a few minutes to peel off the clothes I'd been wearing for two days and take a shower in a bathroom down the hall from Giulia's room that the aide had pointed out to me.

When I rejoined Giulia, she'd had her evening medication, and some of the strain I'd seen in her face was eased. She beamed at me. I was now scrubbed, my hair neatly braided, and wearing fresh clothes.

"Sweetheart, did you bring the things I asked for?"

I patted the tote bag. "It's all in here, Nana. Do you want anything now?"

She wavered, but then threw up her hands as if surrendering to an irresistible need.

"The box. The cigar box. You found it, where I said to look?"

I nodded and dug it out of the bag. "Here it is, Nana."

She took the box and stroked the outside of it, tracing the colorful image of Francisco Fonseca. Then she held the box to her breast, cradling it with her eyes shut. At last, she lifted the cover and stared at the stacks of letters before slipping one out from its ribbon binding. She closed the box and brought the single letter to her lips before unfolding it.

For a few moments I watched as she scanned the lines. I thought she was reading, but then she turned to me in restless exasperation.

"My eyes are no good at night. I can't see the words. Sweetheart, you've done so much, just to come, but do this for me. Read to me. Read me the letter."

She handed me the blue sheet of paper.

I took it hesitantly.

"Are you sure you want me to read this, Nana?"

She looked at me and the letter in my hand, agitation rising in her as she struggled between the absolute sanctity of the message in the letter and the urgency she felt to hear it again.

"I need to hear it tonight, Cara. Go ahead. I trust you."

And so I began to read the words on the page—an elegant, flowing Italian script. At first, my brain attempted to translate silently for myself as I read the Italian out loud, but after a few minutes, I stopped trying to decipher the meaning and simply pronounced the words. I felt as if I were singing a song whose soul and emotion were in the music, not the lyrics.

Dearest Giulia,

Don't forget what I asked you last night—to find five or ten minutes before noon. I have the most important things to communicate to you. If you only knew how much I suffered this morning, to go to work without even seeing you or telling you that I love you.

I am crazy with love. I have never loved with so much devotion. You are the star that shines brightly, a sparkling beam, and you adorn my poor heart with infinite madness. Now that I am writing to you, I believe I have you near me. It seems as if we are talking. How I long to embrace you!

I cover your face with my tears, and dry them with my kisses.

Most faithfully,

Paolo

When I finished, I glanced up. Giulia's eyes were closed and the agitation that had disturbed her earlier was gone. I gently removed the cigar box from her lap and put it on her bedside table. As I reached to turn out the light, she stirred and touched my wrist.

"Grazie, figlia mia."

I slipped into the cot, the words of my grandfather Paolo echoing in my head.

Chapter 3

The Beginning

THE NEXT MORNING I accustomed myself to the week-day pace of San Giuseppe Moscati. Breakfast trays, medication, bath, changes of bed linen. I could see the distress in my grandmother's face, the tension in her body, as the procession of nurses' aides and nuns moved in and out of her room. She scolded a cleaning woman who attempted to move the cigar box of letters that I had placed on the bedside table.

"I'll put it in a safe place, Nana," I reassured her as the bustle around her continued. "We can read more later, when it's not so busy."

The surgeon showed up around ten. He was in his late thirties, a trim, athletic-looking man, wearing a stylish blue shirt under his white coat. His eyes, also blue, conveyed intelligence and compassion. After he'd checked on my grandmother, I conferred with him in the hall, along with Reverend Mother and the sister in charge of the orthopedic ward.

He had scheduled Giulia's surgery for Tuesday morning and felt she'd need at least ten days of recuperation before I could take her home. He explained the details of the operation and his expectations for her recovery. I brought up my concerns about her medication and the discomfort I was witnessing, and he agreed to make adjustments, giving the sisters some latitude in monitoring her painkillers. Within ten minutes he was gone.

Before returning to Giulia's room, I leaned against the wall in the corridor and considered what I had just heard. Ten days. This was more than I'd bargained for. More than I thought I could handle. I chafed at missing my family and our long-awaited week at the beach; I worried about upcoming projects at work; I wondered how I'd fill the long hours sitting at Giulia's bedside. But I'd made my choice. I'd said yes, I could do this. I walked back into Giulia's room.

She turned her head as I pushed open the door and she smiled. "I was wondering where you were, sweetheart. I thought maybe I'd only dreamed you were here. But then I saw your valise in the corner and I told myself, 'You may be an old woman, but you're not a confused one.'"

I glanced at her IV and assured myself that it was flowing smoothly. Then I sat in the chair by her bedside. We talked about what the doctor had told me and I pressed her to be vocal when she was in too much pain.

"Don't suffer in silence, Nana. He's written orders to give you more painkillers if you need them, so speak up."

"I don't want to be in a haze, not knowing what's going on around me. Letitia didn't even know I was there at the end."

"This isn't the end for you, Nana! You have a broken hip, not a terminal disease. Dr. Campobasso can replace it and you'll walk again, back in your own home."

"Okay. Okay. But if I start babbling like my crazy cousin Elena, you make them reduce the morphine. I'd rather have a little pain than be seeing visions at the foot of my bed."

I smiled and promised her as I stroked her hand. As I did so, her clenched fingers released their hold on the bedcovers.

"How about a cup of tea and I'll read you another letter?"

She drew my hand to her lips and kissed it.

I went down the hall to the ward kitchen and poured two cups of tea into china cups and brought them back to her room on a tray. When she was settled, I retrieved the box and passed it to her so she could select a letter. She spent some time sifting through the fragile sheets. None of the letters were dated, and the envelopes had no postage or street address, only her name in a flourishing, emphatic script.

She finally pulled one out and gave it to me.

"This one." She leaned her head back and closed her eyes and I began to read.

Adorata Giulia,

I cannot explain in words how my heart beats for you. I dream of you all the time. If you love me as I love you, we would never suffer. We would always be happy. You have become the owner of my heart. I am yours. How can I give back all the love you show me? My love for you grows day by day and nothing can stop it, not even the anger and disapproval of your family. What have I done to these people that they don't want me?

My heart is full of love for you. I adore you and want to kneel at your feet. I will love you always, in spite of what others say. I await your reply.

Paolo

I folded the letter again. Who was this passionate, intemperate man whose blood I carried in my veins? I gazed at my grandmother, the woman he had loved so desperately, who had so consumed him.

"Tell me about my grandfather, Nana. Why did he write you these letters?"

"We had secrets in those days, Paolo and I. Secrets we kept hidden, concealed. But that wasn't the beginning. The beginning was open and innocent, because I was not aware of what lay ahead—with him or my family. I was just a girl. A girl newly arrived in America who didn't want to be there. I believed my parents were punishing me by sending me to America. It was killing me, breaking my heart, to leave Italy."

She turned her face to the window; the late-morning light filtered through white curtains. Beyond lay the rock-strewn hills of her childhood.

"The beginning, the girl I was when I met Paolo, started out there." She thrust out her chin and gestured toward the window.

"My own grandmother Giuseppina was a *maga*. I suppose now people would call her a sorceress," Giulia began, and I listened.

Chapter 4

─◆─◎◎◎─◆─

The Convent of Santa Margareta
Giulia

IN MY GRANDMOTHER Giuseppina's garden grew the plants she mixed into her medicines; in her head lived the magic words she sang to release her spells; in her fingertips danced the powers she used to heal. She cured the pains and the sorrows of those who came to her, who asked her to speak for them to the saints.

She was known outside our village of Venticano. People came from Pietradefusi and Pano di Greci, some even from as far as Avellino. She turned no one away.

I have a distant memory—sometimes I think it was a dream. In it, Giuseppina, speaking to my mother, raised her very dark eyebrows and nodded in my direction. "I'm watching that one."

I was three years old, feeling only Giuseppina's eyes—loving and burning—upon me. Not long after, my mother was confined to bed with the twins she was carrying and everyone was sure she would lose. Giuseppina came that day with her daily infusion for my mother, which she always swallowed reluctantly. Giuseppina saw the state of affairs: my mother exhausted, sleepless, with barely enough will to get herself through the pregnancy, let alone pay attention to the youngest of her six children. My brother Claudio was the oldest, followed by my sisters, Letitia, Philippina (whom we called Pip), and Domitilla (whom we called Tilly) and then my brother Aldo and me. Even with my father's sister, Pasqualina, helping in the household, this seventh pregnancy was tapping all my mother's strength.

"You need more rest and less worry, Anna. It's Giulia. She's too much for you right now. The others, they're old enough, they take care of themselves, they obey Pasqualina, but not that one. You need peace and quiet, not listening with one ear to what's going on in the rest of the house.

"I'll bring Giulia to my house. I can take care of her better than Pasqualina with everything she has to do here. Now close your eyes. Don't even think about it. In a few months you'll have your babies and everything will be back to normal."

My mother, too drained to fight, acquiesced. That night, Giuseppina took me home with her. My mother delivered the twins—Giovanni and Frankie—early, but Giovanni was sickly and did not survive more than three months.

My mother's loss and subsequent depression gave Giuseppina more reason to keep me, and ultimately I stayed for seven years.

From my very first day in her house, I barely left her side. If we happened to be separated and she wanted me, she never called me. Somehow, whether she was across the room or across the courtyard, a voice inside my head spoke the name *Giuseppina* and I knew to look for her.

When I found her, she'd nod and touch my head with her hand, smudged with dirt from the roots of her plants and smelling of garlic and fennel. Maybe it was my nose that led me to Giuseppina. Giuseppina told me I had a "good" nose, that it was important to smell the sickness in order to identify it.

So many people came to her aching, unable to sleep, unable to eat. She put poultices on their sore muscles, gave them powders to bring on sleep or stimulate their appetites, and coaxed the pains out of their bodies with the touch of her hands. But as she murmured her spells, she was also listening to their stories, the secrets they knew were safe with her. Giuseppina absorbed their suffering, drawing it out of their bodies and taking it into her own.

Giuseppina's house was on the other side of the village piazza from my parents'. When they were first married, Papa and my mother had lived with Giuseppina. But my mother, distressed by the constant parade of sick and troubled people through the place, had cried to Papa that she needed her own house. My mother, too, had a sensitive nose, and she could not bear the smells so vital to Giuseppina's healing ways.

There were many other things my mother could not bear— untidiness, or inelegance, or ignorance. Especially ignorance. That's why she sent me to the Convent of Santa Margareta, with all my sisters—Letitia and Pip and Tilly—and took me away from Giuseppina.

"I let Giuseppina take Giulia seven years ago, but now it is time to reclaim my daughter," she told Papa.

My mother wanted us to be educated, to learn to read and write as she did. My Zia Pasqualina, Papa's sister, did not understand my mother's influence over Papa. My mother was not a woman who drew other women to rally around her— at least, not other women from Venticano. She came from the city, from Benevento. Every summer, she left my brothers and sisters with Zia Pasqualina, a childless widow, and Zia Teresia, her simple-minded younger sister. For all of August, my mother took the baths in Ischia with her childhood friends from Benevento. Papa's business provided the family with a comfortable life; he was the proprietor of the only livery stable in the mountains south of Avellino, with carriages that made deliveries and carried passengers. But Zia Pasqualina believed he indulged my mother in "extravagances."

My mother and Giuseppina argued about me. Giuseppina could see no use for the nuns and their teaching. She wanted Papa to let me stay in Venticano, but my mother was insistent.

"Felice, who can teach her here, in this pitiful school?" my mother demanded of Papa one night before he went off to his card game. "I want only the best for our children!"

Giuseppina, who could not read or write, stalked off from that battle with her head shaking. She told Papa he could bring me to the nuns, but he was a fool if he believed I'd learn anything from them. Papa's cousin Elisabetta was a sister at Santa Margareta. "Everybody knows how stupid she is," Giuseppina reminded Papa.

And so in August of 1900, even though much still needed to be harvested in Giuseppina's garden, Papa hitched up his best wagon, the one he used in his business for the daily trip to Napoli, and headed south with us to Sorrento. I did not cry as we departed the piazza and Giuseppina turned her back on my mother's dream. I did not cry as we rode through the gate of the Convent of Santa Margareta and were surrounded by walls twice as high as my head.

I never cried. Instead, I counted beans.

Beans like stones. We all took a handful from the bowl by the holy water when we came into the chapel at six in the morning. Sister Philomena watched. My hands were small. One morning, the beans spilled; Sister Philomena frowned and grunted. She was too fat to get down to help me pick them up. The big girls up front turned to frown also, except Pip, who buried her face in her hands, pretending to pray, trying to hide her shame that I was her sister.

I got on my knees, looking for all the beans. One had rolled far under the corner of the last pew, in the dark near the confessional where the padre sat on Friday mornings. I left it. Perhaps it would sprout in the dirt and the damp, send its tendrils out around the ankle of a sinner.

I went to my place in the row with the rest of my class. Sister Philomena followed me, watched as I set my beans in two piles on the stone floor and then knelt on top of the beans. Satisfied, she heaved herself into her priedieu and made the sign of the cross.

The beans were supposed to be a reminder to us of Christ's suffering on the cross; a small sacrifice to offer up as penance for whatever transgressions we had committed as sinful girls.

Nobody else wriggled or shifted against the hard white lumps biting into our knees. But I felt them. I didn't pretend they weren't there. Sometimes, when Sister Philomena wasn't paying attention, I scooped the beans into my pocket and stuck my tongue out at anyone who noticed. In the classroom, I was just as fidgety. I hated sitting still to recite lessons or listen to the endless droning of the nuns. To relieve my boredom I drew caricatures of Reverend Mother in the margins of my notebook. The girls sitting nearby would whisper and point and giggle, breaking up the monotony of the day, even if it meant a scolding.

One morning after breakfast, it was gray outside the high windows of the refectory. In that entire convent, there were no windows low enough to sit by and look out to see the garden, the trees or the hills beyond the walls.

I cleared away my dish and cup and took the broom from the cupboard. It was my day to sweep. I swept the crumbs from the corners and under the tables and moved toward the door to the loggia. Sister Elisabetta, Papa's cousin, unlocked the bolt so I could push the crumbs outside. She was supposed to wait and then bolt the door again when I was finished. But there was a crash from the kitchen and the hysterical screams of too many girls, so she rushed off with the keys in her hand and I was still outside, listening to the drizzle beyond the loggia, breathing in air that wasn't stale with the sleep and whispers of all the girls in that house.

The kitchen garden was on this side—clumps of basil and parsley and rosemary and oregano, just like Giuseppina's. It had always been my job to pick the basil for her gravy, parsley for the *brazziola* and the meatballs.

I peeked back into the building and saw no sign of Elisabetta. She was still fixing the disaster in the kitchen. So I dragged the heavy door closed behind me and turned, stepping off the loggia and into the garden.

The path was brick, slippery from the rain and the snails, but I raced along it, faster and faster the farther I got from the house. I raced past the garden and then off the path through the orchard of oranges and apricots and olives.

It began to rain harder. The raindrops pummeled my face, washing away the milk that had dried above my lip. Pip always gestured, exasperated, across the refectory, trying to get my attention. She'd pick up her napkin and in large gestures, demonstrate how I was to wipe my mouth like a lady.

My legs kept moving, carrying me beyond the orchard to the pond. I unbuttoned my shoes and peeled off my stockings and sank into the mud at the edge of the water. A family of ducks rose up squawking. I waded into the water. My dress billowed around me. I leaned back and floated, my arms stretched out, my mouth open to the rain, the clouds in my mind cleared away by the stillness. I was alone. I was free.

I don't know how long I floated before Aurelio, the old

337

gardener, came along the path trundling his muddy wheelbarrow, singing hoarsely. He was not bent like the old men in our village, but stood tall and straight. His yellow-white hair stuck out from beneath a brown wool cap.

He sang his song—a hymn we sometimes sang to the Blessed Virgin—over and over again until he stopped suddenly in the middle of a verse. His hoe and scythe fell to the rocks and his boots sloshed into the water.

The mud at the bottom sucked at his feet and turned the water into a murky soup the color of lentils. When the water became too deep, he thrashed and pushed his way toward me and scooped me up in his arms. All this time, I had listened with my eyes shut tight against the rain, against this rescue.

Aurelio carried me through the water and put me down tenderly on the matted reeds near where I'd left my shoes and stockings. He placed two fingers on my neck and bent his ear to listen for my breath. Although I could hold my breath for a long time (I always won in contests with my brothers), I did not know how to stop my heart from beating. So I couldn't pretend to be dead. I fluttered my eyes and opened them and Aurelio knelt by my side and sobbed. I could see the skin around his neck, rubbed raw by the blackened chain he wore as a penance for some long-forgotten sin.

"*Mi dispiace,*" I whispered. *I am sorry.* I hadn't meant to frighten him. I had only wanted to be outside. To smell the earth. To feel the water holding me.

He reached into his pocket and pulled out an orange. He peeled it with his fingers, digging into the center to tear back the skin with his thumbnail, broken and embedded with the loam of the garden. When it was all peeled—a single spiral coil—he broke the orange into sections and held them out in his palm. I took one and bit into it, the juice exploding into my mouth and dribbling down my chin. I hadn't tasted an orange since I'd been at home with Giuseppina. Giuseppina sliced her oranges across with a knife, making circles of different sizes. Aurelio didn't use a knife, just his hands.

The rain was coming down harder, filling my shoes and the wheelbarrow, sticking my muddy dress to my back and flattening my curly hair. I was happy. For the first time since I'd been at Santa Margareta.

In the distance, past the fruit trees, toward the house, I heard the sound of the bell and then the muffled notes of my own name. They were looking for me.

Aurelio heard it, too. He got up from his haunches and tossed the orange skin onto a pile of rotting weeds. He dumped the water out of my shoes and placed them with my stockings in the wheelbarrow, then piled his tools on top.

He held out his hand and helped me to my feet. Together we walked back to the convent, leaving the quiet of the rain dancing on the surface of the pond, slowly crossing the orchard toward the clamor and agitation around the house. Up ahead, Elisabetta—her veil drenched and heavy—and Sister Philomena with an umbrella, searched the bushes for me.

When Elisabetta saw me she gasped, fell to her knees with the sign of the cross and just as quickly rose and ran to me, the key ring jangling at her waist.

"Thank God! Thank God! You're safe!" She embraced me, then stepped back and slapped me across the face.

"Well, this time you've gone and done it! I can't protect you from Reverend Mother now. The house is in an uproar, your sisters are all in tears, no one's settled down for lessons because of worry over you, and Reverend Mother is pacing the hallways in a fury."

Aurelio bent down into the wheelbarrow and got out my shoes and stockings. He passed them to me with a wink.

Elisabetta finally noticed that I was shivering.

"*Grazie, grazie, Fratello* Aurelio, for bringing her back."

As we walked back toward the house, I turned to the old man and curtsied.

"*Addio!*" I whispered.

He touched his hand to his hat, lifted the wheelbarrow and returned to the orchard.

Papa came to fetch me after Aurelio found me. I waited for him in the hallway outside the Reverend Mother's office, listening to the rise and fall of her complaints. Despite my mother's hastily worded letter of entreaty and promises of generous gifts to the convent, Reverend Mother refused to let me stay at school with Letitia and Pip and Tilly.

"I am throwing up my hands, Signore Fiorillo! I can do nothing with the child. Not only does she disrupt classes and—Mother of God—Holy Mass, making the other girls giggle at her antics. But this running away is the limit. For the sake of the other girls, I have no choice but to send Giulia home."

Chapter 5

Signore Ventuolo's Lessons

I RETURNED TO GIUSEPPINA'S house after Reverend Mother had sent me away from the convent. Papa had gotten my mother to agree that Giuseppina needed someone to help her. Since she was unwilling to give up either Pasqualina or Teresia, she acquiesced to my resuming my role as Giuseppina's helpmate.

Giuseppina greeted me with tears in her eyes the night Papa brought me home. She checked me carefully for fever and other ailments she was certain I'd contracted from the pond. She also examined my head for lice, since no bed was as clean as my own—although we brought our bed linens home from school every week for Teresia to boil and starch before we went back on Monday.

Then she sat me down at the table by the stove, warm from a day of baking and cooking. She fed me *pastina* in *brodo,* manicotti, chicken salmi, rabe and *zeppula con alice.* All my favorite foods in the same meal. Papa ate with us, but my mother had declined. She was disappointed in me, since I'd displeased the Reverend Mother so much. I had disgraced my family. I knew

my sisters were holding their heads high, ignoring the whispers
that followed them through the hallways, but inside they were
mortified by my shameful disobedience. The nuns now eyed
them suspiciously, waiting for any one of them to exhibit the
family trait so flagrant in me. Their embarrassment had trig-
gered a renewal of my mother's headaches. She had one the
evening Papa brought me home. I was permitted into her
room to greet her upon my return. The curtains were drawn
against the late-afternoon sunlight and the air smelled faintly
of eau de cologne. My mother lay propped up against several
pillows, a dampened linen cloth pressed over her eyes.

"I cannot say that I am glad to see you, Giulia."

"I know, Mother, but I am glad to be back."

"In a few days, we'll talk about this. Now run along and
get yourself settled at your grandmother's place."

It took my mother more than a few days to recover and
decide what to do with me. So in the meantime, I was just
happy to be home in Giuseppina's house. I took off the
scratchy uniform we'd had to wear at the convent and worked
barefoot in Giuseppina's garden, pulling up the stalks of harvested vegetables, turning over the soil, chasing away the crows
from what was still left on the vine. At noon, Giuseppina
called me in for soup and bread and I washed the earth from
my hands in the bucket outside the kitchen door. After siesta,
I played with my little brothers and we ate figs from Giuseppina's tree.

Every day I also went to visit my mother, and when she was
feeling better she began to question me about what I'd learned
from the nuns. I didn't think it was much. My letters, my
prayers, my sums. I recited for my mother, read to her from
the prayer book she'd given me at my First Communion,
showed her the small piece of embroidery I had begun—blue
cornflowers, along a border. She nodded in satisfaction.

"Well, despite the Reverend Mother's complaints about how little you paid attention, you seem to have learned something. You are by no means a stupid child, Giulia. And I do not intend that you remain an ignorant one."

My mother eyed me firmly.

"But what did I learn?" I stamped my foot. "It was all so boring and so mean. I would rather be ignorant than go to a school like that again."

"To be ignorant is to waste the talents you were born with. To be ignorant is to confine your life to a path no different than the generations before you. We have embarked on a new century, Giulia! Don't turn your back on the higher things—music, art, literature. When you learn to read, you can read more than the holy words between the black covers of that prayer book. Oh, I know the nuns think those words are the only reason to learn how to read. That's their job. But believe me, you will be enthralled by what you discover, how big your world will become.... I am simply heartbroken that you have lost that opportunity."

I could not comprehend my mother's heartbreak. Instead, I peered out the window at my younger brothers throwing clumps of manure at one another in the stable yard as they mucked out stalls.

"Perhaps...perhaps it's simply that the nuns were the wrong teachers for you. They didn't bother me as a girl, but you and I are very different, aren't we?"

I turned back from the window, surprised by my mother's understanding that she and I were different. In the past, I'd been acutely aware that she had disapproved of the life I was leading with Giuseppina. But this time, she seemed to accept that she could not force me to embrace the things she held so dear.

"I must think about this for a few more days, Giulia. Find

a solution that does not waste your gifts but doesn't confine you, either. The answer is more difficult, of course, because the school here is far worse than the nuns, and Papa will not allow me to send you away again."

I smiled to myself at my wonderful Papa, but my joy was short-lived, for my mother solved the dilemma of keeping me in Venticano by finding Signore Ventuolo. She enlisted the help of her lady friends who went with her to Ischia every summer—women she'd known since childhood whose lives revolved around salons and balls. It was Leonora Esposito, who had known Signore Ventuolo's mother before she died, who suggested him. She made all the arrangements, assuring my mother of both his good background and needy circumstances. And so my mother took her summer money and hired me a tutor from the University of Napoli. Instead of soaking in the sulfur baths at Ischia the following August, she endured the mountain heat so that I might be educated.

I hated it when Signore Ventuolo arrived in Venticano. The nuns were by then only a bad taste in my mouth—a kind of suffocating taste, but well behind me. It was January when he first entered my parents' house.

He had ridden home with Papa on the Monday evening carriage, carrying a scuffed and tattered satchel stuffed with books, a copy of the newspaper *Il Corriere della Sera* and a threadbare shirt.

I watched, sullen, from an upstairs window as the carriage rolled into the stable courtyard. Signore Ventuolo climbed awkwardly down from the seat, his short, stocky legs stretching tentatively for the hard-packed earth. Once on the ground, he backed quickly away from the panting, restless horses, who knew that they were home. The climb from the valley had been accomplished, and their grain bags were waiting in the stable.

For Signore Ventuolo, the climb was still ahead—convincing my mother that she had invested wisely, persuading Papa that a daughter's education was worth this much trouble, and, most challenging of all, bringing me down from my angry perch.

I had been summoned from the warmth and familiarity of Giuseppina's kitchen to greet Signore Ventuolo and have dinner with him and my parents. My hair had been freshly braided, my hands were scrubbed, my pinafore was starched. Zia Pasqualina had fed my younger brothers, Frankie and Sandro, earlier, and the older boys, Claudio and Aldo, had found some urgent work in the stables that required their attention (although not so urgent that they couldn't leave it later to peer through the dining-room windows at our unusual guest). My sisters, of course, were all at Santa Margareta on their knees.

Having escaped the horses, Signore Ventuolo gratefully accepted the washbasin offered to him by Zia Pasqualina before greeting my mother, who waited in the parlor, with me called from upstairs to stand by her side. He managed to remove the grime of the journey, but not the beads of sweat that continued to trickle down the sides of his face and onto his frayed collar. Pasqualina's water likewise had little effect on his unruly black hair and untrimmed beard. Shoving his handkerchief back into a pocket, he finally followed Zia Pasqualina out of the kitchen and into the parlor. When he approached my mother, he took the hand she held out and brought it to his lips. Papa had a carefully groomed and waxed mustache, and I watched for my fastidious mother's reaction to the bristling, tightly kinked hairs surrounding Signore Ventuolo's eager mouth. But I detected no distaste on her part.

"Welcome to Venticano, Signore Ventuolo. I'd like you to meet my daughter Giulia."

I curtsied quickly, but kept my hands behind my back.

My mother inquired about the journey, the health of Leonora Esposito and the weather in Napoli. By the time my father appeared, I was sure there was no other topic to discuss and was grateful for his presence, which signaled that food was now on the dining-room table. Zia Pasqualina always orchestrated the serving of a meal with Papa's readiness for it, and, sure enough, she was just setting a steaming bowl of rabbit stew on the table as we entered the dining room.

My mother directed Signore Ventuolo to sit at her right. My usual seat when I ate at my parents' house put me directly across from Signore Ventuolo, where I had a clear view of him throughout the meal. Despite his shabby appearance, I recognized that Signore Ventuolo knew how to conduct himself at a table. I realized, to my dismay, that my mother would note his manners positively, as well. The more he did correctly in my mother's eyes, the less likely he would be on the return carriage to Napoli the next morning.

From my point of view, that first evening could not have gone worse. Papa's suspicions of a man who was eking out a living as a scholar had already been expressed in the house before Signore Ventuolo's arrival, and I was hopeful that he'd be even more dismissive once the man was under his roof. But Signore Ventuolo had clearly read the newspaper that day.

"Signore Fiorillo, has the unrest on the waterfront affected your business? Are you finding it difficult to reach the port?"

Papa's eyes narrowed as he measured a man he had previously imagined in a ruffled shirt, smoking opium and reading Robert Browning. That this scholar could possibly understand the obstacles standing in the way of a businessman's success was unsettling. But even he could hold Papa's attention for just so long, and Papa went off to his card game as soon as he had finished eating.

Signore Ventuolo did not accompany Papa to Auteri's tavern. He stayed behind with my mother and me, drinking black coffee and anisette, entertaining her with stories about the plays he'd seen over the weekend and the art exhibit at the National Gallery. Pasqualina remained in the kitchen after she'd washed up, listening to their conversation with the door half-opened. I was supposed to be listening in the dining room, but I had come into the kitchen for more cookies and something to drink.

"Why are you so interested in what they're saying? It's so boring," I told her.

"It's what they're *not* saying that interests me," she answered, watching intently through the crack in the door. My mother laughed and inclined her head as she poured Signore Ventuolo more anisette.

My mother finally excused me for the evening, and Claudio accompanied me back to Giuseppina's house across the piazza. The next morning, the work for which Signore Ventuolo had been hired began in earnest. I grudgingly retraced my steps to my parents' house, sullen and resistant. I was grouchy and tired the first morning. I didn't like going from the bustle and activity of Giuseppina's house to the stiff-backed chairs and silence of my mother's parlor.

"It is too distracting at Giuseppina's house," said my mother. "Too many people going in and out, too many questions about the stranger."

My mother hovered in the corner with her spectacles, reading while I learned, but listening to every false word I uttered. Signore Ventuolo, after acknowledging her presence, focused all his attention to me. When he read aloud, he used different voices for each character. Listening to him was like watching an entire company of actors on a stage.

After that first week, I had lessons with Signore Ventuolo

every Tuesday and Wednesday in my parents' parlor. I began to look forward to them.

In my whole life, I had never spent so much time with my mother. She was full of sparkle those days, smiling, sitting up with Signore Ventuolo both nights talking instead of going to her room in silence when Papa left for Auteri's. She ordered crates of books from Napoli and began to paint. She set up her easel and her parasol on the balcony and painted the hills or arranged a bowl of peaches on the dining-room table and fussed with the lace at the window until the light slanted across the bowl "just so."

On the days Signore Ventuolo wasn't there, she listened to me read or had me practice my multiplication tables. Pasqualina took the little ones for a walk so my mother and I could study.

My mother said that Signore Ventuolo lived alone in rooms in Napoli, with no mother or wife to cook and wash for him. She told him to bring his laundry when he came, and Zia Teresia starched and ironed so that his shirts, though old, were neat and white.

Zia Pasqualina and Zi'Yolanda, my uncle Tony's wife, sat in the courtyard at Giuseppina's house peeling eggplants one day, several months after Signore Ventuolo had become my tutor.

"Anna would adopt Signore Ventuolo if she could. I don't know what else he's good for. Who ever heard of making a living teaching little girls? Why isn't he out working for his father? I know for a fact that his family is in the textile business. So why is he here instead of in the mill? Did they disown him? Is he one of those anarchists, throwing bombs at his father's factory? Is that why Anna brought him here?" Zia Pasqualina jabbed at the skin of the eggplant as she continued.

"He feeds his belly on my cooking, dumps his dirty clothes in Teresia's wash bucket, drinks Felice's wine. All for such nonsense as teaching Giulia to read and write. Why couldn't they leave well enough alone when the Reverend Mother sent her home? Couldn't they see Giulia wasn't meant to be schooled? Wasn't it enough that the sisters think she's uncontrollable? Do they want her to run away from here, too, for the entire village to see? How long does Anna think Giulia will sit still for these lessons she'll never use? She should be in the kitchen with me, or better yet, here in Giuseppina's garden, helping her grandmother who needs her eyes, her ears and her sturdy legs."

Zi'Yolanda nodded her head in agreement. "All these books will give her too many ideas, make her lazy and useless. Look at Anna, for heaven's sake!"

I had been in my room, reading one of the books from Napoli. I wanted to tell them that I did sit still. I was back in Giuseppina's house, but now a desk stood under the window, stacked with texts and copybooks and ink pots.

"Look at me now, turning the pages of this book, laughing at the stories, going far away in my mind to the places I read about," I wanted to shout at them.

But Pasqualina and Yolanda moved on to another topic, their opinions of my mother and her passion for education falling in a heap with the eggplant skins at their feet.

I wanted to tell them that Signore Ventuolo was not at all like Sister Philomena. He brought me sweets from the *conditoria* in his neighborhood in Napoli. After I read my lessons to him with no mistakes, he rewarded me with a bonbon. Every week he had something different in the white-and-gold bag. Sugarcoated almonds in pale colors of pink and green and lilac, cherries dipped in chocolate, colored fruits and flowers made of almond paste.

The only thing I didn't like about Signore Ventuolo teaching me was the look on Giuseppina's face—her annoyance when I left with my packet of books to walk to my mother's house and her pain when I returned, full of light-heartedness and excitement that I could not share with her.

Chapter 6

❦

A Game Called "America"

THE CHANGES MY MOTHER initiated by educating her daughters were only the beginning. Within two years, the foundation upon which we based our lives began to shift, creating tremors as real as the earthquakes that sent whole villages toppling down the mountainside in our valley. My brother Claudio decided to leave Venticano right after the feast of the Ascension, as soon as he turned eighteen. He wanted to be someone other than what Papa wanted for him. He told us all, in that voice of his that was always so sure, so smart, that there was no better place for him than New York.

In the last months before his leave-taking, Claudio and Papa had done nothing but argue with each other—thunderous shouting matches that began out in the courtyard and carried into the house at dinner.

"Small potatoes," he called Papa's business.

"The world is wider than the road from Venticano to Napoli," Claudio told him. "This is the twentieth century, for

God's sake. This region is dying. Pretty soon you'll only be hauling caskets to the graveyard."

"Hasn't this life given you enough?" Papa demanded. "You, with your fancy suit and the respect you get just because of your name. What do you think bought you that respect? Who built this house that stands higher than any other in Venticano, so that you, too, can hold your head higher? From living over a stable with your grandmother's herbs hanging from the rafters, I have brought all of you to *this*. Stone by stone, this house was built because every day I traveled that road to Napoli—that road you say is so narrow. Every morsel you put in your mouth, every thread on your body…"

"And just as living over a stable wasn't enough for you, staying here in Venticano isn't enough for me! Every day I drive into Napoli I hear the same stories at the docks—the opportunity, the immensity and fertility of the land—that's what I want for myself, a future in America!" Claudio shouted back at Papa.

"You think America is going to give you this and more? You think you're not going to have to work hard? You think you can turn your back on your family, on your heritage, and succeed? Then go. Get out of my sight!"

Papa slammed his fist on the table, my mother caught his flying wineglass, and Claudio grabbed his hat and bolted out the door and down the hill to Auteri's for a glass of grappa. The rest of my brothers and sisters watched wide-eyed and swallowed silently, not wanting to draw Papa's notice and take Claudio's place as the object of his wrath.

"There will come a time he won't come back," warned my mother, mopping up spilled wine.

"Then good riddance. Let him go." And by the middle of June go he did, driven by his own dreams, my Papa's stubbornness, my mother's pride. It was my mother who paid for his passage, selling some of her jewelry to finance his journey.

On the day he left, my mother dressed in her most elegant gown, put on her ruby earrings and stood on the balcony over the front door of her house—the balcony that looks out on the main street of our village and beyond, to the entire valley below. The balcony from which anyone can see and be seen.

She stood there without tears while everyone else wailed and sobbed, her face shielded from the scorching sun by her wide-brimmed silk hat with the blue feathers, as Claudio walked out of the village and down into the valley on his way to America. She stayed there hours after he was no longer visible to us, but I think she saw him in a way no one else could—his safe journey, his arrival, his triumph. I remember the look on her face, her belief in the rightness of what Claudio was doing.

For Papa, however, Claudio's leaving was a defeat. Claudio *walked* away because Papa refused to take him in his own carriage. Papa spent the day in a darkened corner of Auteri's tavern and spit on what he called Claudio's worthless dreams. Claudio had wanted nothing that Papa could give him.

My parents' house was very quiet in the days after Claudio went.

But his going left a hole in our lives. My family had been in Venticano for nearly five hundred years. How many times had I heard Giuseppina recite the litany that began with Alessandro Fiorillo, the crossbowman who'd sailed from Barcelona to invade Napoli under Alfonso the Magnanimous of Aragon? He never returned to Spain. Instead, he fell in love with the beautiful Maria and remained to cultivate a patch of earth and father her babies.

Giuseppina could not comprehend Claudio's leaving Italy. When he set off from Venticano, Giuseppina had taken a lock of his dark hair, his fingernail clippings and a milk tooth she'd saved since his babyhood. She kept them in a pouch, blessing them every year on the anniversary of his departure.

For us children, the pain of Claudio's departure had been much simpler. We could not understand, could not forgive his leaving *us*. The only people before Claudio who'd left Venticano, never to return, were the dead. What was this place America—farther than Avellino in the valley, farther than Napoli on the sea—that had swallowed up our brother?

In America, Claudio was successful right away. The money began arriving that August. I think my mother knew how well it would go for Claudio—how well it would go for all of us. When Claudio started sending us money, he also sent us letters filled with stories. He recreated for us the streets of New York, teeming with people and commerce. It was the commerce, especially, that fascinated Claudio and presented him with opportunity. In Little Italy, he saw the pushcarts laden with vegetables and fish and shoes and pots that provided the daily necessities to the tenements. Uptown, he saw the glass-fronted shops, their shelves filled with goods—goods he knew had to come from somewhere outside the city. Goods that had to be hauled from where they were made to where they were sold. And so, after a few months of laboring for someone else, Claudio turned in his shovel, and with the money he'd saved, together with what remained of the money my mother had given him, he bought a horse and wagon and began hauling everything the city needed. He had found a place that, unlike Venticano, was not shriveling in the sun but was expanding, exploding.

What we gleaned from Claudio's letters was the sheer immensity of America. So many people, so many streets, long vistas that stretched as far as the eye could see or dream. And one by one, my brothers—first Aldo, and then Frankie and Sandro, who are even younger than me—begged to join him. The hole created by Claudio's departure did not close. Instead, it widened, tearing apart the life my family had known.

My oldest sister, Letitia, had married six months before, a marriage arranged by my parents with the jeweler Samuel Rassina, the son of one of Papa's business associates. She was eighteen and already bitter. She seemed to spend most of her time in the church, "praying for babies, instead of staying home making them," her mother-in-law complained.

I knew, from observing other girls in the village, what lay ahead for me. A year or two of meeting stiff and boring boys at gatherings with families like ours, always under the extremely watchful eye of my mother. And then, after the families nodded and whispered, the women sitting on the sofa and hiding their conversations behind painted fans, the men out on the porch with their cigars and their eyes narrowed, estimating the worth of the girl's family or the boy's land—then, the banns of marriage would be announced in both churches. A string of novenas would follow, the girl's grandmothers and aunts praying that no unforeseen obstacles would tumble into the couple's path, like the loose boulders that had slid off the mountain, crushing five of the village goats and blocking the road to Pano di Greci for three days. Praying that the wedding would take place before the girl had a chance to disgrace the family with a baby born too soon, like Constanza Berti. She'd come to the doorstep of my cousin Arturo's house and thrown the baby into the arms of Arturo's mother, screaming, "Here, this is yours!" My aunt and uncle had made Arturo marry her and take her and the baby away.

My mother wanted no Constanza Bertis in our family.

"You are not peasants! You are the daughters of Felice Fiorillo." Her greatest weapon in her defense of our honor was our pride. From the time we were small, she had Zia Pasqualina scrubbing us and dressing us in starched white dresses while the other children in the village ran around barefoot and in tatters. When the money from Claudio began coming, the dresses became finer, and we ordered fabrics from Napoli for the bed linens we were to take to our marriage beds.

Painstakingly, under the instruction of Zia Pasqualina, I embroidered red silk *GF*s on the elaborate pillowcases I sewed, festooned with tucks and elegant lace. My fingers cramped from the tiny stitches. My mother held up these beautiful objects to us like Giuseppina's talismans. If we wanted a life filled with beauty and elegance, a life where we could rest our heads on an embroidered pillowcase, rather than a life spent washing someone else's pillowcases, then we had to remember that its cost was far more than the silver she'd paid for this linen. How would we be able to put our heads on these pristine objects if we ourselves were soiled?

My sisters soaked up these lessons without question. They were willing to sit for hours with their needles and thread, gossiping about wedding dresses and arguing over the placement of a flower. They looked at the not-married and the married in our family, in our village, and had decided which side they wanted to be on. I was not so sure.

I was haunted by Letitia's heartache. How lonely she seemed! Her husband had no brothers and sisters, and he was often away, leaving Letitia alone with his nagging mother. "No wonder she seeks refuge in the church," my mother muttered one day.

The lonelier and more withdrawn Letitia became, the more I began to share my brothers' growing excitement with each letter from Claudio. I was still young enough to be granted an occasional excuse from the sewing circle, and then I went off with Aldo and Frankie and Sandro to the hills and played "America"—the rules defined by whatever wonders Claudio had described in his most recent letter. The more I learned from Claudio, the less willing I was to do as my mother expected.

I wanted to laugh, I wanted to dance. I did not want to spend the rest of my life praying to the Blessed Virgin in a village church.

Chapter 7

The Spell

ON CHRISTMAS EVE every year the entire family gathered at my parents' house to celebrate—my grandmother, Giuseppina; my sister Letitia, her husband and his widowed mother; Papa's estranged brother Tony, who had begun to talk about following Claudio to America with his wife Yolanda and their son Peppino; Zia Pasqualina and Zia Teresia, who did all the cooking for the feast of seven fishes, the traditional Christmas Eve meal; and all my brothers and sisters who were still at home. In the two years since he'd been gone, my mother had also set a place for Claudio on Christmas Eve, an empty chair she allowed no one else to sit in. She did not set a place for the wife Claudio had written us about in October of that year.

The house was ablaze with light. Every candlestick in the house had been polished and arranged on the table, the credenza, even the windowsills. My mother and Pip had laid the table with a damask cloth, heavy silver and platters painted with cherubs and goddesses. For one night, everyone put aside grudges and resentments, ate abundantly and then walked across the piazza to attend midnight Mass together. At the end of the service, as the bells chimed "Adeste Fidelis" and the snow swirled around our feet, we bid one another *"Buon Natale"* and separated.

After we returned to my grandmother's house, I started toward my bed, but Giuseppina reached out for me with her blue-veined hand. My Christmas Eve was not yet over.

"Wait," she said. "I want to show you something, *figlia mia.*"

She gestured for me to follow her to the kitchen, where she stirred the coal embers in the grate and then sat on her chair— the stool where she sat every day when "the parade of the afflicted," as my mother called them, came for her ministrations and her medicines.

"How old are you, Giulia?"

She asked a question she knew the answer to. This was just like Giuseppina. She often asked the simplest of questions, questions whose answers seemed so commonplace, so obvious, that at first you worried she was becoming feebleminded and forgetful. But then, when you answered her question, scoffing, "But, *Nonna,* you know already!" you found that your answer meant something else entirely.

"I'm fourteen, *Nonna,*" I answered, puzzled by what Giuseppina was seeking, by what my answer would reveal to us both.

"Ah," she sighed. "Fourteen. Yes, I thought so."

Giuseppina did not keep track of time the way my mother did. She could not read the baptismal certificates pressed between the thin pages of my mother's Bible that recorded our names and the years of our births. She had no calendar hanging on the wall next to the washbasin advertising the granary in Avellino. She had no gold-leaf clock sitting on a mantel that needed winding with a key. Giuseppina measured time by the season. Planting, tending, harvesting. She measured time by the length and warmth of the day. She measured time by the flame in her votive candles.

She looked at me then and measured another kind of time—one that marks the distance between the three-year-old chatterbox she took under her roof and her wing, and the almost-woman who, cicada-like, filled the silences in her house with words, questions, songs and stories. She eyed me, in my fine Christmas dress, my face still flushed from wine, the walk home in the cold air, the warmth rising up from the stove.

"When I was fourteen, I had already been promised to your grandfather Antonio," she mused.

Has she found me a husband? I wondered. Was that it? I was old enough to be married off? What about Tilly and Pip? Weren't they supposed to go before me? I wasn't prepared for this, if this was what fourteen meant to my grandmother.

"When I was fourteen, I also sat with my *nonna* on Christmas Eve." She waved a hand in front of her eyes as if to clear away the clouds that obscured the memory of another old woman and her granddaughter. I was more comfortable with this image. A girl sits at the feet of her *nonna,* listening and watching.

"It's a sacred time," whispered Giuseppina, "for the *maghe.*"

A shiver of recognition rippled its way from my hairline down my spine. I was no longer comfortable, but I was also not unwilling. With relief, I realized that Giuseppina did not see me on the threshold of marriage, as she had been at fourteen. But I understood that she did see me as her heir in something far more mysterious, far more powerful. My heart was pounding.

"You are ready," she announced to me, taking my hands in hers. "Ready to learn the first spells."

We were facing each other and she moved closer, so that our knees touched. She then guided my right hand to her forehead and flattened my thumb against her brown and spotted skin, starting my hand in a rotating motion.

"First, you must listen with your *skin,* your *blood.* Hear the blood of the other, take in its message through your fingertips."

My eyes were wide-open, staring into hers, looking for what I was supposed to find.

"No," she said, "not with your eyes." She passed her hand over my eyelids, brushing them closed. This time I clenched them tightly shut, trying very hard to do what she'd told me. I felt her hand again, hovering lightly over my eyes.

"You are trying too hard, *figlia mia.* Do not try at all. Do not think. Just listen."

We sat quietly for many minutes, her hand at first suspended in front of my eyes and then no longer there. I don't remember the moment when she took it away. In the beginning I heard the hiss of the fire, the rustle of the wind, the banging of a loose shutter, even the braying of the padre's mule. My hand continued to move in the gentle rhythm she had set for it, across the fragile folds of her aged face. Again at a point I don't remember, the sounds of the night receded and I heard nothing; and then I heard something. Not words. Not direction, or explanation, or even *yes* or *no.* But I know what I heard was Giuseppina.

Then for the first time in my life I began to speak aloud the words of the spell. I had heard them since I was an infant, so Giuseppina did not have to say them to teach or even remind me. But that night they became *my* words. I said the names in order, the list of the saints and spirits called upon to provide protection and blessing. I made the request for help, for the ring of goodness to surround her. I offered the honor and gratitude for their assistance, and then I repeated the names again, beginning with the least and ending with the Great Intercessor, the Holy Virgin herself.

I was trembling and breathless when I finished. I waited for Giuseppina's judgment. But it did not come. I cautiously opened my eyes. Her head had fallen forward, her heavy silver earrings resting on the crocheted shawl she always wore draped across her shoulders, her chin pressed into the large cameo at her neck. Her eyes were closed and fluttering under the folds of her eyelids. Her breasts rose and fell in the rhythm of my circles. She had fallen asleep, brought to a place of peace and repose by *my* spell. By *my* words. I covered her with a blanket, banked the fire and made myself a bed at her feet.

After that night, she allowed me to do the spell for the colicky babies brought to her by distraught and exhausted mothers, and for the mothers themselves. Soon they no longer waited for Giuseppina, or turned to me reluctantly when Giuseppina was overwhelmed by the numbers seeking assistance. They began to ask first for me.

Chapter 8

La Danza

THE SUMMER I TURNED sixteen, a group of us—cousins and friends who had played together since we were children—gathered in the late evenings behind the Cucino brothers' barn. Mario Cucino had a fiddle, and on moonlit nights, amid the crickets and fireflies, someone would signal with the rhythmic cadence of clapping hands and the music began. We danced. Whirling, wild, joyous, the letting go of winter's confinement and—for me—my mother's constrictions.

I lived for those summer nights. For the moist darkness, a reprieve from the scorching heat and the eyes of the village gossips; for the feeling of breathlessness and weightlessness that overcame me as I spun in circles, my arms outstretched and my castanets alive; for the smells of wine, honeysuckle, hay, sweat. For the aching nearness of Vito Cipriano, shirtless, brown from his endless days in the fields. For what I felt coursing through me—new, delicious and forbidden. For what I had discovered with Vito.

One searing day, Giuseppina and I had gone up into the hills to gather angelica when the heat overwhelmed her and she sought refuge in a small grove. I gave her a few sips of water to drink. She leaned back against a tree and fell immediately into her customary snoring sleep.

I sat with her for a while, but I was neither hot nor tired, so I picked up my basket and continued over the rise to the meadow where the last of the angelica grew. I was crouched there, cutting the stems with my knife, when I saw the shadow. I turned quickly, my knife ready to plunge, to protect myself. But it was Vito.

The grass was very tall; there was no one to see us except the hawks. Vito and I had kissed before that day—sweet kisses on the path back from Cucino's in the half darkness, hurried and cautious, always listening for the sound of footsteps or a shutter opening as one of the sleepless sought the relief of the night air. But in the meadow was different. In the meadow…I let him touch me.

I knew the length and depth of Giuseppina's siestas. And I could still hear her snoring. At first, Vito's kisses were as urgent as the night and I kissed him back with the hunger that had been building to a frenzy all summer long. But then we stopped for breath. He tilted his head to gaze at me and began to stroke my hair and my face. I have a vein in my neck that always swells and pumps visibly when I am nervous. I felt it surging, revealing my emotions. He touched it with his fingertips, then buried his face in the hollow right below it. I could smell the earth on his hands. He had had no time to wash, had come to me directly from the fields when he'd seen me with my basket walking up the rocky path. I felt his hand glide from my neck, along my arm and back up again to the drawstring of my blouse. My hand closed over his as he attempted to loosen the string. *"Per favore,"* he whispered, begging me with his eyes. I hesitated. He released the string, but then brushed his hand across my blouse, over my breast. No one had ever touched me there before. I hadn't known how it would feel, had not known the ripple of desire it could set off. I struggled with the warnings and admonitions of my mother. But this discovery was so extraordinary to me, this moment of our unexpected solitude so magical, that I pushed aside the voice of my mother and bent my ear once again to the voice of Vito.

"I want to touch you," he told me.

"Yes," I answered.

He undid the string and lifted my blouse over my head, then my camisole. This nakedness in the brilliance of midday, in the presence of Vito, was so surprising and so thrilling that I lost my breath. Then I felt his hands, callused and eager. That my body could feel this way! I reached out for him and pulled him toward me and gasped when I felt his own naked chest for the first time against mine. I had watched since childhood the calm and the absolute pleasure on the faces of babies when they nestled against the bare breasts of their mothers, and that's what I knew when Vito extended his body over mine. For a few abandoned moments, surrounded by the drone of the cicadas, the biting fragrance of the grass crushed beneath us, I was aware only of my longing. But in the distance, in a place inside my head that stayed apart, I still listened for Giuseppina's snores and I still measured Vito's every move. I knew I was in danger—from discovery, from desire.

I stopped Vito when his hand reached under my skirt. His face clouded with frustration and anger. I felt a sharp twinge of fear—that I might not be able to hold him back, might not want to. But then we both heard the sound of my name, frantic, wild. He rolled off me, cursing, staying low, and I grabbed for my clothes and wriggled into them.

"Stay down," I hissed, and then rose with my basket to see

the top of Giuseppina's head coming up over the rise. I waved and hurried toward her, brushing the grass from my hair, my back.

"Are you crazy to wander off by yourself! Never again, do you hear me!" She vented the fear she must have felt when she woke to find me missing. "You look flushed, feverish," she observed as I came nearer. "You've been too long in the sun." She saw the mound of flowers in my basket. "That's enough for today. The fright you gave me has worn me out."

We set off down to the village. I didn't turn to look back.

But that night I couldn't wait to return to the dance and Vito's arms. Those hours contained everything my mother had tried to keep me from. I danced barefoot, like the daughters of Tomasino the goatherder, feeling the earth, damp with dew, between my toes. In the early hours of morning, when I returned in exhaustion to Giuseppina's, I poured water into the speckled washbasin and thoroughly scrubbed my feet before slipping back between the sheets of my bed. Giuseppina might not have seen the smudged evidence, but she would certainly have smelled the loamy traces still clinging to my skin.

But my ablutions were not enough to hide my secret life.

Mario Cucino's cousin Clara betrayed me. Clara had watched Vito and me all summer from the corners and the shadows, a skinny, sallow-faced girl who was always chewing on a strand of her hair and did not know how to laugh.

She shrewdly enlisted my brother Aldo as her accomplice. Aldo had embraced his position as Papa's favored son after Claudio left us. He postured in front of the hallway mirror, mimicking Papa's elegant style of dress. He passionately remade himself in Papa's image, taking meticulous care not only of his wardrobe but also of the wagons and horses. He polished, he groomed. He seemed determined to earn Papa's respect, eagerly volunteering for the hardest routes, even passing up the usual entertainments of the other boys in the village to pore over the ledger books late into the night. Papa rewarded him when he turned eighteen, entrusting him with the busy Avellino route.

Aldo had never ventured to Cucino's. He had never experienced the need to break free of the confining Fiorillo name—not as Claudio had by leaving Venticano altogether, nor as I had, in my own fledgling way, by dancing, by dreaming. If he knew about Cucino's, he'd chosen to ignore it, until Clara, recognizing in Aldo a younger version of Felice Fiorillo, whispered in his ear one day. My little brother Sandro, who sometimes tagged after Aldo, witnessed that encounter and later told me about it.

Clara had been invisible to young men, especially young men like Aldo. But then, Clara realized she had something Aldo might want, something that would earn him more favor with the father he seemed so intent on pleasing. She pushed that perpetually loose strand of hair behind her ear, smoothed her dress and approached him.

"You're Giulia's older brother, aren't you?"

Aldo nodded, but eyed her quizzically. "How do *you* know Giulia?" he asked, the surprise in his voice undisguised.

Clara smiled disingenuously. "She comes dancing at Cucino's sometimes. Weren't you aware? I had heard she was hiding it from her grandmother, but I thought she might have trusted you. You must know about Vito?" She looked at Aldo, offering her sympathy to the shocked brother. "Oh, no, I haven't said too much, have I?"

"Not at all. I'm grateful to you, *Signorina*."

Very few young men had addressed her as *Signorina*.

That night, Aldo waited under Giuseppina's mulberry tree and watched me lower myself over the ledge of the window. When my feet touched the ground he sprang forward and tackled me, knocking me breathless into the flower bed. I shrieked and kicked, not knowing it was my own brother. Our scuffling, of course, roused Giuseppina, who threw open her shuttered window, muttering and cursing the disturbance until she saw who it was and—more pertinently—how I was dressed. I was no longer in the nightgown I'd been wearing when I'd said good-night to her an hour earlier, but rather in my flounced skirt and bodice, with no blouse underneath. My arms and shoulders were bare. My hair, now unbraided, tumbled loosely down my back, somewhat unkempt thanks to the tousle with Aldo. As Giuseppina took in my appearance and realized what it meant, she began to wail and keen as if it were my stiff and lifeless corpse lying beneath her window. It might as well have been, given the catastrophic aftermath of Giuseppina's discovery.

In the midst of her lamentation, she ordered me into the house. But she could not prevent Aldo from running to fetch Papa. I cursed at his retreating footsteps. Papa arrived from his card game in a frenzy.

"You whore," he roared and slapped me twice, once on each cheek. "I forbid you to go to Cucino's again. If you disobey me, I swear I'll bring you back to my house and keep you under lock and key."

I spent the rest of the night in Giuseppina's bed with her. When she finally fell asleep, I crept over to the window. Not to escape again, but merely to catch a glimpse of the night and hope that Vito was hovering somewhere in the shadows.

The next morning my mother made her entrance. (No one had dared wake her the night before.) Her outrage was focused not so much on the dishonor that had provoked my father's anger as on the company I had chosen to keep and the manner in which I'd chosen to keep it.

"Dancing in the mud with a Cipriano! Haven't I taught you

to expect more? Will you throw your life away to bear the squalling babies of an uneducated peasant, just because you admire the shape of his buttocks?" she shrieked at me. Then she quieted and narrowed her eyes as a question—more a demand—formed in her head.

"Are you pregnant?"

"Mama! I've only danced with him!" I protested quickly, knowing that dancing alone was enough to anger her, hoping it was enough to keep her from suspecting more.

"Well, thank the Blessed Virgin for that."

My mother did not know—and I did not reveal to her— what I felt when I danced. She could never have known the force of the yearning and urgency that propelled me. She shifted her fury to Giuseppina, not for failing to guard me or seal me in, but for making me susceptible to the night.

"It's you who've cultivated this wildness in her! You've encouraged her to befriend these people, to partake in their primitive pleasures. You let her go off into the hills alone to gather your weeds and look what she brings back! She should've been reading books, not mixing potions for the lovesick."

Giuseppina was no less upset with me than my mother was, but for other reasons. Giuseppina understood the longing. She had taught me the power of the feelings, the dreams that burned inside of people. She believed that to disown what you felt made you sick—sick at heart, sick in the head.

Over the years, most often in arguments about me, Giuseppina and my mother had done their own dance around each other. This time was no exception. My mother, normally decorous and contained, unleashed her words, her pitch, her pace. She brimmed with uncontrollable passion. Giuseppina, on the other hand, became impassive, impenetrable. My mother shrilled her words as if they were fists beating, hammering in futility at the wall of Giuseppina's silence. When my mother finished her tirade, Giuseppina dismissed her with the peremptory gesture of impatience she reserved for the truly stupid with whom she wouldn't even deign to speak. Once again, my mother was forced to retreat.

When she was gone, Giuseppina said, "Before you find yourself pregnant, come to me first."

She turned away from me without her customary penetrating glance. I was expected to understand; she would protect me, as she'd been unable to protect me the night before from Aldo's spying and its consequences. She was angry with me for exposing her lapse, for making her look like a fool and for taking risks with my reputation. But she was also letting me know that she forgave me.

My parents, however, were not ready to forgive. My mother, especially, was determined to protect me in her own way from the dangers she saw lurking behind the eyes of every young man in the village, and within my own emerging womanhood.

Her solution came quickly.

My sister Pip had made a rash promise to a young man in Pano di Greci. She was nearly twenty, but she had no experience of men, as I did. Her embroidery stitches were neat; she followed all the rules at the Convent of Santa Margareta; she would make someone an obedient, if foolish wife. But not this someone in Pano di Greci, my mother decided. Not knowing her own heart, Pip was relieved at my mother's intervention. She floated this way and that, always doing what she was told. The family of the young man, however, was enraged, raining curses and threats upon Pip's empty head.

My mother and father conferred noisily, Papa at first resisting my mother's radical suggestion. Ever since Claudio had left, Papa had refused to even read any of the letters from America, let alone respond. But my mother, summoning all her emotional power, prevailed. A letter was hurriedly sent to Claudio.

Pip, in the meantime, was kept at home, not even allowed to go to the market for fear she would be kidnapped in broad daylight crossing the piazza.

To all outward appearances, life in the Fiorillo households— my parents' and my grandmother's—remained as it had been, except for Pip's and my confinement. But my mother's days had taken on a kind of silent intensity as she worked out in elaborate detail what she considered to be the rescue not only of Pip, but of me and Tilly, as well.

She told none of us, for fear of alerting the enemy in Pano di Greci or arousing the rebel in me.

She did not tell me, in fact, until she had the passage booked, the steamship tickets in her hand, my father's horses practically bridled and ready to drive me to the pier.

"Aiuta me!" I wailed to Giuseppina when my mother marched to her house and ordered me to pack my trunks. *Help me.*

"She cannot help you this time. Your sister will be killed or worse if she remains here, and she can't go alone. She and Tilly can't manage such a journey by themselves. You're the only one with enough sense to see you all safely to Claudio. Venticano is no life for any of my daughters, but believe me, Giulia, it is especially no life for you. You are going now, before you're ruined by what you have clearly never learned to control."

She stood over me while I gathered my belongings together. The tears flooded my cheeks, spilling over onto my clothes. Giuseppina wandered around the house, muttering her incantations, burning incense, tucking her blessings among my possessions as I packed.

"You'll leave before sunrise tomorrow, on your father's

normal run to Napoli, so as not to arouse suspicion. The boys will come this evening after dark to take your trunks to the house, and you will come with them. You'll sleep with Tilly in her bed tonight. I forbid you to breathe a word of this to anyone, especially Cipriano or any of the Cucinos. If you do, you threaten not only your sister's life, but your own, as well."

My mother's voice was taut; her face revealed the sleeplessness and strain of the last few weeks. But just below the surface of her exhaustion, her rigid instructions, I thought I saw a kind of rejoicing—that she was going to be successful in getting us out of here, this village and this life that had been such a trap for her. And I hated her for it.

"I don't want to go!" I screamed at her. "What about Giuseppina? Who will help her?"

"Don't make me laugh! You don't want Giuseppina's life any more than I do! I know you, Giulia. Giuseppina may have taken you from my side, but she can't take me out of you. You are *my* blood. Your tears are not for Giuseppina, but for something walking around out there with bulging pants. Believe me, you'll find a hundred just like him in America. And—like your brother Claudio—they will have money, they will have a future, they will have a life to offer you."

Giuseppina's mutterings became louder, more intense.

My mother simply could not understand my heartache. I didn't want a hundred other boyfriends. I wanted Vito.

When my trunks were packed, my mother had no patience to listen to my sobs for the rest of the day. She locked the trunks herself after she was satisfied that they contained everything I'd need in the life she was sending me to. She took the keys and added them to her own ring of household keys, telling me she'd return them to me before we departed in the morning. What did I believe? That I would forget them? That I would add unsuitable items to the trunks after she left—talismans and powders from Giuseppina's trove? That I would dump the contents of the trunks in the mud of the piazza in a fury of final rebellion? Perhaps that was it. But I felt her taking the keys as another slap.

The trunks sat all day in the middle of my bedroom as an affront, an immovable reminder of my mother's resolve.

I could not stop my tears. At times they were simply silent streams, slick on my cheeks, trickling down my neck. At other times they were wild sobs, engulfing my entire body, starting in some place so deep inside me that I'd never felt it before— deeper even than the longing that had entered me this summer when I'd danced with Vito. I did not know myself. Did not know I could feel such sorrow, such fear.

Giuseppina fed me broth at midday, holding me in her arms like a baby, spooning the warmth into my mouth where it mingled with the salt of my sorrows.

She put me in her own bed at siesta to keep my emotions from being heightened by the massive trunks near my bedside. She lay with me, murmuring the words of her simplest spell.

In her bed, awaiting the evening and its further agonies, I didn't think I'd be able to let go of the thoughts crowding my head. But her words washed over me until they were no longer words. Her hands stroked at the pain until they were no longer hands. I fell asleep.

When I woke it was nearly dusk. Giuseppina was gone from the bed and I heard her in the kitchen, clattering pots and pans. I smelled the extraordinary smells of roasting lamb and freshly cut oranges. I went into the kitchen and then helped Giuseppina in silence, slicing tomatoes and unwrapping the mozzarella. A small bowl of figs sat on the table. She must have walked down to the orchard to pick them in the afternoon, while I'd slept. She was now trimming the shank of prosciutto, shaving thin slices from the cut end. The kitchen was stifling from the fire in the oven, combined with the oppressive July heat. No one cooked like this in summer. The aromas of rosemary and garlic mingled with the red wine she had poured over the lamb. Despite my sadness and my unwillingness to eat at midday, my body now gave in to hunger.

I devoured the meal, savoring every mouthful. Giuseppina sat across from me, watching me eat silently.

I helped her clear away the meal and wash up. By the time we finished, the darkness was spreading and deepening. My brothers would be arriving soon. She took me into her room. We stood in front of her shrine, before the flickering candles in their red pots, the faces of Mary, the Sacred Heart, Saint Anne, Saint Joseph—her own saint—glowing and gazing out at us. She blessed me and whispered her strongest spell of protection. Then she kissed me, unfastened the clasp of the amulet she wore and draped it around my neck.

There was a knock at the door. I began to shake and my tears returned.

Aldo and Frankie were here, neither of them understanding my grief and both wishing it was they who were on their way to America and not their sisters. Giuseppina had decided not to come to my parents' house. As the boys hoisted the trunks onto their shoulders, she cast one final blessing upon my things and then took me in her arms.

I wanted to collapse at her feet, throw my arms around her knees and not let go. But she held me up—for an old woman she had moments of surprising strength.

"*Figlia mia,* don't do this to yourself. Don't shame yourself in front of your brothers, who will only drag you to your father's house. Go now. Remember everything I have taught you. My blessings are with you. You will find what you long for in your life. Cherish it. Protect it. You carry my gifts within you, too, not just the blood of your mother."

It was the first and only occasion Giuseppina had openly countered my mother's words to me. She released me into the protection of my brothers.

We walked silently across the piazza. Aldo kept one hand in his pocket, closed over a bulge I soon recognized as my father's gun. Both boys kept glancing from side to side. Frankie's baby face twitched every time we heard a cat wail or a bucket of dishwater splash upon the stones. But we met no one else. Before we left the piazza, I glanced back. Giuseppina stood in the light of her doorway, still watching us. I could no longer see her face, only the outline of her body standing sentinel until we turned the corner. I lifted my arm in farewell and saw hers go up in response.

At my parents' house, a brittle calm filled every room, every face. Pip twittered nervously, remembering every five minutes yet one more item she'd forgotten. She babbled about the outfit she was going to wear tomorrow, couldn't decide which hat, fretted about her tendency to become nauseated when traveling. Tilly sat in the kitchen, baffled and frightened by this extraordinary change in our lives.

In contrast to Pip's chatter and Tilly's confusion, I was sullen. The boys joked and teased, but their resentment was unmistakable. My aunts—Pasqualina, the childless widow who wasn't sure whether she adored Papa or my brother Sandro more, and Teresia, the one whose mind had never grown beyond childhood—hovered anxiously, saying their prayers and jumping every time they heard a noise outside. I secretly hoped that one of those noises was Vito, somehow aware of my predicament, emboldened to rescue me. But I was not allowed near a window, and they were all shuttered anyway.

My mother, still tense, sent Pip and Tilly and me to bed with the admonition that we were to be up and ready to depart at 4:00 a.m. I slept very little without the solace of Giuseppina and with my own heartache. I awoke to a smoky lamp in my face, my mother's voice urging me to get dressed. Tilly's side of the bed was already empty. I moved unwillingly, but I moved, remembering Giuseppina's warning not to disgrace myself. I dressed in the dim light, half listening to Pip's whimpering from her bed. Silly Pip, whose thoughts had been filled with fashion the night before, had suddenly realized what was going to happen today. So it was Pip my mother had to struggle with, had to coax, and soothe and finally order out of bed. Tilly and I were at the kitchen table, forcing down cups of Pasqualina's coffee and a slice of bread, when Pip came downstairs, her eyes swollen and red, her nose running, her shoes unbuttoned.

My father and Aldo, who was to accompany us to Napoli, were out in the courtyard preparing the horses and loading the carriage. Teresia wiped the tears from her face with the edge of her apron. Pasqualina finished wrapping the provolone she was adding to a basket densely packed with provisions—salami, soprasatta, olives, bread, figs, even a glass jar of last year's eggplant. She handed it over to me, rattling off a list of instructions that began with when and what to eat, but rapidly advanced to the dangers that lay ahead of us among strangers and how we were to protect ourselves. Pasqualina, who had never ventured farther than Avellino in her entire thirty-eight years, was giving us travel advice.

My father's command from the courtyard interrupted her, and we all scrambled to gather together the last of what we were taking with us, to put on our hats and gloves, to kiss one another goodbye. Frankie and Sandro, sleepy-eyed and not completely dressed, had tumbled down the stairs for a final hug. My mother handed me the keys to my trunks.

"Your father has all the papers. He will give them to you at the pier. Claudio will be waiting for you in New York. Go with no one else, no matter what they say to you. Stay in your cabin except for meals. We've bought you first-class tickets so there's no need for you to have anything to do with the unfortunates in steerage. Take care of one another. Don't venture anywhere without the others. Do us honor when you arrive. Be good girls. You know that we'll hear about it if you are not. Write to us. Now, off you go. God be with you."

She held each one of us in a strong, swift embrace.

Pip's chin began to tremble again, but my father barked his final order and she climbed into the carriage. The first pink streaks of dawn were edging over the horizon and my father wanted to be well over the mountain by daylight.

Aldo hopped up onto the seat next to my father in front. I parted the curtain in the carriage to grab one last look at my family before we headed out of the courtyard and onto the Avellino road. My mother shed no tears, just as she hadn't four years ago when Claudio had left. She closed the gate after us, a look of satisfaction, the fulfillment of a dream, on her face.

I drew the curtain back and settled into a numbing doze. I was in a temporary state of resignation, following my parents' wishes by sitting in this carriage, but unable to bring myself to feel any emotion other than a silent rage.

My mother's plans were so carefully constructed, my father's carrying out of them so thorough, that we arrived in Napoli early that afternoon without incident. My mother later wrote us that no one in the village even suspected we were gone until nearly a week had passed.

We ate with my father at a restaurant run by a friend of his and then drove on to the harbor. I had never been to Napoli before. By this time, safe from curious eyes, we were allowed to open the curtains and glimpse the city. It was huge, teeming, loud, confusing. Everywhere there were people. Soldiers on horseback with plumed hats, ladies with brightly colored faces, beggars.

377

As we approached the wide expanse of the Bay, we were stalled in a river of wagons, carts, men on foot with awkwardly shaped bundles strapped to their backs or bulging valises in their hands, women struggling with wailing babies in their arms and small children clinging to their skirts, dressed in several layers of clothing. Lining the avenue to the harbor were food vendors of all sorts, men in suits and hats offering their assistance with the paperwork required for passage, *capos* shouting for able-bodied men who wanted work on the rails, on the roads. Pip cowered in her corner of the carriage. "They're all so dirty!" She acted as if merely looking at them would defile her.

I leaned forward at the window, straining to see ahead, to catch a glimpse of bay or smokestack, but nothing was visible. I smelled raw fish, roasting chestnuts, rotting fruit, horse droppings, grilled sausages and peppers, the sweat of a thousand people. I could not yet smell the sea.

The carriage suddenly lurched forward. Wagons and carts ahead of us had begun to move. I leaned back and closed my eyes to shut out what I could of my anger. I saw Vito's face—laughing, coaxing, teasing. I saw him dancing, his bare arms raised above his head, clapping out the rhythm. I saw him coming in from the fields, wiping his face with a large blue bandanna. I saw him at the feast of the Madonna, dressed in a starched shirt, hoisting the statue onto his shoulder in the piazza. I saw him lying in the meadow with me.

The carriage jolted to a halt, and I heard the voice of my father in heated discussion with someone on the street. I opened my eyes, returned to the present, to the aching in my heart, the aching between my legs. We had reached the pier. Ahead of us loomed the steamship, swarming with activity. Beyond it shimmered the dazzling vastness of the light upon the Bay. Behind us towered Vesuvio, the layered hills, my own dreams. I opened the carriage door and stepped out, setting one foot ahead of the other in the direction of America.

Chapter 9

Laughter

PAOLO SERAFINI HEARD my laughter before he saw me—a cascade of joy, he told me later, rising above the jabbering of the women behind the house of my brother Claudio, his friend and business partner, the man he loved more than a brother. That I was laughing at all was a miracle. It protected me from the desolation I felt at being uprooted from Italy.

Claudio and Paolo were partners in one of Claudio's business ventures—a saloon that provided them both with some income. Claudio had told Paolo that his three unmarried sisters had arrived from Italy, but Paolo had been so busy that he hadn't gotten over to make his "welcome to America" speech until we'd been there almost a month. He did not knock on Claudio's door panting with expectation, or even curiosity. It was purely a duty call: offer his services to the family of his best friend as if they were his friends. Before that day, he believed that he would have done anything for Claudio. But he had not realized that "anything" could include loving his sister.

We were all out in the back of Claudio's house in Mount

Vernon—Pip and Tilly and I, Claudio's wife, Angelina, her sister and a couple of her cousins—sitting on a little spit of stone between the kitchen door and the pathetic garden Angelina had tried to plant. With our sleeves rolled up and knives flailing, great mounds of purple-black eggplants fell victim to our energies. Like Paolo's mother in Napoli, like our aunts up in the hills, we were slicing and salting, laying up *melanzane* in big crocks that Angelina had somehow managed to cram onto that tiny terrace.

I had my back to him, my whole body relaxed with mirth, wisps of my hair escaping from its clasp. When I lifted my right arm—the one without the knife—and wiped away tears of merriment with my outstretched palm, Paolo watched the soft curve of my breasts beneath my flower-sprigged cotton dress.

He reached his hand into his pocket, withdrew his handkerchief—freshly laundered by his sister Flora—and held it out to me.

I turned my face toward him, for the first time registering his presence, and swallowed him with my eyes without once losing the rhythm of my laughter.

Una bella figura. A handsome man with hair the color of Zia Pasqualina's polished copper pots and eyes a transparent, dreamy blue. He was dressed in a brown suit, and his fingernails were clean. Not at all like Claudio.

"Ooh, Paolo!" shrieked one of the others, but I didn't hesitate or even lower my gaze.

I took the handkerchief, brushing my eggplant-stained fingertips along his hand—lightly enough to escape the notice of the others, but long enough for him to recognize that it was deliberate.

He was not a man from the hills, with little experience of the world and even less to say about it. And he was no greenhorn—he'd been in America for ten years. He knew the life, he knew the streets, he knew women. He knew the words they liked to hear.

But he stood before me, watching me press my face into his handkerchief, and imagining himself taking that same handkerchief in his hands and drinking in my fragrance, tasting the salt of my tears—and every sound he had ever uttered to a woman failed him. This is what he told me later.

"So you're Paolo. Claudio wrote us about you. I'm Giulia."

"Claudio's *baby* sister," Angelina put in, wiping her hands on her apron, about to take charge. Angelina didn't like him. She jumped up, all tense and formal and placed herself between us. So just to give her a little more *agita* (as if she didn't create enough for herself every day), I played up to him with my eyes. Didn't say anything. Just looked. Boldly. It made the other girls giggle and Angelina furious. Claudio had told her why I'd been sent away by my mother, so Angelina believed that if she didn't watch me every minute, I would disgrace her.

Paolo saw from Angelina's stance that she would have built a fortress around me, the same way she pulled her baby boys close when danger was near. Angelina, whether she wanted to be or not, was mother-in-absentia to us, and she had just realized that, with me, this was going to be no easy task. *Keep away, Paolo,* she was ordering him.

"This is Philippina." Angelina laid her hand on Pip's shoulder. "And this is Tilly." Paolo took in the funhouse-mirror images of my two sisters. Pip was all bony and angular, a skeleton on which her clothes fluttered, and Tilly was as lumpy and pasty as gnocchi—but they both had the square-jawed Fiorillo face. Tilly seemed planted in her seat, as if she wanted to take root in her corner of the terrace like a waxy palmetto, not move out into the world at all.

By then, Paolo had regained his words. He upended one

of the empty eggplant crates and sat down—to Angelina's visible relief—across from rather than next to me. He, too, needed some distance. He chatted with everyone, asked the expected questions about the land left behind, the journey completed, the strange new world encountered since we'd set foot on Ellis Island. The other women in the group, all worldly veterans of two or three years here, teased us newcomers for our wide-eyed wonder. But not without a tinge of homesickness, an evanescent longing that all of them, even Paolo, at one time or another experienced, and sometimes denied. For him, it was the memory of walking along the jetty at Santa Lucia; ahead of him was the light—lavish and prodigal upon the Bay—and to the east, over the city, the shadow of Vesuvio, hovering.

I said almost nothing as the others talked. But my eyes, glistening with interest and amusement, never left Paolo's face—a caress, I knew, that was as deft as that of my fingertips.

Not only was he unlike Claudio, there had been no one in all of Venticano to compare to him. Not even my father—the coddled brother of his widowed and never-married sisters, the successful businessman, the product of my mother's ever-intensifying drive for betterment—not even he possessed Paolo's elegance. Claudio said that Paolo was an educated man, a man of letters, with piles of books in his rooms and the manner of a scholar. But it was more than his culture and refinement that set him apart from the life that had surrounded me in Italy. He was also different in the way he returned my gaze. Neither red-cheeked and flustered nor swaggering like the boys back home, who teased or made crude jokes when they thought you were interested in them. Paolo looked at me deeply, without embarrassment, with candor. I could tell that he admired me. I enjoyed such attention.

But what would I do with it, with him? He was older than

Claudio, almost thirty, a man of the New World. Too old for me. Letitia's husband was much older than she was, and that had brought her only dissatisfaction.

I looked, but I was not ready to feel. There was too much of this new life to understand. The voices were so strange and raucous, the streets so numerous and confusing. There were so many people whose faces I didn't know, who did not even nod in greeting. I laughed in the garden with the women during the day; I poked fun at Angelina and her proprieties. But at night I was still terrified. I missed both the stillness and the music of Venticano; the faces of Giuseppina and my little brothers; and I missed Vito Cipriano—the roughness of his coarsely shaven cheek and the apple scent of the pomade he wore too thickly on his curly black hair.

I didn't want to be here.

The morning was passing rapidly, and the pile of eggplants had not diminished noticeably since Paolo had appeared in our midst. He could sense, once again, Angelina's slightly veiled impatience. He knew he was going to need Angelina on his side. So he rose from his perch, ready to make his farewell, and with a grin and a flourish, invited all of us sisters for a stroll and then the band concert in Hartley Park on Sunday. Pip and Tilly beamed and giggled. Angelina shot a look of gratitude at Paolo for the gift of a Sunday afternoon free of her sisters-in-law. And I, a smile of acknowledgment spreading across my face, leaned my head back and laughed.

As Paolo walked away, he slipped his hand inside his pocket and clutched the handkerchief, still damp with my laughter.

Chapter 10

Hartley Park

PAOLO TOOK US THREE sisters to Hartley Park, as he had promised. On Sunday afternoons the footpaths in the park were crowded, the crunch of leather on stone a backdrop to the German and Yiddish and Italian conversations wending their circuitous way to the band shell.

That Sunday, the musicians were performing selections from Scott Joplin and George M. Cohan. Paolo picked us up promptly at three. Angelina had not invited him to Sunday dinner, which I thought was ungracious, but I was learning after only a few weeks in America that customs were different here.

Paolo lived alone in a rooming house a few blocks from Claudio's. His married sister Flora also lived in Mount Vernon, and he'd borrowed a blanket from her that she did not object to our spreading on the grass. He had also stopped at Barletta's on the way to Claudio's and picked up three small nosegays of lilies of the valley and forget-me-nots—identical, except that he'd asked Vinnie Barletta to put a single red rose in the middle of one.

When he got to the house, Tilly and Pip were waiting, gloved and anxious. He swept off his hat and presented them with the bouquets, careful to hold back the one with the rose.

"Oh, Paolo! *Grazie!* How thoughtful! What a gentleman!"

A few minutes later I came down the stairs.

"*Come sta,* Paolo! You're here so soon! You don't give a girl a chance to take off her apron."

Paolo turned to me with the flowers. I noticed that my bouquet was unusual—not a match to the others now in the hands of my sisters—but I didn't react. Instead, I took it with a smile and a curtsy. Although I'd flirted with him yesterday over the eggplants, I couldn't imagine him as anything more than a *simpatico* friend of my brother's, a man who was showing me some kindness in this strange new land.

We walked down to the park, Paolo in the middle between my sisters, me on the periphery, laughing, almost skipping, re-lishing my freedom from Angelina's kitchen and laundry and damp babies.

When we got to the park, we looked for a comfortable patch of grass. I wanted to be near the music and strode toward the band shell, stepping carefully around the early arrivals sprawled around their picnic baskets.

Pip didn't want to sit on the ground, not even on Flora's blanket; she didn't want to be so close to other people—to the smells of their food and their unfamiliar bodies, to the sounds of their unrecognizable tongues. She hung back near a bench by the path. Tilly was torn between my pleasure in the outing and Pip's fears and disdain. She was following me, somewhat breathlessly and clumsily, when Pip's bony hand stretched out to hold her back.

Paolo was coming up in the rear, carrying the blanket as well as a cardboard box tied with multicolored string and filled with cannoli from Artuso's bakery. Pip stood in rigid exasperation; Tilly in flustered confusion.

"Oh, Paolo, stop her!" I heard Pip say. "Look at her parading up there. Who does she think she is? A child at a carnival? Isn't there some quiet bench we can sit on out of the way? Look, over there under the trees."

I was up ahead, waving to indicate that I'd found a spot.

Paolo moved toward me, not seeming to care if Pip stood waiting on the path, arms crossed and foot tapping, for the entire concert.

"Paolo, Paolo, over here," I called. "This is a good spot, don't you think? Let me help you with the blanket. I'm so excited! This is the first time I've heard music since I left Italy—what a wonderful idea! Claudio doesn't think of things like this. He doesn't understand that people need more than work, more than money. Did you know that he almost didn't let us come when Tilly told him you'd invited us? We've been so cooped up in that house, barely allowed out to do the marketing. He's worse than my Zia Pasqualina with his worries and warnings."

I couldn't stop babbling, I was so thrilled to be away from everything that had oppressed me since coming to America. I shook out the blanket with a vigorous snap.

"Oh, I've been longing for a day like this! To be outdoors among the trees and flowers, to smell the air, feel the sun, to put on my fine dress instead of trudging around day after day in a housedress and apron with my hair tied up in a rag. Angelina thinks we're her servants. She either doesn't know or doesn't want to know what we came from, how we lived in Venticano."

I finally noticed that my sisters were still not as eager as I was to embrace the day in the park in the midst of strangers.

"Pip, Tilly, over here!" I stood again and waved. Pip, red-faced, lips set in a taut line, came gingerly toward us.

"Giulia, this is not appropriate. I will not stay here in front of all these strange people and I do not want to sit on the ground. And why must you always bring such attention to yourself—chattering and waving like a silly child. You continue to be an absolute embarrassment to me, no matter where we are."

She turned to Paolo to seek his agreement.

"Paolo, I expected you, of all people, to behave in keeping with the trust Claudio placed in you as our escort," she said sternly.

I was annoyed. "Oh, Mother of God, Pip, sit down and enjoy yourself and leave Paolo alone. If it really disturbs you to sit on the blanket, go find a bench. You do manage to drain the last ounce of pleasure out of your life, don't you? Why did you even come? To torment me?"

The people seated around us were beginning to notice. Although they probably couldn't understand a word Pip and I were saying, they could surely hear the scolding in our voices. The concert was about to begin. People were coughing, re-settling themselves, gathering their children into quiet heaps, and packing away the remnants of cold chicken and pickles.

Tilly, an expression of hopefulness on her face, piped in blithely, "So we're sitting here after all, are we? I do think we'll hear the music better. Oh, look, there's the concertmaster already. We'd better all sit down or we'll block the view of the people behind us."

Paolo and I took the opportunity of Tilly's timely arrival to find our places on the blanket and join in the overall hushing that whispered across the lawn. Paolo took care not to sit too close to me and made space for Tilly, who seemed relieved to finally be at rest.

Pip remained standing, her defeat spreading up her face. She took a half turn, looking back over her shoulder at the bench, now half-occupied by an elderly couple with cane and parasol. There was room for Pip, but it was unthinkable that she'd sit alone.

From her stance of rigid refusal, Pip crumpled into an awkward pile on the blanket. She sat as far apart from us as she could, first brushing away small flecks of dried leaves and tiny pebbles before she arranged herself, smoothing her skirt over and over. She did not speak to us for the rest of the afternoon, not even to take a cannoli when Paolo finally opened the box during intermission.

I quickly forgot about the unpleasantness and absorbed myself in the music. In contrast to my sisters, I couldn't sit still. I was in motion even as I sat, legs tucked under me. My hands lightly tapped out a rhythm at times on my thigh, at times on the blanket beside me. I swayed, my shoulders loose, fluid, an elixir of life running beneath my clothing, animating the dress like some puppeteer bringing a costumed marionette to life.

My fingers played the blanket like a keyboard or the strings of a guitar; my body danced; I breathed the music into my lungs and exhaled it as joyous movement.

Once or twice I glanced at Paolo, acknowledging his presence and sending him a smile of appreciation. He had chosen well: the music wafting through the early September air, the afternoon sunlight filtering through the trees, the aromas of freshly mowed grass and chrysanthemums filling our lungs. Not Italy, no, I can't say that it resembled closely any Sunday memory that I carried. But the afternoon held some familiarity for me, some joy, some spark that reunited me with home. Paolo had given me a small gift by bringing me here.

Chapter 11

The Palace

ABOUT A YEAR BEFORE Pip and Tilly and I arrived in America, Claudio and Paolo had stumbled across a building. It was a place nobody had wanted then—filthy, abandoned, something without any value to those who saw it only with the eyes of realists, not with the eyes of dreamers. But Claudio and Paolo were dreamers. That was why they'd come to America.

Claudio's dreams were all about money and doing better than Papa. He fled across the ocean to a land where no one knew him, no one expected something from him just because he was Felice Fiorillo's oldest son—and what did he do? He bought himself a bay and a black horse and started hauling goods in a wagon, just like Papa. But before you knew it, it wasn't just one wagon, it was four. And a stable on Fourth Avenue to house the horses he picked up, one or two at a time when he had the cash. Driving all over New York, bringing the stone, the wood, the bricks that were building the city, he met people, he talked them up, he imagined the possibilities. Anything with a dollar sign in its future, Claudio latched on to, cut himself into the deal. That was why he bought the decaying place he and Paolo named the Palace of Dreams. But Claudio was shrewd. He knew he didn't have the patience to run it once he'd created it, so he made a three-way deal—Claudio, Paolo and Willie Rupert, who owned a brewery.

The Palace was a dump in the beginning, but a dump in the right place, close to the factories and the rail line. Claudio and Paolo cleaned it up, hauling away the debris in Claudio's wagons, bringing in furniture and fixtures that Claudio was able to trade for—a chandelier to hang over the bar, even an old piano. Willie's brewery provided the beer. Paolo did the books and managed the place. He was usually at the Palace every evening after he finished work as a union secretary with the IWW.

Before long, they started getting customers—the men coming off their shifts at Ward Leonard and Pioneer Watchworks, the conductors and engineers from the New Haven and Hartford Railroad, Claudio's business associates from around the city. As the whistles blew, you could hear them.

"Stop by the Palace for a round."

"Meet me at the Palace."

"Comin' to the Palace tonight, lad?"

They came for a couple of drinks and a card game, just like the men in Venticano had made their way to Auteri's every night. They unwound, looking for a little time for themselves before they plodded home. They left some of their worries on the table; they left a few dollars, too. Soon, like everything Claudio touched, it was a success.

Chapter 12

The Blouse Factory

NOT LONG AFTER WE'D ARRIVED in Mount Vernon, Claudio got us jobs at the blouse factory over on the South Side. Claudio's businesses were expanding, but with our three additional mouths to feed, plus his own growing family, his resentment at having to support us was mounting. It had all started with Claudio's wife. I was out sweeping the front stoop when our ignorant neighbor across the street, Carmella Polito, leaned out her window to shake her dust mop.

"Eh, enjoy what you're doing now, because it won't be long," she called.

I pretended not to hear her, but she went on anyway.

"Just you wait. That wife of your brother's ain't gonna stay quiet about you girls not bringing any money into the house. He's gonna make you go to work."

The know-it-all slammed her window shut when I continued to ignore her, but I didn't forget what she'd said. A couple of weeks later, I walked past Claudio and Angelina's bedroom one evening and heard them fighting. Angelina's voice was rapid, complaining. Once or twice she said my name. Claudio was gruff and irritable. Finally, he silenced her with an explosive and exasperated, "*Va bene!* Okay, okay, I'll see what I can do. But I don't think there's much of a market for anything those nuns taught them." I tiptoed quickly down the hall before he opened the door.

Within a couple of days he'd made the rounds of those who owed him favors and came up with three seats behind the sewing machines on John Molloy's shift at the blouse factory. Tilly, Pip and I were to start right away.

It was not what my mother had imagined for us when she sent us to America. Claudio's descriptions of his success in his letters to her had ignored the tough, gritty work that had produced that success. For Claudio, our jobs at the factory were the equivalent of the pick and shovel that had been thrust into his hands when he'd first set foot on American soil.

We had trouble from the first day. I had never sewn on a machine before. Zia Pasqualina and, later, the nuns in Sorrento, had taught me fine hand-stitching, embroidery, elegant work for objects of quality. In America, they didn't know about such things. You looked at the American girls on the streets; their clothes had none of the finer details. The rich ones, they went to the immigrant dressmakers, schooled like us in convents. But those factory-made clothes! We were sewing women's blouses. Fifty of us in a room, the din of the machines unbearable, the dust, the unending piles of fabric arriving constantly from the cutters, the squabbles between girls from different neighborhoods, the ever-watchful eyes of Molloy. This was not the life my mother had imagined for us.

I had headaches by the end of the day. My shoulders and neck were in knots. My fingertips felt numb. Sometimes, in the afternoons, when the sun came through the dirt-caked windows and beat on my back, when the drone of the machines filled my ears so that I couldn't hear even my own daydreams, when Molloy was at the other end of the room with his clipboard—I allowed myself a few minutes of escape, pressed my head against the enameled black metal of my Singer and closed my eyes.

I thought about being someplace else. Sometimes it was back in Venticano, working with Giuseppina in the garden, the earth clinging to my hands, getting under my fingernails. I pulled up a carrot, its feathery greens brushing my bare arm. I rinsed the carrot in the metal water bucket and bit into it, tasting the soil and the sun, tasting Italy.

Or I thought about Saturday nights—the one just past or the one to come—and dancing at the Hillcrest Hotel with Roberto Scarpa. His sister Antonietta worked the machine next to mine and she was the one who'd told Tilly and Pip and me about the dances. I had to beg Claudio for weeks to take us, pleading with him as if he were Papa, reminding him that this was America now. If he could send us to work in a factory like the American girls, then he could let us dance like the American girls on Saturday night! He finally gave in, but full of rules and orders about how we were to behave and who we could associate with. He took us there around eight and then hung out on the porch smoking with his friends, poking his head inside every now and then to make sure we were still there and hadn't sneaked out with some boy he didn't approve of. If he only knew!

"Where's Giulia?" he barked one night to Tilly when he stepped in to make his hourly check and I was nowhere to be seen among the swirling skirts and tapping feet.

"She's gone to the toilet." She gave her well-rehearsed reply, for once not fumbling in anticipation of his rage should he realize she was covering for me. She took a deep breath when he apparently believed her and went back to his friends. But she came scurrying to the small parlor, where I was sitting in deep conversation with Roberto, who was holding my hand and whispering in my ear.

"Claudio's looking for you!" she hissed. "You'd better get back soon or he won't let us come next week!"

I rolled my eyes at Roberto to let him know how miffed I was by the interruption. "Okay, okay, I'll be there in a minute," I said and shooed her back to the dance floor. I turned back to Roberto. "She's right, you know. Claudio's very strict. I don't want to provoke him." I got up off the sofa, but continued to hold his hand. I squeezed it and whispered, "I don't want to lose the opportunity to be with you."

I meant what I said. But I also didn't want him to think I was going to be easy. I sat with him in the back parlor, but you wouldn't catch me like some of the girls I knew from the factory. They went out with men alone; they didn't just meet them at dances. They didn't live with their families. They had no protection. Claudio's vigilance irritated me, but because the men knew he was my brother, they didn't try anything.

Roberto and I walked separately to the dance floor and I stopped to talk with his sister, who had introduced us. Antonietta had talked incessantly about Roberto at work. He was the oldest of her brothers, the tallest, the handsomest. I hadn't believed her until I saw him for myself. He was blond, with long arms and legs and powerful hands. When he danced with me (and by then, I was the only one he danced with), I felt the strength of his grip around my waist. I saw my hand disappear inside his. I'd always been small for my age. Even then, at sixteen, I still wore a child's-size shoe and glove.

People watched us when we danced. Roberto was so big that everyone gave him room. But despite his size, he was very graceful.

Dancing at the Hillcrest was different from dancing at

Cucino's. People were more *watchful*—of others and of themselves. They cared more about what other people thought than we had dancing in the dirt in our bare feet. In Mount Vernon, all the girls spent hours during the week talking about what they'd wear, who they hoped to dance with. We then spent more hours Saturday evening getting ready, borrowing from one another, coaxing our hair into the styles we saw in the magazines that got passed around at lunchtime, trying to find some happy medium in the way we were dressed so that we'd be allowed out of the house but still look stylish. So much energy went into these preparations! It made Tilly giddy and brought nervous shrieks even to Pip's serious countenance.

The other difference between Cucino's and the Hillcrest, like everything else in America, was how big these dances were. At Cucino's, we were maybe a dozen, and all of us had grown up together. Here, the ballroom was a crush of people—fifty, a hundred sometimes. So many strangers. People came up from the city, from the Bronx mostly, because of the Hillcrest's reputation. The musicians were the best. Paolo Serafini played the piano. Claudio said it was a way for him to pick up a few extra dollars every week, since he was never going to get rich working for "that union." But the way Paolo played, you could hear that it wasn't just for the money. He knew all the popular songs. Claudio said he even wrote songs himself, but I'd never heard him play them at the dances. What he did play was wonderful dance music, music that had people moving and laughing and clapping their hands. The ballroom at the Hillcrest on Saturday nights was a blur of color, a haze of voices, a release of all that weariness and longing from the week before. What would we have done without those dances? Nothing to relieve the chill of my sister-in-law's house, the loneliness of my new life, the tedium of broadcloth that faced me every day.

I felt a kick abruptly interrupt my thoughts, a warning from Tilly, who sat at the machine behind me, that Molloy was on his way back here. We had, each of us, already been caught dozing at our tables. Molloy cautioned us not to do it again. So we took turns, one watching out and warning while the others slept.

We had other troubles with Molloy, as well. Getting to work on time was a struggle. There was no peace in my brother's household in the morning. Claudio and Angelina's babies clamored from hunger and dampness. Pip and Tilly and I groped for clothing, for the hairbrush, for coffee. Still in his bed, Claudio muttered at the noise, exhausted from a day at work and a night at the Palace. He stayed hidden until we were all gone and the boys were fed and dry. Pip would snatch the broom, Tilly washed the dishes, I chopped the onions and the garlic for that night's marinara and sliced bread and provolone for us to take to work.

One early November morning, I poured some olive oil into Angelina's heavy pot. It was good quality oil, thick and green. Claudio got it from the DiDonato family, the ones with the importing business. Back then, Americans didn't know what olive oil was. I got the onions started, then ran out to pluck some *basilico*. It was almost finished, all scrawny and leggy. Any night soon we'd have a frost. But even in the intensity of summer, this basil hadn't grown. I hadn't been in Mount Vernon long enough to figure out if it was Angelina or America. But this was not a garden I knew. When I had stood in the middle of Giuseppina's garden, I found myself in a fresco, like the one imbedded in the wall of Santa Maria dei Miracoli. All around me was color: the red tomatoes and peppers, the purple eggplants and fava beans, six different shades of green—zucchini, broccoli rabe, *basilico,* artichoke, escarole, *fagiolini*. Perhaps it was the sun, which was so different from the sun in America. I asked myself, isn't it the same? How can the light, the warmth, be so alien to me? In Italy, the sun released, set free the growing things, splurged itself in unrelenting generosity. In America, the sun was wan, stingy, exacting. It was no wonder these basil plants had to stretch themselves, strain for their meager ration.

I pulled my sweater tighter around me against the cold morning and raced back to my onions. Tilly had, thankfully, finished washing up and was crushing and straining the tomatoes.

"Be careful that no seeds get through. You know how bitter they'll make the gravy and I don't want to listen to Claudio complain after I've had a long day at work."

"Maybe *you* want to strain, to make sure it's perfect?" There was an edge to Tilly's voice. As sweet as she was, she didn't like to take direction from me. But they all knew I was the better cook. Giuseppina had taught me. In my mother's house, Pasqualina had hoarded her skills, unwilling to share Papa's appreciation for a well-cooked meal. And my mother believed there were better things to learn than how to cook.

Of course, here in America, Pip and Tilly had no Pasqualina to bury her arms in flour and eggs every Saturday morning to make the pasta. In fact the three of us were Angelina's Pasqualina. The sisters of her husband, given refuge, a roof, in exchange for our domestic services.

I chopped the basil and threw it together with the tomatoes into the pot. I jumped back as the contents of the pot flashed and sizzled, sending up a hot red spray. I didn't want to have to change my blouse. A flick or two with my spoon and I set the pot on the back burner for Angelina to watch during the day.

I raced upstairs to wash and run a brush through my hair.

"Hurry up! We're going to be late again and Molloy will

be furious! He'll go right to Claudio, too. Why can't you ever be ready when it's time to leave?"

Pip and Tilly waited for me in the front hall. I slipped in the last hairpin on my way down the stairs, the soles of my boots slapping urgently against the wood as Claudio grumbled in annoyance. Coat and hat, a last glance in the mirror by the door, and we were off—coffee and tomato and warm stove left behind in Angelina's kitchen, a ten-block walk ahead of us, Molloy and his clock waiting.

I hated that walk. I hated the dim early morning light and the chill that put an ache in my toes. I hated leaving the familiar streets of the neighborhood. We walked down to the corner, past Our Lady of Victory and the tenements on the other side. Then the houses started to dwindle as we approached the New Haven Railroad line. Because there was no bridge at the bottom of this street, we had to turn left down by the tracks and walk east to the bridge at Fourth Avenue. On the other side of the tracks, we had to walk two blocks west again and then another three blocks south to the factory.

Sometimes we walked with a couple of other girls from the neighborhood and then it was not so bad. We joked along the way about Molloy or talked about the dance, or even stopped to look in the window of the Tabu dress shop on the corner. But this morning we were so late that Annunziata and Carmen hadn't waited for us and we were trudging alone, our steps quickening to a run when we passed the clock in the window of Ruggierio's Shoe Repair.

"We can't be late again. Molloy said—"

"I know what Molloy said. Don't talk. Keep moving."

Just then we heard the screech of the five-to-seven whistle. From this side of the tracks we wouldn't make it in five minutes.

Tilly, Pip and I looked at one another and agreed without

speaking to take our shortcut. Instead of turning toward the Fourth Avenue bridge, we wriggled through the fencing and raced down the rocky slope toward the railroad tracks. We had done this many times before. Milkweed and the shriveled blossoms of goldenrod and thistle caught and clung to our skirts and sleeves. My boots skidded on the crumbled dirt and gravel, and I slid the rest of the way down on my backside. Tilly and Pip reached the bottom ahead of me and started over the tracks. We were a few blocks west of the station, where the tracks branched out five across. I brushed myself off and followed them.

I was almost across the third track when I stumbled, falling to my knees as I tripped over the hem of my skirt. *Va Napoli,* I muttered to myself as I heard it rip. Something else to mend, as if there weren't enough of Claudio's shirts and my nephews' overalls in the basket that waited for me every night. I pulled myself to my feet. My hands stung from where they'd slammed against the gravel bed and my chin felt wet and raw. I knew Molloy would send me to the washroom to clean my bloody face—and dock my pay before he'd let me near his blouses. For the second time that morning, I brushed myself off and started off. But I couldn't move. My left foot remained rooted to the ground, like an unfamiliar weight at the end of my leg when I tried to lift it and take a step. I raised my skirt.

My boot heel had become wedged in the space between the ties, clutched by the resin-soaked wood. A chill climbed its frantic way up my back. My hand reached without thought for Giuseppina's medal around my neck. Then I pulled at the boot with all my strength and will, but it wouldn't budge. I tried wriggling my foot as if I were about to dance. I was so distracted, so consumed by my entrapment, that I didn't notice Tilly and Pip, who'd already made it to the other side and begun to scramble up the embankment. Suddenly, I heard Pip's voice, but not in the scolding tone she used when I lagged behind and she was nervous about Molloy's clock.

"Giulia! Giulia!" she shrieked, a knife edge of hysteria, a bow drawn across a tightly strung violin. "The train! The train!"

I jerked my head up, first in Tilly and Pip's direction, then to the left, where Pip was frantically gesturing. A locomotive was heading toward me from the station. I couldn't see if it was traveling on the middle track.

I grabbed Giuseppina's medal once again as it dangled over the boot, kissed it and rapidly mumbled a prayer. Then I placed both my hands around my ankle and struggled again to lift the boot free. But it still wouldn't come loose.

"Untie the boot! Untie the boot!" Pip's hands stabbed the air in a pantomime.

But I didn't want to. My boot! My mother had sent them, exquisite butter–yellow boots with black trim and laces. They fit me perfectly, narrow and graceful around the ankles, the leather as soft as the satin bags my sisters and I embroidered to hold our wedding tributes. Those boots were my memento of all that I'd left behind in Italy.

The locomotive was looming; I could feel the tracks starting to heave; I could hear the hiss and clang. My fingers somehow found the ends of the laces and pulled them loose. I lifted out my foot and hobbled to the other side where Pip and Tilly waited, white-faced. I flung myself into the bushes at the edge of the southern slope as the train passed.

Chapter 13

The Keys to the Store

THINGS HAPPEN FOR a reason. My scratched and bleeding face, my lost boot, cost Tilly and Pip and me our jobs with Molloy. Claudio roared for a few days—first at our insanity in crossing the tracks, next for our inability to get to work on time and keep Molloy happy. Angelina sulked to have us back in the house all day, but I think she was also secretly pleased that my boot had been destroyed. I kept busy, washing and starching the curtains, beating the carpets, emptying the cupboard of all the glassware and dishes and washing everything till it gleamed. The house reeked of ammonia and lemon oil.

By that time, wooed by Claudio's success and his own disaffection with Papa, my uncle Tony had brought his wife, Yolanda, and their son, Peppino, to America. Claudio had found both Tony and Peppino jobs on a construction crew and they lived not far from us in Mount Vernon.

On Sundays they always joined us for dinner, recreating a small piece of Venticano life. A few weeks after Molloy fired us, Claudio settled into his Sunday pasta with more than his usual appetite.

"I bought another building," he announced, "down on Fourth. There's a store on the ground floor. The old lady who ran it died last month. Her sons don't want it—it's full of buttons and thread and dress patterns. What do they know about dressmaking?"

He turned to Tilly and Pip and me.

"It's yours. Since you girls can't seem to work for somebody else, work for yourselves. I don't want to hear another Molloy complaining to me. And I don't want you crying to me if you fail. This is the last job I'm gonna dig up for you. Don't let the vendors charge you too much or convince you to buy anything you don't need. Don't give your customers too much credit. Work hard. I'll check the books once a month."

He threw the keys on the table, finished his wine and left for the Palace.

Tilly, Pip and I looked at one another. We were proprietors now, over thread and yarn and buttons and lace. We were respectable. Our mother would be proud.

Chapter 14

———❦———

"Divina e Bella"

PAOLO WROTE POEMS. His little nephew, Nino, brought one to me.

I saw Nino almost every day, on the Avenue when I went down to do the marketing. He was so funny. A skinny little fellow, full of energy, always running, playing. His mother, Paolo's sister Flora, kept him very clean, his clothes always well mended. The first time he saw me, he called out, *"Bellissima!"* and clutched his heart and fell in a swoon at my feet. He won me over. I couldn't resist him. After that, he followed me around from shop to shop, carrying my basket, offering his advice on the quality of the vegetables, babbling about his American teacher at the No. 10 School. He was learning English. He showed off his new words like a new toy. I often bought him a peppermint at Artuso's.

"I'll tell Zio Paolo I saw you today," he said whenever we parted on the corner—Flora didn't allow him to leave the block. "He'll be jealous. He'll wish he could be me, walking by your side and making you laugh."

I always laughed in spite of myself and shooed him back to

his games. He started to bring me little presents. A flower plucked from the vacant lot across from the school; a drawing he'd sketched on the back of an envelope; a piece of his mother's coconut cake neatly wrapped in a cloth. Then one day, he greeted me with a carefully folded sheet of blue note-paper.

All this time, he'd been as if an emissary from his uncle. "Zio Paolo did this, and Zio Paolo did that…" Paolo's name and deeds were never far from Nino's lips.

I didn't have time on the street to read what Nino had given me, so I took it home and opened it in the kitchen. On the blue notepaper were words written in Paolo's strong and elegant hand. I recognized the handwriting from the papers Claudio sometimes brought home. It was a poem, entitled *"Divina e Bella."*

> *I was so lost in thought this morning.*
> *I could not take another step but*
> *Found myself rooted, waiting,*
> *Hoping that Giulia would pass by*
> *And bestow upon me*
> *The dazzling beam of her smile.*
> *But my Beauty does not show herself!*
> *Thoughts of her crowd out all else,*
> *Throng around me with doubts.*
> *Perhaps she feels nothing of what*
> *I feel for her?*
> *I swear, if I do not see her*
> *My heart will shatter.*

I folded the note and placed it inside my blouse. I didn't tell my sisters, and I didn't tease Paolo. I was afraid Nino had stolen the poem. Paolo certainly hadn't asked him to give it to me.

The next day, when I saw Nino, I gave it back, scolding him that he must replace it in Paolo's papers undisturbed, that he had no right to let me have it.

Paolo's poem set off such confusion in my head. I was flattered by the intensity of his feelings for me. But I was unused to men who hid their emotions behind words written in silence and locked away in a drawer. I preferred to be whirled around a dance floor, to feel Roberto's desire for me in the press of his hand on my back. But I was beginning to see that, except for those moments on the dance floor, Roberto and I had little else to share with each other.

I returned the blue notepaper to Nino, but I didn't forget the poem. I kept the words enclosed in my heart.

Chapter 15

The Christening

ON A SUNDAY in February, my friend Antonietta christened her firstborn, a little boy she had named Natale. Half the neighborhood turned out for the celebration. Her husband, Giacomo DiDonato, was well-known in Mount Vernon. People didn't ignore his invitations. Not even the police ignored this event, although it was hard to believe they'd been invited by Giacomo. But they were there, standing outside Our Lady of Victory during the Mass and later, more of them, down the block near the hall. Somebody must have warned them that there might be trouble, that there were those in both Giacomo's and Antonietta's families who would've preferred that such a cause for celebration never come to pass.

People were lined up outside the hall waiting to get in, clutching their envelopes, their medals, their blessings for the baby boy. The priest had done his work in the church, but now the old women with powers were ready to add their voices, murmur their spells that would protect the boy in ways the Irish priest couldn't even imagine.

It had snowed on Thursday and it was frigid, but still people waited, small bursts of conversation or the brittle tinkling of gold charms dangling from gloved fingers piercing the February air. The police had built a fire in an ash can on the corner of Fifth and Prospect to warm themselves, scowling over the flames at the bad luck of drawing such a duty.

Antonietta's brothers were also outside—having a smoke, watching the line of well-wishers, watching the police. My Roberto was there—the one they called the Scarecrow, the one with whom I'd been keeping company.

What happened next was unclear, full of the scum of rumor, self-deception, self-aggrandizement. The newspapers, based on police reports, gave one account. Eyewitnesses—the aunts and cousins, the countrymen on both sides who were standing in the line—gave other versions, each containing some elements that coincided, some of their own embroidery. Antonietta's family remained silent.

There was one element that recurred in all accounts—that the origin of the afternoon's events was a conversation in the line questioning the paternity of the child. It was Antonietta's brothers who overheard the provocative comments. And it was Roberto, as oldest, who led them to avenge the besmirched honor of their sister.

Fists let loose. Women screamed. Crucifixes and medals of Saint Anthony were hurled into the snow. The throng surged as if caught in a maelstrom. The police, roused from their resentful apathy, descended with truncheons at the ready. Words, shouts, the quickening ripple of danger, like an animal beating its hoof on the ground to warn its herd, reached those inside. People rushed out into the snow, to defend, to witness. Antonietta, faltering and confused, clutched the baby, paralyzed by what had happened to her celebration until her mother grabbed them both—as well as the white satin bag filled with the gifts of well-wishers—and led them to a small room that led onto the alley. I myself stood in the doorway as people rushed in one direction or another.

The Scarecrow was at the center of the confrontation, his towering height an easy target for the cops, who were making their way toward him. And then it happened. A uniformed arm reached around from behind, encircling Roberto's neck. The cop's other hand then covered Roberto's face, trying to pull him back. Suddenly, the hand flew away, blood pumping, spewing all those surrounding Roberto. The arm around Roberto's neck released its hold as the cop sought to stem his own blood. Roberto ducked and disappeared. But not before he turned his head—his mouth a twisted, carmine slash—and spit out a finger.

The smell of blood sent another tremor through the crowd. As abruptly as they had converged upon the fight—the men compelled to defend the honor of one family or another, the young boys driven simply to partake in the frenzy, the old women bound by ancient oaths to fling their curses—they now scattered, flying from the fringes in all directions.

An ambulance and police wagons began to arrive, bells furiously sending out yet another warning to those still engaged in the melee, police reinforcements pouring out of the wagons onto the street to subdue the violence of the mob with a violence of their own.

In contrast to the fury and confusion outside, a hollow and desolate silence had seeped into the hall. Without an audience, the musicians had long since ceased their rondos and ballads. The floor, only minutes before filled with knots of chatting neighbors and romping children, was now strewn with remnants of food half-eaten, coats forgotten in the madness to join the brawl, a shoe lost in the press of the curious. The last of the mothers had shepherded her children out the same door through which Antonietta had been led to safety. My own family had all left before the fight, but I'd stayed behind to enjoy the waning moments of the party, to listen to the music, hoping to dance one last time with Roberto.

Earlier in the day, I'd darted about from one group to the next, a playful sprite. First dancing with the children, then whispering playfully into the ear of Roberto. I had felt as if a scherzo played in my head.

But the liveliness and joy that had animated me were drained from my body. I was alone; I was not safe. I backed away from the front door, feeling stricken. I thought the hall was empty. Then I heard the sound of footsteps racing down the stairs two at a time and a voice calling my name. My head jerked toward the voice, my eyes charged with terror. It was Paolo. I felt a fleeting relief wash over me, but then my attention was immediately drawn back to the door by renewed wailing and screams. In a few seconds, the cops would be inside.

Paolo reached me and reached out for me, taking my trembling body into his arms and guiding me toward the alley door. I knew only that I had to get out of there, away from the fighting, away from the cops. I was terrified of what would happen if someone told them I was Roberto's girl.

The alley was still clear, and Paolo hurried us over the hard-packed snow, throwing his coat over my shoulders because we hadn't had time to search for mine. It wasn't far to Claudio's house—just a couple of blocks over on Sixth. But the way was rutted and slippery, slowing our silent progress. Halfway there, I stopped, twisting my body away from his side. I grabbed the rough bark of a tree for support, bent into the road and began to retch.

Paolo held me from behind, brushing away the stray curls that had fallen into my face. At first, I resisted his help, pushing

his hand away; but then, overwhelmed by my heaving, I submitted. I even allowed him to wipe my mouth when, spent
and exhausted, I lifted my head and leaned against the tree,
eyes closed against the demons I'd seen that afternoon.

We had barely spoken since he'd called out my name. What
words could I utter? How could I describe to him what I'd
seen? But he did not ask me for words. He put his arm around
me again, taking more of my weight than before. Paolo knew
I was still unsafe out there on the street. We could still hear
the strident call of the wagons and the shouts of those chasing
and being chased.

I had been depleted by the vomiting, in my will to reach
safety as well as my physical strength to do so. But Paolo made
us keep moving.

Up ahead, a man approached us. It was Claudio. Word had
reached him of the fight and he'd come to find me.

"You should've gone home with the rest of us," he barked.
He raised his hand to strike me. Instead of flinching, my
response was merely a sullen and wan silence. "Get in the
house!" He gestured dismissively with the raised hand. I
trudged up the stairs and slammed the door behind me, but
not before I saw a look of disbelief and disapproval on Paolo's
face. He seemed to be assessing my brother in a different way
that afternoon, judging him not as a business partner, but as a
man who might mistreat a woman.

Claudio and Paolo remained outside in the snow. Paolo described the chaos and offered to return to the hall to retrieve
my things, but Claudio decided to go back with him.

When they arrived, the last police wagon was pulling
away. One of Antonietta's aunts emerged from the alley and
began gathering the medals and charms that lay scattered in
the snow. She would have to purify them and bless them
again. Any of the magic they'd once possessed was now

lost—especially if they'd been trampled or splashed by the blood whose traces lay everywhere.

On Monday afternoon when Paolo opened the Palace, the place vibrated with the drone of hushed, excited voices. The newspapers had reported that morning that the finger had not been found; neither had Roberto. He had vanished, protected by the silence of his family. There was talk of nothing except the christening and the ferocity of Roberto. If the rumors hovering above the whiskey glasses and distracted card games were true, Roberto was on his way to Italy.

Chapter 16

The Iron

ANOTHER LOSS WRENCHED from me, this time in the other direction. Back to Italy, they all said. Disappeared, hidden, flown. The blood wiped from his mouth, the memories of eyewitnesses wiped clean. Did I want that mouth on my mouth again? Did I want to taste that blood over and over again in my dreams?

I felt so alone. The feelings I thought I had for Roberto seemed no more than a foolish girl's daydreams. The thrill of being held by him in a dance was now overshadowed by the realization that there'd been nothing of substance—only heat—between us.

The days since he'd been gone were my undoing. The warmth with which our connection had surrounded me was unraveling like a poorly knit sweater. I dragged myself to the store every day and pretended to some industry, but I was weighted down by my worries, by the fatigue that overtook me until I could not lift my body one more time in any kind of movement. I collapsed onto the bench in the waning afternoon sunlight and leaned my head against the wall.

Claudio came almost every day to inspect, to check up, to spy. He had not forgiven me for the taint I carried by my connection to Roberto. The cops even came to question *him,* big Claudio, with all his friends in the right places. People had been whispering to Claudio, people who thought they knew things, who thought they could gain Claudio's favor with their revelations. After that visit from the cops, he raged into the store. Tilly was in the back sorting spools of thread; I was up front, doing the tallies from the previous day, waiting for customers. He drew his hand across the countertop, leaving a track in the dust, and began to rant about how filthy I was, how lazy. I suspected this had nothing to do with my housekeeping, but I didn't keep my thoughts to myself. I yelled back. Big Claudio! Trying to keep his sister in line! That's it, isn't it? The neighborhood's saying, Look who he lets her get mixed up with.

So Claudio didn't want to hear any more. He wanted me to shut up. He grabbed the first thing his hand touched, which was one of the irons we sold. Not the buttons or the packets of needles in five different sizes or the bolts of rickrack or satin ribbons. An iron. We kept about five of them out on the shelf. He did it so quickly, I didn't have time to duck, didn't have time to protect myself. The iron met the side of my head.

He didn't even turn to see the damage he'd done, the blood, *my* blood, not some cop's blood, seeping through the fingers I had clutched to my scalp. He raged out the same way he'd raged in, my life a personal affront to his dignity. Tilly, who'd been cowering, hiding in the back room, crept out to help me.

But I didn't want help. I ran out onto the sidewalk, screaming at my brother, screaming at the mess my life had become.

Claudio strode away from me, putting the winter city landscape—of slushy paths and buttoned-up people, hurrying with their heads down—between us. When I reached the corner, shivering and hoarse, he was already two blocks ahead of me. Whatever had fueled me was used up and I felt the cold, the throbbing in my head, the sticky matting of my hair.

Broken, I turned back—again—to the sudden, solid presence of Paolo.

Chapter 17

———⊱✦⊰———

Tears and Blood

PAOLO TOOK ME to his sister Flora's house. She drew a basin of warm water and sponged away the blood from my face and hair.

"*Ai,* you poor child," she consoled me as she ministered to me. I could not see the wound, but I'd felt it with my fingers, felt the flesh ripped jaggedly apart exposing something soft and wet. My head throbbed, my throat ached. I wanted to lie down and pull the covers over my face.

Flora did not have the skill of Giuseppina, but she had a gentle touch and a kindness I hadn't experienced since setting foot in America. She turned to Paolo.

"What Claudio has done to this child is a sin! You find him and tell him that! And tell him you're not bringing her back to his house."

I wasn't afraid to go back to Claudio's. But to defy Claudio, to fling his anger back in his face by not returning home, was an idea that seized me.

Paolo was silent. Did he agree with Flora? Would he shield me from Claudio, even though he was Claudio's best friend?

I looked at his face, so familiar to me. The neighborhood saw my brother Claudio with respect—for his success, his powerful friends. But for Paolo they had a kind of deference—for his intelligence and his learning. It was Claudio they came to when they needed a favor, but it was Paolo they turned to when they couldn't understand something—a paper from the government, a letter from home they couldn't read or respond to. It set him apart, put him a little on the outside of the everyday life we were all caught up in. It made him lonely, in spite of his connection with Claudio.

I had for so long purposely ignored Paolo's presence in my day-to-day life or, at least, treated him lightly. A friendly voice, a smile, a hand with my packages, a handkerchief for my tears, an arm to support me over the rutted ice. I had only seen these small parts of him, offered with such restraint and graciousness, because I had not wanted to see the passion and the will restraining that passion. I had not been willing to see the whole man.

Flora's baby started to wail in her crib. Flora put aside the cloth and went down the hallway to tend to her. The blood was still trickling down my forehead, mingling with my tears. I grappled for the cloth and held it against the wound.

"Here, let me help you," Paolo whispered. He eased the cloth from my hand and tentatively dabbed. "I don't want to hurt you. Let me know if I do." He was hesitant. Almost afraid to touch me—not because of the blood but for other reasons.

Paolo stood before me, his head and heart filled with words that he did not utter out loud to me, and his hand—in a gesture that felt, at that moment, closer than an embrace—stained with my blood.

The intense pain of the last hour, the gnawing emptiness

of the last weeks, even the longing for my home and family in Italy that I thought I'd put behind me after all these months, suddenly filled my vision. I began to cry, wildly, unrestrained, huge tears spilling down my face.

I felt Paolo's hand lift from my forehead in a moment of confusion. "Am I pressing too hard?" I shook my head, not knowing how to express my own confusion—sadness, despair, loneliness, gratitude, hope. How could I be feeling so many different, conflicting emotions? I did not know myself. I had always been so *sure,* the roots of my self so well-planted and nourished by Giuseppina's teaching. Perhaps in this cold and lightless city I had lost my bearings. I did not know which way to turn toward the sun and so I revolved as if on the carousel that came to Venticano every August, dragged in pieces in a wagon pulled by four massive horses and assembled in the piazza before us eager and curious children. It spun us around and around until we were dizzy with glee and abandon and the delicious fear that if we let go of our painted horses we'd be thrown off over the edge of the cliff to which the piazza clung. That was how I felt at that moment with Paolo—dizzy with the fear that I was about to be hurled into the unknown.

And just as I was about to fly out of control, engulfed by my pain, Paolo caught me. He reached out his arms—his confusion and hesitancy wiped away in an instant of recognition and understanding—and pulled me toward him. My tears and my blood mingled on his starched white shirtfront.

There, within the circle of his arms, I stayed.

Chapter 18

"YOU'VE DONE A GOOD job in my absence, Paolo," Flora said when she returned to the kitchen with the baby in her arms. "Not only has the bleeding slowed down, you've actually brought a smile to Giulia's face."

Paolo and I abruptly pulled away from each other, away from warmth, from the sound of his heart beating beneath my ear, from the threshold we had apparently just crossed. I looked into his eyes and saw my own reflection.

"I think I can bandage that now, Giulia." She handed the baby to Paolo, who nuzzled her belly and then balanced her on his knee while Flora wrapped a strip of torn toweling around my forehead. When she was satisfied with her work, she knelt in front of me, took my hands in hers, and spoke to me intently.

"Giulia, I told you when Paolo brought you here that I would not willingly let you return to Claudio's tonight. I mean that. But I don't think it's wise for you to spend the night here. I am not your family. Perhaps they'll understand if you don't go back, but I know they won't understand if you stay here. They won't trust me if they suspect even a fraction of what I saw a minute ago between you and Paolo. They'll think I'm offering you a haven for lovemaking.

"I'm sorry if this is embarrassing you. But you both know that's what they'll think. And Claudio could come storming up here demanding you back. We must find another place for you, safe, with family. Is there anyone we can turn to?"

Who in my family would shelter me against Claudio? Tilly had hidden herself in the back room. Pip, when she heard what had happened, would purse her lips in a thin line and think I got what I deserved for being Roberto's girl. My cousin Peppino, who did Claudio's errands, fetched him his morning coffee? His father, Tony, Papa's younger brother? Maybe. He admired Claudio's shrewdness, his success in making a life for himself in America. That was why Uncle Tony came here in the first place, awakened by Claudio's success, tempted to create his own out from under Papa's shadow. But Claudio had become another Papa. Peppino worked for Claudio, not for his father. Perhaps Uncle Tony was the right choice, in fact, my *only* choice.

Flora bundled up the baby, and she and I set off for Tony's apartment. Paolo left with us but then turned off to his own pursuits. It was best that he not be with us, that he not be the one standing between my brother and me.

Zi'Yolanda opened the door with a shriek.

"Giulia! Giulia! What has happened to you? Did you fall in the street? Come in, come in. And who is this with you? Ah, yes, Flora. God bless you for bringing our Giulia…but isn't Angelina at home? Why didn't you go home, sweetheart? Wasn't Tilly with you? Oh, my God, oh, my God. Something terrible has happened, hasn't it? Shall I send for Claudio?"

Zi'Yolanda twisted her hands in mounting confusion and concern as she asked her questions without stopping for answers, racing from one possibility to another, a crescendo of disaster and the incomprehensible rising in her voice.

"Tell me, tell me everything. *Someone,* not something, has done this to you, am I right? I knew it—I knew it as soon as I saw your face. Here, here. I just made a pot of coffee. Have a piece of anisette bread—it's all I have in the house. I don't bake until Friday. Uncle Tony likes his ricotta pie fresh for the weekend. No, you're not hungry? Of course not. But tell me. Oh, wait till Claudio finds out! Was it one of those DiDonatos looking for information about Roberto? As if you knew anything—"

"Zi'Yolanda, be still for a minute. Listen to me."

"I'm trying, sweetheart, I'm trying. Do you want a glass of brandy?"

"Zi'Yolanda! Come away from the cabinet for a minute. Put the glass down. Claudio did this to me, Zi'Yolanda."

She dropped the glass.

Flora's baby started to cry.

Zi'Yolanda, finally, was speechless.

"I need a place to stay, Zi'Yolanda. I don't want to go back to Claudio's house tonight. May I sleep here?"

Zi'Yolanda knelt down to pick up the glass shards.

"Claudio? Claudio? In all my days, I would never have thought… Your father is a loud man, he pounded his fist on the table now and then, but something like *this,* never, never. Uncle Tony, too. He barks a lot, but raise his hand to me—I swear to you on my mother's grave—never. Where does this come from? How does Claudio think he can do this? Of course you can stay tonight. And if I know your uncle Tony, he'll go get your things out of Claudio's house and move you in here permanently."

She got out her dustpan and broom and swept up the splinters. She looked up at Flora with the baby on her shoulder.

"You're a good friend to Giulia?" She wasn't sure, I could hear it in her voice, see it in the narrowing of her eyes.

Flora nodded as she patted her daughter's back.

"Then you'll keep your mouth shut about this? This kind of thing, it shouldn't go outside the family." To me, she said, "Why didn't you come here first, sweetheart? Didn't you trust Uncle Tony and me to take care of you? You had to go to a stranger?"

I started to explain that it wasn't my choice. I was going to tell her that Paolo had brought me to his sister, but Flora interrupted me.

"Signora Fiorillo, Giulia meant no disrespect. There was a lot of blood at first. I live close to the store—that's where it happened. I think Giulia realized how much attention she'd attract if she came all the way here with a bloody head. So I cleaned her up a little before bringing her to you. I don't know much more about what happened. I'm a good friend to Giulia, *Signora*. And I'm not a gossip."

Yolanda emptied the glass bits into the bin. She seemed satisfied with Flora's answer, but I could see she wanted to hear more about what had happened and didn't want to ask me in Flora's presence, especially if Flora knew as little as she professed to know.

"No, no. Please don't be offended, my dear. I'm grateful to you for taking care of her and for bringing her here, you with the baby, too. Your first? No? So, you must have a lot to do at home, supper to prepare, the baby to put down. I won't keep you. Giulia is quite safe with us."

After Flora left, Zi'Yolanda stopped her fussing with the broom.

"So, you wanna lie down, sweetheart? I'll make up Pepe's bed nice and clean for you. Or you wanna talk about it?"

"I think I'll lie down, Zi'Yolanda. There's not much to say. Claudio came into the store. He got mad. He picked up an iron and threw it at me."

"He ever hit you before this?"

"No, never."

"I don't understand it. Well, when Uncle Tony gets home, you can bet he'll have a word or two to say to your brother."

I shrugged. Claudio listened to nobody, not even Uncle Tony. Any words Uncle Tony might shout or scold would be ignored, just like Claudio used to ignore Papa.

"Maybe I'll have that glass of brandy before I lie down."

When I woke up it was dark. My head throbbed but the bandage wasn't leaking. The bleeding had stopped. Peppino's bed was in a corner of the dining room, and Zi'Yolanda was setting the table. I smelled soup.

"You feeling a little better, angel? I made some 'scarole and meatballs. Uncle Tony's washing up in the kitchen. You wanna sit up and eat something with us?"

When Uncle Tony came to the table he took one look at my head and started to curse.

"That son of a bitch. He should be my son. If he were, I'd teach him once and for all not to lay a hand on his own sister. God Almighty! That's who he thinks he is. I'll tell you one thing. I'm not letting you go back to his house. Not tonight, not any night.

"He can bang on my door all night long. Wake up the whole damn neighborhood, for all I care. You hear that, Pepe?" He turned to my cousin.

"You tell your boss this is where his sister is and this is where she's going to stay."

After supper, Peppino went out. He had barely looked at me during the meal. I had never seen Uncle Tony so angry or so determined. Something had happened to our whole family that afternoon when Claudio had hit me and I had accepted refuge from Flora and Paolo. Something like this would not—could not—have happened in Venticano. So much damage in one afternoon…so little protection for me…so little solidarity in the family. I saw at supper that this was going to rend us apart. Already Tony and Peppino had chosen sides—one to stand by me, the other to follow Claudio.

This frightened me more than the blow from Claudio. What would my sisters do, sheltered under Claudio's roof? What would my parents say when they were informed? Why weren't they here now, to protect me, to prevent the catastrophe I feared when Claudio came storming up the stairs to fetch me home?

Or would he not come at all? Would he leave me here with Tony and Yolanda, cutting himself off?

Another home for me. I was no longer welcome in the house of my brother, nor my grandmother, nor my mother and father.

How I longed for a home that I could call mine.

Chapter 19

The First Letter

I WAITED INTO THE night for Claudio to come raging into Yolanda and Tony's the way he'd raged into the store that afternoon.

Yolanda jumped at every slammed door, every footfall on the stairs, pricking herself with her darning needle more than once during the evening as she sat at the cleared dining table with a pile of Peppino's and Tony's shirts and socks.

My head hurt too much to sit up with her after we ate. I didn't even help her wash the dishes. She had shooed me back into the bed.

"I'll take care of this tonight, sweetheart. You go and lie down."

I turned my body to the wall, grateful not to have to listen to Yolanda's worries, Yolanda's gossip, Yolanda's aches and pains. Even Yolanda's criticism of the absent Peppino didn't interest me. Peppino had been my least favorite cousin when we were children. He was a tease who'd once brought me a rose he'd doused with pepper. I had sneezed and coughed for almost an hour. But what had hurt the most was his ridicule. I had thought he liked me, was offering me a special gift with the rose. When I held it up to my nose to admire it and began to sneeze so hard that tears welled up in my eyes, he whooped and hooted with laughter, and his friends leaped out from their hiding places to laugh and taunt with him. I threw the rose down and stomped on it with my foot and kicked Peppino before I turned my back on him and walked home with as much dignity as I could.

Now I was lying in his bed, huddled against the wall, waiting for my brother to show himself.

But he never came. No pounding on the door, no shouted curses, no scenes between the blustering Claudio in charge of everything and the outraged Tony, protector of his niece.

I began to drift off to sleep, floating in and out of dreams, when I heard a respectful knock at the door and then muffled voices. It was late, the room already dark, Yolanda and her darning basket gone.

I heard Uncle Tony speaking quietly and without excitement to whoever had come to the door. It could not be Claudio. The voices were too reasonable. The way one talks to strangers, not to family.

Zi'Yolanda's voice pierced the calm. "Tony, Tony? Who's there? What is it? What does he want?"

"It's all right, Yolly. It's Paolo Serafini. Go back to bed. Everything's okay."

Peppino's bed was positioned so that I couldn't see through the archway between the dining room and the front room, where Uncle Tony stood talking to Paolo. Paolo, here. A few feet away across a darkened room. I sat up, straining to hear his voice, wishing I could go out to him but not trusting myself, afraid that I'd throw myself into his arms, sure that if I did so he'd return the embrace. And there would stand Uncle

Tony, mouth agape, not believing his eyes for a few seconds, then jumping from the scene before him to my brother's rage. Tony would explode, feeling betrayed. Yolanda would come running in her nightclothes and grasp whatever fragments she could to feed the clothesline crowd in the morning.

No, I had to remain in bed, show indifference, feign sleep. Anything to prevent them from recognizing the wildness beating in my heart, the agitation I felt knowing he was just beyond reach.

"Tony, I stopped by Claudio's house early this evening to tell Angelina and the girls that Giulia is safe with you. Claudio I haven't seen. He hasn't shown up at the Palace yet. Angelina said he had a meeting in New York and she wasn't expecting him home till late, so I don't think you'll see him here tonight. Unless he runs into somebody like Pepe, he's not even going to know where Giulia is. So rest easy. Maybe by tomorrow he'll have cooled off." He paused. "How's Giulia doing? The girls were upset, wanted her home with them, but I said leave her alone, let her rest out of Claudio's way."

"Thanks, Paolo. That son-of-a-bitch nephew better not show his face around here for a few days. His father should only be here. He'd kill him for touching a hair on his sister's head. I may do it for him.

"I understand your sister fixed her up. God bless her. Giulia's indebted to her and to you."

"Flora would've done nothing less. It's how she is. Look, I'll try to talk to Claudio as soon as I see him. He listens to me…sometimes. Anyway, I just wanted you to know. I've got to get back to the Palace."

"Keep an eye on my son. He hasn't learned to control himself yet. Thinks the night should never end, you know what I mean?"

I heard the door latch, the lumbering of Tony's feet back

to bed with Yolanda, the brisk tap of Paolo's shoes on the stairs that ran along the outside wall next to my bed.

I moved from the bed to the front window, reaching it in time to see him stride from the building. I pressed my palms against the glass, wishing he'd turn around and glance up. But he walked off into the night, his head down against the cold wind, his hands thrust into his pockets.

A blue envelope arrived at eight the next morning, delivered by Nino. He was on his way to school and had run to Yolanda and Tony's in order not to be late.

He knocked on the door in a rapid, impatient-little-boy way. "Giulia? Giulia? I'm looking for Giulia Fiorillo. Is she here?"

I heard his voice on the landing, breathless, loud, for all the building to hear.

Peppino opened the door in his undershirt, sullen from being roused at too early an hour, from having to sleep on the sofa when he came in at four in the morning, since Zi'Yolanda had put me in his bed.

"Yeah, what do you want?"

"Is Giulia here?"

"Yeah. Why?"

"This is for her. Give it to her, please." Nino tossed the envelope to Peppino and flew down the stairs.

Peppino took the envelope and studied it as closely as his sleep-heavy, wine-blurred eyes allowed. He turned it over in his hand, studied the inscription, checked to see if the envelope had been sealed. I watched from the archway of the dining room as he slid his grimy thumbnail under the flap.

"Is that for me, Peppino?" I crossed the room in two swift steps and put my hand on the envelope, my thumb pressing down on the flap Peppino had begun to peel open.

He kept his hand on the blue paper, not releasing it to me.

"Whose brat was that? And who's sending you letters through him?"

"I won't know that until I open the letter, Peppino."

"Is this the reason Claudio hit you?" His hand tugged against mine.

"It's none of your business. You're not my brother. And neither one of you is Papa. Give me the letter."

He still wouldn't let go. The struggle over this piece of paper was waking him up.

"Something's not right," Peppino challenged me. "Some stranger early in the morning. What is it, a love letter? Why so urgent? And how did he know you were here?"

"Peppino, I told you. I have no idea who wrote this because you won't let me open it. And even if I did, I wouldn't tell you."

But I did know, of course. I knew the blue paper. I knew the flourish of the pen. I knew Nino. I was desperate to read the words, but kept my longing to myself. I didn't need to give Peppino, with his nosy questions and his big mouth and his loyalty to Claudio, the opportunity to learn such a secret about me. The secret was still so new that I'd lain awake all night, bewildered. What was I to do with this knowledge? This man who'd been a steady, silent presence in my life had now spoken, had now taken me into his arms. How could my understanding of him, my feelings for him, change so much in just one day? People around me thought my world had turned upside down because Claudio had hurt me so savagely. But they were wrong. I was not going to let my life fall apart because my brother couldn't hold himself in check. He had made me angry but he had not made me afraid. What made me afraid right then were my feelings for Paolo. I was not looking for this; I had not asked for it in my prayers or even my dreams.

I had been thrown off balance by Paolo. I had no warning, no months of preparation and anticipation for the way I felt.

This brought so much unease to my heart. I felt out of control, bobbing and diving among turbulent waves that washed over me with ever-increasing height. Volumes of emotion. Voices within my head expressing doubt, telling me this shouldn't be. I shouldn't feel this way—so suddenly, so differently. I was too confused. I needed to understand more. I needed to anchor myself, to keep myself tethered to something real….

I needed the letter, becoming tattered and smudged in Peppino's hands and mine. We were scrabbling like two children over a chestnut. One taunting, the other clutching.

"Pepe, what are you doing up so early?" Zi'Yolanda shoved her head out the kitchen door. "You wanna cup of coffee? Who was that at the door?"

Her hair was still down in a graying braid behind her back, her cotton housedress protected by a flowered apron. My own mother, her hair still black, never appeared even for morning coffee without her hair smoothly pinned in place.

"What's that? You two look like you're fighting over the last piece of cake. Did someone bring a message? From Claudio?"

"It's for me, Zi'Yolanda. But I don't know who it's from because your son won't let me have it."

"If it's from someone in the family, why didn't they come in person?" Peppino jumped in. "And if it's from a stranger, it's not right…."

"Since when did you become a judge of what's proper and what's not? You with your American girlfriend who stays out with you half the night like a *putana?*" Zi'Yolanda was warming to my side.

"Look, why don't you give me the letter and I'll open it right here in front of your mother and you."

Zi'Yolanda gestured to Peppino to let go of the letter. She was as curious as he, but for more benevolent reasons— romance, gossip.

"Maybe it's about Roberto," she ventured with a mixture of hope and fascination.

Peppino reluctantly loosened his fingers and I slipped the envelope out of his grasp. I opened it calmly, careful not to tear the paper, not to betray my mounting agitation.

Inside the blue envelope lay a folded sheet of blue paper, covered on all four sides with writing. I didn't want to read the entire letter in front of Peppino and Yolanda. Even if I read silently, I was afraid that the emotions expressed on paper would spill over into my eyes, my face, betraying me to those I was least willing to reveal myself to.

"Oh, look, it's from Flora! How sweet!"

Peppino and Yolanda nodded in satisfaction. Yolanda couldn't read a word beyond her own name. Peppino thought he could read, but I'd seen him struggle with simple words. They probably wouldn't know, had they taken the sheet from me and pored over it, heads together, whether it was a grocery list or a death threat.

A friendly note of concern, asking whether I'd spent the night comfortably, hoping the bandages had served me well. That's what I told Yolanda and Peppino. And that was, in part, what the letter said. Except that it had been written by Paolo and not Flora. The rest of the note I resolved to read in private, so I refolded it, replaced it in the envelope and tucked the envelope inside the sleeve of my blouse.

Peppino, deprived of the opportunity for outrage, sulked into the kitchen, Zi'Yolanda padding behind him to serve him a cup of coffee.

Later in the morning, on her way back from doing the marketing, Yolanda decided to stop by Angelina and Claudio's to get me some fresh clothes. Uncle Tony didn't want me out of the house yet. He didn't want me running into Claudio alone before someone—preferably Uncle Tony—had had a chance to talk to him.

Zi'Yolanda was gone a long time. Long enough, I'm sure, to have a cup of coffee with Angelina and fill her in on all she, Yolanda, was privileged to know. Angelina must have been relieved to learn that she'd lost one of her boarders, even if only temporarily. But after a few days without my cooking and entertaining her sons, she might come to appreciate me. God knows, she hadn't yet.

I wondered if Angelina was surprised. Had Claudio ever hit her? I'd never seen or heard anything in all the time I lived with them. A lot of gruff words, shouting matches at the table, Angelina petulant and whining and ultimately punishing Claudio by leaving him to brood alone while she went upstairs to be by herself. Leaving us with the dishes and the sweeping and picking up the broken pieces of whatever Claudio had flung from the table. Not so different from my parents' house.

But I never saw him hit her. And I never came home from work to find her with a swollen lip or a bruised face. Not that she would've confided in me if he *had* hit her—in some place covered up, hidden by her skirt or blouse. But I don't believe he ever did.

Claudio had a violent temper, but until that day he had exercised it with his voice, his words, his smashing of objects that had sentimental worth to Angelina, like the china fruit bowl she'd kept on the sideboard, carried with her from Abruzzi, wrapped in layer upon layer of bedding. It had survived the land journey to Napoli, the ocean crossing, the trolley to Mount Vernon. But it had sat there by the dining table for three years, ever ready, ever in Claudio's view, within reach when he was provoked to new heights of anger. Who knows? Claudio was so adamant about his disdain for Italy. He believed he'd escaped a place of fools and losers. He had no good memories, no lingering doubts about his decision to leave. So maybe Angelina's bowl had sat there all those years shouting

Italy to him. And when the moment had come—some disappointment, some failure he could throw off onto the deficiencies of our homeland—he'd picked up this symbol of Italy accorded a place of honor in his own house and thrown it out the window. Which fortunately had been open, so we didn't have to replace the glass. But the bowl had fallen to the stone terrace behind the house, smashed among the begonias withering in clay pots and the toys belonging to his sons.

Angelina hadn't spoken to him for two weeks. Had Claudio possessed an object of equal emotional importance to him, I'm sure she would have smashed it with a furious pleasure. But what was important to Claudio? His horses? They were his livelihood, but I don't remember him speaking affectionately about a single one of them. He called them "the bay," "the chestnut," "the gray." He didn't even give them names.

What mattered to Claudio were his deals—getting something worth more than he'd had to pay for it. But Claudio treasure something, preserve it, keep it? I didn't think so. He would tell you that he was always facing forward. He didn't look back—not to the business he would've joined with Papa, not to the early days here in America with no horses, no money.

"I keep my eye on tomorrow," he said. "I keep my eye on the other guy. Where's he going, how's he going to make his mistake."

But this time, it was Claudio who'd made the mistake.

Maybe I should've sat at Yolanda's table considering my own mistake as I shelled the peas Yolanda had left for me. Maybe I should've whimpered for Claudio to forgive me for being lazy. Wasn't that what he'd said in the store, tracing his finger through the dust on the counter? Or maybe for dancing with Roberto? Couldn't I see he'd be the kind to get mixed up with the law in a way that brought too much attention upon himself, upon me, and then upon Claudio? Or maybe, like Angelina's china bowl, for just being around in Claudio's life. Standing there in the store, provoking him to rage simply because he had to look at me every day and be reminded of something he couldn't control.

I didn't think so. I didn't think it was my mistake. If Claudio opened my head with a flat iron, it was Claudio who had done something wrong. And who was going to tell him that? Uncle Tony was full of big words, calling Claudio a son of a bitch, but not to his face. Paolo? As much as he loved me, was he ready to choose between Claudio and me? Or did he think he could be the go-between? The man of honor who restored peace to our family?

I didn't want peace right then. I wanted people to look at the horror on my forehead and feel the anger that I felt. But who could I count on for that?

Even Yolanda, concerned as she was and unable to understand how this could happen, was afraid of Claudio. I could hear it in her voice when Paolo came to the door. The tremor, the crack, the waiting in anxiety for hell to break loose or break down the door. Tilly was also afraid. From the first moment, when Claudio had heaved into the store, she'd hidden in the back, making herself small. When we were children and Papa was yelling at the dinner table, Tilly and I had closed our eyes fiercely tight, believing that if we couldn't see him, he couldn't see us and make us his next target.

Everyone here still seemed to believe the same magic. They closed their eyes to Claudio.

But I looked my brother in the eye.

Chapter 20

Paolo's Words

THE GASH CLAUDIO put in my head put a rift between him and Paolo. After Claudio hit me, Paolo's friendship with him became strained. He spent less and less time with Claudio. In the past, they'd often stayed late together at the Palace, closing up the place with a few glasses of grappa and a card game after they'd counted up the till. But after, it was all business between them. Paolo continued to keep an eye on the place in the evenings from the piano and he did the books, but he left as soon as the money was counted for the night. If Claudio wanted to smoke a cigar and play a few rounds, he did it with Peppino and his ruffian friends.

Paolo removed himself from Claudio's presence because otherwise he would have attacked him for what he'd done to me. He wrote to me that he could not control the anger that rose in him when he remembered finding me that day on the street. It blinded him, the thought of my blood and my pain. The only reason he didn't go after Claudio was to protect our secret, to keep our love from those who would try to drive us apart.

Each morning a letter had come for me since that first one I'd wrested from Peppino's filthy hand. But even though I'd received a letter every day, I had not seen Paolo since I watched from the window that first night at Yolanda and Tony's as he'd walked away into the darkness.

He had attempted to keep what was happening between us as private as possible. He did not want to cloud the situation between Claudio and me—did not want to give Claudio more ammunition. It wouldn't take much for Claudio to accuse me of being a whore. God knows, I had demonstrated neither the propriety of Pip nor the innocence of Tilly in my history with men.

Only Flora had Paolo's confidence. After the first day, he did not send Nino with the letters. Flora brought the others, stopping by for a brief daily visit, passing the blue envelope to me when Yolanda's attention was occupied elsewhere, taking the white envelope that enclosed what I had written in secret in response to Paolo's letter of the day before.

Flora brought me Paolo's letters with such discretion that Yolanda never suspected. I don't think she could even imagine that a man would court a woman in such a way. It was not within her experience of life.

I don't think I imagined it myself before I began to read Paolo's words and was engulfed by them. Signore Ventuolo had taught me the power of words on a page—but those were words written for many eyes. Paolo's words were written only for me.

My mother wrote letters. I remember, on the days the post came, how Mama's face would light up at the stack of envelopes—from her friends in Benevento, her own mother and later, from Signore Ventuolo. She would retreat to her room and only emerge when all the letters had been read and answered. She might say twenty words to Papa all week, but she filled pages in her letters. The envelopes going out in the next day's post were always thick, heavy with whatever it was she found the need to say.

Paolo's letters spoke for him as my mother's did for her.

In them, I began to discover the complex man who had been hidden from me. In them, he began to reveal himself. I learned of his passions—for me, for his work, for his music.

He wrote to me that he'd never loved another woman with such intensity, that my beauty and gentleness brought him so much happiness—happiness that he wanted only to give back to me. He told me that I owned his heart.

He wrote to me about his work with the union. Other unions, like the Knights of Labor and the AFL, kept the Italians out. But the Wobblies, the International Workers of the World, had opened its doors to men like Paolo, and he went barreling through that door brandishing his pen like a sword and pouring his outrage at the injustices suffered by laborers into speeches and strikes. He was the secretary of the union. It sounds so quiet, so innocuous—recording the minutes of meetings and writing the broadsides that were handed out to workers and sent to newspapers. But I knew that the words Paolo was writing were not so quiet.

He wrote to me about what he did late at night at the Palace. When things quieted down and everybody had a drink, he stole a few minutes at the piano, composing a song he wanted Caruso to sing. As he composed, he heard the notes sung in Caruso's inimitable voice and knew that only Caruso could bring the music to life. Paolo carried a sheaf of creased staff paper in his coat pocket, folded up at the end of the night after he locked the Palace. Each evening, he retrieved it, unfolded it and placed it on the top of the piano. He studied the marks he'd made, replaying their pattern lightly on the worn keys and then fingering the next measure. Around him were murmurs or shouts, the splash of whiskey in glass, the scrape of heavy boot on oak floor. Still, he listened and called up the voice he'd only heard once but held in his memory like a mother recognizing the cry of her newborn infant. And then he wrote, furiously, passionately, his hand moving as if guided by Caruso himself.

These were Paolo's words; this was Paolo's world.

If I had not had his letters, I would have felt abandoned. But I knew that he kept away, sending the letters as his substitute, to protect me from prying eyes and damaging rumors and to protect us in this fragile state of early love from the interfering words and innuendo that can pull lovers apart.

Chapter 21

Back to Work

I WENT BACK TO THE store after two weeks. Pip had been ill and Tilly had her hands full managing alone. She'd always been the backroom person, content to count spools and organize piles of merchandise. She liked to climb up on her stepladder and restore order to a shelf I'd been haphazardly emptying and refilling. She found satisfaction in those tasks. But as soon as a customer entered the shop, the little bell over the door tinkling, Tilly ducked her head, descended from the ladder and retreated to the back of the store to fetch me and then hide. She was desperately shy, barely able to whisper a greeting.

I was good in the front of the shop. I chatted with customers, discovered what was going on in their lives, found ways to encourage them to buy things they hadn't thought of when they'd arrived at the store.

After two weeks of confinement in Yolanda's house, I saw the store as an opportunity. I wanted Paolo to walk through the door. There was no Yolanda to rush off to Angelina's with a report. Tilly would be mildly perplexed by his visit, but would not be able to hear what was unsaid.

I spent the first day back alternating between reverie and commerce, longing for Paolo to appear but often too busy to notice that he wasn't there. I was a dreamer, but not when doing business. The last customer of the day was indecisive. I took down half our supplies before she made up her mind. She chose six buttons and complained about their price, their quality. When she finally left, I had a pile of boxes on the counter to replace and a throbbing headache. I wanted to leave the mess for Tilly but when I turned to ask her for help she was already putting on her hat and primping in front of the mirror. Shy Tilly had a suitor—Gaetano Novelli. He was as round as she was and his cheeks and nose were chafed a permanent red in the bitter chill of that winter. He had invited her to coffee.

She was gay with anticipation, and I hadn't the heart to make her stay and help me clean up. As soon as she left, I pulled the shades and started putting away boxes. I was on the stepladder, shoving the last carton onto its shelf and imagining myself walking, not back to Yolanda and Tony's that night, but to the Palace to find Paolo, when the bell sounded. I thought I'd locked the door!

"I'm sorry, but we're closed…" I swiveled on the ladder to face the door. It was Peppino.

"Pop sent me down to walk you home. Don't expect this every night. I've got more important things to do than be your nursemaid."

"You don't even have to do it tonight, Pepe. I can get myself to your house just fine."

"Yeah, and if I show up without you, I'll have to listen to my old man rag on me about family responsibility and I'll have to pick my mother up off the kitchen floor where she'll have fallen in a faint, screaming, 'I knew it! I knew we shouldn't have trusted him.' No, cousin. Spare the family at least one night of hysteria. Come home like a good girl, keep Tony and Yolanda happy and out of Pepe's hair, and Pepe will stay out of your business in return."

"I have no business for you to keep out of, Peppino."

"Right. That's why you're in so much trouble with Claudio, why you have to come running to your uncle Tony to protect you. You've got some business, girl. Seems to me this family spends too much time straightening out Giulia's escapades, protecting the almighty Fiorillo name and reputation."

"It's your name, too, and I don't see you doing all that much to keep it untarnished. How much money do you owe, Pepe, to keep playing cards at the Palace every night? Does my brother pay your debts for you? I'll bet it's not your father. Does he even know about the gambling? Or does Yolanda protect you?"

"You have a big mouth, Giulia. But I can hurt you more. Pop would get angry about the gambling, but in the end he'd have to give up, say, 'Boys will be boys,' and 'Let him ruin his own life.' But a daughter with a reputation, that's another story. Nobody wants a whore in the family, Giulia. Least of all the Fiorillos. So get your coat and lock up. My mother's got dinner waiting."

I slammed the last box onto the shelf. Pepe and I trudged home in silence.

Chapter 22

Unwelcome

AFTER A MONTH, my welcome at Yolanda and Tony's was growing thin. Uncle Tony had not confronted Claudio, and Claudio, of course, did not come to Uncle Tony. If Claudio was upset that I hadn't come back to his house, he didn't show it. Instead of yelling and hitting, he acted as if I didn't exist. He had wiped me away, like some fly on one of his horses' flanks. Like the dust he'd dragged his finger through on the counter just before he'd hit me.

Good riddance! I'm sure he thought. One less mouth to feed, one less mouth to listen to in his household of women.

Tony avoided my face when he came home at night. His gaze no longer took in the fading bruise on my forehead. He scrubbed the dirt from his hands but he was never able to get all of it out. His palms seemed permanently crazed with thin black lines of embedded grit from his work as a laborer on a road construction crew. He also could not wash from his face the years of exposure to sun and wind, and here in America, bitter cold. After he washed, he sat at the table, already set by me. Yolanda's things weren't as fine as my mother's. Cotton tablecloth, not damask. But starched and ironed. Heavy, plain stoneware dishes, not painted bone china. Yolanda served Tony immediately, the steam rising off the mounded food on his plate. He ate his macaroni in silence, drank his two glasses of wine and fell asleep in the chair in the front room.

Pepe watched me from across the table. Glowering with resentment, searching for secrets. Pepe was annoyed by my presence in his house, so he made himself as annoying to me as possible. He scratched his bare chest in my face, his pale skin soaked in sweat. He threw to the floor the few clothes Yolanda had fetched for me when he was looking for something that he claimed I'd misplaced. I took all of Paolo's letters with me when I went to the store. I was afraid that Pepe would find them if I left them at Yolanda's—not accidentally, but deliberately. I didn't trust him. He was a violator. Careless of himself, careless of his mother's devotion to him, her only son. He mocked her behind her back. Ignored her pleas that he make something of his life. Took her money—that she slipped to him when Tony wasn't around—to pay off the debts he never seemed to be free of.

I knew that Pepe had begun to complain to Yolanda about my presence. I had taken his bed, I knew his games, I heard his lies. I didn't hear him talking to Yolanda, but I heard his words coming out of Yolanda's mouth. After Claudio had left them alone, she'd begun to convince herself that his silence was reconciliation. If Claudio wasn't breaking the door down, then everything must be okay. She didn't see his refusal to talk to Tony or me as the smoldering fire it could very well be. A few more weeks of my defiance and Claudio's refusal to acknowledge it, and we could've had a conflagration, a fireball that would probably have been seen back in Venticano.

But Yolanda, fed by Pepe, chose to see the fire banked,

muffled, maybe even extinguished by the other, more important concerns in Claudio's powerful life. I was a speck. Blown
away by the wind, washed out of Claudio's eye, brushed off
by a preoccupied hand. Yolanda saw what she wanted to see.
Life goes on. Everybody make nice like nothing happened.
See, the bruises are fading, the cut is healing. In a few weeks
you won't even know anything happened.

"So, sweetheart, you miss your sisters?" she asked me one
morning, a month into my stay. "You wish you could be back
with them? Maybe we should have a family dinner. I'll invite
them all, make a nice *antipast'*. A little minestrone, some
manicott'. Mercurio's got some good breast of veal this week.
I could stuff it with *alice* and hard-boiled eggs. What do you
say? We'll fill their bellies, raise a few glasses of Uncle Tony's
Chianti, clear all of this up. Then you could go home."

"Claudio's house is not my home anymore. I don't want
to share a roof with a man who acts like he did, even if he
is my brother."

"What do you want to do, spend the rest of your life not
talking to your brother? Look at your uncle Tony and your
papa. How many civil words have they said to each other in
ten years? They can't even live in the same country. Uncle
Tony would never admit it, but believe me, it eats away at him.
And over what? Some slight, some insult that I bet neither one
of them remembers. It shouldn't be like that, it shouldn't. Not
when it's family."

Chapter 23

Anna Directs from Afar

BUT NO DINNER of Yolanda's was going to move my brother. Only my mother could do that. She wrote to Claudio, as she wrote to all of us, every month. When she learned of what Claudio had done, she picked up her pen with a vengeance, and she sent me a copy.

Figlio mio,
Your last letter has arrived safely and the money has been put to good use, paying for Aldo and Frankie's next semester of study with the Franciscans. Frankie, as I've written you before, is an especially apt pupil. Father Bruno says he will be ready for the university in two years. If only I had been able to offer you the same opportunity! I look at Frankie and I see you at that age—the same intelligence, the same ambition. But you have put your sharp mind to good use nevertheless, as I never doubted. I shall always be grateful to you, Claudio, for what you now make possible for your brothers, and for the safety you have provided your sisters.

You know I have always trusted you, had faith in you. And you have never disappointed me. I could always hold my head high—with your father, with his sisters, with the gossips in this village—whenever your name was mentioned. I have been proud to say, "That is Claudio Alfonso Fiorillo, my firstborn. A man of honor, of respect, of success." Even when you left here, stubborn and embittered, I knew in my heart that you were doing the right thing, the thing I had raised you to do. Who, after all, found you the money to leave? Whose jewelry was pressed into your hand to buy you passage to your dreams?

That is why I cannot believe what I have learned in a letter from Tilly that arrived the same day as your money. Why I cannot accept that my faith in you has been rewarded by behavior I would expect of a lowlife like your cousin Peppino, but not of my own son.

Tell me that the event Tilly described to me did not take place. I would rather have her be a liar than know that a son of mine has laid a hand on his sister. The man who has done this is a stranger to me, cannot have my blood in his veins.

But if it is true, and you wish me to acknowledge you as my son, then go to your sister and beg her forgiveness. Give her back the safety and protection of her family. God knows what will become of her if you do not. Far worse than the laziness of which you accused her. And far worse than any pride you have to swallow to go to her. Do not bring any further public disgrace upon this family by abandoning your sister to a life on her own. You know as well as I do that she will not stay with Tony and Yolanda. Where will she go? To some American boardinghouse where no one knows who she is or cares when she comes or goes? Do you want your sister to be seen as no better than the village whore?

Has America done this?

I shall wait to hear that both my daughter and my son have been restored to me.

Your loving mother,

Anna

Chapter 24

The Apology

I WAS HELPING Yolanda dry the dishes after supper. Uncle
Tony had gone down the street to his neighbor Fat Eddie's to
play cards and Pepe had told his mother he was going to work
at the Palace. We were alone.

The knock on the door startled Yolanda, and the pot she was
scrubbing slipped from her soapy hands and clattered into the
sink.

"Who, at this hour?"

"I'll go, Zi'Yolanda," I told her, wiping my hands on my
apron. Before she could hold me back I was in the front room.

"Who's there?" I asked through the door.

"Claudio."

My hand flew to my head, to the slight ridge of the scar
that had formed at my hairline, pressing the memory of that
blow, that day, into my fingertips.

"Open up, Giulia. I've come with a message from Mama."

I straightened my back, willing myself to be strong, to with-
stand the power on the other side of the door. I lifted my chin,

seeing in my mind's eye the stubborn tilt of my mother's face defying the sun, defying the murmurs in her own house as well as in the village on the day Claudio left for America. My hand came down from my head and touched Giuseppina's amulet that I wore under my blouse.

Then I opened the door.

Claudio filled the room, taking possession of it without looking at me.

Zi'Yolanda was frozen in the kitchen doorway, twisting her hands.

"Claudio, Claudio. You've come. If I'd known, I would've had something ready. You hungry? I got some broccoli rabe and beans from supper. No? You want a drink? Some anisette? Uncle Tony, he's not here. You want me to go get him? He's just down the street...."

"I came to talk to Giulia."

I was still standing by the door, my arms now folded across my breast, holding myself together. I waited.

"Mama has written. She says you belong at home with your sisters. With me. You're my responsibility. No offense, Zi'Yolanda, but Giulia has a home with us. The boys, they ask for you every day. Angelina has her hands full without you. Pip doesn't know what to do with a runny nose and Tilly spends all her time at the store counting straight pins as far as I can tell.

"People are starting to talk, to say you don't live with us anymore. They think you're on your own, with nobody watching out for you. No sister of mine should be the subject of such gossip. It reflects on the family. On me."

"*I've* given them nothing to gossip about. I go to work. I take care of business, I come home and help Zi'Yolanda in the house. If people are whispering, Claudio, it's not because of anything *I've* done."

"This has gone on long enough. You've made your point. I lost my temper. I throw things all the time when I get angry enough. And that day you made me plenty angry and you happened to be in the way when I let go.

"But I've calmed down. I can live with a little dirt in the store. But I won't put up with your stubbornness about not coming back to my house. I've come to take you home."

I looked at Claudio. All the time he'd been talking, his eyes had been somewhere else, not meeting mine.

"Mama wrote to me, too," I said. This time he looked at me.

"She told me that when you came to me asking forgiveness, I should be ready to give it."

"So, I've come."

I shook my head. "She didn't say I should forgive you when you *came* to me. She said I should forgive you when you *asked* me to forgive you."

Zi'Yolanda gasped.

I knew from the copy of the letter she'd sent me that my mother had told Claudio to ask me for forgiveness. Did she do this for me? Or to restore the image of Claudio that she burnished every day, held up to the light of my father's disdain and my aunts' clucking. Claudio her star, her salvation, her reward. It didn't matter to me why. She had done it. Had been the only one in the family with the will to confront him and the wits to corner him.

I forced myself to move away from Claudio. I turned my back to him and crossed the room to sit in Uncle Tony's chair. I struggled to still my voice, to still my trembling hands. I had always been the chatterbox in our family. The one who always had something to say—a joke or a riddle in the chapel at Santa Margareta when I should have been whispering the rosary, or my insistent interruptions at the dinner table at my parents' house, my chattering stories.

But this was not the time to distract my audience. I bit my tongue, nearly drawing blood, as I waited for Claudio—to erupt, to leave, or to listen.

He began to mutter dismissive curses, throwing his hand in the air, gesturing at no one except perhaps our distant mother.

The trolley clattered by on the street below.

Zi'Yolanda retreated to the kitchen—in fear, in confusion, or perhaps hoping to find some morsel she could offer Claudio to appease him. When Claudio realized we were alone, he looked at me, not with the eyes of a cornered animal, but with those of a shrewd one. He hissed the words at me, in a barely audible voice.

"I'm sorry."

His tone wasn't one of defeat, but of dismissal. As if the apology wasn't important to him. As if he could afford to be magnanimous, generous. But he had said the words.

I stood up.

"I accept your apology," I said.

Chapter 25

In Hiding

I WENT BACK TO LIVE at Claudio's house after he apologized. It meant that I was under more scrutiny at home as well as at the store. But as our love deepened, Paolo and I began to take more risks. We continued to write to each other every day and found ways to meet, sometimes openly on the street, engaging in a few minutes of polite conversation while we stared hungrily into each other's eyes, sometimes secretly in the back of the store.

One Sunday afternoon when I'd gone down to the store by myself to unpack a shipment of fabric, Paolo surprised me. He had brought a small cake for us from Artuso's bakery. He told me he wished he could have brought the piano from the Palace, too, because he had a song he wanted to play for me. I asked him to sing it. At first, he protested. He was a piano player, not a singer. But I coaxed him—how else would I ever hear it? I asked. Claudio certainly wasn't about to let me come to the Palace some night. So Paolo relented and began to sing for me. As he did, I lifted my arms and began to dance around him. Then he reached out for me and took me in his arms. We continued to dance around the storeroom, his lips close to my ear, filling it with song.

Flora lived right across the street from the store, and Paolo allowed Nino to carry the letters when Flora couldn't get over. Everybody knew he was my special boy, my little sweetheart. It was natural for him to dash into the store on his way to school to grab a peppermint. That he also slipped me a blue envelope with a wink and a grin—well, I took care to call him to the back of the store for our exchange.

But Paolo's life at that time was becoming one of *nascondiglio,* concealment. Not only were we hiding our love from my family, but he was also hiding his other life from the police. He was often gone, to New York City or upstate, as his work with the union consumed more and more of his life and put him in more and more danger.

The newspaper of the Italian immigrant community—*Il Progresso Italo-Americano*—was filled with stories about the horrors in sweatshops and the brutality of the police and the bosses against workers who only wanted to put food on the table. The IWW was in the middle of the unrest, and the politicians and American newspapers were furious.

I held my breath every time Paolo left Mount Vernon. I never knew if he was just going to a meeting or if the police had stopped him somewhere and found his papers with their incendiary words. It made him ill sometimes, the passion he poured into expressing his ideas about justice; and it frightened me. The risks he was taking, the enemies he was making.

Claudio thought he was an idealistic fool, a Don Quixote jousting at windmills. But Claudio had no sympathy for workers. Claudio had never sat behind a sewing machine in a factory or worked in the Pennsylvania coal mines. His time with a pick and shovel in New York had been short. He prided himself on figuring it out—using his brains as well as his brawn. He saw quickly that he wasn't going to reach his dream digging ditches for someone else. My mother's jewelry had paid for more than his passage to America. He bought his first team and wagon with money from her. She put the reins in his hands.

Paolo had no gems from his mother. But he had a degree from the University of Napoli and had worked on an Italian labor newspaper before he'd arrived in America. It was that experience and the people he knew from *Il Germe* that brought him into the IWW. Paolo was a man of ideas who threw himself into action.

If I thought his feelings for me would slow him down, hold him back from doing something rash, I was wrong. Trouble was brewing in Schenectady at the General Electric plant and *Il Progresso* printed a story about the involvement of some of the men from the IWW. A knot grew in my heart with every word I read.

One afternoon, Tilly and Pip had gone to do errands. It was lunchtime, a quiet lull when I could steal a few minutes with Paolo, face-to-face in the back of the store. With half an ear I listened for the bell on the front door. The heavy curtain between the front of the shop and the storeroom was closed.

"Here, I have something for you," he whispered as he emptied his pocket onto the counter to retrieve a new poem for me. He took my face in his hands as he kissed me and then began to read the poem. But out of the corner of my eye, I saw on the counter a train ticket to Schenectady.

I let him finish his poem and kissed him again, but my mind and my heart were pulled in the direction of that ticket.

"What takes you to Schenectady?"

"Business. Don't worry. It's not another girl."

"I don't worry about other girls. But I worry about business. Are you going because of General Electric?"

"What do you know about GE?"

"What I read in *Il Progresso*. Tell me you're going for some other reason, not for the union. Tell me it's just a coincidence that you're going to Schenectady."

He looked away from my gaze and put the ticket and other loose papers back in his pocket. I pulled him toward me again and pounded my fists against his chest.

"Don't go! I can't bear the thought of you in the midst of that trouble. You'll be hurt. You'll be arrested. I won't sleep knowing you're in danger. Don't go!"

He pushed my hands away.

"I have to go. You don't understand. It's who I am."

The bell jangled in the front. He kissed me once again, hard, and went out the back door.

The next day, he went to Schenectady.

I couldn't tell anyone of my worries. Instead, I retrieved Claudio's crumpled copy of *Il Progresso* every night from the table where he tossed it after dinner. I took it to my bed and smoothed it out, looking for dispatches about the strike. I pored over the pages, hoping to catch a glimpse of Paolo's face in the grainy photographs, but of course the workers were inside the plant, in the first sit-down strike in American history, and the newspaper only ran a photo of the building surrounded by police and soldiers. I didn't know if Paolo was inside, giving courage to the strikers, or outside, making trouble for the authorities. I searched for any fragment of news that might reveal to me that Paolo was safe. I found nothing, only reports of brutality and fury.

Every morning I returned to the store, hoping this would be the day I would see Paolo again. Finally he returned. I saw him walking down the hill toward the Palace, looking as if he'd seen a ghost. A thin scab extended across his forehead and he was limping. His steps were measured and careful, not the usual swagger and energy that was so characteristic of him. I wondered about the bruises I couldn't see.

He did not come to the store that day or the next, and Nino did not appear with a message from him. Knowing he was back and not hearing from him was in some ways worse than when I had no knowledge of him at all. I didn't know why he was ignoring me. I was afraid of what had happened to him in Schenectady.

I attacked the dust on the floor as if my broom were a weapon. At home, I slaughtered onions with my knife, furiously chopping them into hundreds of pieces while the tears streamed down my cheeks. I swallowed my loneliness, unable to tell anyone of my fears. I cried myself to sleep thinking he had no more words for me.

Finally, one morning at the store as I was sorting through the bills that had arrived in the post, I found a letter addressed to me and postmarked Schenectady. I tore it open, heedless of my sisters. I read the letter quickly, scanning it for the familiar words of passion and longing. I found those words, with relief. But then I read on.

Forgive the smudges on the page, my beloved. My hand is bleeding from a scrape suffered when the police shoved me against the pavement and I haven't had time to tend to it. I have seen too much today that I cannot describe to you—desperate men, impoverished but determined, making history here, but at great cost. I am tortured by what I am witnessing. This is everything I work for and believe in, but I fear I am asking too much of you to share in it. I have realized today that the life I have chosen is incompatible with loving a woman.

I stifled a cry and shoved the letter into my pocket. I knew I had to see him, had to talk to him. But I also needed to understand in my heart what it would mean for me to stand by him, to know that the man I loved could face imprisonment or worse.

I watched for Nino that afternoon as he returned home from school and slipped him a note for Paolo, along with a piece of chocolate. In the note, I begged Paolo to meet with me in the store at closing time. I waited anxiously as the day darkened, knowing that I could not delay my arrival home without arousing suspicion. Just as I was about to give up hope that he would come, I heard a light tapping on the back door.

I let him in and turned out the light so no one could see us. I reached out for him, afraid he might not return my embrace, afraid I might hurt his battered body. But he took me in his arms, gently and tenderly.

"I've missed you so much!"

"I've missed you, too. Did you get my letter from Schenectady?"

"This morning."

"It was agonizing to write. I adore you, Giulia. But I cannot ask you to love me in return when the path I am on is so precarious, so dangerous."

"I've thought about your words all day today, preparing myself for this conversation. I searched my soul to know if I could accept this part of you. Paolo, I do not want to lose you. I know now that this is your life, that I can't make you turn away from it because of my fears. I will stand by you, Paolo. I will never stand in your way or hold you back from your calling."

"Are you sure? I can never give you the kind of security Claudio provides for Angelina, or that your sisters expect."

"I have never wanted what my sisters want. What I want is you. All of you."

He kissed me lightly on the lips. "You have me."

The city-hall clock tolled faintly in the distance.

"I have to get home or they'll send someone to look for me."

"*Addio*. I'll write you tomorrow."

He slipped out the back door and I locked it behind him. I left by the front door and made my way back to Claudio's, my heart both light and solemn.

Chapter 26

Secrets

SECRETS ARE HARD to bear, hard to conceal, when one is in love. We had continued to hide our feelings because my family, led by Claudio, had decided that my recklessness with men—first Vito in Venticano, now Roberto in Mount Vernon—had to stop. I had behaved once too often in a way that flouted the proprieties my family expected of its women. But despite Paolo's and my efforts at discretion, my sisters began to suspect that something was going on and were furious with me. My emotions were written all over my face. If I hadn't seen Paolo on the street early in the morning on my way to the store, or if Nino hadn't come by on his way to school with a letter for me, I was desolate. I went through the motions of restocking the shelves or waiting on customers, but my mind was on the emptiness, the aching, the longing to hear Paolo's voice or feel his lips on mine.

We were like crazy people, addicted to each other. We continued to meet in the back of the store. A few moments behind the curtain, his arms around me, pulling me close, covering my face with kisses, pressing his body against mine.

I was breathless; I was excruciatingly happy to be near him. I didn't care what people thought.

But my sisters cared. One morning, Pip noticed my flushed face and the disarray of my hair as I hastily smoothed back the loose strands when she called me from the front of the store. There were half a dozen customers waiting to be served.

"What are you doing back there, Giulia? Daydreaming? Didn't you hear the bell jangle five times?"

She looked at me sharply when she saw two of our customers eyeing me up and down as if I'd walked out in my underwear.

"She's been unloading boxes all morning. We should've gotten my cousin Peppino to do it, but you know, the boys are never around when you want them for any heavy work." Pip made up the story hastily to deflect the gossips.

I took my place behind the counter and helped Josephina Simonetti find the fabric she needed to reline her husband's coat, trying not to get lost in the memory of Paolo's lips grazing my neck as he eased himself out the door to the alley.

When the store was quiet again, Pip let me have it.

"I don't know what you were doing back there, but I pray to Jesus, Mary and Joseph that you were alone. If something's going on behind our backs, Giulia, don't think you can hide it forever. I guarantee you that within fifteen minutes of leaving here, that Simonetti woman was telling whoever would listen that you came out of the back looking as if you'd just gotten out of bed."

"I don't care what Josephina Simonetti thinks of me."

"Well, *I* care, and Tilly and Claudio and Uncle Tony and Zi'Yolanda. People talk. This is America, with no mother and father to protect you, to show you how to behave. We don't want people in the streets whispering about you, saying no one controls you."

Before I could respond, she went on.

"If someone's visiting you in the back, God forbid, it's got to stop. Sooner or later somebody will see him and sure as hell won't think it's a delivery boy."

She grabbed a box overflowing with trim.

"Stay up front and straighten this out."

Later that day I wrote to Paolo about Pip's suspicions and her watchfulness. Every time I went to the back room, she moved in that direction, too, her ear cocked to catch the sound of the door opening or another voice. I felt like a caged bird, flitting from one end of its prison to the other without hope of finding a way out. By the time I got home, I was distraught, frantic at the thought that Paolo and I had no safe place to meet. I knew we could defy Pip, but that increased our risk of being discovered. And then what? Would my family forbid me to see him?

Paolo saw the toll our secret was taking on me, how unhappy I was when I couldn't see him, how worn down I was by the berating of my sister, her demand that I not bring shame to the family but act with propriety. My freedom to come and go was restricted. Pip or Tilly did the marketing in the early morning before we opened the store. Paolo and I had counted on those morning excursions as an opportunity, however brief and wordless, to feast our eyes on each other as we passed on the street. He had swallowed me with the piercing blue of his deep-set eyes. My pulse quickened as we passed within a few feet, the air between us stirring and our hunger for each other leaping across the chasm of the sidewalk. It was enough, that glance that took in all of me, embraced me with the pleasure and appreciation of his whole being. It got me through the day.

But my family put a stop to even that. They didn't know who was admiring me, but they believed if they kept me out of sight, whatever fire I had kindled would die down, cooled by my disappearance.

But the longing only increased, the fire raging even stronger because we were denied one another. Somehow, despite our loss of those precious moments of public contact, we managed to sustain the private exchange of words. The letters continued, written in secret on my part, passed with a packet of fine-gauge cotton to Flora or left under a rock behind the store for Nino to retrieve and bring to his uncle.

We filled the letters with our dreams and our tears. He wrote to me:

> *I cannot explain in words how my heart beats for you. I dream of you all the time....When I write, I am so happy because I have your image in front of me. I'm crazy about you, Giulia. You are home cleaning the house, but I feel you next to me. I was suffering terribly earlier today when I had to go to work and didn't see you. I needed to tell you I love you. How much longer do we have to wait? Our hearts are suffering, and for me, it's painful to stay away from you.*

The torture of separation was too much. Paolo watched the store whenever he could get away from work early and waited for my sisters to leave. One day Pip went to New York to shop for new stock. I offered to close the store at the end of the day so Tilly could go home and start supper. I was sweeping up when I heard a tap on the back door.

I thought it might be Claudio or Peppino checking up on me again, but when I looked through the glass and saw that it was Paolo, I dropped the broom and leaped into his arms. Tears filled my eyes as he held me.

"Listen to me, Giulia. I've made a decision. Flora has convinced me that this secret we carry in our hearts is dangerous. To go on hiding like this could end in disaster with your family if they find out. I've decided to speak to Claudio, to tell him I want to marry you." He stepped away from me for a moment to see my face and watch my reaction. I saw a flicker of doubt in his eyes. He was questioning whether I'd heard him clearly, whether I believed him, whether I would accept him in front of my family.

"You would tell Claudio that? I am bursting with joy, Paolo. But what if he says no? What will we do?"

"Believe me, Giulia. It's the best way. We act honorably. We can be honest about how we feel in front of the world instead of this concealment. I will present myself as a respectable man, calling on you at your home instead of hidden in back rooms. As much as I desire you, it shames me that I have to treat you like this, sneaking behind your family's back, risking your reputation. No, I'm determined to do the right thing. I'll convince Claudio that I respect him and your family. I'm not a stranger. Let me do this for us."

He promised to come to my house the next night to speak to Claudio. I was agitated the whole day, jumping every time the bell rang over the door, dropping a whole tray filled with spools of thread and having to get down on my hands and knees to retrieve them. When I got home that night, I washed up and combed my hair after supper.

"Who are you primping for?" Pip wanted to know. "What's going on? Don't think you're leaving the house at this hour of the night."

"I'm not going anywhere. I'm expecting a visitor who's coming to talk to Claudio."

It was Pip's turn to be agitated. I picked up a stack of shirts that needed darning and calmed myself by threading a needle and starting to stitch while I waited for the doorbell to ring.

463

At eight o'clock, I heard a familiar voice at the door, and Angelina called out from the hall.

"Claudio, Paolo Serafini is here. If you want a cup of coffee, ask one of your sisters to make it. I'm still putting the children to bed."

Pip looked at me. "I don't believe it! Not him. No. No. No! What a mistake. This must be a joke or a bad dream. He's nothing but trouble, him and his union. You'd be better off in a convent than keeping company with him."

Pip fretted in the kitchen, banging pots on shelves and furiously scrubbing the sink, muttering some kind of litany under her breath while she anxiously eyed the closed door to the parlor, where Paolo and Claudio were drinking their coffee. I strained to hear their words over the angry din Pip was making. Finally, Angelina yelled from upstairs that she couldn't get the kids to sleep because of the noise. The baby started wailing. I kept my head down over the mending, trying not to prick my finger.

I worried that Paolo's plan to be open was a mistake. As difficult as it had been to hide from my family, to write my letters in secret, to sneak an embrace in the back room, at least I hadn't been forced to confront their anger. What if Claudio said no? What if that provoked my sisters to an even stricter watch over me? I might not be allowed out of the house at all, not even to go to the store.

My mind began to race ahead, to scenes of disobedience and defiance. I had climbed out of windows before; I knew I'd do it again to be with Paolo, not just to dance for an evening in the moonlight, but to run away with him. A recklessness rose up inside me as I contemplated the aftermath of Paolo's conversation with Claudio. I was ready to walk out of the house with him that evening if my family forbade me to see him.

The door to the parlor opened and a haze of cigar smoke wafted into the kitchen. Pip stopped her scrubbing and turned around, her hands dripping and red. I stood up from the table.

Paolo came out first and turned toward me, with a gentle smile and a nod. He reached for my hand and brought it to his lips.

Pip threw her dishrag in the sink.

"Are you crazy?" She directed her wrath at Claudio. "What do you think Papa would've said? Do you think he would have allowed this?"

"This is my house. My America. I make the rules here. If she goes back to Italy, Papa can tell her what to do, but for now, it's my decision. Better for her to see someone I know than a stranger. Better that Paolo come to me honestly than to have her hiding."

Claudio and Pip acted as if Paolo and I weren't there. Let them battle with each other rather than with me, I thought. Pip's mistake had been to call up Papa's name.

I walked Paolo to the door, ignoring my brother and sister. He took my face in his hands and kissed me publicly for the first time. It was another turning point for us, this acknowledgment in front of others. But the recklessness I had felt while waiting for Claudio and Paolo to finish their conversation fled in the face of Pip's animosity. I was no longer sure how wise it would be, even with Claudio's permission, to flaunt our love.

The doubts I felt that night were accurate. The women in the family almost immediately began an assault on my relationship with Paolo. They shook their heads; they whispered knowingly to one another, mouth to ear, eyes cast quickly back at me; they clucked in disapproval or pursed their lips.

"He's so wrong for you, Giulia. Think of what Mama will say, what she expects. A good partner for Claudio, yes, he's good with the books. But he'd be nothing, *have* nothing, without Claudio carrying him along. What does he do with himself, when he isn't doing Claudio's business, except moon over that piano fingering tunes? It's nice to have him around on a Saturday night, but what about the rest of the week when you need to put food on the table?"

"What kind of life can you expect from an agitator like Paolo? Somebody in the neighborhood with a cousin upstate told me Paolo was involved in that GE strike. With the life he leads, he could be thrown in prison any minute. And *then* where would you be?"

"You think you can eat those letters after you marry him, or use them to put clothes on the backs of your children? Do you expect Claudio to keep you, like he does now, after you marry?"

"You had a much better prospect in Roberto, Giulia. His family has a good business. He's got the same instincts as Claudio. You'll see. Roberto will be back, ready to step into his father's place. I heard that the old man's sick. Roberto's just waiting for the right moment, a quiet moment when the cops are occupied with someone else. Then he'll show up, looking for you. And where will you be? In some tenement with two bawling kids and not enough to feed them, with your body sagging, your fingers rough, and your husband playing the piano every night, or worse, in jail. Wait for Roberto, Giulia."

"Paolo's so funny-looking with that red hair. Remember how you used to swoon over Roberto's looks? Remember how elegant he was, how everyone noticed him at the dances? All the other girls envied you, wishing he had chosen them."

"You need to *think,* Giulia, instead of peeking out the curtains every five minutes. Who needs it, I ask you? It's like you're sick. A sickness in the head. You act like you'll die without his love poems every day. Pretty words on a page. I can live without those, thank you very much."

Chapter 27

Funeral

ROBERTO SCARPA'S FATHER finally died after all the murmuring speculation that he was mortally ill. Some people said he died of a broken heart; others that it was from anger over Roberto's rash stupidity. Some, the police included, thought Roberto might come back to bury his father. The family held off putting him in the ground for a few days and the rumors that the Scarpas were waiting for Roberto could not be contained.

No fragment, no matter how absurd, escaped my sisters or Yolanda, who sat every afternoon with the grieving widow. In the evenings at dinner, each scrap of information was dutifully brought to our table for discussion and, of course, for my continued indoctrination in the wisdom of waiting for Roberto and abandoning Paolo.

"Zi'Yolanda says she and Signora Scarpa are saying the rosary twice every afternoon at four o'clock. Once for the soul of the father, that he'll make a good journey home to God, and once for the heart of the son, that he'll make a good journey home to his mother who needs him," Tilly reported earnestly.

"I heard that one of the brothers sent a telegram to Italy even before they had the priest in to hear their father's last confession," said Pip.

Even Angelina had news. "One of the boys said the cops have been watching the house ever since the old man died. They got a tip that Roberto was already on his way."

Everyone had an opinion, a theory. How quickly had Roberto's family gotten word to him? When was the next ship leaving Napoli? How would Roberto disguise himself to thwart the police?

Zi'Yolanda's prayers were as fervent as those of the distraught Signora Scarpa, abandoned by her husband in death and by her oldest son in his flight from the law. Zi'Yolanda held out hope of Roberto's return, convinced that I would leave Paolo and fly willingly into Roberto's arms over the coffin of his father.

What did they feed each other, Signora Scarpa and my aunt, as they bent and muttered over their clacking beads? Two crazy old women concocting a frothy zabaglione of despair and fantasy that was all air—no eggs.

And my sisters? How they ate it up every evening when Yolanda made her daily report. They concocted fantasies themselves, remembered swirling dances and whispered intimacies in the parlor of the Hillcrest Hotel. They weren't there at the christening. They didn't have the memories I did, of swirling snow flecked with blood and screamed obscenities. They heard the music of the piano on Saturday nights. I heard the silence in the hall on Sunday afternoon: a suddenly emptied room encircled by sirens, shouts, the crack of baton upon head. A suddenly emptied life, adrift and cut off from the dreams and illusions that had fled through the crack forced open by my lover's brutality.

They all prodded me, wondering if—hoping that—I had

doubts about my fledgling love for Paolo, faced with the prospect of Roberto's return.

I went to the Scarpa funeral. Antonietta was my friend, after all, before her brother had become my dance partner. She was pregnant again. Natale was a robust little baby despite the difficult omens at his christening, and he appeared to resemble his father more and more with every passing day, putting to rest—or at least putting behind closed doors—whatever wild accusations had ignited the events at the christening.

Antonietta did not look well. I think it was more than burying her father and holding up her desolate mother. She was not the girl who'd giggled and daydreamed with me behind John Molloy's back. But then, neither was I.

The Scarpas had waited a week before asking the priest to say the Mass of the Dead. Not enough time for Roberto to travel from Italy. Roberto's younger brothers, convinced of the futility of waiting, finally extracted permission from their grief-crazed mother to lay their father to rest without Roberto as witness. Antonietta, who seemed so weakened by her situation in life, missed Roberto terribly and blamed herself for his forced disappearance. She'd probably been right there with Signora Scarpa and Yolanda praying for Roberto's secret return.

During all the heated speculation before the funeral, Paolo said nothing to me. If he burned with the same question as my sisters—"If Roberto comes back, Giulia, whom will you choose?"—he kept those fires to himself. Paolo did not go to the funeral. He made some excuse about needing to be in the city that morning, leaving me to go with my sisters. Leaving me to make my choice, if I had to, without his presence.

The Mass at Our Lady of Mount Carmel was full, and I took a seat toward the back with Zi'Yolanda and my sisters.

Claudio had paid his respects at the house. He spent as little time inside a church as possible.

The priest droned, banks of candles blazed—all lit by the obsessive grief of Signora Scarpa—and a pungent incense wafted from the nave, attempting to mask the odor of the decaying body.

More than once, Antonietta and her brothers searched the congregation, only to whisper with shaking heads to their bent and wailing mother, "No, Mama. He's not here."

At the final blessing, the five boys took their positions at their father's casket, leaving an empty place where Roberto should have stood to shoulder the weight. At the sight of her sons, Signora Scarpa accelerated her keening, and Antonietta, awkward and heavy, struggled to support her mother as they followed the casket out of the church. Zi'Yolanda cast a meaningful glance at me as the brothers marched past us, but I focused on the eyes of my friend and offered her my blessing.

Zi'Yolanda was determined to accompany the body to its final resting place, not out of respect for the ritual but in anticipation of the drama that would still, she was convinced, play itself out. She had talked Claudio into providing us with a carriage for the trip to the cemetery in Riverdale, so we joined the cortege threading its way through the Bronx.

By the time we arrived at the grave site, the tension that had filled the church had lessened. Only a small group of family and friends had made the trip, and if the police were watching, they were well hidden. The grave was a short walk uphill from the drive where we left the carriages. The flowers had arrived ahead of us and were piled around the recently dug hole. Mountains of flowers, wreaths, hearts, sprays of lilies and carnations, ribbons printed with endearments or prayers, a profusion of familial grief and community solidarity. Somewhere in the masses of blooms was one with the

Fiorillo name attached. Up close, one could see that the edges of the flowers were already tinged with brown.

We clustered around the grave. The Scarpa boys, their father's coffin safely positioned at the side of the hole, gathered around their mother. My sisters and I and Yolanda were opposite them and to the rear.

The priest intoned the Latin prayers for the dead. Then the grave diggers, who had been standing at the periphery, leaning on their shovels, moved forward, slipped two canvas straps under the coffin and lowered it. Michele, the second-oldest son, held his mother back as she attempted to throw herself across the polished wood of her husband's coffin. The grave diggers, used to the hysteria of widows, continued methodically. Shovelful by shovelful, they began to fill the grave. The rest of us began the final procession, grabbing a handful of dirt and tossing it into the hole. As I reached the edge, I looked across at one of the grave diggers, at his long, muscled forearms and powerful hands gripping the wooden shaft of his shovel. I held my breath as I raised my eyes to his face, obscured by beard and visored cap pulled well over his brow. For an instant, he lifted his head and looked directly into my eyes without breaking the rhythm of his shoveling. In his gaze was recognition and defiance, pride, cunning, warning.

I saw new lines around familiar eyes, pressed into flesh that had become reacquainted with the sun. I saw, still smoldering, the glint of desire that had once pulled me into feverish dances and intimate conversations. I saw the man I had lost, not only to Italy but also to violence. I knelt to fill my hand with earth, my lungs with air. The movement brought me close enough to see the hairs on his long fingers bleached even lighter now; close enough to remember my hand enclosed within those fingers. This was no apparition. No figment conjured up by the crude chants of my aunt. No dim memory that I

471

could conveniently wipe away or easily put aside with false assuredness.

This was flesh and bone and breath, inches away from mine. Defying me to reveal him, daring me to leap across his father's grave, full of a man's confidence that I would do as he demanded—stay or come, be silent or profess my desire.

I stood again to steady myself, to hear my own thoughts instead of his. And as I slowly sprinkled the earth over his father's coffin, I let him slip through my fingers as well, brushing the last bits of dust from my palms.

Chapter 28

———⟡———

Flora's House

FLORA CAME TO THE store to ask me a favor. She had become a friend to me, offering me welcome and kindness. I found myself so lonely at home, no one taking my side, no one wishing me well. I was so exhausted by the voices battering at me every day—my aunt and my sisters, harpies who conducted my life like an orchestra leader with his baton; the neighbors, who watched every step I took, whether alone or accompanied. My own voice, that used to sing, chant, cast simple spells, spin funny stories, was now stilled, dumbstruck, seeking words that did not want to be found.

So Flora was a relief—like a sensible, solid hearth. She baked me delicious coconut cakes and listened to me. It was automatic for me to agree to the favor. She and her husband had to go to New York City, something legal they had to attend to. She wanted me to come and stay with the baby. Nino was in school most of the day, so it was only the baby who needed tending. I told Tilly and Pip I wouldn't be in the store and steeled myself against their complaints.

"She has no sister to help her," I told them. "If you want, I'll take the accounts with me and work on them while the baby sleeps."

I got to Flora's apartment early enough to catch a smile from Nino as he left for school. I slipped him the sour ball I had waiting for him in my pocket. I winked as he shoved it into his mouth, shifting it with his tongue to hide it from his mother as she kissed him goodbye.

"God bless you for doing this, Giulia. There isn't anyone else I'd trust with Rosina. Is there anything I should explain to you?"

"I don't think so, Flora. I've taken care of my share of babies, from my little brothers to Claudio's boys. I don't expect any surprises. And Rosina knows me. She'll be fine. Go, go. Look after your business and don't worry about us. That's my girl!"

I took Rosina into my arms and sang her one of our child-hood rhymes. Then I swept her into the kitchen for her porridge while Flora and her husband quietly left.

Rosina scooped up tiny fistfuls of oatmeal and licked it from her fingers as I assisted her with a slender silver spoon—a christening gift from Paolo, Flora had told me. She was hungry and abandoned herself to the milky pleasure, humming softly as she sucked on her fingers, leaning eagerly forward every time I approached her with the spoon. She laughed and opened her mouth.

When she was full, she turned her head in distraction toward the window, the light and shadow, the sounds of the street below: the screech of the trolley, the clatter of horse and wagon, the urgency of voices greeting, bargaining, arguing. Food no longer held her interest. The life all around was calling to her.

I took my cue, and wiped up the remnants of her oatmeal,

playing the finger games Giuseppina had sung to me. Then I lifted her from her chair and carried her over to the window so that she could see what had so attracted her.

Rosina slapped her hand against the glass, making her own music, trying to get the attention of those in the street below. The avenue was just coming to life. Mercurio the butcher was rolling out the awning over his shop window to shade the rabbits hanging from metal hooks, the tripe mounded in bowls over ice. Ferruzzi the greengrocer was filling his sidewalk bins with potatoes and onions. Tilly was removing her key from her bag and about to open the door of the shop.

Rosina was growing tired of the display of sunlight and street life at the window and began to tug on my right earring. I carried her to the corner where Flora had a small box of amusements for the children—a rag doll and a cigar box filled with wooden blocks. I sat cross-legged and stacked the blocks for her to tumble with a gleeful swipe—a game I'd seen her play with Nino more than once. But Nino had far more patience than I, far more playfulness. In time, however, Rosina knocked over her last column of blocks, crawled to her doll and, clutching it, climbed into my lap with drooping eyes.

I crooned no more than a few minutes before her head fell heavy against my breast. I sat still, accepting the stillness, enjoying the moment of doing absolutely nothing except feeling this baby sleep contentedly in my arms.

As I sat, I heard a knock, a man's voice, Flora's name called from the other side of the apartment door.

I rose carefully, shifted Rosina's weight to my shoulder and went to answer the door.

"Who is it?" Flora had not told me to expect anyone. What man would visit her during the day?

"It's Paolo."

I opened the door immediately.

"Giulia! I didn't see you this morning on your way to the store and I thought that I'd missed you—that I'd been too lazy to get up as early as you and was being punished for my laziness. But here you are! What brings you here? Is Flora ill? Is that why you're holding the baby?"

"Oh, Paolo. What a surprise! A wonderful surprise! No, no. Flora's not ill. She and Giorgio had an appointment in the city. She asked me to take care of Rosina for a few hours and I knew Tilly and Pip could spare me at the store for a day."

Paolo took off his hat and entered the apartment, giving me a tentative and awkward kiss on the cheek as he reached around the sleeping Rosina. It was not our usual embrace.

"I was just about to put Rosina down. I'll be right back. Do you have time for a cup of coffee, or are you on your way somewhere?"

"It can wait." He unbuttoned his jacket as I moved down the hallway to Rosina's bed. She stirred and fumbled for her doll as I laid her as softly as I could upon her mattress. I did not want her to wake up at this moment.

Paolo and I had experienced great intimacy in these few short months. But it had been mostly an intimacy of words. When we'd been together—our encounters on the street, his stealing into the back of the store—we had never been truly alone. Bodies, voices—noisy and inquiring or merely haphazardly aware of us—all encroached upon us, obstructed us from that final intimacy.

I knew so much about Paolo. How he thought, how he felt, how he spent his days and nights. But I did not know the warmth of his bare chest, the shape of his back, the weight of his body molded to fit the hollows and curves of my own.

I walked back down the hall to Paolo after assuring myself that Rosina slept. I walked slowly, soundlessly. I did not want to wake her; I did not want to reveal myself to any listeners lurking beyond the walls and windows. I wanted to be silent, invisible. I did not want to exist at that moment to anyone except Paolo.

Chapter 29

❦

Stillness

PAOLO LIFTED HIS HEAD as I approached. He had bolted
the door to the landing, drawn the curtains in the front room.
Done what he could to shield us.

I saw the flicker of longing in his eyes. A smile on his lips,
opening his heart to me. A stillness. No words. No gestures.
Not even that nervous habit he had of pushing his hat back,
running his fingers through his hair. No movement at all. It
was just Paolo and Giulia facing each other in a dim room.
The space between us was a gulf, an Atlantic Ocean of the
unknown, the uncertain. Potential destruction or potential
happiness. We did not move toward each other. We did not
turn away, breaking the stillness with a gesture or a word.

Part of me was ready to jump into my silly chatter—to be
the girl peeling eggplants so long ago who took a man's handkerchief so unknowingly, who gave it back saturated with
unspoken and unrecognized promise.

I felt no certainty in that moment. I looked across the space
between Paolo and me and saw my future, my pain, my sal-

vation, my honor, my desire, my dreams. I felt the blood begin to surge into the vein on my neck, swelling it to a knot. My hand fluttered, then rose to cover the vein as if it were my private parts, some shame that I must hide. Did Paolo feel the same hesitancy? The same sense that stepping forward was stepping off the edge of the world?

I looked into the blueness of his eyes. So transparent, so clear. I felt that I could look through them. Not like Claudio's almost black eyes—guarded, hidden, a mask. Paolo wore no mask, at least not with me.

What did I see during that silence between us? Heartache. Hope. A questioning. Not a demand, not an order, not an expectation. He was asking, "Do you want me? Will you have me? Are you willing to step to my side, separate yourself from your family?"

And I asked myself, *am I?* Do I move into the circle of Paolo's arms and leave the grasp and clamor of my sisters and aunts, the rules of my mother, the protection of Claudio? Can Paolo protect me? Can he place his body between the world and me? In his arms, in his bed, will I find a refuge? Will I find a life? Not only food on my table and in the mouths of our children, but also nourishment for my loneliness and weariness. Will he be able to feed me with his words, his music? Will he sing to me in our bed? He had told me that I came to him in his dreams. So real that he thought I was already there, in his arms, in his bed. He woke up sweating, breathless, spent, as if I had embraced him. He woke up, he said, filled with my light.

I moved toward him.

"This is unbelievable to me. To have you here." I drew briefly back. "Did anyone see you come in? Does anyone know that you're here?" My face constricted in fear of this last obstacle.

"No one knows where I am. And Flora wasn't expecting me. I stopped by on a whim, without a plan. Just a good morning to my sister was all I had on my mind. Now, of course, there's much more...." He smiled and pulled me back into his embrace.

We held each other in silence and at length. There was, for the first time, no urgency, no anxious listening for the approach of others, no bittersweet sense that this joy would be cut off long before we wished it to be. We had *time*.

I didn't know when he was expected elsewhere. He did not inquire when Flora and Giorgio were returning. Neither one of us tried to calculate how long Rosina might doze.

I think we both imagined that by not asking, by not recognizing time, we could, for once, ignore it. The sheer luxury of holding him without the ever-present knowledge that we might have to break away at a second's notice was exhilarating.

I felt every inch of him: the rough wool of his jacket, the starched cotton of his shirt; his arms around my waist, not poised to release but still, firm, a brace against everything that battered at me and pulled me away from him. I was aware, as well, of the firmness between his legs.

I was no longer afraid. I welcomed this moment and what it promised. We made love slowly, not in a crazed and frenzied way, although that was how I had felt all the times before, when we'd been able to capture only fragments of our passion for each other. He undressed me one button at a time, a kiss placed on each inch of flesh revealed with each succeeding button.

When he took off his own shirt I saw and felt the curling red-blond hair and pressed my face into his chest. We lay on the floor, stretched out upon a patterned red carpet filled with flowers of many colors twisting and entwining themselves. We faced each other, belly against belly, hands clasped, in relief, in disbelief.

For the first time since I'd known him, Paolo was wordless. Instead of creating eloquence with pen on paper, he wrote that morning on me, his fingers describing his love on my skin. When he stopped I took the hand and kissed each of his fingertips, lingering on the third, the ink-stained sign of his writing life.

"Your lips will turn blue," he murmured.

"My family will simply believe that I'm crazier than ever for you, kissing the letters that you write to me, trying to swallow your words."

Down the hall, Rosina's voice mewled plaintively.

I kissed Paolo one more time and then gathered my clothes together.

Chapter 30

Anna's Advice

IT WAS MY MOTHER'S intervention that finally stilled the voices of my family and dismissed Yolanda's objections to Paolo as if they were the mutterings of a fool. Even from a great distance, her voice and her decisions carried weight. She wrote to me as soon as she knew what was going on.

> *Figlia Mia,*
> *I have just received a letter from Zi'Yolanda concerning your recent attachment to Claudio's business partner, Serafini. She wrote—or rather, your sister Pip has written for her, because poor Yolanda didn't have the advantages you girls have had—that everyone, your uncle Antonio and herself, your sisters and your cousins, disapproves of your rushing into Paolo's arms.*
>
> *Zi'Yolanda entreated me to write to you as a mother. How else would I have, except as a mother? Whether you will heed me as a daughter is another question entirely. As I said, Zi'Yolanda claimed to have the support of the entire family. She said you have been foolishly swayed by Paolo's courtship, besieged*

daily by his love poems. You listen to no one, apparently, stomping from the kitchen with hands over your ears, seeking refuge in the home of his sister Flora instead of among your own sisters. You have always been the defiant one, never linking yourself, even as a little girl, to any of the others. Perhaps I shouldn't have let Giuseppina take you when she did, or keep you so long. But what was I to do at the time, forced to my bed to prevent the twins from coming too soon, and then losing Giovanni when he and Frankie were only three months old? My worry for him and my helplessness and grief when he died were overwhelming. Mark my words: you cannot know greater pain as a woman than to have a child die before you do. May you never experience it.

May you also never experience the pain of a daughter who thinks she can find her own way, unheeding the advice and wisdom of family in the matter of men. May you not know the ingratitude and shame of a daughter who whirls from one man to the next, not knowing what she seeks.

However, as disappointed as I am in your flightiness, I am extremely reluctant to rely upon the judgment of Yolanda. She is a fool, and you will be more of a fool if you heed the yammering around you. In this Papa and I concur—one of the few times in twenty years that we have agreed on something.

I do trust Claudio. He obviously has great respect for Paolo. It would certainly be good for the partnership to bring Paolo into the family.

We have heard through Claudio that Paolo has asked for your hand. Papa and I are prepared to accept.

I shall write to Yolanda myself. Be a good girl. Write to me. Your loving and concerned mother

Chapter 31

❦

The Veil

STANDING IN FRONT of the altar at Our Lady of Mount Carmel, I saw a flash of light, as if there were a halo around my head. Tilly, at my side, screamed. And then Paolo's hands were upon me, ripping the veil from my hair, my face. I breathed a choking smoke. My eyes filled with water and a searing pain. I gagged on the smell—acrid, bitter. Then I heard the wailing behind me, the mutterings of the old women. I had been too close to the candles.

I turned to where Paolo had flung the veil, where he was stamping out the flames on the marble steps by the Madonna's altar. It was a blackened tangle of strands, like an old cobweb hanging from the rafters of a barn. Ashes. I felt the color, the life, seep out of my face, slowly dripping into a puddle of fear at my feet. Paolo saw me, took two strides to my side and caught me as I began to sink, to crumple. He cradled me, surrounded me, whispered into my ear, kissed the singed ends of my curls. I noticed the black smudges on his fingertips, the fine, powdery soot on his white shirt cuffs.

Tilly was whimpering. The priest was fumbling with his spectacles and his prayer book. He had just risen to his feet after checking the damage to the carpet.

Paolo coughed, still holding me tightly, and said quietly to the priest, "Father, I think we can continue now."

The words droned past me without any meaning. I felt Paolo squeeze me gently when I was supposed to answer. Tilly composed herself enough to help me take off my glove and Paolo caressed the ring onto my trembling finger.

I could not think. I could not rejoice. I heard only the terrified gasp reverberating through the church, the hum of prayers trying to dispel the evil omens hovering amid the candles. I saw only the consuming flash that followed the thousand glimmering filaments embracing my head. I smelled only candle wax, burning silk, charred hair. I buried my face in the white roses and lilies that I carried, but their fragrance was denied to me, overpowered by this memory that I also carried out of the church, into my life.

Somehow, Paolo propelled me away from the priest, down the aisle, out into the fresh air. At the foot of the steps waited the carriage. Two white horses. Paolo had ordered them especially for today, with flowers entwined in their harness. Paolo lifted me into the carriage and kissed my ankle as he settled me against the cushions. He climbed up next to me, and in this moment of repose, removed his handkerchief from his jacket to wipe first my forehead and then his own fingers. He signaled the driver to start. Behind us were the carriages of our families, other people on foot. It wasn't far to the grand salon of the Hillcrest Hotel, just across the railroad bridge on Gramatan Avenue.

We moved forward slowly. I hid my head in Paolo's shoulder. I had no desire to rise up, to display myself to the family behind us, to the strangers who lined the road, to the children waving. Because my head was down I did not see the speeding truck that suddenly startled the horses. I only heard the frantic neighing of first one and then the other animal, the rough, angry shout of the driver, the grating of the wheels, the lurching and twisting of the carriage and then a frenzy of movement, a loss of control, the carriage hurtling, the clatter of the wooden bridge under us, the carriage lifting, straining, shouts, wood splintering. Paolo's body was tense, once again surrounding me, protecting me.

Suddenly, we came to a jolting, thudding stillness. There were more shouts, the shuddering, heaving sound of the horses panting. In one swift, unwavering movement, Paolo lifted me from the carriage and into the urgent arms of Claudio, who had rushed up from the carriage behind us.

Paolo stepped down and together the two men flanked me, walked me around the carriage to the other side of the bridge. I turned and looked back. The bridge was beginning to swarm with people—the families who had followed us, the onlookers along the road. The driver unhitched the horses. The carriage was tilted against the shattered railing of the bridge, halted in its plunge by a single metal post.

I turned away from this vision of what might have been, from the erupting hysteria of my sisters and aunt, from the horror of my uncle. Up ahead, through the windows of the Hillcrest Hotel, wafted the music of a piano.

My wedding day.

From the very first days of our marriage, Paolo brought us out of the shadows where we had been hiding our love for one another. On Sunday afternoons I'd put on my red dress and take his arm as we walked down the hill to Hartley Park, retracing our steps on that Sunday long before when he had escorted Pip and Tilly and me to the band concert for the first time.

Paolo usually couldn't wait to get to the park, his exuberance infectious and childlike. He'd clipped the concert schedule out of the *Daily Argus* and always knew exactly what band would be playing. Often, as we walked, he'd be whistling songs he knew to be on the program, entertaining us with a prelude before we even arrived at the park gate. One Sunday he told me he had a surprise for me, a discovery he'd made. I was eager to know what it was and cajoled and pleaded with him all the way down the hill, but he insisted that I had to wait until we were inside the park. Once there, instead of heading toward the band shell, he led me away toward a grove of arborvitae growing in a semicircle. Within the grove he stopped and put his finger to his lips as I started to question him.

"Wait and listen," he said.

Within a few minutes, I heard the tap of the bandleader's baton on the wooden podium and then the opening notes of the tune Paolo had been whistling. The music was as clear as if we had been sitting in front of the bandstand. But instead of being in the midst of a hundred others, we were alone in the grove.

He bowed deeply and said to me, "Signora Serafini, may I have this dance?"

And then he took me in his arms and swept me over the grass in time with the music. I felt his arm around my waist, his hand caressing the small of my back and sometimes wandering lower. His other hand was tightly entwined with mine, as if he never wanted to let go of me.

We danced that Sunday through the entire concert, until we were breathless and a little dizzy from the warmth generated between us. For the rest of the summer we danced to the concerts from within the grove, alone with each other and the music.

Chapter 32

The Strike

ABOVE THE PALACE were two apartments. Claudio gave Paolo and me one as a wedding gift. We had three rooms—a kitchen in the middle with a room in front that we used as a parlor and one in back that was our bedroom. The toilet was out in the hall between the two apartments. Paolo and I had fixed up the rooms since we'd been there, but they were narrow and dark. I could not see any trees when I looked out the windows. In the summer, I put some pots of begonias on the fire escape.

One morning, I had just returned from the market, my basket heavy with onions and broccoli rabe and peppers, when I found Paolo in the kitchen. We were four months married, my breasts already tender, my belly slightly swelled with the baby that had taken hold inside me that first time, at Flora's.

I remembered the morning he'd come to Flora's, seeking his sister but finding me, my longing, my readiness. Was this the reason for his unexpected appearance—was he looking for the same thing now? I put my basket down and went to him. He was seated at the kitchen table, a cigarette in one hand, his pen in the other, a loose sheaf of papers spread across the table-cloth—columns of figures, cryptic words. No poetry this morning.

I put my arms around him, kissing the part of his neck that was exposed above his collar.

"*Buon giorno, Signore Serafini. Come sta?*"

He patted my hand and kissed it absentmindedly. This was not a man hungry for his wife's body. His face was pinched and furrowed, and I could detect the signs of an oncoming headache. He crushed the cigarette in a coffee saucer, threw down the pen and pushed back his chair. The pen scattered drops of blue ink across the cloth. I picked up the saucer and brought it to the sink. He knew I hated the stench and the dirt when he brought cigarettes into the apartment.

He paced the floor, moving from the kitchen to the front room and back. He stopped at the windows that overlooked the street, but stood to the side, by the curtains, so that someone looking up couldn't see him.

I rinsed the saucer and pulled the tablecloth off the table, first gathering his papers together in a pile.

He jumped at me. "What are you doing? Don't touch them. It's business." He grabbed the loose papers from my hand. "They are none of your concern." He stuffed the papers into his pocket.

Tears stung my eyes and I pressed them back with the palm of my hand. His words had been like a slap across my face.

"I'm a businesswoman. I understand business. How can you not talk to me about business, especially if it affects you? Don't you trust me to understand?"

I saw the pains shoot across his face, the color drain from his skin. Even his copper hair looked dull, leaden.

"Are you in trouble? Do you owe someone? Tell me. Tell me."

I went to him, held his face in my hands. I wanted to scream at him. I wanted to caress him. Take away his pain. Take away his false pride. If I could help him, he had to let me.

He took my hands and pulled them away.

"I shouldn't have come home. I'm going out."

He left the apartment. But when he left the building, he didn't use the street entrance. Instead, he went through the Palace and out through the alley.

He didn't come home for supper that evening. I put a covered plate in the icebox and climbed into bed with one of the books my mother had sent. Around ten, I heard the piano downstairs in the Palace and knew it was Paolo. I was able then to sleep, listening to his melancholy music.

Sometime around three, I heard him on the stairs and then in the kitchen. He ate the *pasta e fagioli* I had made for him, cold and in the dark, his spoon grazing the bottom of the bowl with every stroke. When he was finished, he put his dishes in the sink and left his shoes by the door.

I waited, my back turned away from him, my breathing steady. I wanted no more words that night. He undressed slowly, placing his watch and cuff links in their box on the dresser, hanging his shirt and trousers methodically. When he lifted the covers to climb into bed, I could smell the wine, the homemade Chianti he and Claudio sold by the gallon downstairs. His body, normally so taut and strong, was slack and heavy as he settled beside me. He muttered my name as he buried his face in my hair. Within minutes, he was asleep. He slept fitfully, calling out unintelligible sounds and moving his legs uncontrollably. At five, as a gray light filtered over our bed, I could see that he was soaked in sweat, his face the same color as the early morning sky.

I got up and took a soft towel from my linen cupboard. I filled the washbasin with water and brought it to his bedside. I washed his body. Although he stirred at first in protest, he subsided and submitted, finally drifting into a less troubled sleep.

I dressed and made a pot of coffee. In the pocket of his jacket, hanging on the kitchen hook, I could see the papers, still there, crammed as they had been earlier.

My mother would've taken those papers, studied them, deciphered them. She would have confronted Papa and then presented a solution. She was often furious with Papa, but they were always united. More than once, she'd accused him of generating disasters and then reached into her reserves of cunning and intelligence and will to rebuild from the ashes of my father's failures.

What failure was Paolo hiding? What loss could he not share with his wife? I believed he still saw me as a spoiled child, a privileged daughter, unused to financial uncertainty. I was determined to show him I was not fragile. That I could shoulder his pain, not just wipe the sweat from his troubled face.

I could hear his breathing in the next room, the sounds of the street coming alive below us, the factory whistles starting their round, the trains heading for New York with New Rochelle businessmen aboard on their way to banks and shipping firms and law offices.

I left the papers in his jacket. I didn't need to spy to know it had to do with money. Money he didn't have—that we didn't have. I got dressed, not in my marketing clothes, but in my shop clothes. Clothes I hadn't worn since my marriage and the family's decision to sell the store. Pip had left to marry and move to New York, and Tilly's husband, Gaetano, whom she had married a month after my wedding, made enough to relieve her, as well. Whatever profit Claudio had realized when the final papers had been signed he had kept for himself. Between Paolo's salary from the union and his share of the profits from the Palace, we had thought there would be enough for us. But now I understood from Paolo's fear that there wasn't.

I went downstairs and left word at the Palace that I wanted to speak with Claudio. Then I walked over to his stables and found him in his office. We spoke. I made my offer; he accepted.

The next day, the Palace would begin serving lunch and dinner. I was to give Claudio twenty-five percent of the profits and keep the rest for my family.

It had been easier to talk to Claudio than to Paolo. By the time I'd gotten back from the stables, Paolo was already gone, the bed a damp and rumpled pile of sheets. I changed out of my street clothes and stripped and scrubbed the bedding. Better to begin the evening with fresh linens, a fresh heart. I hung the sheets on the line above the alley, ironed the tablecloth that I'd soaked in bleach the day before. The ink spots had disappeared as if they had never marred it.

In the afternoon, I made lists of provisions I would need for the Palace, rolled up the sleeves of my housedress and began to scrub the unused kitchen behind the bar. When Paolo stayed away again at dinnertime, I put his plate in the icebox and sat at the kitchen table writing menu cards in the hand the nuns had taught me at Santa Margareta.

I heard no piano playing downstairs that night, so I was startled when the doorknob turned shortly after ten. I'd just spread the cards out to dry.

"What's this?" He thrust his chin at the table.

"My answer," I replied.

"To what question?"

"My own. How can I be a good wife, a woman, not a child? I don't want to be your burden."

"You're not a burden."

"I made you angry yesterday with my fears."

"I was angry with myself, not you."

"Do you think I can't understand your problems?"

"You shouldn't have to."

"You admire Flora, don't you?"

"I love her. She's my sister."

"But you approve of her, how she handles herself, her affairs?"

"Yes, always. I have great respect for Flora."

"I want you to have respect for me, as well."

"I adore you, Giulia. That's why I anger myself. That I can't provide for you, for the baby—what you deserve. There. I've said it. I can't provide."

He sat with his head in his hands.

"The union is going out on strike again. We only organized the workers a few months ago, and the leadership is calling for a strike at the clockworks. What little steady income I brought in from the IWW will be wiped out."

"Paolo, look at me. Take your hands away from your eyes. Look at me. I am no precious china doll, with feet good only for dancing and hands made only for holding sweets. These feet are planted firmly on the ground. These hips have balanced laundry baskets and bolts of fabric and Claudio's sons—and, soon, God willing, our own. These hands have harvested my grandmother's garden and counted the till at the shop at the end of the day and kept the books. We're going to survive, Paolo. Strike or no strike. The women in my family don't sit fanning themselves while their men sweat.

"Do you think I married you because of your job? Do you think I defied all the curses and the advice of my sisters and my aunts because of money? Do you think I gave you my heart and my soul because you bring home a steady paycheck?

"You provide, Paolo. You provide nourishment for my soul.

You provide music that makes me soar. You provide a joy in my life I did not know existed. Never, never tell me again that you can't provide. *We* provide. For each other."

I was kneeling in front of him, holding his face in my hands. Praying silently to every saint I could remember to help me rescue him, rescue us. And I called upon my mother for her strength of purpose. Her stubbornness. Her unwillingness to accept defeat.

That night I felt a shift take place between Paolo and me. For the first time, I understood what it meant to be a woman. It had nothing to do with the power I had discovered as a young girl in Italy—the hunger I could elicit in Vito's eyes with a bared shoulder or a quickening castanet. Nor was it the satisfaction I had gained in Paolo's arms, from those first precious moments on Flora's carpet of many flowers to our own marriage bed. It was not even my changing body as the child inside me grew and took shape.

It was something entirely apart from my physical self. It was a recognition of my own *serieta*—my solidity, my strength, when confronted with the doubt-ridden soul whose face I held in my hands, whose future rested in my arms. Up until that moment, it was Paolo who'd been strong—Paolo who had caught me in my fall from my own family, Paolo who had snatched the burning veil from my head, Paolo who had lifted me from the carriage run amok. But Paolo's courage—the courage of men—seemed limited to the physical dangers of the world. Soldiers in war, hunters, builders of bridges and tunnels. The courage of women is much more subtle. Builders of the home, protectors of the man's image of himself. Feed the family without destroying his pride. Be resourceful without undermining his own faith in himself. Be the beating heart that fuels his hope.

I told Paolo the next morning that I was growing bored

without the store. Claudio had mentioned how hungry the men were who came to the Palace—how he could keep them longer, attract more to the bar if he could offer a meal now and then. Sonny behind the bar knew how to pour a drink, but couldn't even light the stove. It would give me something to do during the day, if I cooked for the Palace customers. Claudio was willing to let me try. We'd see if these Americans would eat my sausage and peppers.

I slipped into the kitchen as the watchmakers began their strike. It kept my mind off the fury surrounding the clock-works, the picket lines, the shouting, the cops. Paolo came home at night exhausted from shuttling back and forth between the owners and the workers, between the local and the national union. One time, he arrived with a bloody head, a bruised arm.

He was too tired, too preoccupied, to notice the money filling the jewelry box in my top drawer. He was simply grateful for the warm meal I put in front of him and the warm body I welcomed him with every night.

Chapter 33

───❦───

Carmine

WHEN THE PAINS started one afternoon I dismissed them, ignored them, went on with preparing the evening meal for the Palace. But the pains didn't stop, didn't fade away as they had in the past. I managed to serve dinner to the men who'd come to depend on my cooking, who had helped my business flourish in only a few short months. But when Paolo arrived to play the piano, I told him it was time to fetch Flora and Tilly. He had rushed, white-faced, to bring them to me.

I had tried to appear calm when I'd told Paolo, but I was so frightened. I wasn't ready. It was too soon. This baby was not due for two more months.

I should have remembered. Somewhere in me should have been Giuseppina's wisdom, her healing, her hands on my belly. But nothing. I searched frantically, calling her name, wandering through the past as if through the rooms of her house. Where was she?

Oh—another one…too long…no rest.

I was cold, my body was shaking, the sweat ran down my cheeks, my neck. I heard the voices of Tilly and Flora.

"She's so tiny. How will she ever manage?" someone whispered, thinking I couldn't hear.

If Giuseppina had been there, she would have shown me, guided me. Why couldn't I remember? Why hadn't I paid attention?

How long had this been going on? I couldn't remember. I couldn't take another minute, another pain. The light—I saw the light through the window—was it morning already? Why didn't it stop? Why didn't the baby come?

"The head, here's the head." A voice, agitated. A flurry of activity around me.

"Just a few more minutes, Giulia. It's time to push." Tilly bent close to my ear.

I couldn't bear this pain for a few more minutes. It was tearing me apart. Giuseppina!

A darkness, a silence. It was over.

I turned my head to Tilly; my hands reached out, beseeching, for the life that had just struggled and ripped its way through me.

But Tilly came toward me empty-handed, empty-eyed.

I released a wail that came from no place I had known before, not even in those lost moments of pain from the last hours. In that agony had at least been hope, life.

There was no other sound except mine—blood-soaked, emptying, the howling of a she-wolf in the mountains above our village.

Someone tried to hold me, to comfort me with chamomile tea and a cool cloth pressed to my forehead—as if the pain were in my belly or my head, as if there were some simple remedy to restore me.

But I was broken, shattered as though I'd been hurled from a bridge onto stones below. My body lay curled in on itself, hollow.

In the corner I saw Tilly fumbling with a match and a red glass. She lit the votive candle and set it down on the dresser. I heard her droning prayers to saints I no longer remembered, to a God who had, in this moment, turned away from me.

I turned away, as well, from Tilly's piety. In the other corner I saw Flora at the table with a basin. She was washing the baby's body with great tenderness.

I did not even know if it was a girl or a boy. I begged Flora for the child. She faced me. Without hesitation, with understanding, she carried the swaddled corpse over to me.

I raised myself up, felt the blood leaving my body, leaned back against the pillows. I took the silent, still-warm body into my arms and unwrapped it.

A son. Paolo's son. "Carmine," I said.

His skin was a purple-blue. His eyelids were nearly transparent. His hair was the color of a sunset. He had all his parts—nothing missing, nothing damaged. The only thing missing was breath.

It was my turn to bathe him now. My tears came, huge drops that fell from my eyes to his fragile chest. I felt as if I would lose my own breath, my grief came so fast, so relentlessly. I clutched at Carmine, unable to accept that in these last seven months I had been unable to give him life.

He had kicked me two nights before. So resounding, so full of himself that Paolo had felt it, too, lying next to me. Paolo had cradled my belly in his hands, then, pressing his ear to it, listened for his child. I had always felt cherished by Paolo, but this pregnancy had turned me into an object of such adoration and desire it had been almost impossible to fathom the depth of his feeling for me. Whenever my mother was pregnant, I remember my father's eye wandering farther and farther away the bigger her belly grew. But Paolo had been drawn closer and closer with each passing month. He found me so beautiful.

Paolo…Paolo. Where was he? Had someone told him? Or had they all been so preoccupied here with me, with death?

Flora came and gently took the baby away from my grasp. "I'm going to dress him now, Giulia, before he—" She stopped, not wanting to say what would happen, what would take him farther away from the living child I thought I'd be holding now. He would grow cold. He would stiffen. He would rot.

I released him to her. The clothes I'd made for him lay wrapped in tissue paper in the top drawer of the dresser. A jacket, a gown, booties, a hat. Crocheted with a 00 hook and the finest gauge cotton. My aunts had written with suggestions for more useful things, without ornamentation, that would stand up well to repeated washings. Practical quilted kimonos and plain muslin gowns. I had made those, too, dutifully.

The stitches on the baby's jacket were tight and smooth. When I brushed it along the side of my cheek, it glided like silk. There were no mistakes, no dropped stitches or uneven edges. If I had discovered a problem as I was working, I ripped out what I'd done and redid it. It was perfect.

But it was too big. He would never grow into it.

There was a small cross and a medal to pin to his shirt, in the wooden box next to Tilly's candle. "Say a prayer when you put them on him," I told Tilly. "I can't."

Tilly did not know my emptiness. She fussed, she prayed, she changed the sheets.

Paolo wasn't there in those early morning hours to hear my screams and then the baby's silence. Flora had sent him away during the night to sleep at her apartment when she'd realized how much farther I'd had to go in my labor. He returned home around eight in the morning to a desolate quiet. Tilly had already gone; Flora had put on a pot of coffee and was sitting at the kitchen table. I could see her through the door as Paolo walked in. No words passed between them. A question in Paolo's eyes was answered by the mute shaking of Flora's head. Then a sound emerged from Paolo's throat, a sound of such despair and abandonment that I wanted only to rise from my own pain to comfort him.

"Giulia! Giulia! How could God have taken her from me!"

He'd mistakenly thought from Flora's gesture that he had lost *me*.

Flora quickly got up from the table and put her arm around her brother, directing him toward the bedroom. "No! No! Giulia's here, Paolo. Weak, but alive. It's your son we've lost."

Paolo stumbled into the bedroom and knelt at the side of the bed, resting his head on my empty belly. He put his arms around me and I found the strength to return his embrace, feeling his relief and gratitude that I had survived. For all the comfort and solicitous care I'd received from Flora and Tilly in the last few hours, they hadn't shared my grief the way Paolo now did. We mourned our dead son together, holding one another until our tears subsided.

Chapter 34

Milk

CARMELLA COLAVITA ACROSS the alley had no milk. Flora told me this the morning after Carmine's birth and death, when she came over to help me do the wash. She was elbow-deep in soapy water scrubbing the bloody sheets Tilly had set to soak in bleach the day before.

I waited. Was this neighborly concern or an attempt to demonstrate to me that others, within sight of my own windows, had their problems, too? But Flora did not seem to be concerned about my sinking into misery. She looked at me directly, matter-of-factly.

"So will you help?"

I looked down at my breasts, heavy and aching. I had put hot compresses on them the night before to ease the tenderness. How many days before the milk dried up, unused, unneeded, and my body forgot the last seven months?

I remembered the women in Venticano who appeared like angels at the bedside of a mother who had died giving birth, offering nourishment to a wailing, hungry child. Or who came to the aid of women like my mother, bedridden for months carrying twins, unable to feed both adequately. Who were these women, with their generous breasts, their open arms? My brother Frankie, the twin who survived, could always find refuge in the skirts of Lucia Russo. As a boy of five he'd been chased by some bullies and our older brothers had been nowhere to be found. He'd raced frantically to Lucia's cottage and she'd protected him, chasing the other boys away with her cast-iron pan as she'd cursed them for daring to threaten Frankie.

As a little girl, I hadn't given a second thought to the women like Lucia. She used to come with Frankie and sit by Giuseppina's fire in the winter. She'd felt more welcome there than in my mother's house.

Giuseppina had her remedies, her teas and herbs, for the women whose milk was scarce or thin, but in the end, Lucia was her ally, her final choice, in the battle to keep her grandson alive and growing.

I had no need of Giuseppina's medicines. My blouse was already wet, two round circles of dampness spreading across the front. I folded my arms across my chest to stem the surge of milk. What a waste, I thought.

"Of course I'll help," I told Flora, who nodded.

"She'll be so relieved. She's been frantic with worry. 'It's not like the village at home,' she told me, 'where someone would be on your doorstep in an instant to feed an undernourished baby.' The poor girl has no one here. She came as a bride with her husband. All her own family is still back home."

Carmella brought me the baby that afternoon. Flora had already hung the sheets on the line out the kitchen window. The day was windless but brilliantly sunny and the sheets fell straight and still as if this were August in my mother's courtyard on Pasqualina's wash day. The sheets betrayed no sign of the struggle. They were restored to their original whiteness.

Flora left a soup for Paolo's dinner before going home to cook for her own family.

Carmella's little girl appeared sickly. She was very fretful, did not know what to do with a nipple. Moved her little face from side to side, screaming.

Carmella could not keep her hands still as she watched her daughter against my unfamiliar body. Her hands were rough, worn, not at all the hands of a woman younger than I was. She grasped the cloth of her skirt and bunched it in her fist, then released it, repeating the gesture as she muttered some words—prayers, a lullaby? I tried to coax the baby to turn toward my breast but she did not stop screaming. She was so hungry.

When she opened her tiny mouth to scream, I slid in my finger. She stopped abruptly and sucked my finger. With my finger still in her mouth I eased her to my breast. She continued to suck. Her mother took a deep breath. My milk surged into my breasts, so painfully that I gasped. The baby's blue-veined eyelids fluttered and then closed. Her agitated, frantic body slowed its kicking and grasping. Little noises of content-ment filtered up. I watched her face; I watched her mother's face. The baby finally fell asleep at my breast, and the tiny fists that had been pummeling the air were splayed across my lap.

I sat staring at her for several more minutes while her mother's tears fell quietly. I did not want to let go of her. I wanted to feel that weight leaning into me, to hear and measure that breathing, to smell that mixture of soap and milk.

But then I handed her back to her mother.

"*Grazie,* Signora Giulia," she whispered.

"Bring her back later when she wakes up."

When she left, I placed my hands on my breasts. They felt lighter. A gift, I thought. For me, for this baby, for this mother.

503

I turned and lit the stove under the soup and began to set the table for Paolo. I knew that he expected me to be still resting, not up and about, and I wanted to surprise him.

I no longer felt tired.

Chapter 35

Bread and Roses

AFTER CARMINE DIED, I got pregnant again, and again carried the baby for seven months. It was such a tiny thing, tinier than Carmine. A little girl. Emilia, I named her. I can say her name now, in a soft voice, but the memories of those dead babies haunt me still. My mother was right. There is no other pain, not even the pain of bearing those children, of giving birth to them, that is greater than the pain of losing them. Take my arm, my eye, cut me up piece by piece. That is what it's like to have a child snatched from life.

The winter after I lost Emilia was bitterly cold. It drove us all inside, including the customers of the Palace. The bar was full every evening and I kept warm over the stove in the kitchen, burying my grief by filling large pots with meatballs and sausage.

Paolo's grief was as raw as mine, but his pain was compounded by guilt and fear. Guilt that it was his passion, his desire for me that had caused us these losses; and fear that the next time he would lose me as well as his child. A man does not know how to behave at these times. When he should have been able to walk down the street with his son riding on his shoulders and screaming with delight, "*Babbo, Babbo,* look at the sky," he had only an empty cradle and an empty wife.

It is no wonder to me that he turned outside, taking refuge in his work with the union in the same way I had hidden in the Palace's kitchen. I didn't have the will to hold him back or even question him, as his days and then his nights became consumed.

One night in January when he'd returned from New York City, I came up the stairs from the Palace to give him his dinner. I found him packing, throwing shirts, socks, his notebook and pen into an open bag on our bed.

I watched, my already pale face and slumping body losing whatever was left that had held me together over the last few months. I felt myself sink to my knees and leaned against the door frame for support.

"What's this all about, Paolo? Where are you going?"

"Lawrence, in Massachusetts. Twenty thousand workers have walked out of the woolen mills. Many of them are women and children, mostly Italians. In the last two days they've stopped production in thirty-four mills. New York got a telegram this morning. This isn't something that the cops or the state militia are going to quash in a couple of days. The workers need help, a strike committee, organized relief. Joe Ettor and Arturo Giovanitti are going, and I'm going with them. I know the leaders—I worked with them when I was up there last year. They need me."

He was almost feverish as he moved around the room grabbing clothes from a drawer, sweeping his books from the night table into a pile that he thrust into the bag. He was no longer the shell of a man who'd only been going through the motions of life in the last two months. He had reignited the fire within himself and it was smoldering in our bedroom. His face was flushed and his eyes glistened as he ticked off a mental list of what to take.

"When are you leaving?"

"Tonight. I'm meeting Joe and Arturo at the train station."

He was a man of action that night, a man with a destination and a purpose. He was also a man who did not see me trying to cling to something solid and permanent as I was about to lose him to history yet again. I remembered Schenectady, and how little power I had to hold him back.

"Why now? Why the urgency? Why do they need you if the others are going?"

"Because this is momentous. Twenty thousand people, Giulia. It's what we've been waiting for. They believe in us, they hear what we've been trying to tell them for years—that their power is in their collective voice."

I pulled myself to my feet. My face felt as flushed as Paolo's. I was jealous. Jealous of the passion he was feeling, not for me, but for a cause, for twenty thousand human beings struggling to put a loaf of bread on the table and clothes on the backs of their families. And I admired him, too, for the role he was about to play.

But watching him prepare to leave was killing me. My hands were shaking and I could feel the tears stinging my eyes. Other women, my sisters and mother included, had to endure the callousness and betrayal of husbands whose eyes and hands wandered, who thought nothing of keeping a mistress on the side. I knew I was the only woman Paolo loved. I had no doubts about his faithfulness. Even when he was gone to the city overnight. Even though I knew there were women involved in the union movement—American women who saw marriage as a convention of constraint. Even when Pip or Zi'Yolanda would insert the knife of their own discontent tipped with the poison of rumor and conjecture.

Pip, especially, who lived in New York and who believed herself to be the authority on everything that happened there.

"How can you continue to tolerate his involvement? It's bad enough that the Wobblies are preaching anarchy and would kill us all if they could. But *that woman,* Elizabeth Gurley Flynn, that intellectual up on the platform with them—how many of the men do you suppose *she's* slept with? How do you know she hasn't invited Paolo into her bed when he's working late on one of those speeches that get him into trouble with the police? I warned you, Giulia, when you were first seeing him, what a mistake it would be."

Pip's words were seeds she tried to plant, hoping they'd force their way into my heart the way weeds here break through the cracks in the sidewalk. But I had no cracks. My love for Paolo, my faith in him, was as strong as on our wedding day. I didn't believe her. I didn't believe the muck and the dirt she tried to drag into my home.

But I knew that although I was the only woman in Paolo's heart, I had to share space in there with his work. It wasn't some American girl who was my rival, but an ideal. How do you overcome that? How could my kisses, my warm and pliant body, the safety and repose he found in my arms, measure up to the excitement and sense of being on a fast-moving train hurtling toward his goal?

Standing there, holding back my tears, I saw that I could not be a substitute for that. I went to the laundry basket where I'd stacked the ironing I'd done the night before. I plucked three neatly folded handkerchiefs from the pile.

"Here, you'll need these."

He took them from me, placed them on top of his other things and closed the bag. He looked at me, at the weariness staring out at him from my dark-circled eyes, but he also saw my acceptance and resignation. He realized that I would not try to hold him back, and I imagine he was grateful for that. He took me in his arms and held me, wordless.

"I'll write. I don't know how long it will take."

I broke the embrace first. I did not want to remember him pulling away from me.

"Stay safe," I said as he turned and walked down the stairs. *Come back,* I thought, *because I'm pregnant again and I don't want to raise this child alone.*

Chapter 36

Letters from Lawrence
January 18, 1912

My dearest Giulia,

I am writing this on Thursday night from the rooming house where our group from New York has found lodging. In only a week, Joe Ettor has organized a strike committee and our leaflets have blanketed the town. On Monday morning, afraid of the message that is reaching the workers, the mayor ordered in the local militia. They are patrolling the streets—college boys from Harvard who have no idea what it means to lose the money in your paycheck that paid for three loaves of bread each week. That is what drove the workers from their looms—a reduction of two hours' pay because of new, faster machines.

Already, the spirit in the streets is alive, crackling. Thousands of workers are marching and picketing, a surge of humanity that is like one organism. Even when repulsed, like storm waves hitting the beach, they surge again. This afternoon, at a demonstration in front of the A&P Mills, the company goons drenched us with fire hoses. The temperature was so cold that the water turned quickly to ice on the streets, freezing into icicles on the men's beards and the women's eyebrows. But instead of being pushed back and dispersed, the crowd retaliated. The younger ones picked up chunks of dirty, ice-hardened snow along the road and flung it back at the goons. The police, who'd been on the periphery of the crowd, waiting for them to give up in fear, saw that something different was happening. Something defiant, something unified. They moved in and began arresting people, throwing them into wagons. Don't worry. I managed to elude them. They only got a few people—thirty at most—and there are twenty thousand of us still in the streets. They cannot arrest us all. They cannot ignore us.

Per la vita,
Paolo

January 29, 1912

My darling Giulia,
Another cold and dark night in Lawrence. This afternoon, Joe Ettor spoke to a mass meeting on the Lawrence Common. He is a voice of calm and reason. He has managed to bring together so many nationalities—Italians, Poles, Germans, French, Syrians—with the power of his ideas. No one else could do it—no other union even wanted these poor, unskilled, uneducated ragged folk. I heard him up there on the platform we had built out of scrap wood, a man inspired by the faces in front of him, raw from the cold and the days of picketing, but warmed by the fire of his words. I stood behind him, scribbling down phrases as he spoke them, my fingers clutching my pen as I tried to capture what he was saying. Then he jumped down into the crowd and led them on a march downtown.

While Ettor has been leading the strike, Arturo Giovanitti put together the relief committees. Soup kitchens, food distribution, doctors—the striking families are being cared for so that no one feels compelled to go back to work out of desperation.

I cannot express to you how proud I am to be a part of this, to see my people stand up against the tyranny of the mill owners and the complicity and enmity of the government. The governor ordered in the state militia and the state police. They are afraid—of women and children with no weapons except their own sense of justice.

I want you to know how much I miss your loving arms around me. I have only these words that I write to you to warm my soul. Per sempre,
Paolo

February 1, 1912

Dearest Giulia,
As you have no doubt read, Ettor and Giovanitti have been arrested, falsely accused of a murder that occurred miles away from where they were. The government believes it can disrupt the strike by imprisoning them. Already, martial law has been imposed. Public meetings have been declared illegal, and even more militiamen are patrolling the streets. Everywhere you turn stands a soldier with a gun.

But we are not alone. At the behest of the strike committee, I telegrammed the IWW in New York. More organizers are on their way to Lawrence, including my compadre, Claudio Tresca, from Naples.
All is not lost.
Paolo

February 5, 1912

Dearest Giulia,

It was thrilling. I can still hear the strains of the "Internation-
ale" sung in nine languages by twenty-five thousand workers.
Bill Haywood, one of the leaders of the IWW, arrived on the
train this afternoon and fifteen thousand of us met him and carried him to the Common to speak to the others gathered there.
Haywood is full of tactics for passive resistance. We picket the
mills constantly, our white armbands proclaiming our unity.

My beloved, I know I have asked so much of you already by
leaving you alone while I fight this battle. But I have one more
request.

Because the strike shows no sign of waning, we think it best
to find a safe place for the children, away from the danger here.
The Italian Socialist Federation is organizing safe homes for
them. I beg you, take one or two of these children into our home.
I know you will care for them as the loving mother you will one
day become to our own children. Let these children experience
your warmth while I am away from you.

Yours forever,

Paolo

Chapter 37

The Children's Exodus

BECAUSE HE ASKED ME, I said yes. My family, of course, was outraged. Claudio was already irritated that Paolo had gone to Lawrence. He was less concerned about Paolo's leaving me alone than the fact that he had no one he trusted managing the Palace. It meant that Claudio's activities were constrained; that he had to spend more time at the Palace. Claudio didn't like the monotony and restrictions of shopkeeping, of maintaining the day-to-day life of a business. Instead, he preferred to be out in the world, sniffing out the next deal. His presence every night was a burden for me, as well. It provided too many opportunities for him to watch me and criticize me. When he heard about the children from my sisters, he came storming into the Palace's kitchen.

"What's this I hear from Tilly—that you're going to take in some brats from Lawrence? You don't have time to help Angelina with our kids anymore, but you can be a foster mother to strangers?"

Pip's concern, on the other hand, was not my unavailability to be a nanny to Claudio's brood, but the hygiene of the children. "Do you have any idea how filthy they are? They live like animals in the tenements. They'll be full of lice and disease. How can you bring them into your home? And how do you know they won't rob you of what little you have?"

But I would not be swayed. Paolo had begged me to do this, and besides, my heart went out to the mothers trying to care for their children in the midst of all the unrest. In my eyes, these women, as poor and illiterate as they were, were trying to do right by their families. The least I could do was ease their burden somewhat by putting a roof over their children's heads.

I got Claudio to drive me into Manhattan the day the children were to arrive by train. Always looking for ways to appear as prosperous as the American bankers who disdained his success, he had bought one of Henry Ford's Model T town cars the year before and was happy to show it off in Manhattan.

I had packed a basket with some bread filled with peppers and eggs, and I'd collected some warm clothing—coats and mittens and socks—that Flora's children had outgrown. I was unprepared for the spectacle that greeted us. Thousands of socialists from the Italian Federation had gathered to welcome the children. Bands played, banners were flying. I worried about finding the children in the confusion. But somehow, despite the presence of so many supporters, I found them, thanks to the good planning of the women who'd conceived of and organized the children's exodus.

As we drove back to Mount Vernon, they sat in the backseat of the car, wrapped in the too-big coats and devouring my sandwiches. A brother and sister, Tino and Evelina, their pale but clean faces took everything in—Claudio's car, the city outside the windows, the strange lady in the front seat speaking their language.

When we got to Mount Vernon, Claudio left us at the Palace. I led them upstairs to the apartment, where I'd made beds for them in the front room. They had nothing with them, not even a paper bag with a nightshirt or a hairbrush.

The first thing I did was draw them a hot bath in the tub in the kitchen. Their bodies were so scrawny, so undernourished. I put them in two of Paolo's old nightshirts, gave them each a hot bowl of minestrone and put them to bed. The younger one, Evelina, was only five. She sucked her thumb and barely spoke, but she was trembling and close to tears. I took her in my lap in the rocking chair Paolo had bought me to rock our own children in and that I hadn't been able to bring myself to use. I sang her every children's song I could think of. She finally fell asleep, her head heavy and damp against my breast. The baby inside me had not yet begun to flutter and kick. Instead, I held this silent little girl and dreamed that one day I'd hold my own daughter like this.

Tino and Evelina stayed for a month, until the strike was settled. It was sending the children away that had turned the tide. There was so much public sympathy for them that the mayor of Lawrence ordered a halt to the trips. The next time a group attempted to leave, the police attacked the mothers and children, beating them back from the train station. It was a horrific scene, captured by newspapers all over America.

After that, the workers of Lawrence were not alone. Protests and outrage spread around the country, and the mill owners had no alternative but to settle.

The children of Lawrence went home as Paolo returned. They were well fed. I had stitched each of them some warm clothing. I'd learned how to keep a child still long enough to braid her hair and had taught them both the letters of the alphabet and how to write their names.

By the time Paolo walked in the door again, my belly was rounded with our own child.

Chapter 38

Waiting

THE RE WAS NO HIDING that I was pregnant again. But this time, no other woman carrying a child would look at me for fear that her own baby would follow mine into death. If they had to pass me on the street they'd walk to the other side. Old women offered me advice. Eat this. Don't drink that. Don't climb. Don't bend. Don't carry. Pray to Saint Anne. Pray to Saint Jude.

Paolo walked around in a haze of guilt.

"Giulia will die next time!" Pip screamed at him the night we let them all know another was on the way.

He was afraid to touch me, convinced that his passion for me, undiminished after more than three years of marriage, was to blame for the babies' not surviving. We slept separately—I alone in our bed, crying myself softly to sleep, Paolo on the sofa in the front room, tossing fitfully. It was a lonely time. Most nights, he stayed downstairs at the Palace till early in the morning, playing cards with my cousin or writing music to keep from facing sleep alone. I had no such refuge. I fell into bed exhausted from the routines of the day, from the growing heaviness of my body, from the fears of what still lay before me. I listened for the sound of life within me. I measured the vigor of a kick.

Worry filled my nights. The racket of clattering wagons from the street outside, the tinkling of glass and murmured voices downstairs, the shouting from the Colavitas' apartment across the alley—all kept me awake and thinking. This wasn't good for the baby, I thought, lying on my pillow, tears trickling in rivulets down my neck.

During the day, the other women tried to make little of my experience.

"You're not the first to lose a baby, Giulia. Look at Maria Fanelli, at Rosa Spina. Every time they're pregnant they miscarry. Face it. It happens. What are you going to do, stop making love to Paolo? It's life."

"You can't dwell on these things, it'll make you crazy, like Jenny DeVito, remember her? That girl never carried a baby past three months. Started talking to herself, cut off all her hair. They say her husband got some *putana* in Napoli pregnant because he wanted a son and was convinced Jenny would never give him one. At least you're holding on to them, Giulia. They grow with all their parts. You'll get there. And if you don't, you don't. It's what God gives you."

I tried to keep in my head what it had been like in Venticano with Giuseppina. I knew that not all the babies she birthed actually lived. I knew this was a part of a woman's life. But the fear that I'd *never* be able to bear a living child consumed me. I listened to the way other women talked about childless neighbors. How pitiful! God spare me from the fate of my own sister Letitia—eight years married and never even pregnant, praying novenas and making pilgrimages to bless her with a child.

Sometimes I thought that if Giuseppina had been here she'd

know what to do. She knew how to help my mother. My mother bore nine children, all living, breathing, whole. Frankie's twin was three months old when he died, so it wasn't like dying at birth. What had Giuseppina done? What secrets? What herbs? I didn't remember anymore. The older women here, women like my Zi'Yolanda, I did not trust. They didn't have the secrets, the *knowing* that Giuseppina did. They offered a mishmash of household remedies. The nurses from the Social Service came and tried to teach them about germs and hygiene and they half listened. Partly they didn't understand, especially when the nurses shouted at them in baby English and made pantomimes with their hands. After the nurses left, the women laughed at their naïveté, their modern ideas. But sometimes, in spite of their disdain for American ideas, those ideas crept into what they did and they started to forget the old ways. Or they never learned the old ways in the first place.

Yolanda wasn't very smart. She "dropped" her babies, she said, without a thought, without a worry. She could not understand my sleeplessness.

My mother wrote me with advice.

"Get into bed," she cautioned, when she learned of my third pregnancy. "Let the others do for you."

She seemed unaware of what my life here was like. I had no employees in the Palace kitchen to help me prepare and serve fifty meals a day. I had no widowed, childless sisters-in-law as she did to run my household. I had no mother-in-law to whisk away responsibilities and take them under her own roof while I languished, propped up on linen pillowcases. Flora, God bless her, did what she could to allow me some rest from day to day. Pip, in Manhattan with her husband, was a stranger to us. She had finally achieved her dream of a life as a lady. When she came to visit with her husband, Ernesto, she wore an elegant coat trimmed with fur. Her fingers, which a few short years ago had struggled with bobbins and pin and thread, were warmed in a matching fur-lined muff. Her hat, velvet, with a sweeping brim and a feather that arched down across her brow and grazed her left ear, reminded me of the hat my mother used to wear. Pip had a dressmaker to whom she gave meticulous instructions. Like Letitia, she was childless. But she made no pilgrimages. She and Ernesto traveled to Atlantic City. They went to the opera.

Tilly lived only one street over, but she already had two daughters—Annunziata and Dora—and was pregnant as well when my time came.

As distant as I'd been from my mother, I wanted to write to her, "Mama, come now to me, as Giuseppina came to you when you were in need."

But I didn't. She still had Papa and my three brothers at home. I don't think she was prepared to come to America, to leave her life of ease and comfort, her annual sojourns to the sulfur baths at Ischia, her shopping expeditions to Napoli, her correspondence with great minds at the university. What kind of life would she have found here? When she encouraged me to have others do for me, no, I don't think she had herself in mind.

I had made no preparations for this baby. Antonietta said the American girls had a party when someone was pregnant, bringing gifts for the baby before it was born. I shivered when she told me. Such bad luck! I had no cradle, no shirts, no gowns. Nothing to pack away again or stare at lying flat and empty in a corner. I tempted the fates with the white jacket I'd crocheted for Carmine and I got to use it as a shroud. Emilia I buried in a dress Tilly gave me from one of her little girls.

I didn't have time to sew anyway.

In the mornings, I did the marketing and then went downstairs to the Palace kitchen and prepared whatever meal we served customers that day—lasagna, chicken salmi, sausage

and peppers. I often sat outside the back door to peel the vegetables. The cats came around for scraps and sometimes the
girls who worked for Signora Bifaro at the hotel behind us
were out on the steps. They smoked; they played cards; they
were out there in their lingerie as if they didn't care who saw
them. They didn't look after themselves very well, those girls.
Their peignoirs were dirty, the hems trailing in the dirt on the
steps. Their feet and their necks weren't clean, and they wore
makeup to hide their sallow skin—bright patches of rouge on
their cheeks and smeared kohl around their eyes.

Paolo and Claudio pretended I didn't see the men who, after
a round of drinks at the Palace, slipped out the back door, past
the crate where I sat with my garlic and onions, and climbed
the stairs with one of the girls. The girls leaned against the
railing and looked the men up and down. But they didn't look
them in the eye. And when they were chosen, they tossed their
cigarettes over the railing. The cigarettes usually landed at my
feet, still smoldering, stinking, a slash of dark red lipstick at
one end.

Sometimes, when it was slow and the girls were bored with
their card games, they joked with me.

"Hey, Giulia, you're so pretty. You should be up here with
us instead of down there chopping onions and peppers."

"Giulia doesn't need to be up here. She's got that handsome
husband to take care of her. And from the looks of her belly,
Paolo takes very good care of her. Isn't that so, Giulia?"

The girls laughed when I blushed.

One day Claudio came into the kitchen while I was frying
some meatballs. I was busy over the stove, but he wanted to
talk.

"I don't like you sitting out back. It looks bad."

"What, you think somebody's going to mistake me for one
of Bifaro's girls?" I turned so that my belly was unmistakable.

521

"You know what I mean." Claudio thought I should've learned that time he threw the iron at me not to talk fresh to him. But I didn't let Claudio tell me what to do. He was not my father.

"You mean, when I sit there it makes the men uncomfortable. I know who they are. I know their wives. And if they feel too uncomfortable, maybe they're not going to go through the door and up the stairs. Maybe they're not going to spend their money with Bifaro. And if they don't spend their money with Bifaro, then you don't get your cut."

I turned over the meatballs. What did he think, I was some little girl who didn't know what those women did? Did he really believe that I didn't see a connection between him and Bifaro's convenient location?

"You insult me, and you insult Signora Bifaro with your suspicions. Do your cooking in the kitchen, Giulia. You look like some goddamn *cafona* out back with your knife, feeding the cats. Act respectable. Don't give people a reason to talk."

"The only ones who talk, Claudio, are the whores."

My daughter Caterina was born in early November. The late-afternoon light was reaching over the rooftops and through the lace curtains in the bedroom, stretching across the floor and onto the bed. I heard the tiny wail, the first gasp of air and life. Flora lifted her into my arms and I felt the slippery warmth, the fluttering movements that signaled she was alive.

Paolo had retreated downstairs to the Palace, pacing, waiting, not even playing the piano for fear it would disturb me. But when he heard Caterina cry he came bounding up the stairs, a man bursting with hope and pride.

Chapter 39

Z'Amalia's Inheritance

A FEW WEEKS BEFORE Caterina's birth, Papa decided to visit New York. He took the mountain road from Venticano, just as he had the predawn morning he drove Pip and Tilly and me to our destinies. Just as he had, since then, carried more and more of our countrymen away from the village and toward America.

At Avellino, he joined the regional road that leads through the valley to Napoli. At the outskirts of the city, he wove his way through streets, past market stalls and pink-walled tenements, until he reached the wide expanse of the Via Caracciolo. When he arrived at the harbor, however, he did not discharge his passengers and return to the mountains.

He boarded the ship himself.

"I'm coming for a few months," he said. "I do not intend to stay. I come only to decide if Claudio's business warrants the money Claudio, swallowing his pride, has asked me to invest."

Papa had money to invest because Z'Amalia, Giuseppina's wealthy sister, had finally succumbed to her many ailments, her loneliness and her arrogance. She had left everything—her villa on the perimeter of the Parco di Capodimonte in Napoli, her paintings, her piano, her gold accumulated over years of hoarding—to Papa.

The cousins were furious, but Papa said, "Where were you when I visited her every week? Who sat with her in her rooms smelling like death and listened to her complaints? Did any of you bring her a piece of cake or take her for a walk in the garden?" He ignored their outrage. He bought a new suit and sat in the front row at the funeral.

So Claudio, who as a little boy used to endure with Papa his visits to Z'Amalia, her desiccated fingers pinching his cheeks and offering him stale chocolates that had turned dusty white in their satin box, now thought it was time to expand his business. He wanted to build the roads, not just haul the stone for the builders.

But he needed Papa, Papa's money, to do that. I know what it took Claudio to put aside his own bitterness to ask. Greed. Ambition.

And it was my mother who had interceded. A business opportunity, she told Papa. Make the money grow, don't hide it under the bed the way your aunt did. You're no old woman. You're an astute businessman. You said yourself your bones are getting too old to travel these roads day after day. And, even if it's Aldo at the reins, he carries fewer and fewer passengers, except to take them to the ships.

So go see if this is the right business. Decide for yourself. And take the boys with you. They're old enough now, and will give me no peace if you go without them. I can manage here myself while you make up your mind about Claudio's business. Somehow, perhaps appealing to Papa's own greed, she had convinced him.

They were more alike than they cared to admit, Papa and Claudio. Even though they'd parted ten years before without a word between them since.

On the morning of Caterina's birth, Papa arrived in America. He brought with him Z'Amalia's money, my brothers Aldo and Frankie and Sandro—no longer willing to be left behind—and a gift from Giuseppina for the baby she was sure would be born alive.

Their arrival stunned me, emphasizing the passage of time since my own departure. The boys were all tall and strong, their faces the faces of men. Aldo, almost twenty-four, had cultivated his imitation of Papa so well that, from a distance and in dim light, one could be excused for mistaking the two. He had even put on weight and affected the three-piece suits that Papa's tailor in Napoli must have fashioned for him. Our altar boy, Frankie, not even shaving when I'd left, now turned his sixteen-year-old face to me with a finely trimmed mustache. Not the voluminous, waxed statements of Papa and Aldo and all the other men of my family, but an outline, like the charcoal sketch made by da Vinci before creating a masterpiece in full color. Sandro, at fourteen not yet taking a razor to his face, was nonetheless taller than all of them, his little-boy energy transformed into muscle and bone.

They tumbled into Claudio and Angelina's house and into our lives, breathing American air, listening to American voices, walking on American pavement as if they were once again in the hills playing the games inspired by Claudio's letters. They had rehearsed this scene before. They knew their lines.

Papa, however, was a stranger in the home of his oldest son. Angelina did nothing to ease his discomfort, her sense of being put-upon evident in the firmness with which she placed every additional plate on the table. After dinner the evening of their arrival, she herded her brood—Alberto, now eight, Armando, six, Vita, four, and Magdalena, two—up to bed…but first she opened the windows of the dining room to air out the smoke from not only her husband's noxious cigar, but now that of her father-in-law, as well.

What took place that evening Claudio shared with me many years later, because I was able to listen with the ears of a businesswoman, not the ears of his youngest sister.

Claudio sent the boys down to the Palace that night and turned to an impatient father, waiting at the recently cleared table, fingers taking the measure of the damask tablecloth, comparing it to his own.

Claudio put two glasses and a bottle of grappa on the table, watching Papa's hands. They were calloused and toughened, familiar with handling leather reins, lifting heavy freight, evaluating the muscled flanks of his horses. But they were also manicured, as carefully trimmed and buffed as his mustache. Claudio believed he understood Papa.

"So show me," Papa said. "Show me this dream."

Claudio pulled open a drawer in the sideboard and withdrew a brown folder bound with string. He retrieved several pages from the folder and spread them out on the table. Those pages were his translation of what Papa had defined as a dream—a word Papa used to describe the fairy tales of fools, the deluded fiction of those not rooted in reality.

Claudio had first listed what he'd gleaned from fragments of conversations, minutes of municipal meetings, obscure references in the *Daily Argus*. Land that was to be developed. Roads that would need to be paved. Bridges that would need to be erected. Tunnels that would need to be dug. Next, he'd gathered the names and prices of the equipment required to pave and erect and dig. Then he'd calculated the number of men necessary to run the equipment, hold the shovels, heave the picks. He had factored in his relationship with Paolo, his business partner and brother-in-law. If the construction industry became unionized, he'd use that relationship to influence any deal he might be forced to make with the union. And last, he'd predicted what the city of Mount Vernon and the state of New York—what America—would pay to extend its reach, turn woods and fields into city. A great deal, he said. Far more than it would cost him to build.

"There's something missing in your costs," Papa said, looking up over his spectacles from the numbers he'd examined, "unless business is done so differently here that you don't need it."

Claudio removed another sheet from the folder.

"I didn't forget."

He pressed his lips together in a smile of victory. The price of influence was carefully noted on the last sheet, with cryptic initials and amounts, annotations as to what might be required: liquor, women, a cash donation to a campaign chest, a funeral wreath at a mother's untimely passing.

"I'll take the numbers up to bed with me to study, and then sleep on it. How much are you asking me for to underwrite this venture? What are you prepared to give me in return?"

Papa made a few notations in his notebook and took a long draft on his cigar.

Claudio, sure of Papa's interest, but knowing him well enough to understand that he had to come out feeling the victor, made an offer that he was willing to negotiate, but presented as firm. Let Papa mull and calculate and pare and refine. He, Claudio, felt his father's blood in his veins, heard the pace of his breathing in his own breath. After ten years, he had learned that he could not escape his father in himself, and so turned that to his own advantage. That Papa would win something was irrelevant to Claudio because he would win more. An empire. Carried first on his own back, but then on the backs of his sons.

He gathered the papers together and handed them to Papa. He poured them both another shot of grappa and lifted his glass.

"Salute!"

Claudio got more than he bargained for with Papa's investment. They made their deal the next morning after Papa had slept, as he'd promised. In the morning the house was a chaos of small children, hungry and noisy, the two boys being scrubbed and fed and sent off to school, the two girls observing their unfamiliar grandfather across the breakfast table with open mouths. Papa's own sons straggled into the room for coffee after a very late night, groaning with hangovers but eager to hit the sidewalks once again.

Claudio suggested to Papa a walk to the Palace. In the early morning it was deserted, as good a place to conduct business as any. Claudio paused at the front door to pull out his key, savoring the look on Papa's face as he took in the polished oak door, the glass etched with the Fiorillo and Serafini names.

Once inside, Claudio realized how smart he'd been to suggest it as a meeting place. Everything about it spoke of Claudio's success—the marble-topped bar with its brass rail, the mirrors reflecting the shelves of liquor and the light filtering across the expanse of the room, the piano, the chandelier. It *was* a palace.

He pulled out a heavy chair for Papa, offered him a drink, which Papa waved away, and sat down to deal.

Papa would give him the money he'd asked for, but wanted to be more than a silent investor. He wanted to be part of the day-to-day operation. He had intended to sell the business in Venticano anyway. It bored him. This, on the other hand, was greater than an investment. This was new life. Take it or leave it.

Claudio looked into his father's eyes, and took.

He named his new company after the state of New York, not after the family. No need to cloud his opportunities with the taint of Italy. He wanted the business of America. He wanted to *be* America.

Chapter 40

Giuseppina's Goodbye

GIUSEPPINA WAS DYING. Word came in a letter from my mother. She wrote that Giuseppina had suddenly grown tired, forgetful, unable to care for the simplest of her needs. Pasqualina moved into her house to care for her.

Giuseppina lingered in some shrouded corner of her brain. She wandered at night calling out the names of the dead, and when she was quiet sat by the stove unraveling the edge of her shawl. Like her shawl, she was shrinking. She forgot to eat unless Pasqualina fed her *pastina* in *brodo* with a beaten egg. Her eyes were clouded with cataracts. She wet her pants.

My mother was grateful that Pasqualina could nurse Giuseppina, although it left my mother, of course, with more to do in her own house.

I tried to deny these scenes that my mother described. But in my heart, I knew that Giuseppina had begun to die the moment Claudio took his first step off the mountain. My mother herself put the first nails in Giuseppina's coffin when she took me away from her and sent me to America.

That Giuseppina had lived this long was a miracle. My mother attributed it to her stubbornness as well as to her own magic. The order had been reversed. Giuseppina should have been the one to leave first, to say goodbye to us, her blood and bone, as she departed this earth. In truth, Giuseppina stayed alive only to watch each and every one of us leave her.

Chapter 41

Homecoming

WHEN GIUSEPPINA DIED, only a few weeks after beginning her decline, Mama and Pasqualina tied up their hair in kerchiefs, donned their aprons and began to clean out Giuseppina's house of unidentifiable and odiferous objects.

"However did I allow you to live in such squalor?" my mother wrote.

I hadn't remembered it as squalor.

Mama and Pasqualina swept, scrubbed, burned years of accumulated debris, whitewashed walls, and opened to air and light rooms that had been shuttered and forgotten. In all her years as mistress of her own house, I don't think my mother had ever engaged in such vigorous housekeeping. But taking a broom to Giuseppina's hearth seemed to release in her a newfound energy and a desire to sweep away not only the artifacts and shards of Giuseppina's existence, but her own, as well.

Why should I stay any longer in Venticano? she wrote my father. Why should you come back? Most of our children are in America. Even Letitia and Rassina have decided to leave

Italy. Now that Giuseppina is gone, there is nothing to hold us and everything to release us.

Papa, reluctantly seduced by the opportunities that spilled out of every vacant lot where he could envision a building, every rutted path where he imagined a paved road, made a few loud noises, retired to Claudio's dining table to make calculations in a notebook, and finally sent Mama a telegram directing her to come to America.

Pasqualina, who had waited patiently for Papa's return, reacted with panic to the news that he would not be coming back. She adamantly refused to come to America, a place that for her embodied not dreams but nightmares. She was too old to begin again, she said. And what about Teresia? What if they arrived on American shores only to have the authorities refuse her entry because of her simplemindedness? She had heard stories. She knew these things could happen. That one's future and hope could hang on the whim of some uniformed guard with a chip on his shoulder, looking for any reason to keep someone out. No, she didn't want to risk that humiliation. To be sent back. And to what? The house sold to strangers, the land tilled by someone else? And even if they let Teresia in, how would she survive in such a hostile and unwelcoming place? No. Venticano was where she'd been born, and it was where she, like her mother, would die.

My mother, instead of arguing with her or enlisting my father's authority to order her to join the rest of the family, looked instead for a way that would allow Pasqualina and Teresia to remain in Venticano and my mother to leave.

It was another death that gave her what she needed. Silvana Tedesco, the mother of seven children, had died of malaria the year before. Vincente Tedesco, her husband, was ready to seek a new wife for his motherless sons and daughters. He wanted no more children, so a woman of childbearing age was of less importance to him than a robust housekeeper who could tame his unruly sons and comfort his lonely daughters. Mama presented the idea to both Pasqualina and Vincente, separately of course, and won their approval. Teresia was welcome, as well, especially since she could be so helpful to Pasqualina in the household.

Mama gave Pasqualina and Vincente a wedding feast. She hired a small band to play in the courtyard and a photographer to record the couple so that those of us in America could imagine our aunt in her new life. In the photograph, Pasqualina is wearing her black silk dress, its starkness relieved by the addition of a crocheted white collar. Pasqualina's face is also relieved. The panic that she'd felt at the prospect of leaving Italy had been replaced by the promise of her familiar routines—cooking, cleaning, laundering and ministering to the needs of someone else's children.

My mother left Venticano the very next day.

When she landed in America, she stood on the deck of the *Principe di Piemonte* exactly as she'd stood on our balcony more than ten years before, when Claudio had left Venticano. A plumed and silken bird, a brilliant explosion of color amid the drabness and weariness of the other travelers. She had traveled alone.

On the day the *Principe di Piemonte* docked, we all went down to meet her. She would have expected nothing less. Angelina, Tilly and I with all the grandchildren she'd never held; Pip with her fine clothes; Claudio with his car for her trunks; Papa and the boys with arms full of flowers and Hershey's chocolates; Paolo with a book of poetry.

I had dressed Caterina in the outfit Mama had sent for her first birthday. Cream-colored linen, smocked, embroidered with tiny ducks marching around the hemline, a delicate border of feathered blue stitches on the collar and the fluttering sleeves. I was up the night before ironing it, my belly—

large again, hopeful—pushing against the ironing board. I was tired, but the thought of my mother's judgment kept me awake until the dress was perfectly pressed. How I dressed my daughter, how I cared for the clothes Mama herself had provided, how I showed respect to the woman whose drive and ambition and will were the very reasons we all stood there—this was what she'd be looking for as she scanned our faces. Faces she hadn't seen in years; faces she had never seen.

There wasn't a single one of my brothers and sisters whose life had not in some way been directed from across the enormous distance between New York and Venticano by the diminutive, elegant woman approaching us now.

Her decisions, her advice and her control had been conveyed in thousands of words over the years. How does one person amass so much influence? For my mother, it was her ability to sustain her presence in our lives through her words. Like Paolo, her letters had been an extension of herself. I saw what had happened to me and Giuseppina, separated from our daily contact. When I could no longer see her penetrating eye or the jut of her chin moving me in one direction or another, when I could no longer hear her prayers or her spells, when I could no longer taste her herbs or her fruit, I lost her.

But my mother never allowed us to lose *her.*

This was no stranger on the boat, not even to the grand-children. Each of them had something extraordinary from her. For the girls, exquisite dolls and expensive dresses; for the boys, sets of painted soldiers or toy sailboats. And the repeated message, "This is from your *Nonna.* Remember your *Nonna.*"

My mother was a master of the grand gesture. Whatever she sent, it always stood out. Made people notice. Just as people noticed her.

While the other passengers looked anxiously for a familiar face in the crowd, or in total exhaustion and bewilderment at the enormous city rising up beyond the pier, my mother's gaze took it all in like a queen surveying her kingdom. Her gloved hand, raised as if in blessing, was her only acknowledgment that she'd seen us.

If she searched the children's faces for some glimmer of Fiorillo, I didn't see it. Had I been her, I think I would've devoured those children with my eyes, surrounding them with the fierce protectiveness of a she-wolf for her blood, her line. If she looked with another kind of hunger at my father, whom she had not seen in over a year, I missed that, as well.

But I did see her close her eyes and breathe deeply, as if to swallow the city, her waiting family and the air of the New World.

Chapter 42

⁓⁓⁓

Paradise

WHEN MY SON was born, it was my mother who rolled up her sleeves and got me through my labor.

"I'm not Giuseppina, with her potions, and her mumbo jumbo," she said to me when I raised my eyebrows at her suggestion that she stand by me when my time came. "But I bore nine children, Giulia. Each birth different. I think I know how to do this."

So it was she who mopped my brow, who rubbed my back, who made me walk when the pains slowed, who—when I screamed that I could take no more, that this baby would be the one to kill me—insisted that I could and would get through this birth alive. And it was she who, finally, eased the head of her grandson into the light of day and then caught his tiny body in her own hands.

When she handed him up to me, I saw tears in her eyes that she quickly brushed away.

We named the baby Paolino. He was the image of his father. There were times during the day when I sat at my kitchen table, shelling peas or darning Paolo's socks, with the baby beside me in his bassinet, and I was brought to a contemplative stillness. I gazed in awe at his blue eyes absorbed by the play of light upon the wall, his mouth shaping and reshaping nonsense syllables in response to my own, his tiny fingers reaching for the light.

Caterina would climb into my lap and stroke my cheek, pushing past the bowl of peas or the pile of mending, past my own reverie, to find warmth and comfort.

In the evenings, when he returned home from the union office to eat dinner before heading downstairs to the Palace, Paolo surrounded himself with his children. Caterina would squeal with delight when he walked through the door and he always bent to scoop her up. He wrote poems for *her* now, little rhymes that he acted out for her with his fingers racing up her arm or tickling her behind the ear. Paolino heard his voice and began to coo and kick his legs. I was able to finish cooking while he filled the room with the children's laughter.

One Sunday afternoon, Paolo surprised me with an excursion up to Bronxville.

"I want to show you something, *cara mia*. A dream I have, for us, for the children."

It was enough for me to be out in the open air, away from the city. We got off the trolley and he led me a few blocks.

"Only a trolley ride from the city, Giulia, and look—look at this little paradise."

I looked. I saw a pony nibbling on a tuft of grass, its ears pricking up as I approached the fence. I saw more: an apple orchard, a stone house with green shutters, pots of begonias lining the window ledges. On the side of the house was a garden, with row upon row of beans, potatoes, onions, cabbage. In the back, a glimpse of laundry—not strung between tenement windows, but stretched out in fluttering rows like the beans.

Chickens pranced in a small fenced yard next to the pony's shed. A bell hung around the neck of a goat, white bearded, looking to share the grass with the pony.

"Some day I will buy this for you, Giulia. This is my dream—to see on your face every morning the look you have right now. To bring you this land, this happiness."

Chapter 43

Litany

THEY BROUGHT PAOLO to me in the middle of the night. Claudio and Peppino carried him up the stairs and laid him on our bed. The blood was trickling out of his mouth and staining the front of his white shirt.

I stifled the scream that rose up in my throat. I didn't want to wake the babies, and I didn't want to rouse the curiosity of the old crone across the landing, although, God knows, she'd probably heard enough as Claudio and Peppino had struggled up the stairwell.

It was 2:00 a.m. Claudio sent Peppino to get Dottore Solazio, but no one knew where he was; we knew the American doctor wouldn't come in the middle of the night to the Palace's neighborhood.

Claudio helped me undress him. I washed him, trying to cool down his feverish body. He mumbled and thrashed at first. At one point, wild and out of control, he knocked all his books from the bedside table. Then he quieted.

As long as I had something to keep my hands busy I could

keep the fears at bay. Claudio strode back and forth in the front room, his fist aching to pound Paolo's enemy as he used to when they'd defended each other on the streets in the early days. But this time the enemy was unseen. No mean-spirited bully, but an incomprehensible demon eating away at Paolo. For the first time in my life, I saw my brother afraid, power-less.

When he saw me standing in the doorway, he stopped pacing, his face searching mine for some sign of change. I just shook my head quickly and looked down. If I let the fears burning behind his eyes leap across to meet mine, I would shatter like the wineglass my father had smashed the night Claudio had decided to come to America.

"I'll go wake Tilly to come and be with you. You shouldn't be alone. What if the babies wake up?" He, too, needed something to do.

"No! I do not want my sister in this house tonight!" I was adamant. "Go look for the doctor again, if you can't wait with me."

I spit the words out, accusing, raging. There was no one I wanted by my side. I did not know if I could bear their anguish as well as my own.

I listened with my forehead pressed against the ice-cool glass of the door to his footsteps, frenzied and urgent, racing down the stairs as he left me. Then I turned back.

I checked first on the babies. Paolo was slipping out of my arms, out of my life, and my first impulse was to gather his children to me to fill my emptiness. I ached to smell their damp curls, to feel the tenderness of their skin, to crush their mouths in a kiss.

Caterina lay on her back, arms stretched over her head, her body extended to its full length. Every time I saw her like this, I was struck by how much she'd grown, how sturdy and hardy she was. Only eighteen months since I'd pushed her out of my belly, and she was already racing ahead of me, into her own life. I brushed a wet strand of hair from her cheek and watched for a grateful moment, the rhythm of life, the ebb and flow of her dreams.

Paolino, in contrast to his older sister, lay on his belly, restless, his impending hunger about to announce itself in a crescendo that would move from a tentative, mewling murmur to an insistent wail. I scooped him up and brought him with me to the chair by Paolo's bedside. His body, beginning then at six months to fill out, molded itself to my own, yielding his hunger, his loneliness in the night, to the warmth and milk of my breasts.

He fell back to sleep, sated, the last drops of milk sliding from his parted lips down his tiny, exquisite chin. I could not bear to put him down. Instead, I sat with him nestled in the crook of my arm. My other hand I rested lightly on Paolo's chest. I felt the life seeping out of him with every shallow, uneven breath.

I bent my head to his ear and began to whisper a litany. Not the prayers the old women mumbled in the church on Friday evenings—I had no use for their incantations.

The litany I recited to him was the words he'd written to me over the years, the words that had recorded the tumult and passion and anguish and joy of our brief time together. I knew the words by heart. His dreams, his longing, his doubts that I loved him in return. They were all I could think of as I waited with him.

Thoughts of you fill me to overflowing. I swear to you that if I do not see you often enough, I feel my heart breaking. If I had to be away from you for a week, I would go crazy with sorrow.

You are my talisman of enchantment.

I want to amuse you and keep you merry. I want to make you laugh, to hear your beautiful, charming laughter, which both eases and torments me.

I cover your face with my tears, and I wipe them away with my kisses.

I don't know how long I sat there. I don't know if he heard me.

Claudio came back with the doctor at last, but there was little he could do except tell us that it was pneumonia.

At six-thirty in the morning, Paolo died.

I found the shirt later, forgotten in a heap on the floor. I tried to wash out the stains, my back bent over the washboard, my hand clutching the naphtha soap, my arm scrubbing in a rhythm that became frantic as I realized that it was too late. The blood had already dried.

Chapter 44

The Band of the Bersaglieri

THEY WERE BEGINNING to assemble in front of the
Palace, men and women in black waiting in the gray drizzle.
My mother watched from the window upstairs, waiting for the
sound of a wagon, for the sight of horses with black ribbons
on their bridles. Behind her, resting on the table in my front
room, was Paolo's coffin.

She put out one of the cigarettes Claudio's oldest son had
bought for her and straightened her hat in the mirror I kept by
the door. They were simple, those rooms of mine, but well kept.
She remembered the first rooms she and Papa had lived in, over
the stables, with Giuseppina and Antonio snoring close by. No
matter how hard she tried, she had not been able to rid those
rooms of the pungent odors of horses and old woman's medicine.
My home was tinged with the scent of bleach, day-old flowers,
talcum powder and the haze of the cigarettes Papa berated her
for smoking. She waved her hand to dispel the evidence of the
last one and turned to her girls, now gathering themselves for
the descent to the procession forming in the street below.

She appraised them, her fine-looking daughters. Letitia and Philippina carried themselves with pride—long, straight backs; well-made dresses provided by their husbands' money; bodies untouched by childbearing. Tilly was softer, more sweet-faced than our older sisters, not as well dressed and beginning to thicken around her waist after three daughters. My mother made a mental note to suggest a shopping expedition to the corsetiere after the demands of that unsettling week were behind us. I was still in the back room, my face bearing the bruised signs of the last tear-soaked days. At least my hair had been brushed and neatly fastened and my dress had been pressed. Tilly had done that.

My mother plucked a piece of lint from Letitia's shoulder and adjusted the veil on her own hat one more time. She came into the bedroom to fetch me.

I sat in the chair between the bed and Paolino's empty cradle. Claudio's wife, Angelina, was watching all the children over at their house until we got back from the cemetery. My feet were tapping out a pattern on the floor—making the motions of walking, as I would have to do soon, behind the coffin of my husband—but going nowhere. In my hand I clutched Paolo's ring.

"It's time to go, Giulia. They are waiting for you." This was not the first time my mother had said such words to me, sending me off to a new life on each occasion. First as a little girl to Giuseppina's house, then to the convent and, eight years ago, here to America. Each time away, to a life she believed was better for me. What life awaited me now on the other side of this day? My mother had not known widowhood. Papa still sat at the head of our table, grumbling or roaring, but still there.

"Here, put on your veil. I'll help you pin it so it doesn't blow off. And where are your gloves? Do you have a dry handkerchief?" She rattled off her list. These were the things she knew about, could guide me in. She was about to take me, one step at a time, with dignity, through the day.

She got me up out of the chair and linked her arm through mine. She was determined to keep me moving, even though my will to put one foot in front of the other was locked inside that wooden box with the body of my husband.

Claudio came up the stairs then, a man of boundless energy despite the onerous weight that his wagon would carry today, despite the stiff collar cutting into his neck. Behind him, moving more slowly and talking among themselves, followed Paolo's two brothers, who had traveled from Pennsylvania, and my brothers-in-law.

Not one of my sisters' husbands had been friends with Paolo. Rassina, the jeweler; Gaetano, the carpenter; Ernesto, the businessman. My mother looked at them. Not men she would have chosen for herself—but then, she hadn't chosen Papa, either. Gaetano was sleepy. Rassina had no heart. Ernesto was simply ugly. Paolo, however, she knew she would miss. An intelligent man, a man with compassion for a woman who would rather read books than pound dough.

"Mama, Aldo should be turning the corner at North Street with the wagon at any minute. It's time to go down."

The men moved past us to the front room and gathered around the table where the coffin had rested for two days. At Claudio's count they hoisted the box onto their shoulders and edged through the passageway into the kitchen, where my mother waited with my sisters and me.

They stopped for a moment to ready themselves for the long flight down to the street. My mother kept her grip on me in my silence as the muffled whimpering of my sisters began: the drone of Letitia's whispered prayers, the plaintive questioning of Tilly's little-girl voice. As the coffin crossed the threshold onto the landing, an anguished wail rose above the voices and the tears.

"Oh, my God! Paolo! You're leaving this house for the last time! The last time!"

Pip's screams released the cries of the others, shrieks that followed the men down the stairs. All except me, whose stricken face remained frozen, untouched by the abandoned wailing of my sisters.

My mother was exasperated by the unconfined emotion working its way like an infection, or an insidious malaria, through my sisters. Her heart was aching, too, but Paolo was not her husband, not her lover, not her son. To tear her hair out with grief in public was a display she would not allow herself. My sisters did not have the same self-control.

"Subdue yourselves." She spit out the words in a fury. "It's time to follow the men with some semblance of dignity. You are Fiorillos, every single one of you, no matter what your last names are now."

She moved out first, supporting me as I stumbled and faltered, unable to take even a step without assistance. My condition forced her to turn her attention—reluctantly—from the excesses of her other daughters. They continued their keening as they descended behind us to the street.

The wagon was nowhere in sight, Aldo delayed somehow in the few blocks between Claudio's stable and the Palace. Everyone waited restlessly, the men still shouldering the coffin.

My mother wanted to light another cigarette, but she didn't smoke on the street. She held firmly to my arm. The drizzle had let up, leaving a dampness that curled the edges of my hair, a heaviness that muted the shuffle of impatient feet. My sisters, thank God, quieted themselves, resuming their muttered prayers. I stared numbly at the cobbled pattern of the road.

Directly in front of us—waiting as we all were—stood the

Band of the Bersaglieri. At ease in military fashion—feet slightly apart, arms clasped behind their backs, eyes straight ahead—they looked off at some distant point, not at us. Their horns floated in silence, suspended across their chests from a tricolor braided cord slung over their left shoulders. For all their military exactness and their remote bearing, the Bersaglieri were flamboyantly plumed birds.

This was no ragtag jumble of musicians Claudio had collected from some dance hall, with fraying jackets and wrinkled shirts, faces still bearing the traces of too much whiskey. The Bersaglieri were a *fanfara,* the brass band attached to one of the most elite infantry units in Italy. They were touring the East Coast and my mother had managed to engage them for the funeral. They wore well-cut black wool suits trimmed with polished brass buttons and red epaulets that seemed about to take wing, starched white shirts and broadly knotted red ties. This costume alone was enough to turn heads during a procession. But atop their heads, tilted sharply over their right eyes, were wide-brimmed black hats. Exploding from the front of the crown was a red feathered plume of such exuberance that it defied the grayness, the enclosed and suffocating air of grief.

There were those in the neighborhood who found this display ostentatious. There were people like them in Venticano as well, people who have nothing better to do than to pick away at their scabs of discontent and jealousy.

Paolo and I had next to nothing, so Papa and my mother paid for this. I don't know what I would have done if they hadn't—I had barely enough to pay the priest for a Mass or the grave diggers who made room for Paolo next to our babies' graves in the Holy Sepulchre Cemetery in New Rochelle.

I had hardly left Paolo's side in the three days since his death. After sitting with him during the night in death watch,

I had washed his body and dressed him for burial. During the wake, I had been willing to leave his coffin only to feed Paolino. No one could dissuade me. "Have something to eat, Giulia. Keep your strength up." "Rest, Giulia, put your head down for a few minutes." I had ignored them all, all of their ministrations, their offers of assistance. No one could take my place. So my mother took over what I had no heart for. She put everyone to work to prepare for this day. Hired the band, arranged with the priest and the cemetery, organized the women for the food afterward, explained to Claudio how to set up the bier, ordered the lilies from Barletta's. She knew it was easier when it wasn't your own. Your son-in-law instead of your son.

Her final responsibility came that morning as she stood with me on the stoop of the Palace, keeping me upright, feeling the tremor of fear ripple through me as Claudio's wagon rounded the corner at North Street, clattering over the cobbled pavement.

Ever since my wedding day, I had been petrified of horses. As a child, you couldn't tear me away from them. I was always out in the courtyard with my brothers, brushing away the layers of dust the horses had accumulated in their long hauls over the hills, feeding them broken bits of carrots I had snitched from Pasqualina's kitchen garden. Now, I crossed to the other side of the street or backed up against the wall of the nearest building when I saw a horse. This time, as Aldo maneuvered Carl's best team behind the Bersaglieri, I stiffened and pressed my back against the Palace door, covering the Fiorillo and Serafini, Proprietors etched in the middle of the frosted glass.

The wagon stood directly in front of us, draped in black, covered with pots of lilies. The men hoisted the coffin onto the platform. My mother was proud of her choice—a burnished wood, not cheap looking. Papa had balked at first at the expense, but then, that was what he always felt he had to do. Complain about the extravagance, the unreasonableness of her request, and then, in a gesture of magnanimous generosity, buy not only what she'd asked for but also some additional item. This was why, after the men had positioned the box, Claudio placed a brass crucifix on top of it. Papa's contribution.

It was time for us to move into position behind the wagon. The men broke up their knots of conversation—rumors about jobs about to open up or shut down, politics, especially news from the old country, about which they all had opinions. They had less to say about what went on here because they didn't understand or care about it. They took off their hats, put out their cigars, found their wives.

Paolo's sister Flora and her husband joined us. Flora, her face covered with a heavy veil, left her husband's side and approached me as I stood, stiff-backed and frozen, on the stoop. She touched her cheek to mine and whispered in my ear. Her fingers clasped black rosary beads, the silver cross dangling. With her free hand she pried open my fingers, still cramped around Paolo's ring, and pressed the beads into my hand. I bent my head and raised the beads to my lips.

I am not a religious woman. Paolo's death hadn't suddenly converted me. I could not imagine that the next day would find me among the ranks of the women who attend Holy Mass every morning at 6:00 a.m., say the Rosary at noon, and wash and iron the altar's linen for the priest every evening, although, God knows, it's the path more than one widow has taken. But for the rest of the morning, I cradled the beads in my hand, along with the ring, at times rubbing a bead between my thumb and index finger. Not in prayer, no, but moving my hand the same way I'd been moving my foot back and forth in the bedroom.

After Flora spoke to me, she rejoined her husband among

the family gathering behind the coffin. Paolo's associates from the union had arrived to march, my mother was glad to see. A sign of respect for Paolo, for the family. She nodded her head to their tipped hats, their deferential bows.

Claudio conferred with Aldo at the reins and then turned to check the presence of those in the procession. He was ready to give the signal to the bandleader. He glanced over at my mother, his eyebrows raised in a question. To anyone except my mother, it wouldn't have been a question. It would have been an order. Claudio was used to being the boss, to saying, "Now we start to march because I've decided it's time." He did not see his sister paralyzed against the glass. He saw the restless horses, the band that was to be paid, the policemen waiting along the route, hired to clear a path for the cortege.

But because she was his mother, he waited.

She tightened her grip around my shoulders.

"Let's go, *cara mia*. Let's get through this day."

She urged me down the steps and out into the street, directly behind the bier. The fragrance of the lilies crept around us in the muggy air, surrounding us with the smell I have associated with the dead since I was a little girl.

My body was not under my control. My fingers rubbed the bead, and my eyes beneath the veil stared through the coffin, not at it. As slight as I am, my mother did not think she had the strength to support me all the way to Mount Carmel. She motioned to Papa to join us on the other side of me. He took my right arm, which I gave to him without resistance, in a daze.

Claudio strode to the front, signaled to the bandleader, and the Bersaglieri shifted to attention. In unison they raised their horns to their lips and took their first steps as they blew the first note.

The horses reacted to the music piercing the stillness and

tedium of the wait. I heard Aldo speak sharply to them as the wagon lurched abruptly forward. My head jerked up and I sprang back from the wagon, from the mournful tones of the music. I wasn't completely lost. I had some sense of what was going on around me.

We fell into step behind the bier, and the others took their places behind us. My sisters embraced their wailing once again. I remained silent.

Chapter 45

Widow

AFTER THE FUNERAL, Pip got ready to go back to New York. "I'll take Caterina," she informed me. "Ernesto and I have plenty of room."

"It's better for you both," chimed in Tilly, with Claudio watching tensely from the other side of the room, waiting, letting my sisters do the work of convincing me. Sharing the burden of their widowed sister and her children, that was what this carefully rehearsed scene, this artifice of concern and generosity, was all about.

Widow. I turned the word over in my mouth, parched, aching with the memory of Paolo's last kiss. I gagged on it. I wanted to spit it out, this sour, suffocating word.

There was a heaviness and an ugliness to this word that had now attached itself to my life. I saw that ugliness reflected in the eyes of my brother and sisters—eyes that averted, eyes that resented, eyes that blamed. I was weighed down, not only by the fact that Paolo had been ripped from my very being and by fears for my fatherless babies, but also by the anger of my family.

As Tilly and Pip danced with false merriment around the welcome my Caterina would find, a room of her own on Canal Street, I gradually gleaned the true reason she had to be separated from me at all. It was Claudio.

He was forbidding me to remain with the children in the apartment above the Palace. He was forbidding me to continue to work there or to hold Paolo's share of the business.

"It's unseemly. A woman alone. People will talk, make assumptions about you." This from Pip, my most proper of sisters, who had never once set foot in the Palace. She was afraid of even the taint of impropriety. What did she think I would do, bare my breasts as I fried the eggplant? Serve up the macaroni with kisses on the side? Join Signora Bifaro's girls on the back stairs of the hotel?

"You are no longer safe here. You've lost the protection of your husband." I've lost much more than his protection, I wanted to scream at her. But what did she, married to an ignorant, desiccated old man, know of what I'd lost? Did she ever hear such poems as Paolo had whispered to me in the night, lips so close that his very breath was a caress, words so pure, so unrestrained, that their very utterance was something sacred? Did she ever feel such tenderness, such mystery, such surprise as I had felt in his embrace?

Not Pip, not any of them, understood my rage or powerlessness in the face of my empty bed, my empty heart. They only understood their own duty. It was a duty they'd carved out, apportioned among themselves, without asking me. Claudio was taking over my protection. He would house me; he would feed me. I would return to his house, as I had eight years ago when I'd first arrived from Italy. My parents had no room in their own apartment on Eighth Avenue with the three boys still living there. Papa's investment in Claudio's new business had not yet yielded the profits that would later enable him to build a house on the park. Pip was taking Caterina because Claudio's wife said there wasn't room for "all of them." I could keep only one of my children—the baby—with me.

I was numb. I was weary. I had not slept for three days, since the night Claudio had brought Paolo upstairs, bloody and fevered, to die in my arms. I had buried him that morning. I had nothing left in me, neither the words or the strength, to say to Claudio, "No!"

Tilly helped me pack up Caterina's things—a few dresses, stockings, a pair of shoes and the doll my mother had sent just after she was born. Once elegant, the doll had dainty porcelain hands and feet and a porcelain face with painted eyes as blue as Paolo's, a pouty red mouth faded to a pale rose from Caterina's many kisses, golden hair and a chipped ear. Its dress, smocked and cross-stitched in blue, revealed the expensive hand of my mother's dressmaker. A rag doll would've been more appropriate for an infant, but what did my mother know? And Caterina loved that doll. She wouldn't be separated from it. So into the valise it went, to make the journey downtown.

Claudio drove Pip and Caterina back to New York, while Tilly stayed behind to help me pack up my own things for the move to Claudio and Angelina's house.

Chapter 46

─◆─⚬⚬⚬─◆─

Silence

AFTER PAOLO DIED, I stopped living, as well. I spoke to no one. When my sisters tried to cajole and coax and finally scold, I didn't answer them. When Zi'Yolanda came by with pots of food or a dress for Caterina, I didn't thank her. When my mother sat with me and made a list of what I must do to help myself and my children, I didn't acknowledge her. Even when Caterina climbed into my lap whenever Pip and Ernesto brought her to visit, I could only rock with her as both arms reached tightly around me.

I didn't hear the murmurs in the kitchen, the prayers recited before votive lights, the rising tune of late-night conversations. "What are we going to do about Giulia?"

My family had always been asking that question. She runs wild in the hills, she climbs out of windows, she daydreams, she loves the wrong man. We have to do something about her.

So once again they tried to do something, but I didn't let them. It wasn't that I stopped doing *everything*. I still got out of bed in the morning, washed myself, dressed. I knew there were women who, after their husbands died or left, turned into pigs who refused or forgot to care for themselves. Whose hair became matted and caked, whose bodies acquired layer upon layer of dirt and odor. Whose houses became infested with bugs and filth. I wasn't one of them. Every morning, I brushed my hair and secured it at the nape of my neck with two long hairpins. I kept my fingernails clean. I bathed and dressed Paolino in clothes I'd washed and ironed. I swept the floors. I aired the bed linens. I lined Paolo's books up neatly on the night table.

But I did all these things in silence. I had nothing to say to anyone. Most of the time, of course, there was no one there except the children. Claudio was at work and Angelina, leaving me to watch her brood, went off to New York to shop and eat lunch at Schrafft's. What was I to do, talk to myself? Become like Crazy Fabiola in Venticano, who wandered the streets talking to the pigeons?

My words simply disappeared. Words had been life between Paolo and me—the breath, the food that nourished us. Without Paolo, the words stopped.

Chapter 47

Rescue

IT WAS MY MOTHER who rescued me. My mother—pampered, powdered, constantly in stately motion, her life swirling in constellations far removed from us, the children she'd borne and then handed over to someone else. My mother, more familiar with the drape of silk, the poetry of Boccaccio or the variations of azure in Capri's grotto than she was with the terrors that beset her own children. It was my mother who recognized the dark circles under my eyes, who watched me scrubbing the clothes not only of my own son and my nephews, but Angelina's, too, who observed Angelina returning from one of her shopping expeditions laden with boxes of finery for herself, toys for her sons, and not even a piece of candy for my children.

It was my mother who heard my silence and found a way to end it.

"It's so pathetic," she reported one afternoon when she and Tilly and her girls had stopped by. "The little girl—what's her name? Mariangela, that's it. Mariangela he has tied to a chair in the blacksmith shop while he's working so she won't toddle into danger. It's absolutely harrowing—all those tools, all that dirt. So she sits there with those enormous brown eyes, watching, nobody bothering to wipe her nose. She can't be more than eighteen months old. And the two boys, well, half the time they're running around God knows where. I heard that Barbara Nardozzi cooks for them, but I can assure you, nobody's washing them."

"They need a mother." It was Tilly, nodding solemnly in agreement with my mother, who revealed the purpose of their visit to me today. My mother's depiction of the circumstances of the widower Salvatore D'Orazio and his motherless children was intended to do more than just elicit my sympathetic nods.

My mother, continuing her orchestration of what she hoped would be a convincing portrayal of desperate need, cast an expectant look at me.

Salvatore D'Orazio played the accordion. He brought it with him when he first came to call on a Sunday afternoon. He also brought the children. Someone had given them a bath, starched the boys' shirts, put a bow in Mariangela's wispy curls.

He set the accordion down in the parlor and the boys took up positions on either side of it, like little soldiers or altar boys. Mariangela he held on his lap, smoothing her dress with his left hand, the one he used to stroke the buttons of the accordion that play the harmony.

It was March 19, the feast of Saint Joseph. I served him coffee and cream puffs that I'd made earlier that morning, before anyone else was up. It was the only time I was alone, those moments by a hot stove before dawn. The frantic scurry of early morning life when Tilly and Pip and I were working at the factory so many years ago had given way to a different tempo. We were no longer four women straining to fit our lives under the same roof. It was only Angelina and me, and God knows I didn't have to worry about sharing the kitchen or the laundry with her. The difference was the children. The clamor of hungry bellies, the tug of sticky hands. The restlessness of Paolino at night in his crib next to my bed. The books my mother lent me would have gathered dust at my bedside if I didn't have those private moments in the kitchen.

I waited in the parlor that Sunday afternoon. Waited for Salvatore to still his hand, to clear his throat, to shift the weight of his daughter from one knee to the other. I couldn't keep myself from studying his face.

I must admit that when my mother first told me about him, I'd gone out of my way one afternoon to walk past his blacksmith's shop and peer in the half-open door. He didn't see me; he was crouched over the hoof of a tethered horse, intent on prying off a damaged shoe. His face had been streaked with sweat and soot, his hair falling over his forehead and periodically swept away with the back of his hand. In the dim light I couldn't discern with certainty the features of his face—I couldn't tell you if they pleased or repulsed me. But I watched him at his work, saw the strength in his arms, the solidity of his legs, and listened to him calm the horse. I moved from the doorway. Later that day, I let my mother know I would allow him to call on me.

On Sunday, not only the children had been scrubbed. The face opposite me was no longer disguised by his labor. His hair had been slicked away from his forehead, black and wet, the hands now fussing with the baby probably pressed to it a quarter of an hour before, smoothing out whatever unruliness he normally lived with. His mustache, equally black, had been neatly brushed and waxed. It drooped and curved up again. Paolo had always kept his face clean-shaven.

"Don't make comparisons," my mother had said. "You'll never be able to decide if you haul up out of your heart these images that become more beautiful, more precious, the longer you live without him in the flesh."

So I tried not to hold up Paolo's exquisite face as I watched Salvatore in his unfamiliar feast-day clothes. I tried not to hear the poetry that Paolo recited to me as I listened to Salvatore speak of his situation, his prospects, the practical and substantial life he might be willing to offer me. I tried not to remember the piano at the Palace and the strains of Paolo's songs wafting up through the floorboards to our apartment as I studied Salvatore's accordion sitting between his sons and hoped that he would never play it for me.

Chapter 48

———————————

Ice Flowers

THE PANES OF THE windows in Angelina's pantry were thick with frost. If Caterina had been there, she would have carved flowers and stars with her fingernail, scraping away at the papery ice until her fingertips were numb.

But she wasn't there. She was asleep under a crocheted coverlet in Pip's house, her face resting against the porcelain cheek of her doll, her hair neatly braided, her fingers, instead of creating ice fantasies, firmly planted inside her mouth.

I moved the sack of onions on the floor to get at the semolina and the cake flour. I placed eggs into a bowl. I wanted to start the pasta, set the dough to rise for the cream puffs before the boys woke up. It was five in the morning.

There was no daylight yet. I worked by the dim overhead bulb in the kitchen, but I didn't really need to see. I piled a hill of flour onto my board and made a hollow in the top with my fist. One by one, the ten eggs slipped from their shells into the hollow. I plunged my hands into their liquid, working the flour little by little into a mass of dough, exactly as Giuseppina had taught me. I didn't think as my hands moved in a pattern that was as natural to me as planting seeds or weeding a garden. The echoes of Giuseppina's instructions had found their way into my muscles.

I shaped the dough, kneading and pushing it with the rhythm I'd learned from Giuseppina's singing. Now and then, I even found myself singing again. I took my rolling pin, a thin, tapered stick that Tilly's husband had shaped for me, and began to roll out the dough. It resisted at first, a thick slab of creamy yellow that I had to tame until it was a translucent sheet light enough to rise when I blew under it. With a sharp knife, I cut the sheet into strips and then hung the strips to dry on a wooden rack. Fettucini I would serve that afternoon, with porcini mushrooms sent from Salvatore's cousin in Connecticut.

I wiped my hands on my apron and started a pot of coffee. The rest of the house would be waking soon.

That afternoon Pip and Ernesto brought Caterina to Claudio's for dinner. She was dressed in the green merino wool coat and hat they'd bought for her. The conductor lifted her from the iron steps of the train onto the platform and exclaimed how beautiful she was, how perfect. Pip beamed and took her hand in her own gloved one and walked with her—proud, proprietary—out of the station to Claudio, waiting in his new automobile.

Chapter 49

Caterina Dances

PIP AND ERNESTO wanted to adopt Caterina.

She danced in the parlor when they came to visit, twirling in a circle with her arms outstretched. We clapped our hands to the music on the gramophone.

I remembered Salvatore's accordion and thought, *He could play for Caterina*. She could dance in his parlor. My parlor, if I marry him.

I could give her a home again.

I could give me a home again.

I sank into the chair in the corner and watched my daughter, my sister, my mother.

My mother sat in the center of the room, cooing and praising. She touched the edge of Caterina's exquisite dress. She pressed a coin into her tiny hand and Caterina held it high as she continued to circle the room. The coin glinted in the late-afternoon light; it adorned her, like a jewel on her finger or a ribbon in her hair.

Pip did not take her eyes from Caterina. She leaned toward

her as Caterina laughed and floated away. There was a hunger, a longing in Pip's body. I saw her reaching out for my daughter, stroking her hair, adjusting the bow on the sash at her waist. Caterina slithered from her grasp and danced some more.

She stopped in front of me.

"Dance with me, Mama."

She stretched out her hands.

I wanted to refuse. My body had given up that lightness and freedom since Paolo's death. I had no reason to dance, I told myself. My feet trudged to the market, bore the weight of laundry baskets and sleeping children, curled up at night in an empty bed, seeking warmth and finding none. I shook my head and held up my hands in refusal.

"Dance with me. *Per favore*. The way you used to."

Caterina grabbed my hands, holding the coin between us, and tugged at me to get out of the chair.

Pip stopped clapping. She sat back and wrapped her arms tightly in front of her.

I got to my feet and smiled at Caterina as we spun around each other.

Chapter 50

Gardenias

FLOWERS. GARDENIAS. WHITE with dark, glossy leaves. Salvatore bought them for me to carry at the wedding. Pip gave me a navy blue silk dress of hers to wear. My mother offered me her ruby earrings.

In a small cigar box on my dresser lay all the letters Paolo had written me. They were much more precious to me than the jewels Papa had showered upon my mother in appeasement, as substitutes for his attention and love.

I took the box on the morning of my wedding day and wrapped it in one of the embroidered trousseau linens I'd brought from Venticano. I buried the shrouded box out of sight in the bottom drawer with my scapulars and extra votive candles, amid the packets of dried herbs and the cotton towels for my time of the month. Salvatore didn't concern himself with these things, and he had no need to know, to see the letters, to understand why I kept them, cherished them, took them in my hand to feel the weight and smoothness of the paper and to run my fingers over Paolo's words as I'd once run my fingers over Paolo's body. Salvatore never knew those letters existed.

Chapter 51

⊰❦⊱

Gratitude

MARRYING SALVATORE BROUGHT five children to sleep under his roof—Salvatore's three, no longer motherless and neglected; Paolino, and Caterina, restored to me despite Pip's bitter disappointment; and a sixth growing inside me within a few short months.

Pip knew, in giving Caterina back to me, that she stared ahead at a childless life.

"You have so many to take care of, Giulia. Why take her back when Ernesto and I can give her so much?"

But how could I not take her back? Not only my own flesh and blood, but Paolo's? Did I want her to grow up distanced from me, as I'd grown up separated from my own mother? Not only the distance from here to Manhattan—the train ride measured not in the clack of the rails, the minutes from Mount Vernon to Grand Central, but in the journey that separates two households as different as New York and Venticano, as far apart as my mother's parlor and Giuseppina's kitchen.

Before the wedding, I took the train down, to visit Caterina and to get the blue silk dress Pip was lending me because I refused to wear the ivory wedding gown from my first marriage. What kind of an omen was that, I thought, to put on that dress again? I wanted to cut it up, burn it, throw the ashes on Paolo's grave.

I had not been to Pip and Ernesto's house in many years. They didn't entertain the family. When they wanted to see us, they came to us with a box of Schrafft's chocolates. I had forgotten the grandeur, the opulence and the heaviness that Pip had surrounded herself with. The wood was dark, the carpets a deep purple-red, the color of Chianti. The draperies were fringed, tied back with tassels the color of dulled gold. They hid the soot that filmed the outside of the windows. They cut off the light. Even in the middle of the day, she had to light the lamps.

The furniture in Pip's parlor reminded me of my mother's rooms. No comfortable place to sit, the texture of the upholstery unyielding against one's skin.

Her coffee, served in the gold-rimmed bone china my mother had sent each of us years before, was still bitter. Her cake was store-bought.

"There's a wonderful *pasticceria* in the neighborhood," she boasted, as if this made her life better than mine. She reminded me that I was still the poor, widowed sister who did her own baking.

Caterina was dwarfed in her room. There was a pale rose-colored carpet, a white bed, a doll's house that had the instantly recognizable stamp of my mother's extravagance.

How could I take her away from this, you ask? Back to a bed she would share with a stepsister, to a table with clamoring brothers and a father she didn't know?

How could I not?

At first, for Salvatore and me, there was only our gratitude for each other. I rescued his children, who'd been fed at one table or another since their mother's death. With the baby, who'd never known her own mother's milk, never felt the warm breath of a mother's caressing lips placed in a kiss at the nape of her neck, it was easy to scoop her up into my arms. Paolino was already moving away from my skirts, eager to follow his new brothers.

I balanced Mariangela on my hip while I stirred the gravy. I dressed her in Caterina's outgrown dresses. I blessed and pinned a medal of the Virgin Mary on her undershirt.

With the boys, it was harder. Eight and twelve years old, they eyed me suspiciously when I entered their house as their papa's bride. The little one, Patsy, had nightmares and crawled sobbing and terrorized into our bed every night. The older one, Nicky, ignored me. He shrugged off my good-night kisses, claiming he was too old for such things. It was all I could do to make a quick sign of the cross on his forehead at night before he turned away from me in his bed.

Va bene, I thought. I saw that he had enough to eat, clean clothes. I walked him down the street every morning to the corner across from No. 10 School and made sure he went in. In the afternoons, he went to the blacksmith shop and helped his father. When he came home with dirty clothes and a smudged face, I didn't yell.

Salvatore had rescued me. From a life as a burden to my family, from a place in my brother's household as little more than a maid, from my silence.

This gratitude that we felt for each other held nothing of the passion that had sustained Paolo and me. But it sustained us nevertheless. To be touched again, however awkward and unaccustomed the calloused hands, to be protected within the walls of my own home, to be thanked, with eyes that took in his well-cared-for children and my growing belly, was enough.

Chapter 52

The Great War

OVER THE NEXT YEAR we began to build a life together. Salvatore created a garden out of nothing in the back of the house—a vacant lot filled with debris. I sat out there in the spring, braiding Caterina's hair, a brown glistening with the red–gold lights of her father's. The baby, Giuseppina, slept in her carriage beneath the arbor that Salvatore had built to shelter the oilcloth–covered table that sat fourteen. Grapevines planted at the same time had begun their ascent up the posts supporting the roof of the arbor. The leaves formed a delicate curtain around the baby. Next to the shed at the end of the garden, Salvatore had planted a cherry tree, its white blossoms hiding the sheet–metal wall of the garage that backed up against our property. We were content.

Our first challenge together came when the American president brought our new country into the Great War that had been raging across the ocean, and Nicky ran away.

Salvatore had taken us all up to Waterbury to visit his cousin Archimedes. Nicky and Patsy were going to spend two weeks on the farm helping Archimedes with the haying, and we decided to bring the whole family for the ride and a visit with their cousins. We borrowed Claudio's car and drove up the Post Road, the children all in the back, squabbling and restless. By the time we got to the farm, I was happy to have them run off to play in the barn, climb trees, even splash in the muddy pond. We all needed to be in the country. Salvatore and Archimedes took the boys to the river to fish, while Estella and I stayed in the house with the little ones and cooked.

Down at the river, the men talked about the War. Archimedes's younger brother Sebastiano had enlisted in a regiment from New Haven that was mostly Italian, soon to sail to the front and fight for their new country. I don't know what they said, but it was the kind of talk a fourteen-year-old boy, lying on a rock in the sun, bored with his life and feeling encroached upon by his father's growing new family, would listen to. What was it—uniforms, guns, the adventure of sailing across the ocean, of taking part in the Great War? Whatever he heard that day, Nicky took it in and absorbed it, chewing on the idea as if it were a wad of tobacco.

When they all returned from the river for dinner, I noticed how quiet he was, not taking part in the children's banter. For several months, he'd been pulling away, his boy's body shedding the chrysalis of childhood. He'd already begun to shave, and he wanted nothing to do with little-boy games with make-believe swords and guns. Real guns, that was a different matter. But he kept his own counsel at dinner that day, not sharing his fascination with the conflict.

There was no sign of anything amiss when we packed up the car at the end of the day and prepared to say goodbye. The boys, together with Archimedes's sons, were going to sleep in the hayloft in the barn and had picked out their spots earlier. We said our goodbyes and headed back to New York.

It was sometime during the night that Nicky left the barn,

seized by the pull of the War and eager to be free of his father's rule. The younger boys were asleep when he left, and when they woke up and found his corner empty, no one suspected that he'd run away. So he had several hours' head start on his journey to New Haven before Archimedes realized he was gone. He walked many of those miles in the dark and must have hitched a ride with a passing truck as dawn broke.

Archimedes had searched every inch of woods and field, every nook and cranny in the barn and sheds and house, before he sent word to Salvatore that Nicky was gone. Salvatore stopped everything, shut down the forge and took the train back to Connecticut to look for his son. He spent three days combing the countryside around the farm. Sleepless, unable to eat, he was both frantic and furious. He finally gave up and came home without his firstborn, a man upon whom tragedy had descended too many times.

A month went by. Every weekend, Salvatore traveled to Waterbury and walked the streets, questioning people. Archimedes put the word out in the Italian community, hoping someone would have seen Nicky or fed him. It was his own brother, Sebastiano, who finally gave us an answer, in a letter he sent just before his unit sailed for France.

He had come across a young enlistee in his machine gunners' squadron, a boy he thought he recognized. Although the boy had tried to conceal his identity, he eventually admitted to Sebastiano that he was Nicky. Nicky begged him to keep his secret. He had lied about his age and somehow convinced the army that he was eighteen. Thank God, Sebastiano did the right thing and got word to us before it was too late.

Salvatore went to the camp where the men had been training, Nicky's birth certificate in hand. With Sebastiano's help translating, he managed to get Nicky released from service.

I don't think Nicky ever forgave Salvatore for that, robbing him of the chance to be a soldier, a man. He came home sullen and angry. Despite the discipline of the army, the regimentation and orders, he had felt free for that one month. The prospect of going to war had been a promise of excitement, not a fear of the horror and destruction that were too far away for him to understand.

For Nicky, the war had been accounts of Eddie Rickenbacker and Francesco Baracca, the Italian ace who shot down fifty-seven German planes. It was glory and ribbons, not vermin-infested trenches and mustard gas. Sebastiano did not come back. He was killed four months later, along with sixteen other men in the New Haven battalion, on a bitterly cold December day. Nicky didn't grasp that he, too, might have died that day, or another, if Salvatore had let him stay.

Nicky dropped out of school that fall, calling it a place for infants, not men. I thought it was a mistake, but kept my mouth shut. Salvatore's family didn't believe in education the way my mother had. Salvatore's only concern was that Nicky not become a bum. He put him to work at the forge, taught him how to beat and shape metal, made him sweat and ache, and let him pound out his anger with a heavy mallet on hot iron.

Chapter 53

Dancing On Sunday Afternoon

OVER TIME, SALVATORE and I experienced more than gratitude.

Salvatore, with his reserve, his bashful admiration, never asked me what he truly wanted to know: Do you lie in our bed at night dreaming of this hand brushing against the beauty of your body? Do you long for me in ways you find indescribable, every centimeter of your skin crying out to be touched? Salvatore did not know that he had these questions, simmering beneath our everyday discussions of money and household and children. I did not know that, eventually, my answers would be "Yes."

I'd thought we would share a table in the noisy, crowded kitchen filled with our children and never feel that we were the only two people in the world, seeing and hearing only each other. I had thought I could watch him with his work-hardened hand around the cup of black coffee I made for him every night and not imagine that same hand taking shape around my breast. Or see him bring the cup to his lips and not expect to trace with my eyes and my heart every crack in that winter-chafed mouth, envisioning that mouth on my lips.

I was mistaken.

One Sunday afternoon about three years after we were married, Salvatore took out his accordion after we'd eaten dinner and I was cleaning up the kitchen. Until then, he'd let the instrument gather dust, only bringing it down to his club occasionally or taking it along in the summer when we visited Archimedes out in the country. I'd never said anything to him about not wanting to hear him play but, without asking, he had refrained from using the instrument in the house.

But that Sunday, he went down to the cellar with an empty jug. I thought he was going to fill it with wine from one of the casks that lined the wall in the storeroom. He'd begun making wine from the grapes that grew over the arbor in the garden. But instead of coming back upstairs with a full jug, he carried the accordion, retrieved from its case under the stairs.

I think he'd intended only to clean it, because he took it into the parlor with a rag and was wiping the keys when the girls, Caterina and Mariangela and even Giuseppina, began clapping their hands and begging him to play them a song. He ran his fingers quickly over the keys in a children's tune and the girls bounced with delight.

I put down my dishrag in the kitchen and stood in the doorway of the parlor, my arms folded across my breasts, listening and watching as he played and they jumped around the room. When they saw me, they screamed, "Mama, dance!"

I looked across the room at Salvatore, who had stopped playing. He looked back, then put his head down and began to play *"Starai con me."* Not a children's song, but a love song. I stepped into the room and began to glide around my daughters. I raised my arms and coaxed the air with them, swaying my hips.

Salvatore stood and walked across the room. I sensed the strain in his body as he approached me, every muscle poised, held back from an embrace by the tautest wire of will. The air between us became heated, churning, colliding with the unspoken.

I continued to dance, not for the children, but for him.

Chapter 54

San Giuseppe Moscati at Night
Cara Serafini Dedrick

GIULIA HAD SPENT most of that Monday before her surgery recounting to me the hidden story of her love for my grandfather. Throughout the day, despite the interruptions of nurses and preparations for her operation the next morning, she had continued her outpouring, as if this were the only opportunity she'd have to make sure someone else knew what she'd kept in her heart for so long.

I thought she'd be exhausted when evening came and her words ended, her hands making a final graceful gesture in the air, echoing the dancing that had captivated so many on those Sunday afternoons years before.

But that night she couldn't sleep. The hospital had slipped into dim light and muted sounds—the swish of Sister Annunziata's rosary beads against her habit as she moved down the corridor, the click and hiss of respirators, the flicker of green lights casting waterlike reflections on the linoleum floors. Above these muted sounds and through the pale, unearthly light of her IV monitor, I could hear Giulia's moaning and muttering and could see her arms, ghostly, flailing about the sheets.

I sat up in my cot and put my bare feet on the floor. It was cool and smooth. I went to Giulia's bedside. With her right hand she was attempting to pull the IV tube out of her arm. Her lips were parched and chapped.

I placed one hand on her arm and stilled her frantic jerking. With my other hand, I pressed the bell for the nurse and waited for her to respond.

"Are you in pain, Nana?"

She tossed her head back and forth on the pillow, not in denial, but in a repetitive, ritualistic movement. She seemed not to be aware of me. Her eyes were closed and she was reciting some kind of litany.

When Sister arrived, she assessed her condition and checked her chart.

"Unfortunately, she's had the maximum dose I can safely administer tonight. Perhaps you can sit up with her for a while to calm her and help her fall asleep. Let me know if she remains agitated. I don't want to restrain her, but if she tries to pull out her IV again, I'll need to restrict her movement."

I grabbed my sweater, put it on over my nightgown and then resumed my position at Giulia's bedside. I began to stroke her arm to quiet her and keep her from reaching for the IV. I tried to listen to the words she was uttering. At first, it sounded like gibberish, or an incantation. I bent my head close to her lips and listened. Slowly, I began to recognize syllables and familiar Italian words.

I started to repeat the sounds as I heard them, setting up an echo, a reverberation of whatever, whoever, she was calling down to help her.

"*Madre Mia,* protect me. Form a ring around me to wall out evil. Cast off my pain."

Soon, I no longer had to imitate her, but could recite the words with her in unison. It was a kind of music, rising and falling in a rhythm. *Pull me close to you. Throw off this suffering. Pull in. Cast off.*

Without intention, I lifted my hand to her forehead and with my thumb, blessed her with the sign of the cross. My fingers spread out to stroke her brow in a gentle massage. Some ancient memory informed my hand; it seemed to know what to do without my direction.

I don't know how long I sat with her, my voice joining hers and my fingertips smoothing her pale temple. But at some point I heard the quiet, steady breaths of sleep. Her arms were no longer rigid and agitated, but relaxed. Her mouth formed a smile, as if whatever images were forming in her dreams were bringing her joy.

I fell asleep myself, in the chair. I was afraid to slip back into the cot for fear that she'd wake again and I wouldn't hear her. But she slept through the rest of the night.

In the early morning, just as a thin line of pink-hued light appeared at the window, I felt her stroking my hand.

"Figlia mia," she whispered and then brought my hand to her lips and kissed it. "Do you know what *serafini* means in Italian?"

"Yes, Nana. It means *seraphim,* the highest order of angels."

She leaned her head back on the pillow.

"And you are my angel."

Chapter 55

Life After Giulia

GIULIA DIED A LITTLE more than a year later. Oh, her hip operation was a success, and she and I flew back to New York within two weeks of her surgery on a special Alitalia flight arranged by the American ambassador to the Vatican, a childhood friend of my cousin.

She stayed with my parents at first, unable to navigate the stairs in her own home. Giulia approached her rehabilitation with the same steely drive that had kept her alive into her nineties. Every time I went to visit her, she had painstakingly made a little more progress toward walking on her own. She was determined to get back to her home.

She and I did not mention the letters again. "They are for you," she told me before we left Italy. "You alone. You are the only one who knows what to do with them."

By Christmas, Giulia was back in her own house, giving orders to all my aunts and my mother as they hustled around her kitchen on the morning of Christmas Eve, preparing the feast of the seven fishes for that evening. I had left Andrew and my kids at my brother's house so that my sister-in-law Jeannie and I could help. But even though we were grown women, we were relegated to setting the table, Giulia pointing with her cane at the drawer where the embroidered linen tablecloths were kept or instructing us to polish the silver before we laid it on the table.

It was the last Christmas Eve the whole family spent together, the last Christmas Eve Giulia was alive. I remember that night more vividly than her funeral, which, despite her long life, stunned us into an empty, hollow silence.

But that Christmas Eve we were still together, talking over one another, raising glasses of pinot noir, my cousins and I keeping our kids from climbing the walls in anticipation of Santa Claus, our husbands—most of them not Italian—trying to avoid the *baccala* and octopus. And over it all presided Giulia at the head of the table, her oldest son—my father Paolino—and her youngest son, Sal, on either side of her. Three of her children had already passed away before her, and Mariangela had moved to Florida. Only her sons, Caterina, and the baby of the family, my aunt Elena, were still there, held together, as we all were, by the threads that bound us to Giulia.

During the following winter, a bitterly cold January and February filled with record snowstorms, Giulia began to deteriorate. She rarely left the house, and Caterina moved in to take care of her. Once a month I drove up from Jersey to spend a Saturday afternoon with her, stopping first at Artuso's bakery to pick up a cannoli. We sat at the little table in the kitchen to drink our espresso and then she led me into the living room, pushing a walker ahead of her.

The family had ordered a hospital bed and had it set up in the living room so she didn't have to climb the stairs anymore, but she still got up every day, dressed and held court with whoever stopped by to visit her.

Our ritual was the same every time I came. She sat in her chair in the corner, near the votive candles she'd moved down from her dresser in the bedroom. The Metropolitan Opera broadcast played softly on the radio. I sat in front of her as she closed her eyes and I reached up and began to circle her brow.

She was the only one I dared touch in that way, the only one who'd heard me recite the ancient incantations that had sprung from my lips that night in the hospital in Avellino. I didn't trust that what happened when I touched her was anything more than a granddaughter comforting a grandmother. I didn't think it was anything *I* was doing. It seemed only to be Giulia placing her trust in me and feeling better simply because I was there.

I remember once watching a movie about a young woman who marries into a California wine family with an incredibly powerful matriarch who becomes the young woman's nemesis. Ultimately, the young wife triumphs, replacing the matriarch, but in doing so she takes on a striking resemblance to the older woman, even wearing her long, flowing hair in the severe wrapped braids that had been the matriarch's signature. It was as if the older woman had inhabited her.

I wasn't about to start wearing my hair in the style Giulia had favored ever since I'd known her. In a photo taken on my first birthday, Giulia hovers over me as I blow out the candle, her wavy hair pulled back in a bun at the nape of her neck. In fact, true to my baby boomer quest for perpetual youth, I still wore my hair the same way I'd worn it in my high-school yearbook photo. No, I had no intention of imitating my grandmother's looks. But I was also uncomfortable taking on this most mysterious aspect of her life. Like my great-grandmother, who'd dismissed the spells of Giuseppina as so much mumbo jumbo, I did not believe that Giulia's power had anything to do with me.

I wasn't with Giulia when she died. It was 8:00 p.m. on a Thursday night in early August when my mother called me. I had just read my four-year-old twins, David and Matthew, their nightly chapter of *The Lion, the Witch and the Wardrobe*. Joshua, my ten-year-old, was trying to teach my husband, Andrew, how to play Zelda on his new Nintendo, and my only daughter, Julia, was engrossed in dressing the Barbie doll my mother had insisted on giving her for her sixth birthday.

"It didn't do you any harm, so I see no reason why I can't give her one, too," she'd told me over my objections in May.

I sat alone with the news of my grandmother's death, perched at the top of the stairs, remembering the lines of her face under my fingertips.

We buried Giulia in Holy Sepulchre Cemetery in New Rochelle, with Paolo and the two babies she had lost, Carmine and Emilia. The grave is far in the back, against a crumbling wall covered with ivy on the northern edge of the cemetery. The plot, though remote, had been well tended. My father told me that after Salvatore had died, Giulia had arranged for him to be buried in Connecticut with his first wife, the mother of Patsy and Nicky and Mariangela. Giulia made annual visits to that grave but, in her second widowhood, it was to Paolo's grave she returned almost monthly, restoring it from its overgrown and forgotten condition to a neat patch of grass and flowers. She had left instructions with my father and Caterina that it was there she wished to be buried.

The dates on the headstone tell a striking story. Giulia outlived Paolo by seventy years. Carved under their names is a phrase I recognized from his letters:

Per la vita. For life.

★ ★ ★

That was twenty years ago. Although I resisted taking on Giulia's persona and her gift for healing in those last months of her life, I found I could not escape the connection that had been forged between us in our lives together. I look back now and see Giulia's imprint.

Like my grandmother, I had two husbands. Although the first one didn't die as my grandfather Paolo had, like Paolo, Jack Peyton left me with an infant and disappeared quite emphatically and finally from our lives. He might as well have been dead.

And like Giulia, I turned my culinary skills into a business, opening a catering company to support Joshua and myself. I had absorbed the drive and seriousness of purpose Giulia had called upon to survive the loss and hardship in her life, and I became as successful a businesswoman as she'd been.

When I met Andrew Dedrick, we were both trying to rebuild our lives after difficult divorces and were as tentative and cautious of new love as Giulia and Salvatore had been in their courtship. But we plunged ahead nevertheless and created a family, bringing three more children into the world—Julia, Matthew and David—to join Joshua.

Although he didn't play the accordion, Andrew brought music into my life in other ways. He filled our home with his eclectic collection of Mozart and Dylan and later, Loreena McKennitt and Jesse Cook and obscure singers from remote corners of the world whose music he'd heard on equally obscure NPR broadcasts. He encouraged Joshua to play the violin and go on to perform with the Boston Symphony Orchestra. And he enthusiastically endured the twins' experimentation with drums and electric guitars. A rock band performed in our family room throughout their years in high school, with Andrew ever at the ready to haul equipment to a gig on a Saturday night.

Although I resisted taking on Giulia's mantle as a healer, I learned something about the power within myself when David and Matthew were born early and spent the first weeks of their lives hovering precariously between life and death, health and impairment, in a state-of-the-art neonatal intensive-care unit. I sat with them every day between their Isolettes, holding one or the other in my arms, the wires attached to their many monitors draped across my lap. The NICU nurse on duty drew my attention to the monitors one afternoon. The irregularities in their heartbeats and the unevenness in their respiration disappeared as I stroked and murmured to them. When they were released a month after their births, the pediatrician told me, "I'm sending home two normal, healthy babies, and I'm not entirely sure how that happened."

The last echo of Giulia that emerged in my life came about when Andrew taught me how to dance the tango. In his arms I shed one layer of my grandmother's influence—my reserve—to discover another. Her passion for dancing.

Now, when the children return home at Christmas, after we've finished decorating the tree and before we sit down to the feast of the seven fishes, they insist on a tango. Joshua plays a haunting and vibrant tune on his violin, and Andrew and I glide across the floor as our children watch.

★ ★ ★ ★ ★

Rita Brooks can redesign anything—
except her own life.

Acclaimed author

NANCY ROBARDS THOMPSON

delivers another compelling read!

Rita has landed a dream project: transforming a rectory in Avignon into a summer home. But the client insists on hiring local furniture artisan Philippe Beaulieu—and their styles couldn't be more different. His ultra-modern designs definitely clash with Rita's classic tastes. But as the saying goes, Vive la différence!

Working closely in the romantic Provençal countryside, the colleagues discover shared passions outside the studio, and recently widowed Rita throws herself into their affair with appropriate French élan. But with her dreams so tantalizingly close, Rita must find the courage to take hold of them...and never let them go.

AN ANGEL IN PROVENCE

In stores today.

Free bonus book in this volume!
What Happens in Paris (Stays in Paris)
by Nancy Robards Thompson
It's never too late for a Left Bank love affair....

www.eHarlequin.com

**For her fiftieth birthday party,
Ellie Frost will pretend that everything is fine.**

That she's celebrating, not mourning. That she and Curt are
still in love, not mentally signing divorce papers. For one
night, thrown closer together than they've been for months,
Ellie and Curt confront the betrayals and guilt that have
eaten away at their life together. But with love as the
foundation, their "home on Hope Street" still stands—they
just need the courage to cross the threshold again.

HOPE STREET
From acclaimed author
Judith Arnold

Don't miss this wonderful novel, available in stores now.

Free bonus book in this volume!

The Marriage Bed, where there is no room for
secrets between the sheets.

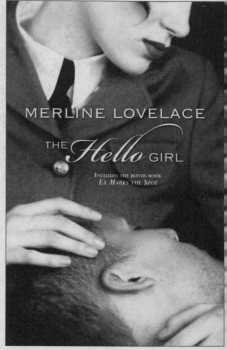